Cynthia Harrod-Eagles

Necrochip

sphere

SPHERE

First published in Great Britain in 1993 by Little, Brown and Company
Paperback published in 1994 by Warner Futura
This reissue published by Sphere in 2019

3 5 7 9 10 8 6 4 2

A CIP catalogue record for this book
is available from the British Library.

ISBN 978-0-7515-7535-4

Typeset in Plantin by Palimpsest Book Production Limited,
Falkirk, Stirlingshire
Printed and bound in Great Britain by Clays Ltd, Elcograf S.p.A.

Papers used by Sphere are from well-managed forests
and other responsible sources.

Sphere
An imprint of
Little, Brown Book Group
Carmelite House
50 Victoria Embankment
London EC4Y 0DZ

An Hachette UK Company
www.hachette.co.uk

www.littlebrown.co.uk

1

Bottle Fatigue

It had been quiet lately, a warm sunny spell after a cold wet spring surprising the General Public into good behaviour. If it went on, of course, the hot weather would generate its own particular rash of crime and they would all be run off their feet, but for the moment people were more interested in enjoying the sunshine than abusing their neighbours.

In the middle of the morning the atmosphere in the canteen at Shepherd's Bush nick was so dense and bland you could have poured it over the apple pie and called it custard. Like trench soldiers during a prolonged pause in hostilities, the troops hung about drinking tea, playing cards, and swapping half-hearted complaints.

Detective Inspector Slider had had a cup of tea brought to him in his office only half an hour ago, but the contagion of lethargy found him joining his bagman, DS Atherton, for another. Some previous occupant of their corner table had managed to persuade the window open a crack, and a green, living sort of smell from the plane tree outside was pervading the normal canteen miasma of chips and sweat.

Slider dunked his teabag aimlessly up and down in the hot water, his mind idling out of gear. He didn't really want the tea. These days there was a choice of teabags at the counter: Earl Grey, Orange Pekoe, Lapsang Souchong, or Breakfast Blend (catering-speak for Bog Standard). It was a move intended to quell the complaints about the change to teabags, which itself had been the response to complaints about the quality of the tea made the old way, which had always been either stewed or transparent. Since Atherton had bought this round, they had both got Earl Grey, which Slider didn't care for. He didn't like to say so, though, for fear of Atherton's left eyebrow, which had a way of rising all on its own at any evidence of philistinism.

Atherton was so bored he had picked up a copy of *The Job*, the official Met newspaper whose explorative prose style brought out the David Attenborough in him. He turned a page now and found a report on an athletics meeting at Sudbury.

'It says here, "After a slip in the 100 metres hurdles, PC Terry Smith remained lying prostate for some minutes." That's a gland way to spend the afternoon.'

Slider looked across at the front page. The picture was of two cute Alsatian puppies sitting in upturned police uniform caps, under the bold headline YAWN PATROL. He began to read the text. *At the moment police work might be nothing more than a playful game of caps and robbers to tiny Dawn and Dynasty, but 12 months from now. . .* He stopped reading hastily. On the back page was more sports news and an achingly unfunny cartoon. Slider remembered Joanna telling him what orchestral trumpet players said about their job: you spend half the time bored to death, and the other half scared to death. She was away on tour at the moment. He had managed to get thinking about her down to once every ten minutes.

Atherton turned a page. 'Hullo,' he said. 'Here's a para on Dickson. Obituary.' He read it in silence. 'Doesn't say much,' he said disapprovingly.

'They never do,' Slider said. Die in harness after thirty years of dedicated service, and you merit less room in the paper than tiny Dawn and Dynasty. Of course, to be honest, Dickson had never been that photogenic. And to be fair, they had been about to execute him when he forestalled them by having a heart attack. 'Anything known about the new bloke?' Slider asked to take his mind off Dickson, whom he missed and whose treatment he bitterly resented. 'What's his name – Boycott?'

'Barrington,' Atherton corrected. 'Detective Superintendent I.V.N. Barrington.'

'I knew it was some cricketer or other.' Atherton, who had never heard of Barrington, looked blank. 'I've never come across him. Have you heard anything?'

'He's from Kensington, apparently; before that I don't know. Originally comes from *oop north* somewhere. Carrot country.' He glanced round at the next table, where DC McLaren – recently transferred from Lambeth to replace Hunt – was reading the *Sun* while slowly consuming a microwave-heated Grunwick meat pie straight from the cellophane. Atherton repressed a shudder. 'Hey, Maurice – you were at Kensington for a while, weren't you? Did you come across this DS Barrington at all? What's he like?'

McLaren looked up, removing his mouth from the pie. A lump of something brown and glutinous slipped out from the pastry crust and slopped onto the table. 'Barrington? Yeah. He's a great big bloke, face all over acne scars. Looks like a blemished lorry.'

'Never mind that, what's he *like?*' Atherton interrupted.

'What would you be like if you'd spent your teenage years

looking like a pepperoni pizza? *And* he's ex-army. Boxed for his unit; fair shot, too. Belongs to some snotty shooting club out Watford way. At Kensington we used to call him Mad Ivan.'

'That's encouraging.'

'Cos of his initials – I.V.N.,' he explained kindly. 'Anyway, he comes from Yorkshire, and you know what it's like out in the sticks – the top bods think they're gods. I mean, Met guv'nors are human at least – more or less—' It was plain that he hadn't seen Slider in the corner. From where he was sitting, Atherton's tall shape must have screened him.

'Disciplinarian, is he?' Atherton interrupted tactfully.

'You might say,' McLaren said with grim relish. 'You lot'll have to pull your socks up. He won't let you get away with murder like old Dickson did. Especially you, Jim. No more lying about the office all day reading *Time Out*, then knocking off early for a trip to Harrods Food Hall.'

'Do you really do that?' Slider enquired mildly of Atherton. 'I didn't know.'

McLaren started, and reddened. 'Sorry, Guv. I didn't see you there.'

'That's all right. This is most enlightening. So Mr Barrington's a spit and polish man, is he?'

'Ex-army. Some said he was in the paras, but I dunno if that's true. But he likes everything smart.'

'Well, that suits me,' Atherton said languidly, leaning back in his chair and stretching his elegant legs out under the table. 'Maybe he can stop Mackay wearing nylon shirts.'

'I doubt whether his definition of "smart" will coincide exactly with yours,' Slider said. He pushed his now tepid tea away and stood up. 'Ah, well, I suppose I'd better go and do some paperwork.'

* * *

As he walked back to his office, he reflected on the last days of DS Robert Scott Dickson, sometimes referred to – though never in his hearing – as 'George'. He hadn't quite died at his desk, as freshly-reprimanded DCs generation after generation had hopefully predicted, but it was a close thing. He'd been found there unconscious after the first heart attack, and it had taken four of them plus the ambulance crew to extricate him from his furniture and get him downstairs into the ambulance; for Dickson was a big man.

Slider had visited him in hospital the following day, and had found him strangely shrunken, lying immobile in the high white bed, patched in to the National Grid and running half a dozen VDU monitors. Small he looked amongst so much technology, and very clean and pale, as though he'd been shelled and his gnarled old obstreperous personality cleared tidily away by the nurses. Only his hands, resting on the fold of the sheet, had defied the process: the first and second fingers of each were stained orange almost to the knuckle, kippered by a lifetime's nicotine, as though he'd smoked them two at a time. He looked for the first time like an old man, and Slider had been suddenly afraid for him, taken aback by this unexpected hint of mortality in someone he'd regarded as hardly human enough ever to die.

Dickson suffered a second attack the following day, a lesser one, but enough to finish him. But it had not really been that, Slider thought, which killed him. There had long been an element that wanted Dickson out, and that element had been baying more loudly recently, despite the good publicity the Department had gained over the clearing-up of what the tabloids had dubbed the Death Watch Murders. Even there, though presiding over a successful investigation, Dickson had not come across well in front of the news cameras: he was neither a lean, smart, keen-eyed achiever, nor the fatherly, dependable copper of public yearnings. Unpredictable of temper and permanently ash-strewn, like a mobile Mount Etna, he had scowled at the journalists' questions and all but told them to mind their own bloody business. Standing at his elbow and wincing inwardly, Slider had imagined the local editor hastily changing the proposed jocularly approving head-line of DICKSON OF SHEPHERD'S BUSH GREEN for an irate and rhetorical WHO DOES HE THINK HE IS?

In the end if top brass wanted you out, they'd always find a way, and Dickson's faults being as many and manifest as his virtues, he didn't make it hard for them. There had been a certain amount of fancy footwork on the part of the area chiefs, and some flirtatious meetings with members of Dickson's team who were not-so-discreetly pumped for incrim-inating evidence against him. Slider, whom Atherton described affectionately as CSN – conspiratorially sub-normal – hadn't understood at first what was going on. When his own turn came he met both veiled promises and veiled threats with puzzled blankness. Later Atherton and Joanna together explained it all to him, and when he wanted to go back in there and punch noses, they assured him he couldn't know-ingly have done better than he had unwittingly.

But it angered and depressed him all the same. 'If I'd realised what they were getting at—! All those questions – d'you know, the bastards even tried to make out that the old man's racially prejudiced? I didn't twig it then, but I see now why they kept asking why we had no black DCs on our firm—'

'You're not allowed to say "black" any more. You have to say "epidermically challenged".'

'Shut up, Jim,' Joanna said. 'This is serious.'

'I mean, Dickson of all people – he hardly even notices whether people are male or female, never mind what colour they are. And all that guff about his relationship with the

6

press! As if any copper can keep those jackals happy, without feeding them his balls in a buttered roll.'

'We're all going to have to keep our heads down for a while,' Atherton said, suddenly serious. 'When the shit hits the fan, it's better to be a live coward than a dead hero.'

'I hate you when you talk like that,' Joanna interrupted plaintively.

'That's from the Michael Douglas books of aphorisms,' Atherton said in hurt tones.

'You sound like some dickhead junior sales executive trying to impress the typists.'

'But what about loyalty?' Slider asked, still angry and ignoring the asides.

'Depends,' Atherton said, on the defensive. 'Do you think Dickson would be loyal to you?'

'Yes.'

'Not if you'd done wrong.'

'He hasn't done wrong,' Slider said, frustrated.

'Then he's got nothing to fear,' Atherton said with maddening logic.

In the end, the Mighty Ones picked on drink; and Slider heard it first from Dickson himself.

It was at the end of a routine discussion in Dickson's office. Slider, waiting to be dismissed, saw a change come over his boss. Dickson said suddenly, 'I've been offered a posting to the computer centre. Letter here from Reggie Wetherspoon.' He made a flat gesture towards his tottering in-tray. Wetherspoon was the Area Commander.

'Sir?'

'Come on, Bill, don't give me that innocent look! You know what's been going on. You had a cosy little cup of tea with Wetherspoon yourself last week, didn't you?' The irritation was feigned, Slider could see that. Dickson's expression was watchful: a man counting his friends, perhaps? Or perhaps merely assessing his weapons. 'I've been given the choice: sideways promotion, or a formal enquiry into my drinking habits in which I'll be found unfit for duty and required to resign. I can make it easy for myself, Wetherspoon says, or I can do it the hard way. It's up to me.'

'You'll fight them, sir,' Slider said. It wasn't really a question so much as a demand for reassurance. He had seen Dickson over the years in many moods and many modes, but this one was new. He seemed neither angry nor depressed nor even afraid; only very calm and rather distant, as though he had other things on his mind and was trying to be politely attentive to a friend's child at the same time.

'Bottle fatigue,' Dickson said thoughtfully. 'I don't know. That would be a stain on the record, all right.'

'They couldn't make it stick,' Slider said. 'They've no evidence. Everyone here—'

'—will be invited to an official enquiry. Statements will be required. Names taken for future reference, absences noted, apologies not accepted. If you're not a friend you're an enemy. Remember that.'

'I'll pick my own friends,' Slider said angrily.

'Don't be a bloody fool,' Dickson said, quite kindly really. 'They'll take you down with me if you don't co-operate. You're a marked man already, don't forget.'

'I don't care about that—'

'You should care! Christ, this isn't the bloody Boy Scouts! You're here to do a job. I happen to think it's an important job, and what good will it do anyone if you chuck your career away? No, listen to me! If they want a statement, give them a bloody statement. And if I do leave, take your promotion and get out. Go to another station as DCI and do the job you've been trained for.' He forestalled another protest with

8

an irritable gesture of one meaty hand. 'If nothing else, you should be thinking about your pension now. You're not bloody Peter Pan.'

'Sir,' Slider said stubbornly.

Dickson looked suddenly tired. 'All right,' he said, with a gesture of dismissal. 'Suit yourself.'

Slider left him, not without apprehension. The old man would fight – must fight – could not and would not let Them get away with branding him a sot and a failure. Yet there was something detached about him, as though he had already let go; as though the effort of caring about things had become too great.

Slider lived through three days of strange, nervous limbo, waiting for the official notification that there was to be an enquiry, which would be the sign that Dickson had refused the posting to computers. But on the fourth day Dickson had collapsed at his desk, refusing either to be captured or shot, but launching himself instead Butch-Cassidy-style over the precipice where none could follow him.

Slider had sometimes wondered what he would feel in the event of Dickson's departure for that Ground from which no man returns. He had supposed it might be sorrow, though the old man had not been one to court affection or even liking; he had expected a sense of loss. He had not been prepared for this anger and depression; but then he had not expected Dickson to be assassinated. The only small comfort was that Dickson had left the Job and the world with a stainless record after all. Dead hero. Slider reflected that it must have taken the most delicate of footwork for such a nonconformist man thus to avoid the falling fertiliser for thirty years.

At the end of the corridor Slider heard his telephone ringing, but before he reached his door it stopped. He shrugged and went over to his desk to see what had arrived since he had left it half an hour ago. The usual old rubbish. There were periods like this from time to time when nothing much seemed to happen, and his duties became almost completely supervisory and sedentary. He picked up a circulating file he had been putting off reading for days, and felt nothing but gratitude for the interruption of a knock on the door.

Jablowski put her head round. She always wore her hair short and spiky, but when she had just recently had it cut it looked almost painful. Her little pointed ears stood out from the stubble like leverets in a cornfield, exposed and vulnerable with the loss of their habitat.

'Oh! You are there, sir.'

'So it seems. Problem?'

'I've just had Mr Barrington on the line, asking where you were. He said as soon as I found you to ask you to go and see him. He's been ringing your phone.'

'I've only just got back to my desk. Where was he ringing from?'

'Here, sir. I mean, Mr Dickson's office.'

'Already? I thought he wasn't due until Monday.'

Jablowski wrinkled her nose. 'Dead men's shoes. Maybe he's trying to catch us out. Maurice McLaren was saying—'

'I think we ought to try to start without prejudices,' Slider checked her. 'Give the man a fair chance.'

'Yes Guv. If you say so,' Jablowski said with profound disagreement.

It was unnerving to tap on Dickson's door and hear a strange voice answer.

'Come!'

Slider's heart sank. He felt that someone too busy to get to the end of a sentence as short as 'Come in' would not prove to be a restful companion. He entered, and true to his principles searched around for a friendly and cheerful expression as he presented himself for inspection.

'Slider, sir. You wanted to see me?'

Barrington was standing beside the desk, his back turned to the door, staring out of the window. His hands were down at his side, and the fingers of his right hand were drumming on the desk top. His bulk, coming between the window and the door, darkened the room, for he was both tall and heavily built. It was a solid, hard bulk – muscle, not fat – but he dressed well, so that he gave an impression of being at ease with his size. Slider thought of Atherton's lounging grace which always made him seem apologetic about his height. Still, Atherton would approve of the suit at least. Even Slider, who was a sartorial ignoramus, could see the quality of it. And a quick glance at the shoes – Slider believed shoes were a useful indicator of character – revealed them to be heavy and expensive black Oxfords, polished to that deeply glassy shine that only soldiers ever really master. So far so bad, he thought.

When Barrington turned, it was impossible to look anywhere but at his face. It was a big face, big enough for that huge body, and made bigger by the thick wiry black hair which Slider could see would defy any barber's efforts to make it lie down quietly. It was a big face which might have been strikingly handsome if nature had left it alone, but which in its ruin was simply spectacular. Slider blenched at the thought of what the ravages must have looked like which could have left such scars: Barrington's naturally swarthy skin was gouged and pocked and runnelled like the surface of a space-wandering meteor.

And set in the ruin, under thick black brows, were intelligent hazel eyes, black-fringed; almost feral in their beauty.

With an unwilling access of pity, Slider imagined those eyes as they must have looked out in adolescence from amidst the fresh eruptions; imagined him as a boy carrying his pustular, volcanic face before him into a world which turned from him in helpless distaste. Christ, Barrington, Slider thought, reverting in the depth of his pity to police jargon, ain't life a bitch! He was ready to forgive him even for saying 'Come!'

'Ah yes, Slider,' Barrington said coldly, surveying him minutely. His voice was big, too, resonant and full. It would carry – had carried, perhaps – across a windy northern parade ground. 'We haven't met before, I think. Bill, isn't it?' he asked, having apparently filed Slider's essential features in some mental system of his own. 'Relax. I'm not officially here yet. I thought we might just have a friendly chat, get to know each other.'

'Sir,' said Slider neutrally. The offer to relax was as enticing as a barbed-wire hammock.

Barrington's mouth smiled, but nothing else in the pitted moonscape moved. 'Well. So this is Shepherd's Bush. Bob Dickson's ground – which he made peculiarly his own.'

The last bit did not sound complimentary. 'Did you know him, sir?'

'Oh, yes.' There was no telling whether it had been a pleasure or not. 'We were at Notting Hill at the same time. Some years ago now.'

'I didn't know he'd been at Notting Hill,' Slider said. He felt it was time to nail his colours to the mast. 'His death was a great shock, sir. We'll all miss him.'

'He was a remarkable man,' Barrington said enigmatically. The effort of being nice seemed to be proving a strain. The fingers drummed again. 'Doesn't anyone ever clean the windows here?' he barked abruptly. 'This one's practically opaque.'

12

'They haven't been done since I've been here, sir,' Slider said.

'Then we'll have them done. A lick of paint here and there wouldn't come amiss, either; and a few pot-plants. I'm surprised the typists haven't brought in pot-plants. The two usually go together.'

'We've always been short of civilian staff here, sir,' Slider said neutrally.

'I want the place brightened up,' Barrington rode over the objection. 'Can't expect people to behave smartly if their surroundings are dingy.'

He paused to let Slider agree or disagree, but Slider let the trap yawn unstepped-in. The bright eyes grew harder.

'I was ringing your office for quite a while, trying to reach you. You weren't at your desk.'

'No, sir,' Slider agreed, looking back steadily. Now was definitely the moment to get a few ground rules clear.

After a moment it was Barrington who looked away. 'Things are pretty quiet at the moment,' he said, moving round the desk and pulling out the chair as if he meant to sit down.

'We're always busy, sir. But there's nothing special on at the moment.'

'Good. Then it's the right time to do some reorganising.' He changed his mind about sitting down, and leaned on the chair back instead. Slider thought he was like an actor during a long speech, finding bits of stage business to occupy his body. 'Organisation is the first essential – of people as well as the place. I want to find out what everybody's good for.'

'We've got a good team, sir,' Slider said. 'I've worked with them for some time now—'

Barrington made a small movement, like a cat in the grass spotting a bird landing nearby. 'You refused your promotion to Chief Inspector, I understand. Why was that?'

13

'I wanted to stay operational, sir.' Slider had been prepared for that question, at least. 'I've never been fond of desk work and meetings.'

'None of us are,' Barrington said firmly. 'But it has to be done. Someone has to do it.' To which Slider's inward answers were – Not true, So what? and As long as it's not me. 'I expect everyone in my team to pull his full weight. No free-loaders. No weak links.' There seemed to be nothing to say to that, so Slider said it. 'We've got the chance for a new start here. Bob Dickson had his own ways of doing things, and sometimes they paid off. But his ways are not my ways. He's gone now, and you've got me to answer to. I expect *absolute loyalty*. And I think you can tell the men that in return they will get absolute loyalty from me.'

'I'll tell them that, sir.'

Barrington studied the answer for a moment and seemed to find it short on fervour. 'Some things are going to have to change around here,' he went on. 'Things have been let go. I'm not blaming anyone. It happens. But not when I'm in charge. I like to run a smart outfit. People are happier when they know what's expected of them.'

'Sir,' Slider said. He was puzzled. The man was talking like a complete arse, and yet he got the feeling of real menace. It was as if the worn cliches were a crude code used by a being from a superior species who thought they were good enough for poor old dumb *homo sapiens,* Barrington's higher thought processes were deemed to be too subtle for Slider to understand. And why had he not liked Dickson? Was it merely a spit and polish man's irritation with the effective slob, or was there something else behind it? It must have been a fairly steep sort of annoyance for him to let it show like this.

Slider had evidently had his allotted time. Barrington came

back round the desk and held out his hand. 'Glad we've had this little chat.'

Slider's hand was gripped, wrung and let go all in one movement, and Barrington was opening the door for him and ushering him out with the sheer force of his physical size. Norma, approaching along the corridor, stopped on seeing Slider, and then somehow stopped again from a stationary position on seeing Barrington. He smiled at her with his automatic, unmoving smile, his eyes photographing and filing her.

'I don't think we've met,' he said. 'Barrington.'

'Swilley,' she responded, mesmerised.

'WDC Swilley—' Slider began to explain, but Barrington cut him off.

'Fine. I'll get to know you all in due course,' he said, and popped back through his trap door like the Demon King.

Norma turned open-mouthed to Slider, who shook his head and walked away along the corridor. He wouldn't put it past Barrington to be standing just by the door to hear what they said about him.

When they had turned the corner and were safe she burst out in a low gasp, 'Who is that extraordinary, *sexy* man?'

'Sexy?' Slider said, wounded. 'With those acne scars?'

'I can't help it,' she said in a baffled voice. 'I know he oughtn't to be, but, God! He made my knees go weak.'

'He's the new DS. Stepped into Dickson's shoes. At Kensington they called him Mad Ivan.'

'I bet they did! He's breathtaking!'

'You're dribbling,' Slider told her coldly. 'What did you want, anyway?'

'I was looking for you, Guv. A call's just come in from Dave's Fish Bar in Uxbridge Road – chip shop, corner of Adelaide Grove—'

'Yes, I know it.'

'A customer just bought a thirty pee portion of chips and found a finger in it.'

'A finger of what?' Slider asked absently.

'A human finger.'

He wrinkled his nose. 'Someone else can deal with it, surely? I'm not a public health inspector.'

Norma looked offended. 'I thought you'd find it amusing, that's all. There's so little to do around here. Atherton's gone,' she added cunningly.

'You're quite right, of course. Anything's better than going back and reading circulation files.'

'You never know,' she said encouragingly, following him down the corridor. 'You might find the rest of the body attached to it.'

'I'm never that lucky,' he said.

2

A Finger in Every Pie

Cheryl Makepeace, aged fifteen, had been on her way to school – Hammersmith County, at the far end of Bloemfontein Road. She'd been to the doctor that morning, to consult about what her mother referred to with breathless Jamaican delicacy as *Ladies' Problems*, and since her appointment had been for ten forty-five she'd decided happily it wasn't worth going into school beforehand. Coming out of the surgery in Becklow Road and seeing the sunshine, she thought she might as well make the whole thing last out until lunchtime.

She crossed the Uxbridge Road and mooched along in the sunshine looking idly at the shops. The chippy had just opened, and the smell of frying wafted delightfully down to her, spiced with a whiff of solvents from the dry-cleaners next door. It reminded her she was hungry. Thirty pee's worth of chips would just last her nicely down Bloemfontein Road, she thought.

The chip shop was in a short row of five shops on the main road between two side turnings. There was the photographic shop (portraits in the back and a fast printing service in the front) which had just opened, called Developing World. Cheryl, who hadn't got the joke, thought the name was poncey and that the shop wouldn't last long in that neighbourhood, in which she showed a business judgement beyond her years. Next to it stood the Golden Kebab Take Away, which was run by two devoted Lebanese brothers who shared everything, including profits and a wife and three children, and allowed themselves to be called Ali quite indiscriminately by the local customers, who all looked alike to them.

Next to the Golden Kebab was the Chinese restaurant which had used to be called the Joy Luck Wonderful Garden, but had recently been redecorated, and rechristened, for inscrutable oriental reasons, Hung Fat. Next door to that was Mr and Mrs Patel's dry-cleaning emporium, and then Dave's Fish and Chip Bar – Eat Here or Take Away. On the other side of Dave's was the alley which gave access to the backs of the shops down the next side-street and, incidentally, to Dave's own back yard.

These details did not impinge much upon Cheryl's consciousness as she entered the Fish and Chip Bar, and were even less to the forefront of her mind five minutes later when she shook vinegar over her bag of chips and saw that one of them was a finger – pallid, greasy, but well-fried.

Afterwards when she told the story to her friends – and she was to tell it often – she always said 'I just stood there and screamed'. But in fact she didn't scream, or make any sound at all. Instead she demonstrated an extraordinary, atavistic reaction arising from a deeply hidden race memory of poisonous snakes and spiders: she flung the chip-bag instantly and violently away from her with a two-handed upward and outward jerk, which sent its contents flying across the front shop. They hit the reproduction Coca-Cola mirror and scattered over and under the small metal table-and-seats composite screwed to the wall, which constituted the restaurant and fulfilled the Eat Here part of Dave's advertised promise.

Dave himself, in the person of one Ronnie Slaughter, made a sound expressive of indignation and annoyance, but one glance at his customer's dilated eyes and flared nostrils convinced him she was not simply messing about. Naturally enough he didn't believe her when she said there'd been a finger in her chips, not until a hands-and-knees clear-up of the mess under the table had discovered the offending object nestling along the skirting board. He expressed the opinion that it was just a pencil or a felt-tip pen or something like that and picked it up boldly, only to demonstrate the same animal instinct of rejection, which because of the confined space in which he was kneeling resulted in his banging his head quite sharply and painfully on the metal underside of the table.

'I told you so,' Cheryl moaned, clutching her school blouse tight at the neck as though she feared the finger might scuttle across the floor, spring for her throat and wriggle down inside her clothing. 'Whose is it?'

'Well it's not fucking mine,' Slaughter shouted, perhaps forgivably in the circumstances, and telephoned for the police.

By the time Slider got there the uniformed constable, Elkins, who had been despatched by the section sergeant, was holding the door of the shop against a knot of idlers who had gathered to see what was going on. On the other side of the plate-glass window, like a depressed goldfish in a bowl, Slaughter was sitting at the table hiding his head in his hands.

Atherton came to meet Slider as he went in.

'You didn't waste much time,' Slider said sternly.

'I like to keep my hand in,' Atherton smirked.

19

'Oh God, don't start that. Where's exhibit A?'

'On the counter, wrapped in paper.'

'And the customer who found it?'

'She seemed to think it was time she had hysterics, so I sent her next door for a cup of tea. Mrs Patel's making her one in the back room of the dry-cleaner's. It's all right,' he forestalled Slider's question, 'Polish is with her, trying to get some sense out of her.'

'What's Jablowski doing here?'

'Well, seeing she didn't have anything particular to do, and as it's so near lunchtime—' Atherton said beguilingly. 'We weren't expecting you to come as well, Guv.'

'So it seems. Well, now you're here, you'd better make yourself useful. Go and have a look round out the back, and see if there's anything—'

'Fishy?'

'Out of the ordinary,' Slider corrected firmly. 'I'll have a word with this bloke. What's his name?'

Atherton told him. 'He's a bit nervous, Guv – afraid we're going to finger him for the crime.'

'Just go, will you?' Slider said patiently.

'Even police work's gone digital these days,' Atherton said, going.

Ronnie Slaughter was an overweight, pudgy-faced man in his late twenties who had already gone shiningly bald on the front and top of his head. Perhaps to compensate, he had grown his hair long at the back, and it straggled weakly over his collar, making him look as though his whole scalp was slipping off backwards like an eiderdown in the night. He was dressed, unsurprisingly for the 1990s, in jeans, T-shirt and the regulation filthy trainers. A bump was rising raffishly on the right side of his forehead, which combined with the single earring – a plain gold sleeper – in his left ear and the rose tattooed on his left forearm made him look like a pudgy pirate.

He was obviously upset by his experience. His meaty face was damp and pale, and he lifted strained and reproachful eyes as Slider addressed him pleasantly.

'I'm Detective Inspector Slider. Are you the owner, sir? I'd like to have a little chat with you.'

'I don't know nothing about it,' Slaughter said plaintively. 'I've never had nothing like this happen before. I keep a clean shop, everybody knows that. You ask anyone. I don't know how that bloody thing got in there, and that's the truth. I never—'

'That's all right,' Slider said soothingly. 'Just let's take it from the beginning. What time did you get in this morning?'

'Arpast ten, same as usual.'

'You open at half-past eleven?'

'That's right. Tuesday to Sat'day, arpast eleven till two, arpast four till eleven. Closed Sunday and Monday.' He seemed to find the familiar recital soothing.

'You come in early to prepare things, I suppose?'

'S'right.'

'And where did the chips come from? I suppose you buy them in from a wholesaler?'

Slaughter looked almost scornful. 'Nah, only Wimpy Bars and them sort of places buy their chips in. They're never any good. Fish an' chip shops always make their own.'

'You peel the potatoes and cut the chips yourself?' Slider was mildly surprised.

'Yeah. O' course, in the old days there used to be a potato boy come in to do it. That's how I got started in the trade, as a spud boy, every morning before school. Better than a paper round. Learn the ropes an' that. But nowadays what with the recession and every think I 'ave to do 'em myself.'

21

'You have some kind of machine, I suppose?'

'Yeah, a peeler and a cutter. I'll show you.' He half rose, eager to display his expertise, but Slider checked him gently.

'Yes, later. Just a few more questions. So you cut up a new lot of chips this morning, did you? How do you suppose that finger got into them?'

'I dunno,' he said, shaking his head in perplexity. 'It couldn't have been in the new lot. How could it? I haven't lost a finger.' That seemed indisputable, but he spread his hands out on the table before him, as though for reassurance. 'It *has* happened,' he conceded, 'with the old style of cutters. They was dangerous. There was a bloke over in Acton a couple o' years ago with one of them old sort lost two fingers. But with the new rotaries—' He shrugged, displaying his firmly attached digits again.

'That's what you've got?'

'Yeah. An' they've got safety cut-offs.'

Slider shuddered at the choice of words. 'Who else works here?'

'No one. There's only me, except at weekends for the busy time, then there's the part-timers, school kids mostly. But they only help serve out front. I'm the one that does all the preparation.'

'So the chips you cooked this morning were peeled and cut up this morning by you?' Slider asked.

Slaughter's frown dissolved suddenly. 'Wait a minute, I've just remembered! I had half a bucket of chips left over from last night. They was what I put in first thing when I opened this morning. It must have been in them.' He seemed happy to have solved the mystery.

'And who prepared yesterday's chips? You?'

'Yes. I keep telling you, there is only me,' he said almost crossly.

So they were no further forward. It was a mystery, Slider thought, and not a particularly interesting one, either. Someone must have planted the thing as a joke. 'Let's just take it slowly from the beginning,' he said patiently. 'When you arrived this morning, did you come in by the front door or the back door?'

'Through the shop. I let meself in through the shop like I always do.'

'And did everything seem normal? Was there any sign of disturbance?'

'No, it all looked all right. We've had break-ins before, mostly after the fruit machine. Nicked the 'ole bloody machine once, took it out the bloody front door right in the street in broad daylight – well, under the street lamps. No one saw nothing, o' course,' he added bitterly. 'They never do.'

How true, thought Slider. 'But this morning everything was all right? And what did you do next?'

'Went through into the back room to start work.'

'Did everything seem normal there?'

'I never noticed anything different.'

'The back door was shut?'

'Yeah. I opened it to let some air in. It gets stuffy in there 'cause I had to brick the window in, 'cause kids kept breaking in through it.'

'What sort of lock have you got on the back door?'

'A Yale lock, and two bolts, top and bottom.' He seemed to experience some qualms about this, as though realising it was not much of a high-tech response to the modern crime wave. 'It's kids mostly,' he added apologetically. 'Little bastards.'

'And was the door locked and bolted when you arrived this morning?'

Slaughter hesitated, and then said, 'Yeah, it was bolted.'

'You're quite sure?'

'I always bolt it last thing before I go home. I wouldn't forget that.'

'All right, Mr Slaughter. What did you do next?'

'Just what I always do. Get stuff ready.'

'What stuff is that?'

'Well, I wash out the batter buckets and mix up the new lot, cut up the fish, peel the spuds and cut the chips.' The words recalled him to the present mystery. He shook his head dolefully. 'I dunno how that thing got in there. I cut them chips up yesterday morning. It didn't half give me a shock when I saw it. Bumped my head on the table.' He touched the lump gingerly.

'And were you here alone all day yesterday?'

'Yeah. I only have helpers on Friday night and Sat'day.' He looked up suddenly as an idea occurred to him. 'Maybe that kid put it in herself, for a joke,' he said hopefully.

But before this possibility could be explored to its conclusion, which admittedly would have taken all of a microsecond, they were interrupted. Atherton appeared in the doorway between the front and the back shop, looking distinctly pale. 'Guv?'

Slider got up and went to him. Atherton glanced significantly at Slaughter, and then jerked his head towards the back room.

'Something nasty in the woodshed,' he murmured.

Across the tiny back room the back door stood open, but Slider caught the smell well before he reached it. The sun had risen high enough to clear the surrounding buildings and shine into the tiny yard, which contained an outside lavatory and a number of bulgingly-full black plastic sacks, neatly stacked round the perimeter, their necks tied with string. The sickly stink of rotting fish was terrible, mitigated

24

only now and then by the chemical odour rolling over the fence from the dry-cleaner's next door. Cleaning fluid would not normally have been high on Slider's list of Things to Smell Today, but it was still considerably ahead of rotting fish – if that's what it was.

Breathing shallowly Slider turned, and found that Slaughter had wandered after them and was standing in his back shop, staring in a puzzled way at his equipment as if it might speak and obligingly solve the puzzle.

'Mr Slaughter – does it always smell as bad as this out here?' Slider asked.

Slaughter started a little, plainly having been far away with his thoughts. 'Well,' he said apologetically, 'it does get a bit – you know – whiffy, especially in the warm weather. It's the fish trimmings and that. But the dustmen only come twice a week. I tie the sacks up – well you have to with the cats and everything – but the smell still gets out. You get sort of used to it after a while.'

'You get used to *this*?' Atherton said disbelievingly.

Slaughter took another step or two to the door and sniffed cautiously. 'Maybe it is a bit worse than usual,' he admitted. 'I dunno. I don't think I've got all that much sense of smell, really. Working with fish all the time – and the frying smell gets in your clothes—'

'These bags, sir,' Slider said. He gestured to one at random. 'That one there, for instance. What's in that?'

'Rubbish and that. You know, just the usual. Potato peelings, fish trimmings, left-overs and stuff. Just rubbish.'

'Is that how you tied it up yourself?'

'I suppose so,' said Slaughter cautiously. A certain reluctance was coming into his expression, perhaps as the magnitude of the smell came home to him at last.

'Would you mind opening it, sir?'

25

He plainly would mind, but equally plainly didn't feel he could refuse. He untied the string and parted the neck of the sack, pulling his head back out of the way as the smell rose up. On the top were some broken, soggy chips and several portions of battered fish.

'Red herrings, I suppose?' Atherton enquired.

'Left-overs,' Slaughter corrected him, with some relief.

'The piece of cod which passeth understanding,' said Atherton. 'But what's underneath, I wonder?'

He looked round him, picked up a yard broom, turned it up the other way, and used the end of the handle to push aside the top layer of rubbish. Underneath the left-overs was a left foot.

'Bloody 'ell,' Slaughter said softly, transfixed with horror.

'I thought it'd been too quiet lately,' Slider murmured.

'The game's afoot, Guv,' said Atherton.

'I was afraid you were going to say that,' said Slider.

Slaughter burst surprisingly into tears.

'I think we're going to need help here,' Atherton said under cover of the noise. He licked his lips, and Slider could see that his nostrils were flared with some emotion, distaste or excitement – either would have been appropriate.

'We certainly will. I'm not looking through a sackful of dead fish for evidence,' Slider agreed.

'And that's just one sack. There are enough of them out here to hold the whole body, assuming it's in pieces.'

'Right,' said Slider. 'Take Slaughter inside to the front shop and stay with him. I'll call in. And be gentle with him. If there is a body out here, he must know about it.'

'Okay,' Atherton said. The colour was returning to his face, and with it the blood to his head. 'If there is a body out here,' he gave the words back with minor relish, 'we've got ourselves a murder.'

26

'You don't have to sound so pleased about it.'

'It's better than endless burglaries and domestics.'

'Yes,' Slider assented minimally. His own pulse had quick-ened at this first, far-off sound of the hunt, but he never liked the part of him which felt excited at the beginning of a murder enquiry. It was someone's life, after all. 'Well, get on with it.'

The circus – forensic, fingerprinting, photography – had been and gone, and now Slider stood alone in the back shop looking round it contemplatively. It was small, drab, and even with the door open, stuffy. The floor was tiled in a chequerboard pattern of black and red, scuffed and pitted with age. The walls – what you could see of them – were tiled with large white ceramic tiles of the sort which first gave rise to the expression 'bog standard'. The back door was a massive thing of plain, impanelled wood, painted black, and with a splintered notch three inches above the lock where it had been forced on a previous occasion, according to Slaughter. The window, as Slaughter had said, had been blocked in rather crudely and was still awaiting any kind of finish to its raw bricks and mortar.

Two walls were lined with open shelves on which were stacked bags of powdered batter mix, boxes of Frymax cooking fat, jars of pickled eggs and pickled gherkins, cartons of crisps and outers of soft drinks. Along the third wall were ranged a large fridge which was mostly full of individual meat pies and drink cans; a huge chest freezer which contained nothing more sinister than packets of frozen fish, chicken portions and sausages; and a pallet stacked with paper sacks of potatoes.

Along the fourth wall, nearest the door, was a large sink with a stainless steel drainer to one side and a steel-topped work table to the other, above which, on the wall, was a rack containing an impressive array of butcher's knives. Under the work table there was a small drain set into the floor, and a brief glance around confirmed that the floor was sloped to drain into it, presumably so that the whole thing could be hosed down for ease of cleaning. Next to the work table stood the peeling machine, a large metal drum on a stand, which looked like a cross between an old-fashioned ship's binnacle and a What-The-Butler-Saw machine. Next to that was the chip-cutter. Slider tentatively felt one of its blades, and withdrew his hand hastily.

He stepped again to the back door and looked out. The yard had high wooden fences all round and one gate, secured by a padlock, leading to the alley. The alley had a high brick wall on one side, behind which were the back yards of the shops in the adjacent side-street, and on the other side the gardens of the houses down the opposite side-street. The back windows of those houses were out of sight because of a large sycamore growing in the nearest garden. The only windows which might have a view of the yard were upstairs in the dry-cleaners next door, and he had already ascertained that the Patels used the upper floor only for storage – they lived in a semi-detached house in Perivale. So anyone might have come and gone through the alleyway with a good chance of not being seen.

The pathologist, Freddie Cameron, came looking for him. 'I'm off now, Bill. I'll let you have a preliminary report as soon as possible.'

'What's the hurry?'

'The smell, old boy.' Cameron shuddered delicately. 'It's the sort of stink you can't get out of your nostrils for days.'

'That's something, coming from you,' Slider said.

'Not a Linger Longer Aroma,' Cameron amplified, in retreat.

Slider smiled inwardly, wondering how many people would remember that particular advertisement, and nearly missed

28

his chance. 'Oi! Can't you tell me something before you go? Anything, even if it's only I love you.'

Cameron turned back reluctantly. 'About the body?'

'Certainly about the body. It is animal, vegetable or mineral? Can you eat it?'

'Preliminary shufti suggests there's just enough bits for one male Caucasian, rather small and slightly built, youngish. But it's in a lot of pieces, so I'll have to have time to lay them out before I can tell you any more about it.'

'Have you got a head? If I can get a photograph right away—'

'We've got a head, but I'm afraid a photograph won't do you any good. It's been rather heavily altered. The face has been obliterated.'

'Obliterated?'

'Removed,' Cameron said uncompromisingly. 'I suppose the bits may be in the sacks somewhere, but whether we'll be able to make anything of them—'

'Someone didn't want him recognised, then.'

'Right. And we haven't found the hands, except for the one finger. Oh, and there's no hair, either. The entire scalp has been removed. We may find that, of course, but—'

He let the sentence hang for Slider, who would just as soon not have had it. Scalped? It sounded unpleasantly obsessive. Were they going to have to look for a homicidal Wild West fan?

'I suppose the body's badly decomposed?'

'No, I'd say it was quite fresh. Probably not more than twelve hours old. I think you're probably looking for a murder committed during the dark hours last night.'

'Then it was the fish making the stink?'

'Just the fish,' Cameron agreed. 'Ironic, isn't it? If friend Atherton hadn't been so fastidious, it might all have been carted away by the dustman and no one any the wiser.'

He turned to go again. A murder during the dark hours, Slider pondered. 'Freddie, all this cutting up – wouldn't it have taken a hell of a long time?'

'Not necessarily. There was that case last year, don't you remember, of the serial killer who dismembered his victims. The first took him thirteen hours, the second he managed in just two and a half. It all depends on knowing your way round a carcase. With a skilled hand and good sharp knives – and I'd say this was a skilled hand. There's no haggling. The body's been disjointed very neatly.'

'What about the cause of death?'

'Impossible to say yet. I'll keep you posted.'

'Okay. Thanks,' Slider said absently. A skilled hand and sharp knives – the back room with its steel table and floor drain. And yet Slaughter had seemed genuinely puzzled by the finger. Well, yes, perhaps he was – puzzled by how he came to miss it. A lot of pieces, Cameron said – not surprising one went astray, perhaps. Fell unseen into the chip tub. And Slaughter opened up the shop again just as usual the next morning. He must be a cool hand – God, he had to stop using that word! But then what could he do but open up? Anything else would have been suspicious. And when the schoolgirl began shrieking, what else could he do but call the police?

Step by step, landing himself in the soup. Or, as Atherton would undoubtedly say, the chowder.

3

Definitely Queer

Polly Jablowski, the Polish plonk, was in Slider's office putting a folder on his desk. Slider stopped dead just inside the door, feeling a nameless sense of unease, almost dread. Something was not as it should be. It was like one of those dreams where something enormously familiar, like the house where one was born, suddenly takes on an air of inexplicable menace.

Atherton, just behind him, stopped perforce, and stared hungrily over his shoulder at Jablowski's little spiky head and nude neck. The air crackled with impure thoughts; Slider's ear grew hot.

'Sir?' Polish said, straightening up. Seeing Slider's expression she said defensively, 'I was just delivering this folder—'

'Something's wrong,' he said. 'This is my office, isn't it?'

She grinned. 'The windows have been cleaned, that's all. By order of Mr Barrington.'

'Blimey, he moves fast,' Atherton murmured. 'And when we've just got ourselves a nice murder, too.'

Slider shook his head, bemused. 'It was such a shock.'

'The CID room windows are clean, too,' Polish mentioned.

'There goes our centre-spread in next month's *Toilet and Garden*,' Atherton said sadly. 'That man has no respect for tradition.'

Slider crossed to his desk to look at the folder. It was new, crisp, and had a fresh white label on the cover with the circulation list for checking off. The list was very long. There was also a memo fixed to the cover by a paper-clip.

'From Mr Barrington, sir,' Polish said apologetically.

'So I see,' said Slider. *As of this date, circulation files will be read and passed on within 24 hours of receipt, unless there are exceptional circumstances which prevent this. Such exceptional circumstances must be advised in writing to IVNB.*

'Apparently we're all to see all circulation files from now on,' she explained. 'Mr Barrington says we should be conversant with every new directive, whether it affects us directly or not. So the files have to go round more quickly, so that everyone gets a chance to read them.'

'I see,' Slider said with admirable restraint.

'And the painters are coming in next week,' she added, perhaps by way of providing a counter-irritant.

'Oh, good!'

'There's a colour-chart on its way to you. Mr Carver's got it at the moment'

'Splendid!'

'Shall I get a cup of tea, sir?' she enquired tenderly, like a nurse in casualty department.

'Yes, please. I need one. I think I'm getting a headache,' said Slider.

'The light's shining right in your credulity,' Atherton suggested.

Atherton entered the CID room and sat down on the cold radiator, stretched out his legs and crossed his ankles in a way that was somehow essentially English. Norma glanced across with interest. He had elegant ankles. She secretly suspected him of wearing silk socks.

'Well, it looks cut and dried, doesn't it?' he enquired rhetorically of the air. Beevers at the far desk grunted without looking up, like a sleeping dog hearing its name spoken. 'I don't think this one's going to be a sticker.'

'What, our homicide?' Norma encouraged him kindly. 'We don't even know it's a murder yet.'

'I suppose the victim may have undressed and slipped himself through the chip-cutter for thrills,' Atherton acknowledged. 'Anyway, there's no sign of forcible entry, and Slaughter's at suicidal pains to tell us that no one but him has been in the back room and no one else has a key.'

'I suppose the cutting-up was done there?'

'There were traces of blood on the table, the sink, the drainer, the floor and the floor drain. Also between the blade and the handle of two of the knives.'

'We don't know for certain yet it's human blood,' McLaren offered indistinctly through the Mars Bar he was sucking. 'We had a case once in Lambeth—'

McLaren had always had a case once that topped anyone else's. Norma interrupted him witheringly. 'I wish you'd make up your mind whether you want to eat that thing or mate with it,' she said. 'You have the most disgusting eating habits of anyone I've ever worked with, and that's saying something.'

McLaren opened his mouth to retaliate and Atherton hastily averted his gaze. He felt his speech was losing its audience. 'Well, we know it isn't fish blood,' he said loudly, 'and there's so much of it that the inference is plain.'

'Inference?' McLaren hooted derisively. 'What's that, some kind of in-house conference?'

A blob of half-melted chocolate slipped from his lips as he

spoke and fell onto his powder blue sweater. McLaren was very proud of his sweaters. Atherton smiled tenderly and continued.

'Especially as there were traces of blood and tissue in the chip-cutter. And fragments of fingernail.'

'I suppose that's how the finger got into the chips,' Norma said. 'He shoved a hand through and mislaid one of the digits. What did he do it for, though, I wonder?'

'Probably a joke,' Beevers said.

'If so, it was a bit near the knuckle,' Norma got in first.

'Perhaps he thought it might speed things up,' Atherton said, ignoring her loftily. 'He must have had a lot to do in a short time.'

'Unless he hoped it would obliterate the fingerprints? He seems to have wanted to hide the identity of the victim. Did the scalp turn up, by the way?'

'It wasn't in the sacks. Nor the hands. Nor any of the victim's clothing. God knows where they'll turn up. But what bugs me is that he goes to all that trouble,' Atherton complained, 'and then makes no attempt to give himself an alibi.'

'Perhaps he wants to be punished,' Norma said. 'Remorse. You said he was pretty upset when you found the foot.'

'Yes, but he might have the decency to wriggle a bit, though. The man is not a sport. I mean, where's the challenge for us if he doesn't make a chase of it?'

Mackay came in in time to hear the last bit. 'Oh, has he put his hand up, then, Slaughter?'

'As good as,' Atherton said. 'First he insists he went straight home alone and went to bed'

'Where does he live?' Norma asked.

'Bedsitter in Pembridge Road—'

'Shangri-la!'

'As you say. Then when I pushed him a bit, he changed his story and said he stopped for a drink on the way, didn't speak to anyone in the pub, and *then* went home alone. How can you verify a negative?'

'I thought he didn't shut till eleven o'clock,' McLaren objected. 'How could he get to a pub before closing time?'

'Well spotted. You should be a detective,' Atherton said admiringly. 'Version number two of his non-alibi was that it was so quiet he closed up early, about half-past ten—'

'Which accounts for his having chips left over,' Norma put in intelligently.

'—picked up a taxi to Holland Park Station and went to Bent Bill's.'

'Oh? Is he that way, then?' Mackay asked. Bent Bill's was the aptly named Crooked Billet, a notorious gay pub in Clarendon Road, Notting Hill.

'To the trained observer it's obvious,' Atherton said modestly. 'Anyway, I asked him if he had a girlfriend and he said no. Then I asked if he had a boyfriend and he got upset and went bright red. That's when he changed his story and said he'd gone for a drink. But he still claims he drank all alone, didn't talk to anyone, went home alone.'

'Well, I suppose that's it, then,' Mackay said. 'Bent Bill's is a cruiser's pub. He must have picked the victim up there, taken him back to the shop for a spot of whoopee, and after that—'

'He'd had his chips,' Beevers interrupted eagerly, as though he'd just thought of it.

'These homosexual murders can be very nasty,' Norma said, trying to keep up the tone. 'Look at that Michele Lupo case back in 'eighty-six.'

'We had a case once when I was at Kensington—' McLaren began.

'Have you run a make on Slaughter?' Norma asked hastily.

'Yes, but he's got no form.'

'There always has to be a first time,' she said comfortingly.

'But he still says he knows nothing about the body, so unless he breaks down and tells all we've got a long haul ahead of us. I'm going with the Guv'nor to have a look at his bedsit.'

'What about Bent Bill's?' Norma asked.

'No point in going there until the evening session. It's a different pub during the day. Anyway, it's between you and Andy, Alec. I'm booked, and the Guv'nor won't want to do it himself.'

'What's that, homophobia?' McLaren demanded.

'No, they only keep Watney's,' said Atherton.

The house where Slaughter lived was one of those tall terraced houses so typical of North Kensington, stuccoed and painted dingy cream, with a pillared porch, and steps up to the front door over a half-basement. You could tell the privately owned houses from those divided into flats or bedsits by the condition of the paintwork and the quality of the curtains at the windows. Dead giveaway for a burglar, Slider thought as they trod up the steps.

Beside the door there was a vertical toast-rack of labelled bell-buttons. Three of the bedsits were apparently occupied by the ubiquitous Mr Friedland. The second bell from the top offered *Slaughter,* and Slider pressed it just on the offchance. Nothing happened. Atherton went to press his face to the hammered-glass panel of the door. Slider pressed again, and heard the rattle of a window going up. Stepping back, he saw a pretty, painted face surrounded by fuzzy dun hair hanging out of a second-floor window.

It smiled winningly. 'Are you looking for Mandy?'

'Are you Mandy?'

'That's right.' She leaned out a little further, and Slider caught a glimpse of a scarlet satin dressing-gown. 'Are you Bob?'

Atherton was out of sight under the overhang of the porch. Slider flicked him a glance to keep him there.

'No. Were you expecting him?'

'I don't think he's coming now, he's ever so late.' She looked him over with interest and approval. 'D'you want to come up?'

'Yes, please,' Slider said eagerly.

'Second floor, door on the right.'

The head was withdrawn; the buzzer sounded, and Slider pushed his way in to a narrow hall with very shiny, very old lino, smelling strongly of furniture polish, stretching straight ahead up the stairs. On the second floor Mandy was waiting at the door, her dressing-gown invitingly parted at the neck, one bare knee poking through the folds and a feather-trimmed slipper appearing at the hem. How reassuringly traditional, Slider thought. Under the make-up she looked about nineteen, going on thirty-five.

'That lino's a bit slippery,' he commented.

'Oh, I know, it's lethal. It's Kathleen – the housekeeper – she will polish it. I don't know how many times a week people go arse over tit down the stairs, excuse my French. What's your name, love?'

Slider pulled out his warrant card. 'Detective Inspector Slider.' Her face sagged with dismay at the sight of it, and of Atherton coming up the stairs behind him. 'This is Detective Sergeant Atherton. Don't worry, it's not trouble for you,' he said quickly. 'We just want to ask you some questions about someone who lives here.'

'I haven't done nothing,' she wailed, pulling her dressing-gown tight at the neck with belated modesty.

37

'I know you haven't,' he said soothingly. 'It's all right. We just want to talk to you about Mr Slaughter who lives upstairs. I promise you you're not going to get into trouble. Can we come in?'

Inside, her single room was mostly taken up with a double bed covered by a quilted satin counterpane and crowded with dolls and frilly cushions. It left little room for a wardrobe, an armchair, and tiny table by the window covered in a lace cloth and bearing a vase containing a bunch of plastic violets. There was an old-fashioned gas fire with a mantelpiece crowded with ornaments, cards, letters and photographs, and on the wall above it a mirror in a frame encrusted with sea-shells. In the far corner was a sink with a geyser, and a marble-topped side-table bearing a single gas-ring and a collection of mugs, spoons and coffee-jars.

Slider felt a pang of nostalgia. Barring the personal clutter, it was exactly like the room he and Irene had first lived in when they got married. It even smelled the same, of carpet-dust mingled with the faint but penetrating aroma of tomato soup. And on just such a gas-ring he had cooked exotic one-pot meals for his bride, and they had sat on the bed together and eaten with spoons straight from the saucepan.

Back in prehistory. He shook the thoughts away, and concentrated on reassuring Mandy, who was passing from fear to indignation as she looked from Slider to Atherton and told herself how she'd been tricked. When his fatherliness and Atherton's obvious harmlessness – an effect at which he had worked hard over the years – had won her confidence, she proved both garrulous and inquisitive, and perched on the bed with one leg tucked under her, plainly glad of the company and spoiling for a chat.

'Well, he's gay, of course. I didn't need to be told that, although Maureen next door tried to get friendly with him when she first came. She thought he might bring us home stuff, you know, fish and chips and that, but I said to her what'd be the use of that? They'd be cold by the time he got here, though she's got a little cooker with an oven in her room so we could warm them up. But I don't like warmed-up fish and chips, and anyway, the time he gets home we're always working, and the smell does hang about. It'd put you right off, wouldn't it?'

She paused, seeming to expect an answer. Atherton, unfairly, looked at Slider for it, so he agreed.

Mandy nodded confidently. 'I mean you can smell Ronnie a mile away when he comes home with all that frying smell on his clothes. Not that he doesn't seem a very nice bloke, as they go, and I'm not prejudiced, but I wouldn't like a job like that. I like things nice.' She looked round complacently at her room.

'You've certainly made it very comfortable,' Slider said politely.

The compliment seemed to please her. 'It's not bad here. I've been in lots of other places before that weren't near as nice as this. Kathleen, the housekeeper, she comes in every day and cleans, and I must say she keeps it all, you know, very nice.'

'She doesn't mind about your – er – visitors?' Atherton asked.

'Why should she? She doesn't own the house. It belongs to a man, ever so rich he is, lives in a big house in Chorleywood, so I suppose he doesn't need the money, that's why the rent's so reasonable. He just wants enough to cover the running expenses, so Kathleen told me. She said he bought it for a capital investment, whatever that might be when it's at home. She said to me when I first took the room that it was a quiet house and as long as there was no trouble the owner didn't mind what we did. And there isn't,' she said emphatically, 'because believe you me the last thing *we* want is trouble.'

'Of course not,' Slider concurred. 'And what about Mr Slaughter? How long has he been here?'

'Oh, for ever! Well, I've been here three years, and he was here before me. I've been here the longest now, apart from him. There's a lot of coming and going. Some people only stay a few weeks, and you never see them when they're here. But Maureen and me, and Kim downstairs, we've all been here a while now.'

'Do you see much of Mr Slaughter?'

'Well, he's out at work all day and that, but we say hello if we pass on the stairs or anything, and I've been up to his room a few times for a cup of tea and a chat.' Slider could imagine who did most of the chatting. 'I mean, he's not very exciting, if you know what I mean, but he's a nice enough bloke.'

'Does he have any other friends?' Atherton asked. 'Does anyone visit him?'

'Not really, not regular.' She looked at him confidentially. 'Well, there's pick-ups, but you wouldn't call them friends, would you?'

'Does he often have pick-ups?'

'Not often. Well, he isn't Mr Universe, is he? Just sometimes he'll take someone up there. Never the same one twice, though. Well, that's how it goes, isn't it?'

'He had someone up there last night, didn't he?' Slider put the question as casually as possible, but still she experienced a belated surge of caution.

'I don't know if I ought to be talking about him behind his back. What's he done, anyway?'

'I don't know that he's done anything. I can't go into what it's about, but I can tell you that I'm trying to establish an alibi for him, so if there was someone with him who could vouch for him—'

'Oh well, that's all right then,' she said, instantly satisfied. 'I wouldn't want to get him into trouble, that's all. But he did have someone, in. They were coming up the stairs just when I was coming back from the bathroom – that's down one flight on the half-landing. I said hullo to Ron and he said hullo and they sort of come up the stairs behind me. And I came in here and they went on upstairs to his room.'

'What time would that be?'

'Ooh, I dunno, about half-eleven, quarter to twelve. I couldn't swear to the minute.'

'What did he look like, the other man?'

'I didn't really get a good look at him, only that he was youngish, and slim. Well, Ron's a bit – you know—' she shrugged, 'and I thought to myself he was doing well for himself, picking up a nice-looking lad like that.'

'How was he dressed?'

'What, the other man? He had a leather jacket on, with a sort of white collar. And jeans, I think. I didn't really see his face or anything,' she anticipated. 'He was sort of in the shadow coming up the stairs, and I only got a glimpse of him behind Ronnie. Not to know him again.'

'Where would Ronnie have picked him up?' Atherton asked.

She shrugged. 'One of those gay pubs, I suppose. Naturally I didn't ask. He goes up the Coleherne sometimes, in Earl's Court. And the Billet in Holland Park – that's near here. I expect it was one of those, I couldn't say really.'

'Does he go out often?'

'Not really. Well, he doesn't normally shut the shop until eleven, and he only gets Sunday and Monday nights off. He doesn't usually go out a Sunday night.'

'What does he do for pleasure, then?'

'I don't think he does anything. He just stays in his room and watches telly and plays music.' She made a face. 'Jim Reeves. I can hear it sometimes when it's quiet down here. His room's just above mine. And that Dolly Parton. I can't stand country an' western. Drives me barmy – twang twang twang!'

'Did he play music last night?' Slider asked.

'Yeah. He had it turned up really loud at one point. I think he must have been dancing with his mate, because they were thumping on the floorboards. And then—' She stopped herself and looked at Slider nervously.

'And then? Go on, you'd better tell me. It might be important.'

'Well, at one time they were having a bit of a barney, shouting and that. The music stopped and I could hear them at it. Then he put another tape on, and I didn't hear any more.'

'Did you catch what they were arguing about?' She shook her head. 'Did you hear the other man leave?'

'Yeah, it was about one o'clock, give or take. I was busy,' she said delicately, 'but I heard them go down the stairs talking.'

'How do you know it was them?'

'Well, it had to be. The other room upstairs is empty. There was one of those Chinese men staying there, but he's left now.'

'Chinese?'

She shrugged again. 'We seem to get a lot of Chinese here. I don't know why. I don't mind – they're never any trouble. Quiet. You hardly know they're there.'

'So Ronnie and his friend went out together?' Atherton said.

'Yeah. So they must have made it up,' she added hopefully.

'And did you hear Ronnie come back in again later?' Slider asked.

'Well, it wasn't before four o'clock, because I'd have heard him. After that, I dunno – I was asleep. But I heard him in the bathroom this morning about seven o'clock, so he must have come back, mustn't he?'

Ron Slaughter's bedsit was smaller than Mandy's, but seemed larger because it had only a single bed. It was furnished with much the same equipment, but it was painfully, monastically neat. The bed was tightly made with a white candlewick bedspread folded down and tucked under the turn of the sheet and the pillow severely smoothed. Nothing had been left lying about. A mug, plate and knife and fork which had been washed up and left to dry beside the gas-ring were the sole signs of riot. The sink itself was sparkling clean, and there was a room-freshener on the windowsill making the room smell faintly of synthetic peaches.

On the mantelpiece was a cheap quartz carriage clock and a framed photograph of Slaughter himself, much younger, with his arm round an elderly woman, with a bungalow in the background. His dear old mum, without a doubt, Slider thought. The mirror above the mantelpiece was perfectly plain, but around the walls were four framed, home-made pictures of ladies in crinoline dresses, fashioned out of silver-paper sweet wrappers. Slider shook his head in disbelief. He remembered the craze for making them, but it was too long ago for Slaughter to have experienced it. The Dear Old Mum must have given them to him.

Otherwise, Slaughter's possessions were meagre, and all stored away neatly. There was nothing of interest except for the suitcase under the bed, which contained a stack of gay porn magazines, a red-spotted neckerchief, and a heavy leather

43

belt so encrusted with metal studs it would have dragged any trousers it was attached to down to the knees with its sheer weight.

'No collection of scalps,' Atherton said sadly. 'I was looking forward to seeing them pinned up around the walls like a stag's revenge.'

'No evidence of morbid obsessions at all,' Slider concurred.

'Oh, I don't know,' Atherton said, looking in a drawer. 'It is all far too tidy. He even folds his socks – now that's morbid.'

'There's something odd about this room all the same,' Slider said absently, letting his mind slip out of gear as he stared around.

'How odd do you want it? What kind of a man irons his underpants?'

Slider got it at last. 'There's no reading matter of any kind. No books, newspapers, magazines—'

'Except those under the bed.'

'Well, presumably they're valued more for the illustrations than the text.'

'No *TV Times*,' Atherton acknowledged. 'How does he know what's on?'

'No diary, letters, bills – nothing.' Slider shook his head. 'It's perfectly possible to live a life without paperwork, of course, but it's surely unusual?'

'Nothing in writing. Caution, do you suppose?'

'I don't know. But it's odd.' Slider looked in the wardrobe. The clothes were neatly disposed and looked clean, with the exception of the two pairs of trainers which were, in deference to normal usage, grimy. 'All this will have to be bagged and tested, but it doesn't look as if any of them belonged to the victim.'

'No sign that anyone's been involved in an evening's amateur butchery, either,' Atherton began.

Slider put a warning hand on his arm. A slow footfall was coming up the stairs. They turned towards the open door. A middle-aged woman with permed and dyed black hair rose laboriously into view. She was wearing a green nylon overall with a yellow duster bulging out of one pocket, carpet slippers, and enamelled earrings in the shape of four-leaved clovers. She had a fag clamped in the corner of her mouth and one eye was screwed up against the ascending smoke. She also carried a pair of blue jeans over her arm.

She wheezed as she climbed, concentrating on the stairs, and didn't notice them until she was almost on top of them. Then she started violently, let out a faint shriek, and clutched the jeans to her chest, teetering on the brink of the slippery stairs.

'It's all right,' Slider said hastily, taking a step forward. Any further movement of alarm could prove fatal.

'Who are you?' she spluttered through the cigarette in her lips. 'Dear Baby Jesus, you frightened me nearly to death, jumpin' out on me like that!'

'I'm sorry,' said Slider. 'I didn't mean to startle you.' They showed their briefs, and she looked suspiciously from one to the other.

'What are you doing in Ronnie's room? How did you get in?'

'With the key,' Slider said, displaying it. 'I take it you're the housekeeper, Mrs—?'

'Sullivan. Mrs Kathleen Sullivan and I've been housekeeper here for ten years, as anyone will tell you,' she said emphatically, as though it were a character reference. 'Ronnie Slaughter's a nice boy, hard-working and quiet. Don't tell me he's in trouble because I won't believe you.'

'We hope not. That's what we're trying to find out.' He looked at the jeans over her arm. 'Are those his?'

'That's right. He must have washed them in the bathroom and left them to dry. I was bringing them up for him. I've already done his room – not that there's anything much to do, ever, for he's the cleanest, neatest creature I ever saw, which is not natural in a man, let me tell you! I've been married to two of them, so I know what I'm talking about. Why the good Lord made men messy I don't know, but that's the way of it.'

'Does he usually do his washing in the bathroom?'

'He does not! I wouldn't encourage it. He takes his little bit of a wash down to the launderette of a Sunday morning as a rule.' She held the jeans up judicially before her. 'It is queer,' she acknowledged. 'I suppose he must have spilt something on them. He seems to have got it out, anyway, whatever it was.'

Behind him, Atherton played a little fanfare on a trumpet. No, he didn't really, that was just Slider's imagination. He held out his hand.

'May I?' he said politely.

4

Fillet in your Bones

Tufnell Arceneaux of the Metropolitan Police Forensic Science Laboratory was a raw-boned giant of a man, half Scots, half French and half Swiss-German, as he said of himself. He had fair skin, pale blue eyes, and masses of thick, fuzzy blond hair which sprouted so vigorously from his visible orifices that his inevitable nickname of Tufty Arsehole was less speculative than it might otherwise have been. He had a booming voice, an enormous appetite for work, a new young wife, and eight children at the last count.

'Bill!' he cried in greeting. 'How are you, my old dear? How are the essential juices?'

Slider held the receiver a little further from his ear. 'Flowing, thanks Tufty. What've you got for me?'

'I thought you'd like a preliminary report to be going on with.'

'All contributions gratefully received.'

'In the soup, eh?' the earpiece howled. 'Well, the blood in the shop is human all right. So you're not looking for a mad pork-butcher after all.'

47

'Good.'

'We've typed it against the sample from the body, and we've got a pretty good match. About ninety per cent. Good enough for the Crown Prosecution Service, anyway. We'll do the genetic thingummy on the tissue from the cutting machine, but you know how long that takes. One little old man with a bunsen burner in the lab of a girls' secondary mod in Leicestershire. Be a week, I should think. Still, I think you can reasonably assume that the body was cut up in the back room of the shop.'

'That's a relief. In all the best crime novels the corpse is never the corpse—'

'And the suspect is never the suspect. Quite.'

'Talking of the suspect, have you looked at the jeans?'

'Yes, and we found a bloodstain on the front left side and at the top of the left leg. Human blood.'

'I knew there must be something!'

'The old copper's instinct, eh? Well, we managed to get enough out of the inside of the seam to group it EAPBA, which is the same as the corpse.'

'Halleluja!'

'The bad news,' Tufty roared sympathetically, 'is that it's also the same as one in four of the population at large. And, I'm afraid, his voice surged with regret, 'it's also the same as the suspect, as per samples, intimate, freely donated, innocence for the establishing of.'

'Can't you type it any more closely?'

'Sorry, old mate. The sample just isn't good enough. It was a bit washed out. But never mind,' he subsided to a mere fortissimo, 'something else will turn up. Always does. How are you getting on with the new man, by the way? Barrington?'

'I don't know yet. I've hardly come into contact with him – except for his memos. He seems to be suffering from AIDS.'

'What?'

'Accumulative Inter-office Document Syndrome.'

'You're going to hate him,' Tufty promised in a confidential roar. 'He's dry, old dear, dry – no essential juices at all. You couldn't get an intimate sample out of him with a hundred foot bore. In fact, hundred foot bore just about sums him up.'

'How do you know him?'

'I meet him at dinners all over the place. He's one of Nature's club men. A great Joiner. Belongs to just about everything – golf, cricket, rifles. All the backslappers too: Buffaloes, Rotary, Order of the Honourable Chipmunks – you name it.'

'I'd sooner not,' said Slider mildly.

'Mind you,' Tufty bellowed reasonably, 'I've nothing against that kind of thing in theory. If a man wants to spend his weekends in the Function Room of the Runnymede Sheraton, lifting his trouser leg and swearing eternal loyalty to the Grand High Ferret of the Chasuble, that's his business. But when it gets in the way of his profession, that's another matter.'

'So Barrington's a Mason, is he?'

'I never said a thing, old love. All that panic about Masons is pure paranoia anyway! I don't believe for a minute that they sacrifice newborn babies and drink the blood in bizarre secret rituals. But a man can't be too careful who his friends are. Need I say more?'

'Well, yes, actually, you do,' Slider said, mystified; but it was no use.

'Said too much already! Anyway, I'll send you the full report on the shop as soon as I can find a typist who can spell "immediate". Cheerio, old mate! We must have a drink sometime.'

* * *

Atherton put his head round the door. 'I'm off, Guv, unless you need me for anything else.'

'No overtime for you?'

'Not tonight. I'm cooking dinner for Polish. Three-mushroom terrine, noisettes of lamb with walnuts and gooseberries, and dark and white chocolate mousse.'

'That should do it,' Slider agreed. 'For a dinner like that you could have me on the sofa.'

'When does Joanna come back?' Atherton followed the thought rather than the words.

'Tomorrow. It's been a long two weeks.'

'Longer for her, I should think, doing the whole of North America in a fortnight.'

'Be in early tomorrow.'

'I will. Goodnight.' The head withdrew.

'Make notes!' Slider called after it.

When he got home, the place was deserted. In some ways it was how he liked it best, though even at its best it never really felt like home. In the spotless kitchen he found a note pinned against the refrigerator door by a magnetic strawberry: *Cold meat and salad in the fridge. Please ring Mr Styles about the bath tap if you're not going to do it.* Whatever happened to welcome home darling? he wondered. He opened the fridge and looked in. The salad was laid out on a plate with clingfilm over it: lettuce, green pepper, cucumber, tomato and cold lamb. He'd never liked cold lamb. He shut the fridge and wandered into the living-room.

Irene had been moving the furniture round again. He hated to come home and find things changed, but Joanna said it was a secondary sex characteristic, all men were like that. Something to do with the primitive territorial instinct: you couldn't properly scent-mark things if they moved around from day to day.

He smiled at the memory of her telling him that (in The Bell and Crown at Strand-on-the-Green, it had been, ploughman's and a pint of Fullers, watching and wondering at the cormorants diving for fish in the Thames: the last time he had seen her before she went away) and approached Irene's latest proud acquisition. Her desire to have a conservatory had, of course, arisen from the fact that Marilyn Cripps had one – though hers was Victorian and original to the house. The installation had cost more than Slider had been eager to spend, but he had been unable to think of a convincing reason to refuse it, especially given the elephant of guilt he could always see out of the corner of his eye whenever he was with his wife.

So there it was, gleaming white PVC, octagonal, double-glazed, with black-and-white-tile effect Cushionfloor, and Sanderson print curtains all round – 'So we can entertain in here at night,' Irene had explained when he baulked at the extra cost. The material seemed unnaturally expensive to him, though to be fair Irene had made the curtains up herself and done a beautiful job of it, thermal lining, contrasting piping, pelmets, tie-backs and all. But that was only the beginning: next there had to be special conservatory furniture – a bamboo sofa and chairs with cushions to match the curtains, and a glass-topped coffee table just for starters. More would undoubtedly follow – she had already hinted at an indoor fountain.

'You want it nice now we've got it, don't you?' she had said in wounded tones when Slider protested mildly about the outlay. He thought it had looked nice completely empty, and Matthew had confided in a rare moment of masculine sympathy that it would be perfect for a three-quarter-size snooker table he had seen advertised in a Superman comic his friend Simon had lent him. But Kate, who was growing up horribly fast, had been on her mother's side, and was already promising to make vol-au-vent cases, which she had just learned at school, for the inaugural cocktail party.

Slider went through it and out into the garden: an oblong of grass with a path up one side and a rather drab collection of shrubs round the other two; a paved patio with two half-barrel tubs planted with red geraniums, blue lobelia and white alyssum. He felt another pang of guilt. The garden had always been his responsibility, and he liked gardening, but he had found less and less time to do anything about it, and of late years Irene had taken over the function. As a result, anything that was complicated or involved a lot of work had been quietly eliminated. It looked like her garden now, not his – and whose fault was that?

Standing brooding like a heron, he remembered the garden of his childhood home, the rows and rows of vegetables looking so ugly in the rain (why did he always remember the vegetable garden in the rain?) and the ranks of shaggy chrysanthemums, the fruit trees and the pale rambling rose down the bottom by the potting shed, the hollyhocks which had been his mother's favourites and which were always blighted with some disease or other, chocolate-spot or rust or whatever it was called.

Now that *was* a garden! It smelled like a garden, too, of earth and rot and manure; full of birds and slugs and earwigs; the dank potting-shed a haven of mouldy sacks, cobwebs and woodlice. This present garden had no smell, no wildlife, no natural chaos. It was just an oblong of tidiness, bland and sterile. He stared at it with a sense of loss. He didn't belong. He had been away too long, so that even when he was here the place rejected him. Where were they all, anyway? They no longer even bothered to tell him where they were going, though Irene must have been expecting him back or she wouldn't have laid out the salad.

He had to get out. The fact was that they didn't need him or want him any more. He would take the first opportunity to talk to Irene – calmly and sensibly – tell her everything, tell her he was leaving. She wouldn't really care, not any more.

Not tonight. And not until Joanna was back. But the first chance he had after that.

They came back all together when he was watching the late news on ITV. The children went straight upstairs, as was their wont, to the privacy of their own rooms into which – as guaranteed by Magna Carta, the Bill of Rights, the Geneva Convention *et passim* – no adult might penetrate without express invitation. Irene came in still untying the silk scarf from around her neck. Her face was lightly flushed and her eyes were bright. She looked almost pretty.

'Hullo. Did you have your supper?'

'Yes thanks. Have you been somewhere nice?'

'Just to Marilyn's, for bridge.'

He smiled inwardly at the casualness. Six months ago it would have been 'To MARILYN'S for BRIDGE!' But he would make an effort to be sociable, even though playing bridge seemed to him an extraordinary way for intelligent adults to behave.

'Good game?'

'Yes, not bad. I had a couple of really good hands for a change.'

'Who did you play with?'

'Ernie Newman.'

'Oh, bad luck.'

Irene frowned. 'Look, I don't make fun of your friends. Ernie's a very nice person, and he's got lovely manners, and he's very fond of me. *And* he's a good bridge-player.'

'I'm sorry.' Ernie Newman had been coming up in conversation a good deal lately, partnering Irene to all the things Slider couldn't make, and he probably had been jocular too often at the boring old fart's expense. He changed the subject hastily. 'Where were the kids?'

'I didn't know what time you'd be back, so I left them at Jeanette's and picked them up on the way home.'

'Just as well. I was a bit late. We've got a murder case.'

'Oh,' she said, and seemed to be hesitating between sympathy and disappointment. 'I suppose that means you'll be working all hours again?'

'I suppose so,' he said, thinking of Joanna and how the case would provide all the excuses he needed. But no, he was forgetting, he was going to sort things out; he wouldn't need excuses any more.

'You've been home so much the last couple of weeks, I began to think we might have a proper social life at last,' she said diffidently, folding and refolding her scarf, her eyes on the television screen. He looked at it too, but watched her warily out of the corner of his eye. Was it going to be a row? He didn't want a row tonight. But in the brief silence the moment passed. 'Did you call Mr Styles?' she asked instead.

'Yes, but it was engaged,' he lied.

'All right, I'll ring tomorrow,' she said peaceably. 'That is, if you're not going to fix that tap yourself?'

'I don't think I'm going to have time, what with the case and everything,' he said. The adverts came on, and he shifted his gaze to look at her, unfortunately just at the moment when she looked at him. It made him realise how rarely their eyes ever met these days. She seemed to be studying him thoughtfully, and for a moment he felt completely exposed, as though all his unworthy, craven thoughts were laid out in the open for her to see. Could she possibly know about

Joanna already? No, she couldn't possibly. Not possibly. *Nothing in writing.*

The searchlight moved on past his hiding place: she turned away towards the door. 'I think I'll go and have a quick bath,' she said.

Was that all? In the old days she would have asked him about the case. Even in times of maximum irritation with him, she had always made a point of asking: she believed it was her wifely duty to express an interest in his job. Her slender, retreating back made him feel suddenly lonely, cut off from humanity. He had a contrasting mental flash of Atherton and Jablowski sharing their intimate, candlelit dinner and talking comfortable shop together. Now he felt like the Little Match Girl.

'By the way, the new man's come,' he said desperately as she was about to disappear.

She stopped and half turned. 'Oh? What's he like?'

'Smart. All spit and polish.'

'That'll be an improvement. That Bob Dickson was such a slob.'

He felt wounded by her lack of understanding. She must know by now how he had felt about his late boss. 'He doesn't like me,' he said plaintively.

'The new man?' Now she looked at him again, that same, thoughtful look. 'I wonder why?'

'He didn't like Dickson either.'

'Well, that probably explains it,' she said. 'Everyone in the Job must know you were Dickson's man.'

It was an incisive, even an intelligent comment, but he didn't know whether or not it was also derisive. He couldn't think of anything to say, and she went, leaving him surprised for the first time in God knew how many years of their marriage.

★ ★ ★

55

Dickson's office was Dickson's no more. Fug, filth and fag ash had been swept away by the new broom. The clean windows stood wide open to the traffic roar, there was nothing on top of the filing cabinets but a red Busy Lizzie in a pot, while the only bare bit of the wall was now adorned with a framed print of Annigoni's portrait of the Queen. The desk gleamed with furniture polish and was disconcertingly clear, containing only an in-tray, an out-tray, and between them one of those burgundy leather desk sets for holding your pens and pencils, from the Executive Gift Collection at Marks and Spencer.

The chair was different, too, a black leather, tilt-and-swivel, high-backed, managing director type Menace-the-Minions Special – two hundred and fifty quid if it was a penny. Barrington must have brought it with him, Slider thought as he presented himself in response to summons. You'd have to be a pretty important, influential kind of bloke to take your own chair with you wherever you went. The kind of bloke who'd have a car phone and a Psion organiser too.

'You sent for me, sir?'

'What's the situation with Slaughter?' Barrington asked without preamble. His ruined face and impossible hair had the irresistible magnetism of incongruity amid all that determined neat-and-tidiness.

'He's still sticking to his story, that he went home alone, even though we've told him he was seen going to his room with another man. And he still says he knows nothing about the body.'

'Has he asked for a solicitor?'

'No, sir.'

'Have you told him he can have one on Legal Aid?'

'More than once. He just shakes his head.'

Barrington stirred restively. 'I don't like that. It won't look good in court if he hasn't had access to a brief. If he still refuses one tomorrow, send for one anyway. You've got the name of a good local man, someone we can trust?'

'Yes, sir,' Slider said. 'But—'

'Don't argue. Just do it,' Barrington said shortly. 'I don't know what sort of ship Mr Dickson ran,' he went on with faint derision, 'but when I give an order I expect it to be obeyed without question. And I expect *you* to expect the same thing from your subordinates.'

'Yes, sir,' Slider said faintly. He was experiencing the same insane desire to giggle as when he had been called up before the headmaster of his school for bringing a hedgehog into Prayers. How had this man managed to get so far without being murdered by his subordinates?

'Right. So what have you got on Slaughter?'

'No form, sir. He's not known anywhere. We're still looking for witnesses but so far we can't place him at the scene at the right time.'

'That's all negative. I asked what you'd got, not what you hadn't got. What did he say about the bloodstains on his clothing?'

'He says he had a nosebleed while he was getting dressed, so he took the jeans off and washed them out before it set.'

'It's a pity about that grouping. Still, no one can prove it isn't the victim's. And there's no sign of forcible entry to the premises, and Slaughter's prints are all over everything and on the knives.'

'About those knives, sir—'

'Yes?'

'It strikes me as odd that all but two of them were absolutely clean – no prints at all – and the other two had just single prints of Slaughter's.'

'What's odd about that? He wiped them clean after the

murder, and then used two of them in the morning. He'd have to have done that if he wanted it to look innocent.'

'But the prints on the two knives were of his fingers and thumb only – no palm print. He must have washed and dried the knives and then left the prints putting them back in the rack.'

'Well?'

'But why only those two? There ought to have been similar prints on the others if he wanted it to look natural. And after all, since he works there, there's nothing intrinsically wrong with having his fingerprints on anything, so why go to so much trouble? It makes me uneasy. It's either too clever or too stupid, I don't know which.'

'You want logic from a man like that?' Barrington said impatiently.

'No, sir, only consistency.'

'We're policemen, not psychiatrists. Your business is to collect evidence, and let someone else worry about the implications. Have we got enough to charge him?'

'You're asking my opinion?' Slider asked cautiously.

'I'm not whistling Yankee Doodle.'

'Then – no, sir. Not until we can ID the body, at any rate.'

Barrington frowned, but did not pursue the line. 'What courses of action are you following?'

'House to house is still going on. There's the rest of the residents in Slaughter's house to question. There's the pub he said he visited. Also all the other known gay pubs within reasonable distance. And we're trying to trace all the casuals who've worked at the fish bar in the last six months – there were a couple of other prints in the back shop clear enough to identify and we want to eliminate them.'

'Got enough men?'

'For the moment. Unless we have to start looking for another suspect.'

58

'I want Slaughter kept under wraps,' Barrington said sharply. 'That's why I asked you about charging him.'

'He's co-operating with everything at the moment, sir. He hasn't asked to leave.'

'If he does, let me know immediately,' Barrington said abruptly, and took a file from his in-tray and opened it, to signify that the interview was terminated. 'All right, carry on.'

Slider left, quelling the desire to salute facetiously. Atherton was having a bad effect on his character, he decided.

Beevers had drawn a blank at Bent Bill's.

'In spite of the moustache and chubbiness,' Atherton mourned. 'I thought you'd be very much up their street.'

Beevers shrugged. 'I didn't say I didn't get any offers, only that no one I spoke to would admit knowing Slaughter.'

'What about the barmen?' Slider asked.

'Same thing, Guv. They all went glassy-eyed when they looked at the photo.'

'There'll be other nights and other customers,' Slider said philosophically. 'At least we've got time on this one: Slaughter's going nowhere. Someone else can have a crack at it tonight.'

'Alec looks too much like a policeman. Why not send Norma?' Anderson suggested. 'They might think she's a bloke in drag.'

'I don't mind,' said Norma, splendidly unconcerned. 'Polish can come with me. The older ones might fancy a young boy.'

'A catamite look a queen,' Atherton offered.

'Come again?' Polish said blankly.

'I wish you'd said that last night,' Atherton complained. Slider saw Jablowski blush uncomfortably and hastened to intervene.

'Let's get on. What have we got from the house-to-house?'

'One of the Ali Rebabas confirms that the chip shop was

shut before eleven,' Anderson said. 'He went out to his car for something at about ten-to, and noticed that it was dark.'

'That's helpful corroboration anyway. What else?'

'And a woman living across the road – a Mrs Kostantiou – saw a car parked at the end of the alley at about one a.m., which wasn't there when she got up in the morning, about six o'clock. She thinks it was dark red or dark blue or brown. She doesn't know what make and she couldn't see the registration number.'

'Terrific!' Atherton groaned.

'Slaughter hasn't got a car,' McLaren pointed out.

'Might be the victim's,' Norma said.

'Might not,' said Atherton.

'Never mind,' Slider said. 'Bring her in and let her look at the book, see if she can pick out the model. It could be something. See if any of the other residents saw it arrive or leave. Anything else?'

'We've still got some of the people in the other side-street to do,' said Mackay, 'though given it's their gardens that back onto the alley, it seems unlikely they'll have seen anything in the middle of the night.'

'There is one thing, Guv,' Norma said hesitantly. 'I've been checking into the other helpers at the fish bar, and I haven't been able to get hold of one of the ones who's been doing Friday and Saturday nights.' She looked down at her notebook. 'He's a Peter Leman, lives in a maisonette in Acton Lane. I've called and I've telephoned, but no luck. It might be nothing, of course, but I've got a sort of feeling about it—'

'You think it's worth looking into?' Slider asked.

'She can fillet in her bones,' Atherton said.

'For that,' Slider said, 'you can do Bent Bill's tonight.'

★ ★ ★

60

'I'm back,' said Joanna.

'I can tell,' said Slider.

'How?'

'The receiver's gone all damp and my trousers are too tight.'

'It's just the other way round with me.'

'Where are you?'

'At the airport, waiting for the baggage. I just thought I'd phone you,' she said with a casualness which didn't, thank heaven, fool him.

'How was the tour?'

'Terrible. Three people got food poisoning in a fish restaurant in San Francisco, and one of our cellos fell down some steps in Washington and broke his arm. But New York was heaven. We couldn't get all the desks of first fiddles on the platform at the Carnegie, so Charlie and I got a day off and did the tourist bit. How's the sleuthing business?'

'We've got a murder.'

'What, another one? Shepherd's Bush gets more like Chicago every day.'

'This is one thing you won't get in Chicago – a dismembered body in a fish and chip shop.'

'Most unhygienic.'

'That's just what I said. When am I going to see you?'

'I was going to ask you that,' she said.

'I could probably manage to drop in later. I've got to go to South Acton. But I suppose you must be tired,' he said wistfully. 'You'll want to sleep.'

'I'm jetlagged to hell, so I mustn't sleep until bedtime or I'll never get my clock right. Come whenever you like.'

'I've waited two weeks to hear you say that.'

61

5

Gone to Pieces

The White Horse was open all day, but that was the best thing you could say about it. It was a large 1930s building occupying a corner site, and its original individual bars had been knocked into one vast open-plan office inhabited at all hours by a muted selection of nondescript men in ready-made suits, whose precise function in life was impossible to determine. Some of them had portable phones and some of them didn't, but all of them ought surely to have been at work, or why did they look furtively towards the door every time it opened?

Slider could never fathom the reasoning behind building Shepherd's Bush nick right opposite a Watney's pub. As he said to Cameron, 'It reminds me of the busload of American tourists travelling along the M4 past Windsor, and one says to another, "They must have been mad to build the castle so close to the airport."' He stared sadly into a half pint of Ruddles, which was the nearest thing they had to real ale in the White Horse.

Freddie Cameron was a gold watch man, so it didn't trouble

him. He hitched his dapper little gluteus maximus into a more central position on the bar stool and asked, 'Why is it only in London pubs that you get these things? Most uncomfortable invention. They wouldn't stand for them up north.'

'Our bottoms are different from theirs,' Slider said. 'Surely you've heard of the London Derriere?' He looked at the bar menu. 'Are you having a sandwich?'

'No, thanks, I haven't time. I've got to get across to Harlesden by two o'clock for a PM on that immolation case.'

Slider, who had been toying with the idea of a toasted ham sandwich, changed his mind. 'So, what can you tell me about the Fish Bar victim?' he asked instead. 'Apart from the fact that he'd completely gone to pieces, of course.'

'Young Atherton's been a rotten influence on you,' Cameron said sternly. 'Deceased was male, about five foot seven; slender – weight around ten stone; sallow-skinned; probably dark-haired to judge by the body hair – of which there was very little, by the way. No scars or peculiarities.'

'Age?' Slider asked.

'I put him at first at twentyish, going by the skin and muscle tone, but now I think he was probably older. From the skull sutures I'd say he was nearer thirty. But probably he was young-looking for his age.'

'Have you found a cause of death?'

'Almost certainly a single heavy blow to the back of the neck at the level of the second and third vertebrae.'

'Battered to death,' Slider murmured, somewhat against his will. Still, better out than in.

Freddie didn't flinch. 'Death would have been instantaneous,' he corrected stalwartly. 'Fracture of the spine and rupture of the spinal cord. It was torn about two-thirds of the way across. An expert blow, I'd say – or a damned lucky one.'

'And then the cutting up?'

'With very sharp instruments, as I said before,' Freddie went on. 'I've taken the fingerprint, by the way, of the one finger we had, and sent a copy over to you but I don't think it'll help you much. Deep frying didn't improve it.'

'Yes, I got it, thanks. I wish it had come with a photograph, though.'

'Someone's done a good job on the head,' Cameron admitted gloomily. 'Scalp and face both removed, and the bits we've found of the face are no help at all.'

'You can't put them together again?'

'Diced,' he said succinctly. 'Couldn't do anything with 'em except make a shepherd's pie. Chummy was taking no chances. The scalp and hands are missing, as you know. Oh, we haven't got the eyes, either. But he had a fine set of gnashers. I suppose you want the Tooth Fairy to have a look at them?'

That was the forensic odontologist. 'Yes, please. We'll see what comes of that. If it doesn't lead to an identification, I suppose it'll be a job for Phillips at UCH.'

'The medical illustrator?' Cameron raised his eyebrows. 'Is it that bad, old boy? Won't chummy come across?'

'He's sitting on his hands and keeping his knees tightly together.'

'So what's gone wrong with the old Slider Interview Technique?'

'Look at it from his point of view,' Slider said. 'If he's gone to all that trouble to hide the identity, he's not going to tell us just for the asking who the corpus is. And until we know who, we can't prove Slaughter even knew him, let alone topped him—'

'And chopped him. I can't get over that name – Slaughter!' Cameron said, shaking his head.

'He's obviously banking on the body-work for his salvation. But if we can present him with an identification, I think he may fold up and admit the murder. Otherwise we've a long hard road ahead of us.'

'Have you charged him yet?'

'Barrington's toying with the idea, but I can't see how we can, yet. I'm not too worried about that. If we let him go and he does the off, it's all evidence on our side. And he might just do something really stupid. He doesn't,' he added, 'seem the brightest to me.'

Freddie studied Slider's expression. 'That puzzles you?'

'It does, rather. There's an inconsistency in it all.'

'Human beings aren't machines. Besides, what's so bright about committing a murder and getting yourself taken up for it?'

'He was all we had,' Slider shrugged.

'That's exactly what I mean. Not very clever, setting things up with yourself as the only suspect, is it?'

'That's true,' Slider said. He smiled. 'How you do comfort me, Freddie!'

'Can't have you brooding, old bean,' Cameron said kindly.

The 'maisonette' in Acton was in fact only the upper floor of a dismal turn-of-the-century terraced cottage which should never have been divided in the first place. The short front garden had been concreted over, and the concrete was stained and cracked, sprouting tufts of depressed-looking grass and a few defiant dandelions. The front gate and most of the front wall were missing, and there were only stumps in the ground where the railings that had once divided it from next door had been sawn off, probably during one of the scrap-iron-for-victory drives of the Second World War.

The bricks of the front elevation were blackened with the soot of ages, the paint was peeling off the window frames, and the battered front door had been painted in that one shade of blue which evokes no emotional response at all in the human soul, and which presumably goes on being produced by paint manufacturers through sheer force of habit. Slider trod carefully up the uneven path and rang the bell, setting off a fusillade of barks from somewhere inside.

The occupants of the lower floor were at home. Inside the street door was a tiny hall, about three feet square, with a door straight ahead – across the stairs, of course – and another to the left, leading directly into what had been the best parlour of the original house. Slider was invited in with an eagerness which suggested their lives were yawningly lacking in incident. They sat him down on a sagging sofa upholstered in much-stained orange-and-brown synthetic tweed, pulled the dog off him, and offered him tea.

The room smelled of old tobacco and old carpets and damp and dog. As well as the sofa there were two equally repulsive armchairs, a coffee table decorated with overflowing ashtrays, a large television set, and a clothes horse on which a wash was drying – a faded blue T-shirt and a vast quantity of grey underwear. Perhaps to help the drying process, the two-bar electric fire was on, making the room stiflingly warm and bringing out the full, ripe bouquet of the various smells. On the television Michael Fish was demonstrating the action of an occluded front, and from another room came the sound of disc-jockey babble from a radio. The dog, denied the sexual gratification of Slider's leg, walked round in short circles by the door, barking monotonously.

'It's about Peter upstairs, is it?'

'Do you take milk and sugar?'

'. . . some bits and pieces of rain, working their way slowly across central areas . . .'

'No, no tea, thank you.'

'D'you smoke at all? Chuck us the fags, Bet. Ta, love.'

'. . . tending pretty much to fizzle out, really, by the time . . .'

'Shut up, Shane! Ooh, can't you put him out in the kitchen, Garry?'

'Sorry about this, he gets a bit excited. C'mere you stupid bastard!'

'. . . not nearly as much as is needed, I'm afraid, particularly in the south east . . .'

'I could make you coffee instead, if you like?'

The dog suddenly hairpinned itself and sank its teeth into an itch at the root of its tail.

'No, really, thank you, not for me,' Slider said into the decibel vacuum. 'I had a cup just before I came out. I wonder if you'd mind turning the television off, just while we talk?'

They looked at each other a little blankly, as though the request had come out of left field, barely comprehensible.

'I'll turn it down,' Garry said at last, coming to a management decision.

'Only it's *Neighbours* in a minute,' Bet added anxiously.

The dog finished with its tail and resumed barking, standing still now and staring at the ceiling in a way that suggested it was really going to concentrate this time on making a good job of it. Garry turned the sound down on the television and Michael Fish mouthed silently from behind the glass, sweeping one hand with underwater slowness to indicate the Grampians.

'Oh, take him out, Garry. Shut him in the kitchen for a bit.'

The closing of the kitchen door muted both dog and deejay, and in the blessed near-silence which followed, Slider asked his host and hostess about the upstairs tenant.

'He's a nice boy, Peter – quiet, you know,' Bet offered. 'He's not been here long. There was that couple before—'

'Pakis,' Garry mouthed, nodding significantly at Slider. 'Not that I mind,' he added hastily, 'but they had this baby, cried all the time. And then there was the rows – you never heard nothing like it, all in Swahili or whatever it is—'

'You can hear everything down here,' Bet said with breathless emphasis. 'It's as thin as paper, that ceiling. Even anybody walking about, let alone shouting at each other.'

'And the smell of them curries morning noon and night.'

Slider intervened before they got too carried away. 'So how long has Peter Leman been living there?'

'Oh, it's – what—?' They looked at each other again. 'Three months? About that.'

'Four months. Febry, it was. That's when he came.'

'Febry's three months.'

'Nearly four. It was the beginning of Febry.'

'Do you know where he lived before?'

Garry shook his head sadly, as though loath to deny Slider anything. 'Not to say exactly. Well, Bet talked to him more than me. Did he say where, Bet?'

'No-o,' Bet said reluctantly, 'not really. Not inasmuch as *where*, so to speak. But I think it was somewhere in London. He speaks like a Londoner, anyway.'

'What does he do for a living, do you know?' Slider asked.

'Unemployed,' Garry said tersely. 'Well, who isn't these days?'

'He has just got himself a casual job,' Bet qualified. 'Evenings behind the bar at the Green Man, on the corner. He only started there last week. But Fridays and Saturdays he helps out at this fish and chip shop, doesn't he, Garry?'

'You'd think they'd be the busiest times at the pub,' Slider said.

'Oh, he said about that,' Garry said eagerly. 'He said they asked him to do Fridays and Sat'days, and the money would've been better, but he couldn't let these other people down. But if you ask me, he's scared it might get rough.'

68

'Well, he's only little,' Bet said defensively, as though it had been an accusation. 'I don't blame him. He isn't much bigger than me, and some of them kids that go in there of a weekend – you know, lager louts and that—'

'Doesn't want to spoil his face,' Garry grunted disparagingly.

'Well, he is a nice-looking boy,' Bet said.

'What does he look like? Can you describe him to me?'

But *Neighbours* had come on, and Bet's attention slithered resistlessly to the screen. Garry answered distractedly, watching it sideways. 'Well, he's a short bloke, about five-six or seven, I s'pose. Dark hair.'

'Thin or fat?'

'Slim. But he's fit. I see him jogging and that, sometimes. He's like, athletic, you might say.'

'Clean shaven?'

'What, you mean, like, does he have a beard? No, nothing like that.'

'Age?'

'I dunno really. He looks about twenty-five. Good-looking bloke, like Bet says. Smiles a lot. He's got nice teeth,' Garry added.

Slider thought of Freddie's words: *he had a fine set of gnashers*. So far it was looking good. 'Does he have any friends? Anyone that visits him here?'

'He has a girlfriend,' Garry said. 'What's her name, Suzanne.'

Bet came to, dragging her eyes away from the screen. 'I don't think she's his girlfriend, Gow,' she said earnestly. 'I think she must be his sister. Only I've never spoken to her,' she explained to Slider, 'but I see them come in together sometimes, and she doesn't sort of act like a girlfriend.'

'And when did you last see him?' Slider asked quickly, now he had her attention.

'Well, I see him go out Monday, to the pub. About half-past five that'd be,' she said doubtfully.

'Did you see him come in again?'

'No,' she said regretfully.

'But we heard him,' Garry added proudly. 'He come in about – what would it be—?'

'Half-past eleven?'

'Nearer quarter to twelve,' Garry corrected. 'We heard him bang the door and walk upstairs. Then we heard him, like, walking about up there.'

'Was he alone?'

Garry shrugged. 'We didn't hear no one else.'

'When I took the dog out, about ten minutes later, just in the front garden, I saw his light on in his front room,' Bet offered.

'And what about Tuesday? Did you see him go out on Tuesday?'

'Never saw him, but I heard him come down the stairs. Whistling, he was. And then he banged the door. You have to bang it – it sticks a bit.'

'We never heard him come in from the pub, though,' Garry said.

'And when I took the dog out, there was no light up there,' Bet added.

'We haven't heard any moving about up there, either, not since. And the gas man came yesterday morning to read the meters, and he didn't answer his door, so he couldn't have been in. I said to Bet, I reckon he's done a bunk, didn't I, Bet?'

But Bet's eyes had slid back to the magic screen. A fair-haired young woman with her hands on her hips was plainly telling a firm-jawed young man what she thought of him, while the firm-jawed young man picked sulkily at the back of a sofa, waiting his chance to justify himself. In the kitchen the dog had reached a peak of hysteria and was scrabbling at the closed door with its nails. Garry was lighting a fresh cigarette from the butt of the current one, and the smoke was lying in strata from the ceiling down almost to the level of the washing.

'Could I use your telephone, please?' Slider asked.

The landlord of the Green Man was tall, thin, and sour. His hair was dyed black, and lay reluctantly in separate strands over his skull. His skin was grey, his nose mottled blue, and his eyes congested yellow, and he spoke without moving his lips, as though to open them would be to give away too much of his precious breath.

'I never liked him from the start,' he pronounced. 'What's he done?'

'Nothing, as far as I know,' Slider countered. 'Why don't you like him?'

'Too clever-clever. College boy type. I knew he wouldn't stay.'

'He's a college boy?'

'I said "type". Thinks he knows everything. Lahdidah accent. I said to myself, this one won't stay. He won't want to soil his hands. But he was so keen on the job I took him on against my judgement.'

'Did he come to work on time on Tuesday?'

'Came on time. Then springs it on me that he wants to go off early. Says he's got to meet his sister off some plane at Heathrow. Well, we were quiet, so I said he could go, though I had my doubts. Starting the old nonsense already, I thought – and I was right. He left here at half-past nine, and that's the last I saw of him.'

'He hasn't been in to work since?'

'He has not.' The yellowed eyes met Slider's reluctantly. 'He's got wages owing. Well, he can have them if he comes for them.' He seemed to regret even this momentary lapse into kindness, and tightened his lips more grimly in compensation. 'Too clever by half, that one. He mended my bar video that's been on the blink for a fortnight – knows his way round a circuit board all right. What's a bloke like that doing behind a bar, I ask you? I knew he wouldn't stay.'

By the time Slider got back to the maisonette, Atherton had arrived.

'Shall I break in, or you?' he asked politely.

'You do it so nicely, dear,' Slider said.

'You're going to get me into trouble one of these days,' Atherton grumbled, bending to examaine the lock.

Slider told Atherton what he had learned so far while they looked round. The upper flat was small and dingy, with all the muted horror of a furnished let: nasty wallpaper, nastier carpets, and furniture the nastiest of all. The bottom door let straight onto the stairs, which were narrow and steep. At the top was a tiny half-landing, dominated by a mess of meters and fuse-boxes which seemed in imminent danger of pulling the sagging plaster off the wall. A doorway without a door led to what had originally been the bathroom of the house, and was now a kitchen. It had been divided down its length with a partition wall, behind which a bath, hand-basin and lavatory were crammed into the smallest possible space. From the half-landing four steps led on up to two doors, the bedrooms of the original house, now a bedroom and sitting-room.

The rooms gave every sign of expecting their owner back. In the bedroom the bed was unmade, the duvet flung back from a wrinkled undersheet; wardrobe and drawers were full of clothes, and there were two suitcases, one on top of the wardrobe and one under the bed. He had not packed and gone, that was for sure.

On the kitchen table a coffee mug, a crumby plate and knife, a pat of butter and ajar of Marmite bore witness to a last meal – Tuesday's tea? – and there was food in the fridge: milk, eggs, tomatoes, bacon, a pack of French beans, a packet of lamb cudets – Wednesday's dinner?

In the sitting-room there were newspapers lying around – Monday's *Evening Standard* folded to the jobs page and Tuesday's *Guardian* – and a copy of a paperback Dick Francis was lying on the floor half under the sofa, face down and open at page thirty-six. On the small table there was a half bottle of whisky and a tumbler with a screwed-up crisp packet stuffed in it, and a brown apple core lay in a glass ashtray on the hearth. The television showed a red light, having been turned off from the remote control instead of at the switch.

Yet all the evidence the flat provided was negative. Peter Leman seemed to receive no mail but junk mail. He kept no diary or address book. His books were few, paperback best-sellers. He kept no personal papers in the house, no letters, bills or anything of that sort. The flat gave the appearance of a temporary home.

'It's like a student's term-time place,' Atherton said. 'You get the feeling that there are parents somewhere with a bedroom full of his personal gear. I mean, where's all the normal silt of life?'

'He hadn't been here very long,' Slider reminded him.

'Why was he here at all?' Atherton asked, dissatisfied. 'Because it's cheap, I suppose. Maybe he quarrelled with his parents.'

'Over being gay?'

73

'We don't know that he was. There's the possible girlfriend. And we don't know that Leman was the corpse or that the corpse was the man Slaughter took to his room, or that the man Slaughter took to his room was Leman.'

'We don't know much, and that's a fact,' Slider agreed placidly, amused by his bagman's growing irritation.

They were almost ready to give up when they found, inside a copy of the London *A to Z*, a snapshot of a slim, dark-haired young man in jeans and T-shirt with his arm round a fair-haired, smiling young woman. Pencilled on the inside of the cover of the *A to Z*, there was also a telephone number. Slider tried it while Atherton took the photograph down to Garry and Bet. He returned a few minutes later.

'It's Peter Leman all right. And that's his girlfriend stroke sister—'

'Suzanne.'

'La même. Any luck with the number?'

'Yes and no,' Slider said. 'It's the number of the payphone in the hall of the house where Slaughter lives.'

Atherton brightened. 'But then, that proves—'

'At ease,' Slider said. 'We already know he knows Slaughter. He works at the shop, remember?'

'Curse! If there were any justice in this world, it would have been Suzanne's number,' Atherton grumbled. 'And you realise there could be any number of reasons why he's not come home?'

'Patience, lad. One step at a time. At least we've got the photograph.'

'It's the littlest least you've ever asked me to be glad about,' Atherton said.

'God, this is good!' Slider murmured. He was lying in post-coital bliss on Joanna's saggy old Chesterfield, with Joanna

74

curled up in his arms. Elgar's Second Symphony, which had been on when he arrived, was coming to its close.

'Mmm,' she agreed. 'Did you know that an interviewer once asked Barbirolli if he could nominate the last notes of the last music he would ever conduct, what would he choose? And he chose this.'

'I wasn't talking about the music. But still – I can relate to that, as the Americans say.'

'Oh God, that reminds me – there was a sort of stage manager person at the Carnegie Hall, and whenever something went wrong, he'd come mincing up and enquire politely, 'Is there a concern here?' It made Charlie foam—'

'Charlie?'

'My desk partner. He's an irascible old scrote with a very low pain threshold when it comes to language.'

'He seems to be cropping up in your conversation a good deal.'

She stretched up to kiss his chin. 'You can't be jealous of Charlie,' she decreed. 'Just not possibly.'

'I can be as irrational as the next man when I put my mind to it.'

'I work with him, that's all.'

'I work with Atherton.'

'What makes you think I'm not jealous of Atherton? You spend a lot more time with him than with me.'

He hugged her. 'Ah, but I mean to do something about that.'

'Oh yeah?' she said derisively, though without heat.

'I mean it.'

'Of course you do,' she agreed. 'But not just yet. What's the excuse this time? Irene isn't involved in any school plays and the children haven't got chickenpox or exams coming up.' His own excuses, handed back to him out of context,

75

sounded embarrassingly threadbare. Oh, I forgot, you've got a big case on, of course. That should be good for a few months.'

'Sarcasm is an unlovely trait,' he observed.

She kissed him again, contritely. 'I know. I didn't mean it. I'm just talking to hear myself talk.'

'You've every right, though. I've kept you waiting far too long. It's because—'

'It's because you're a Libra, and see every side of every situation,' she supplied for him.

'All the same, I was thinking about us the other night, and I saw it all very clearly. Case or no case, I'm going to speak to Irene the very first opportunity.'

She still wasn't taking him seriously. 'What constitutes an opportunity?'

'I mean just an opportunity. Both of us in the same room at the same time, alone together.' She was silent. 'Aren't you pleased?' he asked after a moment.

'Yes, of course I am.'

'You don't sound it.'

She looked up at him, suddenly serious. 'Bill, are you sure about this?'

His feet seemed to fill up with cold water. 'Of course I am. God, we've talked about it often enough! What's the matter – aren't you?'

'It isn't me that has to do it,' she said reasonably. 'It's a big step.'

'Are you trying to put me off?'

'No. I just want you to be sure it's what you want.'

'I knew it was what I wanted the first moment I met you. I've never felt like that about anyone else in my life. I know that sounds corny, but it's the literal truth.' He stared at her, puzzled. 'Why am *I* having to convince *you*, all of a sudden?'

Her face cleared and the sun came out. 'I just felt like a change,' she lied. 'Of course, if I didn't love you so much, I could quite happily settle for an affair with you, just as I do with all the others—'

The phone rang.

'What others?' he demanded,

'Sorry, your five minutes is up,' she said, grinning evilly, and reached for the phone. 'Hullo. Oh, hi! Yes, thanks, very nice. Well, when I say very nice – doing the choral symphony three times in a week is no joke. I reckon that Beethoven bloke must have been deaf. Yes, he's here. No, no, we were just talking.' She handed the receiver to Slider. 'From the excitement in his voice,' she said, 'I think that'll be it for the evening.' She got up and left him with a cold space all down his front.

'This had better be important,' Slider said into the mouthpiece.

'Would I disturb you otherwise?' Atherton said, wounded. 'I've been at Bent Bill's, and I've met a dear old couple there who have definitely identified Peter Leman from the photograph.'

'Tell me!' Slider said, struggling up straight and looking for his trousers.

'Well, they like to go there for a midweek drinkie because it's quieter than at weekends. They were there on Tuesday night, and as they were leaving at about half past ten, they saw Leman come in with Slaughter and walk up to the bar to order a drink.'

'How do they know it was Slaughter?'

'They gave me the description, I gave them the photograph.'

'How sure are they?'

'Very. They walked right past them. Slaughter isn't the least memorable man in the world, and they noticed Leman for his nice bum.'

77

'It sounds good. Are they willing to swear a statement?'

'Not willing, but they'll do it. Oh, and one other thing, Guv. They say Leman was wearing a leather flying jacket with a sheepskin lining. And do you remember, the tom in Slaughter's house—'

'Mandy.'

'Yes, Mandy – she said that the man Slaughter brought back with him had a leather jacket with a "sort of white collar". He was coming upstairs in the shadow, remember.'

'Yes,' Slider said. 'It sounds as though we've got him, then. I'll come in. Where are you now?'

'In their flat in Aubrey Road. They were a bit sensitive about talking to me in the pub. I'm getting the statement now, then I'll go back to Bent Bill's and lean on the barman.'

'Be careful you don't break something. I'll see you back at the factory.'

Joanna was looking at him with interest as he put the phone down and stood up.

'Result?' she asked succinctly.

'It could be. At least, it may be enough to persuade the suspect to tell us the rest. He's been on the verge of breakdown anyway for some time.'

She stepped close. 'Good. I'm pleased for you.'

He kissed her. 'I'll have to go now, though,' he said apologetically.

'I know,' she said. 'Don't worry.'

He kissed her again. He was getting an erection. He hoped it was her, and not the excitement of the case. 'If it's not too late, shall I come back afterwards? Or will you be asleep?'

'You can always wake me,' she murmured, lip to lip and hip to hip. 'Sleep I can have any time.'

'All right, then,' he said. Yes, it was definitely her.

6

A Bird in the Strand is Worth Two in Shepherd's Bush

Slaughter was weeping, but still coherent. Slider decided to carry on.

'Come on now, Ronnie. Why don't you get it off your chest? You'll feel better if you tell me all about it.'

'I never killed him! I never!' Slaughter sobbed.

'Killed who? Who was it in those plastic sacks? It was Peter Leman, wasn't it?'

'No! I don't know! I don't know nothing about that. I never done it, I tell you!'

'But you did meet Leman on Tuesday night, didn't you? You went with him to the Crooked Billet?'

Slaughter, who was occupied in wiping his nose with his fingers, reluctantly nodded.

'Was that a yes, Ronnie? You have to say it out loud, for the tape. Was it Leman you met on Tuesday night?'

'Yes,' Slaughter said at last. He was getting rather tangled up in the strings of mucus, and since he had only a short-sleeved T-shirt on, Slider pushed the box of tissues closer to him. Slaughter took one and blew his nose, took another and wiped his mouth. The pale lard of his chops was damp and quivering with distress.

'All right,' Slider said kindly. 'Why don't you start at the beginning and tell me about you and Peter Leman?'

'There's nothing to tell, really,' he mumbled.

'He was a nice-looking man, wasn't he?' Slider offered temptingly.

Slaughter sat up a little straighter, sighed, and smoothed his hair back with both hands. When he lifted his arms, a waft of rank sweat emerged. Tape rooms always smelled of sweat and trainers: it was the essential odour of crime, Slider thought.

'Yeah, he was nice,' Slaughter said. Slider exchanged a glance with Atherton. Slaughter had accepted the past tense and handed it back to them.

'A nice smile, he had, too – I should think he was a friendly kind of person, wasn't he? How did you first meet him?'

'Well, he come to the shop, didn't he? Asked if I needed a part-timer. Well, I had this girl – Karen – but she kept not turning up. So I said yes. So he come in Friday nights and Saturday nights after that.'

'How long ago was this? When did he start with you?'

'It was March, I think. Or Febry.'

'Just Fridays and Saturdays? Did he have another job as well?'

'I dunno. I didn't ask. That's all I needed, just the weekend.'

'Was he good at the job?'

'Yeah. He picked it up all right. He was clever – educated an' that. He spoke nice, too.'

'Too good for the job, was he?' Atherton put in.

'He worked hard, all right,' Slaughter said defensively. 'There wasn't no swank about him. I liked him.'

'And did he like you?' Slider asked.

80

Slaughter blushed furiously and looked down. 'No. I dunno. He never said – I never thought about it. I didn't think he was—'

'That way inclined?' Slider said helpfully.

Slaughter looked up. 'I thought he was straight. Anyway, he was educated and everything. He'd never look at a bloke like me.'

'You're a successful businessman,' Slider suggested. 'For all his education, he hadn't got a job.'

Slaughter only shook his head wordlessly, as if trying to convey the inequality of the situation.

'All right, so when did you first realise that he was interested in you?'

Slaughter looked puzzled. 'He never said nothing. He never so much as looked at me. I mean, you can usually tell, can't you? Right up until that night—'

'Tuesday?'

'Yeah.' He had short circuited himself, and looked to Slider for another question.

'You met him at the Crooked Billet?'

But Slaughter was clear on that point at least. 'No, it was like I told you. The shop was quiet and I was fed up. I was thinking of closing up early, and then Peter comes in and starts chatting to me—'

'What time was that?' Atherton put in.

'Dunno exactly. Be about quarter-past ten, maybe. He goes what about going for a drink. So I goes yeah.'

'You went straight to the Crooked Billet? By taxi?'

'Nah, in his car. He had his car parked outside.'

'What sort of car?'

'It was a nice one. Red, sort of. Like a dark red.'

'What make?' Ronnie shrugged helplessly. 'All right, you went to the Crooked Billet. Did you talk to anyone else in the bar?'

He shook his head, and opened his hands in a gesture of frankness. 'There's a different kind of bloke goes in there midweek. Not my sort. Antique dealers and that – posh queens and couples and that. Anyway, I just wanted a quiet drink with Peter. We had a pint of lager top each. That's what I like, lager top, and he said he'd have the same.'

'And what time did you leave?'

'After drinking-up. About twenty-past eleven, I suppose.'

'And what happened then?'

Ronnie seemed to blush. 'Well, we was just stood there, like, saying goodbye, and he says, he says do I live near there, and I says yes. And then he says – he says—'

'Yes?'

This bit seemed to be difficult. Slaughter's eyes were anywhere but on Slider. 'He asked me if I had a boyfriend, and I said no. Then he said – he said he'd been thinking about me a lot recently.'

He stopped, overcome with emotion, and seemed unable to go on. His eyes started leaking again. Slider nudged the tissue box suggestively and asked, 'Whose idea was it to go back to your place?'

He shook his head, mopping dolefully. 'I dunno, really. He said how about a cup of coffee, and I said okay. And then he said was there anywhere open around there. So then I said—' He stopped.

'You suggested going back to your place for coffee?' Nod. 'Out loud, please.'

'Yeah.'

'And what happened when you got back to your place?'

'We had a coffee.' He stopped again, with an air of finality.

After a moment, Slider said, 'You put some music on, didn't you?'

'Yeah.'

'Did you dance together?'

'Sort of.'

'And then what happened?' Shake of head. 'Did you have sex together?'

Slaughter said nothing, only threw him a brief, reproachful glance.

'I don't want to know all the details, Ronnie. That's your private business. I just want to get clear in my mind what your relationship with Leman was. Did you and he—'

'No,' Slaughter said suddenly, defiantly. 'But he wanted it all right. I mean it was him what was coming on to me, not the other way round. I never thought he'd fancy someone like me, but he was coming on really strong, when we were dancing and everything – you know, like putting it out. But he was like stringing it out, sort of – flirting and teasing, as if he was going to do it, but not yet.'

'Making you wait? Making you want him more?' Atherton suggested.

'Yeah, like that,' Ronnie said eagerly. 'But then, all of a sudden, he changes his mind. And then he starts saying—' He gulped. 'Saying all sorts of things. He hadn't got no call to say things like that. So I got mad.'

'You quarrelled with him, didn't you?'

It came out in an indignant flood. 'He said things. When it turned out, like, he didn't want to – you know – I thought maybe he was shy. So I asked him, well, when we could meet again, and he said never. He said he could do better than me for himself. He said he never wanted to see me again. I couldn't believe it. I mean, we'd been having a good time, hadn't we? And it was all his idea. I wouldn't never have had the nerve to ask him. But now he was, like, making fun of me, and saying rotten things to me. He called me a slob. He said only a blind man would want to go to bed with me.'

Slaughter's hands balled into fists in remembered anguish. 'I got mad at him. I started shouting and, like, slagging him off. I told him he was a slag and a cock-teaser and that, and he was just jeering and laughing at me—' He choked. 'I could have killed him, the rotten little bastard!'

He stopped, and in the silence that followed, his own words must have echoed back to him. The animation of anger slowly drained from his face, to be replaced with a look of hollow dread.

'Yes,' said Slider gently. 'I understand perfectly.'

'No,' Slaughter whispered. 'No, I never done it. I never killed him. You got to believe me.'

'You left your bedsitter with him. You were seen going down the stairs together,' Slider said, to get him back to the narrative. 'How did you persuade him to go back to the shop with you?'

'I never—'

'You pretended to make up the quarrel.'

'That was him, When I got mad he said he was sorry. He said to calm down, he never meant it. He said he liked me really. I didn't believe him, but he asked me to walk with him to his car, 'cos he was scared of the streets.'

'What time was that?'

'I dunno exactly. It must of been about half-past twelve, quarter to one, I suppose.'

'So you walked him to his car – and then what?'

'He just got in and drove off.'

'Are you sure you didn't get in with him?' Slaughter shook his head helplessly. 'His route to South Acton would have taken him right past your shop in the Uxbridge Road. A red car was seen parked outside it at one in the morning – just about the right time for you to get there if you left your house at a quarter to one,' Slider said. Slaughter was staring at him, fascinated. 'I suggest you got in his car with him, persuaded him somehow to stop at the shop and go in with you. And then you killed him.'

'No,' Slaughter moaned.

'You were angry with him for refusing to go to bed with you, for laughing at you. You hit him on the back of the neck with something very heavy—'

'No. No. I never.'

'And then when you found he was dead, you decided to cut him up into pieces and hide him in the rubbish sacks. You thought no one would find him. Wasn't that the way it was?'

'No!'

'You probably didn't mean to kill him, did you, Ronnie? You'd had a quarrel, you were upset and angry. Perhaps you had another quarrel in the shop, and you hit him a bit too hard. Isn't that it?'

'I never killed him. I walked him to his car. He drove off, and I went home—'

'Ah, but you didn't go straight home. Your neighbour swears you didn't come in before four o'clock.'

'I just went for a walk. I couldn't go home right away. I was too upset. I went for a walk, that's all.'

'Where?'

'I don't remember.'

'You walked around all night?'

'I don't know. Not all night. I don't know how long I walked about. I was upset.' Slaughter's face was wet again, but now it was sweat, not tears.

'Ronnie, why don't you just tell me what you did, get it off your chest?'

'I ain't done nothing!'

'Then why have you been lying to me? You've been telling

me from the beginning that you went home alone on Tuesday night. Why didn't you tell me about Peter Leman before?'

'Because I didn't – I didn't want anyone to know.'

'To know that you'd been with him? To know that you killed him?'

'No!' he said desperately. 'I didn't want anyone to know I'm gay!'

Atherton stirred restively. Slider said, 'It isn't a crime any more, Ronnie.'

Slaughter said nothing, staring at the desk with the air of one who had said all he meant to say.

Silence would get them nowhere. Atherton decided on a little shock treatment. 'Everyone's bound to find out anyway when they read about the trial in the paper.'

'Trial?'

'The murder trial,' Atherton said pleasantly.

'But I never done it,' Slaughter protested. 'I never killed him.'

'Killed whom?' asked Atherton.

'Peter. I never killed Peter.'

'So you knew it was Peter's body in the rubbish sacks, did you?' Slider asked gently.

Slaughter stared at him for a moment with his mouth open, and then burst noisily into tears. Slider watched him for a bit, but he obviously wasn't going to stop this time.

'I think we'd better break off for the time being,' he said.

Slider stood watching Barrington read through the statement. It had taken a long time to get it down, with Slaughter breaking down every few sentences; and then when they had told him to read it through and sign it, he had asked them to read it aloud to him, since he didn't have his glasses with him. Slider thought he knew it by heart by now, having gone

86

through it so many times, and it didn't amount to much. Slaughter's clumsy, crabbed signature on the bottom of the page represented hours of work and nothing much worth having.

When he had finished, Barrington sat in silence for a moment, drumming his fingers on his desk top. 'All right,' he said at last. 'Charge him.'

'He still hasn't admitted it, sir,' Slider pointed out.

'Nevertheless,' Barrington said with irritation. 'I don't want him wandering off. We've got enough trouble with villains committing crimes while they're on bail, never mind murderers with access to sharp knives prancing about loose.'

'We still can't place him at the scene of the crime—'

'What the hell are you talking about?' Barrington's eyes sparked like a Brock's Golden Rain. 'It's his shop, isn't it? And no one but him had the key, according to his own admission.'

'That's exactly it, sir. Why would he admit anything so damaging?'

'Because he's stupid!' Barrington frowned. 'I'm not a hundred per cent happy with the way you're handling this, Slider. You're letting a villain with a minus IQ run rings round you. What's your team been doing? Why haven't we got a witness yet? Someone must have seen these two men going into the shop that night – it's on the main road, for God's sake! And where's the rest of the body? He must have put the bits somewhere. I want every inch of ground between the shop and his home covered until you find them.'

For once in his life, the exactly right, the witty, incisive riposte leapt to Slider's lips. 'Yes, sir,' he said.

'Guv? I think I've got something.'

Slider, who was passing the CID room door, stopped and

turned in. Several of the team were going over the house-to-house statements in the hope of turning up a witness. McLaren, whose sweater of the day was a delicate melange of eau-de-nil and lavender rectangles, was eating Pot Noodles with a plastic spoon, filling the air with a smell like rancid laundry. He shoved the statement he was reading to the side of his desk for Slider to look at, and licked a shiny smear of sweet'n'sour sauce off his finger before using it as a pointer.

'Some old dear lives in Dunraven Road – Mrs Violet Stevens. Says she saw a man coming out of the alley in the early hours of Wednesday morning. That's the other end of the alley, of course.'

Slider read in silence. A fair-haired man in a camel overcoat. Tallish, middle-aged. Looked left and right as he emerged and then hurried off towards Galloway Road. Mrs Stevens was very old and lived alone. She said she often wandered about the house at night as she was unable to sleep, and she didn't put the light on for fear of attracting burglars – as though they were some kind of moth. She had seen the man from her sitting-room window as she looked out to see if it was morning yet, and had watched in case he was a burglar. Once she knew he wasn't coming to rob *her*, she lost interest in him and left the window.

'That's it?' Slider asked in disbelief.

'It could be Slaughter,' McLaren prompted eagerly, his eyes fixed appealingly on Slider's face. Slider felt he ought to be feeling in his pocket for the bag of Good Boy Choc Drops. 'In the lamp light, and her being old and shortsighted, she might have taken his bald head for fair hair. It's been known.'

'It hardly makes her much good as a witness, though, does it? She's not absolutely sure if it was Wednesday or Thursday morning, and she doesn't know what time it was except that it was still dark. You put that in the witness box and watch defence counsel make knitting of it. Besides, Slaughter hasn't got a camel overcoat.'

'Not now he hasn't,' McLaren said significantly. 'But suppose he had blood on it, and had to get rid of it—'

'Along with the scalp and hands. I suppose he had them in his pockets? Or did Mrs Stevens say he was carrying a large shopping bag?'

'It doesn't say,' he said, a little crestfallen. 'But it's worth following up, isn't it? Ask if the bloke was carrying anything? And in any case, even if it wasn't Slaughter, if whoever it was was up the alley at the right time, he might be a witness. If we could trace him—'

'Yes, all right,' Slider said. His not to look a gift witness in the mouth, even one as old and spavined as this. Check everything, however small, however unlikely. 'You can go and talk to her. Take the photograph of Slaughter – and take it gently,' he added warningly as McLaren shot to his feet, tipping over the empty noodle pot and flicking the sticky spoon onto the floor. 'Don't press her and put words into her mouth; these lonely old dears can be suggestible if it means company. Let her tell you, not vice versa. And you'd better take Jablowski with you, in case she's scared of men and thinks *you're* a burglar.'

'Right, Guv. Softly softly does it,' McLaren nodded, proving his grasp of the cliche even in a moment of high drama. I'll handle her with kid gloves. Come on, Polish, get your skates on.'

'Time and tide,' Slider murmured as they passed him, 'wait for no rolling stone in the bush.'

Mackay meanwhile was answering the phone. 'Yes, sir. Yes, he's here. Yes, right away sir. Guv?' His expression was rigid, as though the phone had eyes. 'Mr Barrington would like to see you right away.'

Slider managed a fair imitation of rigidity himself. It was not for him to undermine authority by allowing the others to know that a summons to the command centre nowadays filled him with a certain apprehension.

As well as saying 'Come!' instead of 'Come in!', Barrington had the habit – culled, presumably, from The Alphabetical Guide to Management Power Ploys (Volume Two, L to Z) – of continuing to write while whoever had been sent for stood before him wondering whether to cough meaningfully, or to stand in silent contemplation of his master's framed certificates on the wall and absorb a proper sense of his own inferiority.

Slider said politely but firmly, in the manner of a man too busy for executive games, 'You sent for me, sir?'

Barrington looked up and subjected Slider to a keen-eyed examination. 'Ah, yes,' he said in his own good time. 'I have noticed that some of your team are not very particular in their dress. I want every man under my command at all times to wear a suit and tie, with the tie done up properly, and the jacket on.'

Slider was puzzled. 'That's how they do dress.'

Barrington's fingers drummed irritably. 'When I passed the CID room earlier today, I saw collar-buttons undone, ties loosened, two men in shirt-sleeve order, and one wearing a *pullover*.' From the way he said it, it might have been a leopardskin posing-pouch and high heels.

'Only in the office, sir. When they go outside or even down to the front shop—'

'I expect proper dress *at all times*.'

Only the knowledge of what the team would say when he passed that on drove Slider to protest further. 'But surely, sir, where members of the public can't see them—'

Barrington leaned forward sharply, tilting the moonscape

aggressively at Slider. 'You don't know, and I don't know – no one knows – who might walk into that room at any time; and then what sort of confidence would they have in our abilities?' He sat back. 'Besides, a sloppy appearance goes with sloppy thinking and inefficient methods. Do you think they let executives walk about looking like that at ICI or Marks and Spencer's?'

Slider confessed his ignorance on that point.

'We are a service industry. We have customers. Don't ever forget that.'

Slider remained silent.

'You've got into some bad habits in this department,' Barrington said kindly. 'Well, a unit takes the character of its commanding officer, so perhaps it's understandable. But things are going to change around here. I've already told you that, Slider. I hope you believe it now.'

Slider indicated that he did.

'And another thing,' Barrington said just as Slider had decided that was that and began to turn away. He turned back. 'You haven't chosen the colour for your office yet.'

'Sir?'

'You've had the colour chart on your desk for two days. Others must have a chance to look at it.'

'I'll see to it right away,' Slider said.

'In some stations there's just a uniform decoration scheme imposed from the top, whether you like it or not. But I like my officers to have a working environment they feel at home with. Be sure you don't abuse your privileges.'

'I won't, sir,' Slider said gratefully. The man was as sane as a sardine in a thicket. He wondered if he could get out of the office before he started foaming. Fortunately there was a knock at the door.

'Come!' Barrington barked.

Norma put her head round the door. 'Sorry to disturb you, sir, but there's a woman downstairs asking for Mr Slider. Says it's very important, and won't speak to anyone else.'

Barrington nodded his release, and Slider took his grateful departure.

'Who says there's no God?' he murmured to Norma when he got outside.

He recognised the woman at once as the female in the photograph with Peter Leman. She was mid-twenties, pretty and very smart, dressed in a coffee-coloured linen suit, with short fair hair, very professional-looking make-up, and expensive shoes. There was nothing about her that was appropriate to the flat in Acton.

As he approached, she watched him nervously but hopefully. 'Are you Mr Slider?' she asked.

'Detective Inspector Slider. You must be Suzanne,' he said. 'I'm afraid I don't know your other name.'

'Edrich.'

'Ah, another cricketer.'

'I'm sorry?'

'No, nothing. You want to speak to me about Peter Leman, I understand? Who gave you my name?'

'Oh, that lady and man who live downstairs at the flat – I don't know their names. They said you were there asking questions about Peter, so I thought – well, *she* said you seemed nice, so – only I'm so worried about him, you see. Oh, please tell me, what's he done? Where is he?'

Slider put a hand under her elbow. 'I think we'd better go somewhere a bit more private, and have a chat.'

Interview Room 2 was free. Slider sat her at one side of the desk, sat himself at the other and tried to look unthreatening. Her brow was furrowed and she fiddled with the clasp of her handbag, but she seemed well in control. Her eyes were large and blue, and their gaze was level and intelligent.

'Now, Miss Edrich – you're Peter Leman's girlfriend, are you?'

'Yes. Well, I suppose so. I haven't known him very long, but – yes, I suppose I am.'

'How did you meet him?'

'He moved into a flat in my road about six months ago. I used to see him around. Then I got chatting to him at the station on my way to work one day and, well, he asked me out.'

'Your road? You mean Acton Lane?' Slider asked.

'Oh no, I live in Casdenau. Boileau Road. You know, just the other side of Hammersmith Bridge.'

Posh, Slider thought.

'The flat in Acton Lane isn't Peter's,' she explained. 'He's just minding it for a friend.'

'What friend is that? Do you know his name?'

She shook her head. 'Peter never said. Only that this friend's gone abroad for six months or something. Peter just goes over sometimes to see if everything's all right.'

Double life, thought Slider – and this was the Bird in the Strand, of course, somewhat out of her place. 'The people downstairs you mentioned – Mr and Mrs Abbott – say that Peter led them to believe he lived there,' he said. 'They've seen him coming and going – going out to work and coming in late at night.'

'I don't know about that.' She shook her head, plainly bewildered. 'He lives in Boileau Road, the house opposite mine.'

'You're sure about that?'

'Of course. I've been in his flat and everything, with all his things in it. In any case, Acton Lane – well, it's a dump. He wouldn't live in a place like that.'

'You've been there with him, I understand.'

She looked embarrassed. 'Well, you see, the fact is I live with my mum and dad, and Peter's flat being right opposite – well, there'd be no privacy. So we use his friend's place sometimes.'

'Your mother and father wouldn't approve of you going out with Peter?'

She made a face. 'They think there's something funny about him, just because he isn't an accountant or a banker or something boring and respectable like that. Mum keeps on about where his money comes from. She thinks anyone who doesn't work in an office must be a crook.'

'Does he have a lot of money?'

'Enough,' she said with a shrug. 'He has nice clothes and takes me out to nice places, and he has a BMW. He parks it outside, so of course Mum and Dad can't help seeing it.'

'I see. So where does his money come from?'

She stuck her chin up. 'It's none of my business to ask.'

Slider smiled encouragingly. 'All the same, I can't believe an intelligent person like you hasn't wondered about it. If he doesn't appear to have a conventional office job and he isn't short of money—'

'It doesn't mean he's a criminal! There are lots of ways of making money. He has investments. He speculates – you know, on the stock market and things. At least, that's what I think. There's nothing wrong with that, is there?'

'Nothing at all,' Slider said politely.

'Even Dad has stocks and shares,' she said triumphantly, 'though he doesn't do anything with them. But I bet he would if he had the know-how. And Peter buys and sells things – not out of a suitcase,' she added hastily, with a quick smile, 'on commission. Commodities or futures or whatever they're called. He goes abroad quite a bit.'

94

'On business?'

'I don't ask,' she said with a stubborn look. Slider could see the parental disapproval and the family quarrel it caused looming through her statements. 'It isn't my business. I shouldn't expect anyone to question *me* about where I was going and what I was doing.'

'Yes, I see.'

'Only now he's missing—'

'Missing?'

'We were supposed to be going out on Wednesday night. He was going to meet me from work, but he didn't turn up. And he hasn't phoned me or anything since, and he doesn't answer his phone.'

'But how do you know he's missing?'

'He hasn't been home.' She looked a little defiant. 'I've got a key to his place. I've been in there. His mail hasn't been picked up off the mat, and the last lot of washing-up hasn't been done. Peter's always very clean and tidy. Besides, he would never let me down like that, without saying something.'

'Perhaps he went abroad – on business – at short notice?' Slider suggested.

She shook her head. 'He'd have told me if it was that. And his suitcases are still there, so he can't have packed anything. That's why I got worried. I went round to the flat in Acton Lane to see if he was there – I didn't know what else to do – and they said the police had been round asking for him. Oh, please tell me what's happened. Do you know where he is?'

Slider weighed her up carefully, and decided that she would do better and be more forthcoming on the truth. 'I'm rather afraid,' he said slowly, 'that he may be dead.'

She stared, her mind working. 'Don't you know?'

'We have a body which we believe is that of Peter Leman, but we haven't been able to identify it for certain.'

95

She licked her lips. 'Because – because he didn't have any next of kin, you mean? Do you want me – should I—?'

'It isn't that,' he said. 'I'm afraid the body's been knocked about rather badly. Even you wouldn't be able to recognise him.'

She closed her lips tightly, and he could see her jaw muscles working with distress. At last she said, 'So it may not be him?'

'It may not,' Slider says, 'but it seems most likely that it is. And now you've confirmed that he is missing . . .'

'Yes,' she said blankly. She was thinking hard. 'Can you tell me about it?'

'It's a long story,' Slider said. He gauged her fitness once more, but she seemed more thoughtful than distressed. 'Would you be surprised if someone told you that Peter Leman was bisexual?'

'Bisexual? You mean – that he goes with men? But he doesn't. He isn't.' She seemed astonished at first, and then indignant. 'I don't believe you! Who said he was? You couldn't get a more normal man than Peter, as far as *that's* concerned. Someone's putting you on.'

'I think,' said Slider, 'that you and I have rather a lot to tell each other.'

7

Cache and Carry

Peter Leman's Castlenau flat was a world away from the Acton one. It was also a conversion, but of a nice, bay-windowed, red-and-white Edwardian villa in a wide, tree-lined road, where every front garden sported nice rose bushes, and either a lilac or a laburnum.

'There's his car, anyway,' Atherton said as they drew up behind the red BMW. He got out and strolled down to peer through the window. 'He had all the extras,' he said from his pinnacle of knowledge. 'He's added about six K to the basic car, so he couldn't have been short of a bob or two.'

'Could it have been the car Mrs Kostantiou saw parked opposite the alley?' Slider wondered. 'It's red.'

'She picked out a Ford Sierra from the book,' Atherton reminded him.

'Yes, but with hesitation. She says she doesn't know anything about cars; and they're not all that different in shape to a quick glance.'

'If she's that vague about it, she's not going to make much of a witness, though, is she? And anyway, the car being here doesn't fit in, does it? Even if Leman did drive Slaughter to the shop for some obscure reason, how did it get back here after he was murdered?'

'Slaughter drove it.'

'Can Slaughter drive?'

Slider shrugged. 'Can a hedgehog swim?'

'I don't know,' Atherton said. 'Can it?'

'Useless speculation, that's all. We'll take the car in, anyway, and go over it. Might find a handy patch of blood, hair or skin.'

'Twitching curtains at twelve o'clock, Guv,' Atherton said in an undertone.

Slider looked across the road. 'That'll be Suzanne's mother, I suppose. Better have a word with her. Do you want to go and do it, while I have a shufti upstairs?'

Upstairs it was all freshly decorated, newly carpeted, and recently furnished at some expense. There was a large television and video, sound system with plenty of CDs, wardrobe full of expensive clothes, modern kitchen equipped with a microwave and a freezer full of Marks and Spencer ready meals, and a bathroom with gold taps. When Atherton came back, he found his senior going through the contents of the bedroom drawers.

'Phew,' said Atherton, flopping down on the bed.

'That bad?'

'She's living proof of the adage that superficiality is only skin deep. Tongue on wheels, dressed like mutton, obsessed with appearances. Very hot on the subject of Peter Leman not being good enough for her little girl, and so she told him! Flashing his money about – fast cars – and who knew where it all came from? Never had a job as far as she could tell. Here today and gone tomorrow. Probably a drug dealer for all she knew. She'd forbidden her Suzanne to have anything more to do with him, and Daddy agreed with her. Daddy is a bank manager. She was only a bank manager's daughter, but she received many a deposit.'

'Is Suzanne the only child?'

'There's a much older sister, apparently: married to a barrister, three children, two cars, an Irish wolfhound and a swimming pool. Second home in the Dordogne. Private education.'

'Ah.'

'I got the lot. No wonder Suzanne fancied a bit of rough trade. *Nostalgie de la boue.*'

'No wonder she asked no questions.'

'What have you found?'

'He certainly lived here – gubbins everywhere. And he certainly had money, but where it came from, I'm no wiser. I've found his cheque book, bank statements, credit card bills, but no salary slips. He was a sharp dresser and did all his food shopping at Marks and Spencer, and there's a cupboard full of booze – spirits and imported bottled lager – but no cigarettes, syringes or little glass tubes.'

'A clean-living boy.'

'I've also found his passport.'

'Interesting reading?'

'I think the Customs and Excise men would have found it fascinating. He was in and out like lamb's tails. America, Hong Kong, Turkey, Bangkok, Algeria. Last trip San Francisco six weeks ago.' Slider frowned. 'Business of some sort, that's for sure – using the word in its widest sense. Even with his unexplained wealth, he'd hardly be popping back and forth like that for pleasure.'

'Maybe he just liked air stewardesses. Or stewards, come to that. Or both. Hardly matters, though, does it? Wherever his money came from, he's thrown his hand in now.'

'Must you?' said Slider. 'All the same, doesn't it seem strange to you that this flash, jet-setting, BMW-driving, *Guardian*-reading type should take on a part-time job at a fish and chip shop, and then suddenly join up for one night of love with Ronnie Slaughter?'

'Yes,' said Atherton bluntly. 'The words *love* and *Ronnie Slaughter* do not bed down easily together in one sentence. On the other hand, why should Slaughter lie about it? If he was going to lie, he'd lie the other way – especially since he says he doesn't want anyone to know he's gay.'

'Unless the real reason for his meeting Leman was even more dodgy. Remember he didn't say anything about Leman at all until we faced him with the witness statement. Then when he realised we knew it was Leman he'd met, he made up a reason for it.'

'But what a reason! Surely he could have come up with something more convincing than that?'

'But you've just indicated you believe it because it's too incredible to be a lie.'

Atherton raised his eyebrows. '*Credo quia absurdum.* Well, you've got something there, Guv. Except that I don't believe Ronnie Slaughter's that bright.'

'Unless he's so bright he's able to make us think he's stupid,' Slider said tauntingly.

'Oh, nuts,' Atherton said. 'You could go on like that all day.' He wriggled, and felt underneath him. 'What am I sitting on?' He stood up and patted the counterpane, and then whipped the covers back to reveal a man's handkerchief crumpled up in the middle of the bed. 'Hullo-ullo-ullo! What's this?'

'It's used, that's what that is,' Slider said distastefully as Atherton bent down to peer at it.

'Certainly is – and if I'm any judge, it wasn't his nose he blew on it. The lad had nasty habits.'

'At that age, the essential juices flow fast and frequent.'

'I suppose Suzanne was otherwise occupied. Do you suppose he was keeping this for later – a secret cache?'

'Wait a minute,' Slider said suddenly as the idea occurred to him. 'That could be just what we want.'

'Speak for yourself,' Atherton said firmly. 'I'll get pregnant the conventional way, thank you.'

'Have you got any evidence bags?'

'In the car.'

'Get one, then. Don't you realise, whichever nose he blew on it, there's DNA in them thar folds.'

'Of course! We can get a proper match with the corpse at last. Why didn't I think of that?'

'Because I'm brilliant and you're stupid,' Slider said pleasantly.

'I knew there was a reason. I'll go and get the bag.'

Joanna came to meet him for a late lunch, and they went to the Acropolis for steak and kidney pie, mashed potato, carrots, peas and cabbage, prepared and served as only the caffs of old England can do it.

'Do you think you'd be able to tell if a man you were sleeping with was bisexual?' Slider asked.

Joanna looked at him gravely. 'It's Atherton, isn't it?' she asked after a moment.

'Eh?'

'I don't blame you, Bill. God, I've often fancied him myself! But why, *why* didn't you tell me from the beginning?'

'No, seriously, would you? Is it a thing you could tell?'

She made a thoughtful gravy inlet in her island of mashed potato. 'Depends how well I knew him, I suppose. I'd like to think I would, but it doesn't mean that a young, inexperienced girl also would. From what you've said, this Leman type was pretty well leading a double life. Presumably he was skilled at deception, or he'd have been found out long ago.'

'I don't understand the girl,' Slider grumbled. 'She's smart as paint – pretty, intelligent – she's got a job with a publishing company—'

'She's not all that intelligent, then.'

'She could have any man she liked—'

'Men don't like going out with smart, pretty, clever girls. They like to feel superior.'

'All the same,' he said patiently, 'she can't be lacking opportunity. Yet she goes out with this chap she knows virtually nothing about, who has no history or friends or relatives, who won't be pinned down, who comes and goes and is unaccountable. He works in a fish and chip shop two nights a week, and she never even asks him where he gets his money, although she says he had plenty.'

'You think he was a villain, then?'

'*I* don't know. But usually when people won't say where the money comes from, it's because they've got something to hide. And there was nothing in his flat to indicate that he was investing it in any of the usual ways – no share certificates or dealing papers or anything of that sort. But his bank balance was healthy, and he paid in large amounts of cash from time to time. All we know is that he went abroad a lot on short trips.'

'Sinister!'

'But she says he was very fond of her, and seems in no doubt about it. And she's genuinely distressed that he's dead, and quite adamant that he wasn't a bender.'

'Is there no doubt that he went to bed with Slaughter?'

He shrugged. 'He wanted to. Or at least pretended to want to. Unless Slaughter's lying.'

'Well, perhaps he is. I mean, if he fancied Leman and made

a play for him and Leman reacted with horrified rejection, he might not be able to admit it.'

'But that only provides a stronger motive for the murder. And in any case, he *does* say that Leman rejected him.'

'True.'

Slider shook his head. 'And in any case again, Leman certainly went for a drink with Slaughter and then went back to his flat with him. He didn't do that under duress.'

'Still, it doesn't make any difference to the case, does it, whether he wanted Slaughter or only pretended to, or even didn't? He met him for some reason, went home with him for some reason, quarrelled with him about something, went back to the shop with him, and got himself murdered.'

'Quite. But it does help when you present a case to the Great British Public if it has a modicum of credibility and consistency about it.'

'You sounded just like Atherton then.'

'No, no, he sounds like me.'

'Oh, sorry. What about Leman's car, by the way? If he was killed at the chip shop, how did it get back to his flat?'

'We have to assume Slaughter drove it there. Obviously he couldn't leave it outside the shop, and if he was clever enough to conceal the murder, he was clever enough to think of that.'

'Can he drive?'

'He says not, but that doesn't mean anything. Lots of people who've never taken a driving test can drive, and a negative of that sort is impossible to prove, anyway. But if he did drive the car back to Castelnau, he'll be bound to have left some trace of himself in it, even if it's only a single fallen hair, and forensic will find it.'

'I see. Well, the case is pretty well wrapped up now, isn't it? I mean, you've got your man and everything, haven't you? No big problem about it, is there?'

'No more than usual, I suppose,' he said cautiously. 'Why do you ask?'

'Because of my concert tomorrow – you know, the charity gala with the reception afterwards? I've been offered a guest ticket for it, and I'd rather like you to come along.'

He looked doubtful. 'Will I like it? I wouldn't have to wear a dinner jacket, would I?'

'An ordinary suit would do. I'm not proud. And yes, you will enjoy it. The music's lovely. And if the reception's really terrible, we'll sneak out and have a late supper at La Barca, how's that?'

'All right. Why not?' he said.

'You might be a bit more gracious. It's a very grand do, you know. There'll be royalty there, and the stalls will be stuffed with VIPs and hotshots from the world of entertainment, all doing their bit for charity. What you might call a Cause Celeb.'

'In that case, I'd love to come.'

'These tickets are not easily come by,' she told him severely. 'They're changing hands for more money than an unsigned Jeffrey Archer.'

He'd just reached the top of the stairs when the lift door opened and Barrington emerged explosively like the Demon King. The baleful eyes fixed on Slider.

'My office. Five minutes,' he barked, swivelled on the ball of one foot, and dashed off.

Interpreting this as a request rather than a set of random phonemes, Slider plodded after, following the faint whiff of sulphur that lingered on the air. With the difference in their metabolisms, he reckoned, it would take him the five minutes to get there. What would it be this time, he wondered: a window-box for the CID room? The length of Beevers' sideburns? McLaren's edible thumbmarks on his report sheets? The trouble was, it was very hard to learn to care about spit'n'polish. You either did or didn't, quite naturally, from birth – like being able to sing.

Outside the office – which unlike every other DS's office in the land kept its oak inhospitably sported – he waited, consulting his watch, until it was time to rap smartly and listen for the wild bird cry from within.

'Come!'

Since it was plainly still save-a-word week, Slider said nothing as he presented himself. Barrington was not pretending to read, which on the whole seemed ominous. He had his hands on the desk a little farther apart than shoulder width, as if he was about to push himself up by them, and it had the effect of making his upper body look larger and more muscular than ever.

'The department car,' he said abruptly, 'is the blue Fiesta down in the yard, yes?'

'Yes, sir,' said Slider, with the imperturbable air of one no longer to be caught out by life's random demands on his attention.

'It's in a disgusting state. The outside is dirty. There's a chocolate wrapper in the dash compartment and an empty hamburger carton on the floor in the back. And the whole thing stinks of chips.'

McLaren, of course. He grazed all day long like a Canada goose, starting at one end of their ground and working his way across. He usually reached the McDonald's on Shepherd's Bush Green about midday.

'It's not good enough,' Barrington snapped.

'No, sir,' Slider agreed amiably.

'I want it cleaned up. And I want no more eating in the car. Or in the CID room. What do you suppose a member of the public would think if they came in and saw our people eating at their desks?'

Slider declined that invitation to suicide. 'Will that be all, sir?'

Barrington leaned back slightly from his hands, adding another inch or two to his breadth.

'No. I wanted to get the trivial matter out of the way first. I have something much more serious to say.'

Could anything be more serious than McLaren's eating habits? It was hard to imagine. 'Sir?'

'I have had a telephone call – an irate telephone call from Colin Cate. I assume you know who he is?'

'The name sounds vaguely familiar, but I can't quite place—'

'He is a very influential businessman, who used to be in the CID. He sits on various committees, including several police advisory bodies. He is widely consulted by everyone from the local authority to the Royal Commission. He owns a string of properties and businesses all over West London, including several on our ground. Am I ringing any bells yet?'

By the tone of his voice he was more interested in wringing balls. Slider kept a cunning silence.

'Perhaps it would help you if I mentioned that he owns eight fish and chip shops, one of which he drove past this morning, only to find it closed, with police screens all over it. Need any more hints?'

Slider thought he'd better speak before Barrington's voice went off the scale. 'He owns Dave's Fish and Chip Bar?'

'Yes, Inspector, he does. And he was naturally wondering, just by the way, of course, why it was we hadn't contacted him before now – as a matter of courtesy, if not because he might have been able to help us with the *bloody investigation*!'

Whoops, Slider thought. 'We didn't know he owned it, sir. Slaughter told us he was the owner.'

'You should have checked it out! Good God, man, do you really think a slob like Slaughter could run a business? A simple enquiry to the Community Charge office – something which ought to have been pure routine – but of course you wouldn't know about routine, would you? It was something my predecessor despised.'

'I don't think it will make any difference to the case, sir,' Slider began, but Barrington overrode him in a sort of desperate Lionel Jeffries shriek.

'*It makes all the difference!*' Having left himself, vocally speaking, nowhere to go, he dropped back into normal dicdon. 'You're going to have to check every statement and every assumption against the new evidence. If Slaughter has lied about something as basic as that, what else has he lied about? You're going to go back to the beginning and start again, you and your team, and this time you'll do it by the book. I don't want any more mistakes. Colin Cate has got his eye on this one now, and he is not a man to be underestimated. He has the ear of some Very Important People Indeed, do I make myself clear?'

'Perfectly.'

'You're going to have to get a statement from him.'

'Of course. I'll send—'

'As you were! You won't *send* anyone, you'll go yourself. He's not received a very good impression so far, so I want him to have the best possible service from now on.'

'Sir.'

'He'll be at the golf club this afternoon, and he'll see you there, in the clubhouse, at half-past three.'

Too late for lunch and too early for tea, Slider thought. 'Yes, sir.'

'And for God's sake watch what you say. Remember this man was a copper when you were still learning to shave.'

'Yes, sir.'

'Carry on, then.' He waited until Slider reached the door, then added, 'And get that car cleaned up.'

He went downstairs to see his old friend O'Flaherty, who was custody skipper on Early, and found him just going off duty and handing over to Nutty Nicholls.

'Step across the road with me and have a drink,' Fergus invited as he hauled off his tunic and inserted himself into a modest blue anorak. 'I'm as thirsty as a bearer at a Protestant funeral, and there's a pint waitin' over there with me name on it.'

'All fresh is glass,' Nutty observed, sidelong.

'I've got to go and interview someone important,' said Slider. 'I'd better not turn up with booze on my breath.'

'Ah well, come and sip a lemonade and watch me drinking, then.'

'Don't you want to know about your body?' Nicholls enquired in hurt tones as Slider turned away.

'Slaughter? How is he settling in?'

'He's the happiest wee felon I've ever banged up. Chirpy as a budgie now we've charged him – isn't he, Fergus?'

'You'd think we'd done him a favour,' O'Flaherty concurred. 'Thanks us for every little thing. He even likes the canteen food – Ordure of the Day, we call it. Sure God, the man's as daft as a pair of one-legged trousers.'

'Probably a relief to him to hand over responsibility,' Slider said. 'I've seen it before with this sort of murder—'

'*Crime passionelle,*' Nicholls interpreted in his rolling Scottish French.

'No, that's a kind of blancmange,' Fergus corrected.

'God, you two!' Slider exclaimed. 'Talk about Peter Pan and Windy!'

In the pub Fergus collected his pint of Guinness and said, 'D'you want a table, or would you rather sit on one of them things?' He nodded with disfavour at the brown-leather covered bar stools. 'Aptly named, I've always thought.'

'Let's find a table,' Slider said. 'I want to ask you about something.'

'Y've a worn look about you this fine day,' Fergus observed, following him. 'Are you keepin' some woman happier than she deserves?'

'My wife smiled at me across the breakfast table this morning,' Slider said cautiously. 'I don't know what you'd make of that.'

'Sounds ominous.' O'Flaherty sat down and drank deeply, and then wiped the foam from his lip daintily with his little finger. 'But a wife at home and a mistress on the nest, Billy? Christ, I don't know how you do it at your age!'

'I take a young DC and a set of jump leads with me.'

Fergus shook his head. 'I could never be bothered with that malarky. Sure God, there's a lot to be said for starin' at the same face across the cornflakes every day.'

'Cereal monogamy?'

'It's dull, but it's restful.' He eased one huge buttock upwards and aired a nostalgic memory of a steak and onion pie, not lost but gone before. 'But then,' he added succinctly, as the song reminded him, 'my owl woman can cook. So what did you want to talk to me about?'

'Did you ever hear of a man called Cate?' Slider began.

'A man called Kate? You don't mean that cross-dresser, what was his name, Beefy Baverstock? He used to call himself Kate, or Kathy. Used to pose as the Avon lady. Did the old ding-dong, got himself invited in, then lifted the cash and jewellery while the woman o' th'house was makin' a cuppa tea. He came out about four years ago, but the last I heard he was goin' straight – or as straight as any man can go, wearin' a black suspender belt an' a Playtex trainin' bra.'

'No, no, not him. This bloke was a copper, apparently. Colin Cate.'

'Christ, everyone's heard of him,' Fergus said simply.

'Tell me about him,' Slider invited. 'What's he like?'

'Overpaid and underscrupulous, like any successful businessman.'

'You don't like him?'

'I don't like ex-coppers,' Fergus said. 'If you get out, you should get out, not hang around interferin', lookin' over people's shoulders and makin' suggestions you'd never have made when you were in the Job.'

'But he's done well since he left?'

'Oh, he's pots a money. Smart as a rat. Owns property and shops all over the place. He's a big house in Chorleywood looks like a Hollywood ranch – swimmin' pool and the lot.'

'Apparently, he owns Dave's Fish Bar,' Slider said ruefully.

Fergus whistled soundlessly. 'Izzat so? Well now, who'd a thought it?'

'Barrington seems to think we should have.'

'Well, he does own several fish bars, that's true,' Fergus said. 'But then he has that computer retail chain too – Compucate's?'

'Oh, yes. I know. That's his?'

'Yeah. I'd have connected him in me mind with computers sooner than battered fish, but there y'are. We're supposed to know everything, aren't we?'

'So why is Barrington so keen on this Cate bloke, anyway? He was practically having an orgasm telling me how important and influential he is.'

'Ah well, him and Cate go back a bit. Our Mr Dickson too. Did you not know that? They were all together at Notting Hill at the time of the shootin'.'

Slider frowned. 'Do you mean that incident in, when was it, 1982? When two DCs were shot?'

'That's the one.'

'I read about it at the time, but I don't remember the detail. Tell me about it.'

O'Flaherty eyed the level in his glass. 'This'll never last. It's a full pint story.'

Slider fetched another pint of Guinness, and Fergus began. 'Well, now, at the time yer man Cate was the DCS, and Barrington and our Mr Dickson were DIs down at Notting Hill nick. The Area team had been investigatin' a drugs network for a long time, under cover, and now at last it was all comin' good. So they set up this big operation, a raid on the pub where it was all happening – the Carlisle in Ladbroke Grove—'

'Yes, I know it.'

'The Notting Hill lads have still got their eye on it to this day. Funny how some places attract that sort o' thing. Anyway, it was all set up, huge operation, a hundred men or something of that order. It was all worked out in advance like a military campaign, and kept dead secret. Mr Cate was to be the man in charge on the ground, but even he didn't know until the last minute exactly when it was coming off.'

He took a drink, eased his position in the chair, and went on. 'Only come the night somethin' goes wrong. Our Mr Dickson was out in the road at the side of the pub with orders to stay outside so as to catch anyone who might slip the net. Well, in go the troops and there's all the noise and rumpus. Dickson's standing around waiting—'

'Not relishing it very much, I shouldn't think,' Slider put in.

'That's right. Always a man of action, our Mr Dickson. Anyway, suddenly he sees that there's apparently nobody covering the yard at the side where there's a fire door leading out of the function room. So he uses his initiative, grabs these two DCs, Field and Wilson, and goes in there, sees the fire door open, and goes for it.'

He removed his hand from his glass to curl it into a fist and thump the table softly.

'Shots were fired. Field was killed, and Wilson was wounded and spent three months in hospital.'

'Yes,' Slider said thoughtfully. 'I remember reading about it. They got someone for the shooting, though, didn't they?'

'Jimmy Cole and Derek Blackburn. They went down for it. They always swore they didn't do it, though.'

'Well, they would say that, wouldn't they?'

O'Flaherty nodded. 'Blackburn was a scummy little villain, kill his own grandmother for the gold in her teeth. He's dead now – got killed in a brawl inside, to nobody's disappointment. Jimmy Cole, now – he musta come out six-eight weeks ago, f'what I was hearin' from Seedy Barry.'

'Who's Seedy Barry?'

'Him as runs that garden centre th' back o' Brunei Road. Little fella, th' spit o' Leslie Howard.'

'Leslie Howard?'

'*Gone Wit' the Wind*,' Fergus said patiently, and then clasped his hands under his chin, batted his eyelids and slid into an indescribable falsetto. 'Oh, *Ashley!*'

'Now I've lost track. How did we get on to Scarlett O'Hara?'

'I was tellin' you, Seedy Barry's set himself up in business within sight of the Scrubs – says he misses the place when he can't see the old ivory towers. He's been goin' straight fifteen years now, but he keeps up with all the comin's and goin's, does a lot of work for the rehabilitation services. He was sayin' the other day that Jimmy Cole went down very well with the parole board and they let him out a sadder and wiser man.

112

But I was surprised meself at the time that he was mixed up in the shootin'. We'd had him over on our ground enough times before that, and I wouldn't a put him in that league. Strictly a small-time villain. I'd never known him carry a shooter. But Seedy was sayin' over the bedders the other day that the word always was it was Blackburn did the job, and took Cole down with him.'

'So what happened afterwards?' Slider asked. 'From our point of view, I mean. I suppose there was an enquiry?'

'Must a been. But there were no disciplinary actions. Cate left the Job not long afterwards, but he wasn't required to resign or anything o' the sort. He was only second-in-command, but he was the man on the spot. The Commander was co-ordinatin' back at the ranch.'

'I suppose no one likes to lose men,' Slider mused.

'If you're thinkin' he left a broken man, you can think again. He's gone from strength to strength since he went private.'

'And what about Dickson and Barrington?'

'Dickson transferred, just in the natural course o' things. I think that was when he went to Vine Street. Barrington stayed at Notting Hill as far as I know. Why d'you ask?'

'I keep getting the impression Barrington didn't like Dickson, and I wondered if it could be anything to do with that incident.'

Fergus shrugged. 'It might. I've never heard Dickson talk about it – but then he doesn't talk about himself, does he?'

'Not any more.'

'Sure God, I was forgetting. I can't think of him dead, can you?' He eyed Slider curiously. 'If you want to know more about it, why don't you ask his missus? You've met her, haven't you?'

'Yes, once or twice – and at the funeral, of course. I think perhaps I will, if I can find time.'

'I expect she'd like a visit. She must be lonely. They were devoted, y'know.' He sighed sentimentally. 'Sure, isn't it a grand thing to know, that there's someone for everyone, however unlikely it may seem?'

'It's a comforting thought,' said Slider.

8

Hand in Glove

Any man who has worked in a modern police station is likely to feel at home in a modern golf clubhouse: the decor and the assumptions about life are much the same in either.

The lounge to which Slider was directed in his search for Colin Cate had all the true transcontinental glamour of the Manhattan Bar of a Ramada Inn on the ring-road of a North Midlands town. Cate was leaning against the bar laughing loudly with some friends, and he carried on the chaff just a little after he had seen Slider at the door simply to emphasise the difference between them as the detective inspector began the long plod across the stretch of crimson carpet that separated them.

Cate was a tall man beginning to go soft in the middle, but his clothes were too expensive for that to matter. He was subtly resplendent in a light grey Austin Reed suit, an Aquascrotum shirt of broad blue and white stripes, and a dark blue silk tie with a tiny, discreet logo on it – so tiny that its decorative value was nil, so its function must have been to make the onlooker who did not know what it represented feel equally small. His plain onyx and gold cufflinks were large in exactly the same way that the tie-logo wasn't, his watch was a Rolex Oyster, and on the bar next to his drink was a hefty portable telephone and a bunch of keys with a BMW tag. Since the two other men he was standing with had been turned out by the same firm, by the time Slider reached them he felt like a crumpled tourist on a long-haul flight who had wandered accidentally into club-class while looking for the lav.

'Ah, yes, you must be Bill Slider!' Cate hailed him cheerily. Slider agreed, sadly, that he must be. 'What'll you have?' Slider protested mildly about being on duty, but Cate overrode him with the sort of outsize bonhomie men use when they are trying to convince an inferior that they look on him as an equal. 'Bollocks, you must have something! What'll it be? Whisky, brandy, anything you like. Christ, you don't have to put on a show for me – I used to be a copper myself, y'know. Don't worry, I won't tell your boss on you!'

Slider thanked him and asked for a gin and tonic, which gave him the opportunity, while Cate was dealing with the order – 'Same again for you blokes, I suppose? All right, you drunken bastards! Christ knows how you ever manage to run a business,' and so on – to study him. Cate was one of those men who gave the impression of being handsome, though when you examined his face carefully there wasn't a good feature in it: the nose was too narrow and too small, the mouth too soft, the chin too large and long, the cheekbones too wide. He had carefully-styled, silver-white hair which looked as though it had been specially selected by a top-price designer to go with his Playa de las Americas tan. Cate must have been late fifties at least, but the effect of the contrast was to make him look much younger.

It was only when you studied him closely that you could

see the slackness of the face muscles, the tell-tale tiny pouches over the cheekbones, the tiredness of the skin – and there would be few enough people who would ever do that. The hearty palliness was there to keep at bay as much as to put at ease, and the eyes that were screwed up in constant smiles were grey and keen behind the concealing lids. Slider had known policemen like him, and they were often the most successful ones; businessmen too, though the style had so many imitators in commercial life that the real goods like Cate could hide up in a herd of prats and go unnoticed for as long as it was to his advantage.

Having secured the drinks, Cate ushered Slider away from his friends. 'Excuse us, lads – a bit of business to discuss. I'll catch you later. Oh yes, I will – it's your round, you tight-fisted sod! No, seriously, I'll only be about half an hour, all right? Cheers, then.'

He led the way across the room to one of those round bar tables which are too low and too small to be of any use other than to catch you in the knees every time you shift position and make you spill your drink. Cate settled himself, and rested his right hand on the table top beside his drink. It was very brown, and Slider noticed he was wearing a ring on the third finger in the shape of a skull: heavy gold, beautifully wrought, expensive and ugly – a strange thing, he thought, to go with the aforesaid suit, shirt and tie. If it had been silver instead of gold, and much more crude, it might have been a biker's ring. But maybe it was meant simply to surprise – and to warn the business contact that this was not just a rich man, but a tough bastard too.

Cate surveyed Slider's face and slipped into serious man-to-man mode.

'All right, tell me about it. The lad Ronnie's got himself into trouble, has he?'

Slider told him briefly the history of the case. 'He told us that it was his shop, and there seemed no particular reason to doubt him. If anything, it would have been in his interest to make us think there *was* someone else to suspect.'

The eyes crinkled merrily. 'You're not suspecting me, I hope?'

'No, sir,' Slider said solidly. 'I'm just explaining why we didn't doubt he was the owner of the shop.'

Serious mode again. 'It's all right, Bill – I may call you Bill?'

Slider toyed with 'No,' even as his lips were sneaking in with a cowardly 'Yes, of course.'

'Well, Bill, I understand perfectly, of course. I was a bit annoyed at first, I don't mind telling you, that nobody had bothered to let me know. But I know how many things there are to check up on at the beginning of a case. I shan't say any more about it. And I'll make it all right with your Guv'nor.'

He paused for Slider's murmur of gratitude.

'I'm pretty shocked that one of my shops should have been involved in that way, but the public being what they are, it may turn out to bring them in rather than put them off. People can be rotten ghouls. Good for business, you know what I mean? Time will tell. And who is it that Ronnie murdered? One of his boyfriends, I suppose?'

'You knew he was homosexual?'

Cate raised an eyebrow. 'Oh, come on!'

'He seems to hope he can hide it from the world,' Slider said neutrally.

'I knew he was an iron as soon as I saw him, but it didn't bother me. It's not illegal, and I've got no prejudices. What mattered to me was that he knew how to run a fish and chip shop.'

118

'How did you come to employ him in the first place?' Slider asked.

'He answered an advertisement I put in the local rag for a manager. I could tell he wasn't very bright, but he'd been in the trade since he was fourteen, so there wasn't much he didn't know about it. He's turned out to be a good worker, anyway. He never took time off – except occasionally shutting up early if it was quiet – and he never tried to rob me. I shall be sorry to lose him.'

'I'm afraid you'll be losing more than just him. The man he murdered was also one of your employees.'

'Oh?' The grey eyes became serious. 'Who?'

'The man who helped out in the fish bar at weekends – Peter Leman. Did you know him?'

Was there the tiniest of hesitations? No, it must be just inferiority-induced paranoia.

'I didn't know him, as such – I left it to Ronnie to sort out his own helpers – but I think I saw him in the shop once or twice. He seemed like a nice lad. You're not telling me that he and Ronnie—?' He paused suggestively, eyebrows raised.

'It seems so. Certainly the night Leman was killed he met Slaughter and went home with him. They quarrelled about something—'

'Well, that doesn't surprise me! If ever there was a case of beauty and the beast. Still, it sounds as if you've got it all wrapped up. That's quick work. I'm sure Ian will be pleased with you. It looks good in the figures to get it cleared up so fast'

'Ian?'

'Barrington. DS Barrington,' Cate explained. 'He's an old mate of mine. Didn't you know his name was Ian?'

'No sir. Only his initials.'

'He's a good man,' Cate said seriously. 'Sound. He can be

119

a bit of a martinet, I know, but he's a good copper. He gets the job done, and that's all that matters, isn't it?'

Slider took this as a hint, and eased his notebook out of his pocket. 'I hope you won't mind if I ask you a few routine questions, just to clear up one or two points?'

Cate crinkled a smile. 'Not at all. Nice to see you being thorough. What d'you want to know?'

'How often do you visit the Fish Bar?'

'That particular one, not very often. Twice a month maybe, at most. Ronnie's a good manager – or he was, I should say. I just used to pop in when I was passing on the odd occasion to see that everything was all right. I never give my businesses warning that I'm coming – keeps 'em on their toes.'

'Do you remember when you were there last?'

He frowned in thought. 'Hard to remember. Three weeks ago, maybe. About that, anyway.'

'You have a key to the shop, of course? Where do you keep it?'

Cate lifted his hands and laid them on the table on either side of his glass. 'Well, as a matter of fact, I haven't. I did have one, but I lost it – oh, must be two months ago. I was having my office at home redecorated, so I had to clear everything out of it. All the keys were on hooks on a pegboard on the wall by my desk, so of course it had to come down. I put it with the rest of the office gear in a spare bedroom, but when I came to put everything back afterwards, that particular key was missing.'

Slider felt a sinking sensation. If there were a missing key sculling about the universe, it put paid to half the case.

'Could it have been stolen, do you suppose?'

'Well, I suppose it could have. The decorators were in and out of the house and one of them could have gone upstairs when no one was looking. But I've known 'em for years, and I trust 'em. I don't think they'd steal anything – if I did, I wouldn't employ 'em. And besides, it's hard to see why anyone would take that one key and no other. No, I think it must have just fallen off in the spare room and got lost.'

'You searched for it, of course?'

'Of course. It never turned up, though.' There was a breath of a pause, and then Cate continued blandly. 'In any case, I told Ronnie to get the lock changed just to be on the safe side, and he did. I kept meaning to collect the spare key from him, but I haven't got round to it yet.'

Cate was making a monkey of him. Slider controlled his temper and continued to play Plod, while his mind felt about for a reason why Cate should want to bait him. 'So Ronnie is still the only person with a key to the shop?'

'Front door key, yes. I have a key to the back door, but it's always kept bolted on the inside, so I couldn't use it if I wanted to.'

And Slaughter said that the back door was bolted when he came in on the day after the murder. And there was no sign of forcible entry. They were back on safe ground. It had to have been Slaughter after all.

Soon afterwards, Slider was rising to go. Cate extended his hand and shook Slider's firmly: virile, confident, friendly, said that grip.

'It's been nice meeting you, Bill. I hope we can get together again some time. I like having the chance to talk shop occasionally. You must come over to my place one day. Are you married?'

'Yes.'

'Well, come to dinner some time, bring the wife.'

'Thanks. I'd like that.'

'Right! Good! I'll be in touch, then. And tell old Ian to go

121

easy on you, like I did on him when I was his boss! A good man is hard to find, you know.'

According to Joanna, Slider thought on his way out, a hard man is good to find, though he wondered in this case. He was not going to hold his breath waiting for a dinner engagement to materialise; and if Colin Cate, with all his police contacts and committees, needed a lowly and newly acquainted inspector with whom to talk shop, then his arse was an apricot. All the end bit, like all the beginning bit, was insincere, but equally it was not intended to deceive. It served the same social function as eyebrow-raising and bottom-flashing amongst baboons: it established social hierarchy.

That didn't mean to say there was anything wrong with the middle bit, though Slider was at a loss to understand why he had been dragged all this way to go through it, when any DC at any time would have done as well, for all the information Cate was able to add. He supposed demanding Slider's presence so far from home had been Cate's way of flashing his bottom at Barrington: I may have left the Job, but I'm still your superior, laddie, and don't you forget it.

Another little chat with Ronnie was in order, to establish the whereabouts of the second key, and then home.

Not home for much longer, he reminded himself, and felt a sudden surge of nervousness. He still had that hurdle to clear, and it wasn't going to be in one gazelle-like bound, that was for sure.

The effect on Ronnie Slaughter of Cate's name was unexpected. Slider had expected him to look embarrassed or shamefaced at having his self-inflating pose debunked, but instead he seemed terrified. He appeared to crouch lower in his chair, like a motorway verge mouse swept over by a kestrel's shadow, and he fixed frightened eyes on Slider in desperate appeal.

'Oh Gawd, oh Gawd,' he whimpered. You didn't tell him? Oh Gawd, he'll kill me!'

'I had to tell him, Ronnie,' Slider said reasonably. 'It's his shop. He came asking why we'd shut it without asking him. He's got a right to know.'

'He'll kill me! He said there's not got to be no trouble. He said it's got to be a clean shop, no drunks or rowdies, no fights or anything. I promised him. That's why I got the job. He was real good to me, giving me that job. It's the best job I ever had – a real nice shop, respectable and everything. I was that grateful. I'd never do nothing to upset him, and he said if ever the Bill was called in, I was for it.' He rocked in his chair a little and moaned. 'You shouldn't of told him! What did he say? Was he mad?'

'Ronnie, you're in much bigger trouble than worrying about your job with Mr Cate,' Slider said bemusedly, but even the mention of the name made Slaughter wince.

With difficulty he kept Ronnie's attention and asked him about the other key – 'It's in a box in the suitcase under my bed. I told you nobody but me had a key' – and about the bolt on the back door – 'It was bolted, I tell you. I would never forget that. Mr Cate would kill me if I forgot it.'

'Never mind what Mr Cate would think, are you quite sure it was bolted?' Slider pressed him.

Slaughter nodded, his mind clearly on more serious problems. 'You didn't tell him about – about me – you know – about me being gay?'

'He knew about that anyway. *He* told *me*, in fact.'

Slaughter began to cry. 'Oh Gawd, he'll kill me,' he whimpered.

Slider was at a loss to know how to put things into

perspective for this pathetic creature. To be worrying about his boss's disapproval when he was facing life imprisonment for murder suggested a view of life so far askew that it wasn't surprising he had killed and cut up Peter Leman on so small a provocation and with so little apparent compunction.

It was an evening on which Slider desperately needed to see Joanna, in order to have himself reconnected via her with the real world. The day had left a bad taste in his mouth, and he badly needed the sweet and sensual pleasure of her company to soothe his troubled mind and weary body and restore him for the fray tomorrow. But Joanna was what she pleased to call 'up-country', doing a concert in Leeds which was a repeat of one of the tour programmes. She had nobly refrained from pointing out that if he had done his duty and sorted out his personal life by now, she would have come home, albeit very late, to him; but he pointed it out to himself as he drove home along the A40 towards Ruislip. Due west, it was, into the sunset, and a very gaudy one this evening: purple bars across raging crimson and gold on the horizon, and above that streaks of Walt Disney powder pink and baby blue. It made him feel as though he was in the last scene of a movie. He could almost hear the soaring strings and the celestial choir in the background.

Wind the film back a bit. *The first opportunity,* he had promised her. Would there be an opportunity tonight? Oh fearful thought! Why couldn't he skip that bit? He saw himself in a still taken from the movie, facing Irene and telling her about Joanna, telling her he was leaving her. In the still he couldn't see his own face, but he could see hers. How could he do that to her? Well, that had always been the question, hadn't it? And it was unanswerable.

He had stills of the children, too. He saw them not in their

124

usual roles of either defying him, ignoring him, or berating him for failing to reach their high standards of parental expenditure. Here they appeared in vulnerable mode: Kate coming to him weeping because Goldie the Guinea pig had died, Matthew's brow buckled with the weight of anguished responsibility because he had been picked to play for the middle-school eleven and was afraid his batting wasn't good enough.

And what would he say to them? Daddy's leaving you, children. Daddy still loves you very much, but he won't be living here with you and Mummy any more. He'll still come and see you, of course, on Sundays (if he's not on duty) to take you for an outing that's supposed to make up for the fact that he isn't there every day, and for birthday treats and at Christmas. Slider knew how it was done. The police force was a high-divorce industry – he had seen it all before.

How would he bear it when they cried? How would he bear it if they didn't? He was hardly ever at home anyway, hadn't taken them out anywhere in months (years?). Maybe they wouldn't care that he was going. He imagined Matthew taking Kate aside: 'A boy at school's father went away, and now every time he visits, he brings him *brilliant* presents! This boy's got a fifteen-speed bike and a Nintendo Gameboy and his own video . . .' Ah!

There was the alternative, of course: to say goodbye to Joanna, and to serve out his sentence as the disappointing husband and barely tolerated father; without love, without comfort, without appreciation, without conversation – and worse, knowing that Joanna was without those things too, only at the other end of a telephone, within reach, out of reach. Foolishness and waste, the two of them unhappy when they could be happy. Irene and the children would soon get over him, they didn't care that much for him, never had . . .

But he had made promises, taken on responsibilities. How could he go back on them?

But he could fulfil them in other ways – better ways, surely, if he was personally content? He had a responsibility to himself, too. What sort of husband-and-father would he make if he felt miserable, deprived and trapped?

Or was that just a weak justification for doing what he knew was wrong? But *was* it wrong, or was it the best thing for all of them in the long run?

And he had gone through all this before, every argument, every word, a hundred times, maybe a thousand, since he first met Joanna and went over the side – as the police saying was – in an unexpected splash which astonished him and everyone who knew him, left his brains waterlogged and his moral rectitude going down for the third time. It was not as if he had done anything like that before. He had not been a philanderer. He had never even been tempted before. Surely that made a difference? It was not that he had wanted to leave Irene and had latched onto the first available woman. It was Joanna, no one else. He had to have her, or everything else was pointless. And to have her he must leave Irene.

Oh, round the wheel again! He could see his own tail up ahead of him, its fluffy tip ever retreating, beckoning him on. *The first opportunity.* Would there be an opportunity tonight . . .?

She was not in when he got home, but the children were there. Kate was sitting on the floor about eight inches away from the television screen watching *The Young Doctors*. She was addicted to soaps, and absorbed the emotions of the characters, however banal or incomprehensible, like a vicarious black hole. The video recorder was permanently set to tape them all, and she watched them over and over again unless she was stopped.

Matthew and his adenoidal friend Sibod were playing a game which involved much running up and down stairs, slamming doors, and bellowing at each other from opposite ends of the universe. Since the house, built in the worst period of the '70s, was only made of cardboard and Sellotape, it trembled like a frightened dik-dik at every adolescent footfall.

Slider fielded Matthew as he thundered past. 'Are you lot all on your own?'

'Bernice has just gone,' Matthew said, already slithering away. He had a child's ability to remove his bones from a grip, leaving the restrainer with nothing but a handful of clothing. 'Mummy was supposed to be back by now, and Bernice couldn't stay any longer.'

'Have you eaten?'

'We had Turkey Bites,' Matthew replied diminuendo as he retreated upstairs.

'Turkey bites?' Slider said, baffled. Was that food?

'And oven chips. Out of the freezer.' He was almost in his room now. 'Bernice did them in the microwave,' he offered, as if it were the clue to the labyrinth, and the door slammed, shutting off any further possibility of communication. Slider, stranded in the hall on his ebbing wave of parental enquiry, looked through the sitting-room door at Kate, but decided against disturbing her. With her head almost in the set, she was far, far away in a sunnier land, pursuing one of girlhood's most durable dreams in a nurse's uniform.

He went into the kitchen and put the kettle on, and stood leaning against the work surface, his mind for once leaving him alone. The kettle sang companionably, like a cat purring. He would have liked a cat, but Irene always said there was no point when he was barely ever at home, and in any case they were dirty and unhygienic. In vain he pointed out that at least you didn't have to clean up after them like Kate's rabbits and Guinea pig – they did it themselves. But Kate's beasts were kept caged and did it in one place, Irene countered. And in any case, she – Irene – would be the one who'd end up having to look after the thing (which was undeniable) and if she'd wanted a cat she'd have got one for herself long ago. So that was that.

Just as the kettle boiled, there was the sound of a key in the front door, and Irene's voice called, 'Bill? Are you back?'

'In the kitchen,' he shouted. She appeared in the doorway, taking off her coat. 'I didn't hear your car. You must have had the exhaust fixed.'

'It's in the garage. I'm getting it done tomorrow. Marilyn just dropped me off.'

'Oh,' said Slider cautiously. 'I didn't know you were seeing her today.' His wife had a bright-eyed and bushy look to her which boded no good. What was it going to be this time? A roof garden? An en-suite bathroom? A two-week bridge-playing holiday in a heritage hotel in Wiltshire?

'We've just been shopping in Watford. She wanted me to help her choose some curtain material for their dining-room.'

And make the curtains, Slider thought, if he knew anything about it. The she-Cripps, though wealthy beyond repair, was not averse from letting Irene save her money through the labour of her nimble fingers. Perhaps she believed that exploitation was the sincerest form of flattery.

'Are the children all right? Did they have their tea?'

'Bernice brought them back and gave them Turkey Bites, whatever they are. Out of the freezer.'

'It's pieces of turkey breast in breadcrumbs,' Irene said seriously. She dropped her coat over the back of a chair – a most uncharacteristic gesture – and sat down cater-cornered to him. 'We had them last week, don't you remember? With salad. On Tuesday.'

He didn't remember. Food at home was an exercise in nourishment without tears rather than an occasion to cherish in recollection. 'Oh, those,' he said vaguely.

'The children like them,' Irene said defensively, 'and they're quick.' She clasped her thin hands together on the table-top. They were always beautifully kept, with perfect, unchipped nail varnish on the neat oval nails. Joanna's nails had to be cut very short for playing the fiddle, and would have looked wrong painted. He couldn't imagine Irene's hand clasped round a pint glass or throwing a dart. She was everything that was ladylike, neat and feminine. Why didn't he love her? He transferred his gaze from her hands to her face, and found it urgent with hopeful anticipation.

'Bill,' she said, 'you aren't doing anything tomorrow night, are you?'

'Why, what's tomorrow night?' He said it non-committally, though his heart was sinking. It would be harder to pull the usual piles-of-work excuse if he had already had to agree to whatever it was she wanted him to do with her. And anyway, he didn't like letting her down at the last minute, especially since he had so often in their lives had to do it legitimately.

'It's a concert,' she said, serenely unaware of what she was doing to his heart rate. 'The Royal Charity Gala at the Festival Hall – the Duke and Duchess of Kent will be there, and all sorts of celebrities, and there's a sort of reception afterwards to meet them and some of the orchestra. Marilyn's got four tickets – well, David has, really. His firm is one of the sponsors. They're apparently ever so hard to get hold of, the tickets I mean, so I was really flattered when she asked us. Of course I told her I'd have to check with you. I know you've got a case on at the moment, but you did say it was going well and you've charged a man, and that usually means you're a bit less pressed. But Marilyn said she'd like me to come even if you're working, and they'll just keep the other ticket in case you can make it at the last minute or anything.'

Slider marked time in desperation. 'It's rather short notice, isn't it?'

'I expect she's only just got the tickets,' Irene said trustingly. Only just been let down by the first people she invited, Slider corrected inwardly.

'How much does she want for them? If it's a gala, it'll be expensive.'

'She doesn't want *paying* for them,' Irene said, shocked. 'She's invited us as her guests, hers and David's. It's a great compliment. Why do you always think the worst of people?'

'I suppose it is kind of her,' Slider said reluctantly, desperately searching for an excuse. 'I don't know that I'd be very good company, though. You know how tired I get when—'

Irene jumped in, bubbling with excitement and happiness. 'I know, but you like classical music, much more than I do, really, at least you know more about it, and you wouldn't have to talk, would you, just sit and listen. It would be relaxing for you. And, oh Bill, it's so nice that she's asked us to something like this, when everyone must be longing to go, if they could only get the tickets! I'd have been glad enough to go on my own, but if you can come it will make it just perfect – you know how awkward I feel when everyone else has a partner and I don't. And we haven't been out together for such ages! I've only got to ask Bernice to come and sit in with the children, and I can take your dinner suit into that two-hour cleaners in the High Street tomorrow morning, so that'll be all right.'

'Dinner suit?' Slider said dazedly.

'It is a *Gala,*' she reminded him. 'Of course it's black tie! And Marilyn said long dresses,' she added happily. 'It's so nice to have the chance to dress up once in a while, and you

130

look so distinguished in a dinner jacket, it really suits you. People don't wear evening dress often enough nowadays. Everything's so casual, it's a shame. I've hardly worn my long dress and I've had it five years. I expect Marilyn's got a dozen of them, she and David go out so much. I just hope it will be warm enough tomorrow night not to wear a coat. I do think a coat looks so silly over an evening dress, unless it's a fur coat of course, but that's different. A fur stole would be nice. Marilyn's got the most beautiful fox cape – David bought it for her for their first wedding anniversary, she told me. I suppose I could wear a shawl if it's chilly, that would be better than a coat, anyway. I wonder if that one I got in Spain would be all right, or would it look common?'

Slider let the burble pass over his head. This one was going to be a bugger to sort out. He switched his conversation circuits over to automatic pilot and got down to some real industrial-strength worrying.

9

Lying in his Teeth

WDC 'Norma' Swilley glanced up as Atherton came into the CID room, and then as she saw his face she gave him her full sympathetic attention.

'You look terrible.'

'I feel terrible,' he said. 'It's a set.' He slumped down behind his own desk and rubbed his eyes.

'What time did you go to bed last night?'

'Oh, two – three. A low number.'

Beevers from across the room made a vulgar noise of appreciation which in written English is usually rendered along the lines of *hooghoooeragh!* 'Ask him what time he went to sleep, though, Norm!' he advised further. 'Polish come across at last, then, did she? *Corrhh!*'

Atherton yawned without bothering to stifle it. 'If I could yawn with my mouth shut,' he told Beevers conversationally, 'you'd never know how boring you really are.'

'It's funny, you know, Jim,' Norma said seriously, 'I had a strange dream last night. I dreamt I was walking along the beach with my mother, and washed up on the shingle there

132

was a huge, bleached Alec Beevers, its white belly glinting in the sun. I said, "Mummy, can I touch it?" And she said, "Be careful, darling, the dullness rubs off."'

'Oh har har,' Beevers said getting up. 'I'm going to the toilet.'

'It's funny how he always tells us,' Norma said just before Beevers was out of earshot. 'He regresses further every day. I'm sure he's an anal retentive.'

'Just as well,' Atherton responded automatically.

The door slammed. Norma got up and came across to sit on Atherton's desk. Her long, Californian beach-beauty legs disappeared beguilingly under her skirt just about at the level of Atherton's intellect, and it was a sign of his state of mind that he hardly gave them a glance.

'Seriously, though,' she said.

He looked up. 'Seriously, said he with a mocking smile. This is my mocking smile.'

'You can tell me. And I wish you would – I like you, but I'm also fond of Polly. She's a sort of protegee of mine, you know? And if you're going to make her unhappy—'

'No, no, quite the reverse. You don't need to worry about her.' He met Norma's eyes unwillingly. 'It's not debauchery that's giving me bags under my eyes, it's frustration. The fact is, I've always believed in the rule that if you can keep a woman talking until two in the morning, she's yours. It's never failed before, but—' He shrugged.

'It failed last night?'

'Polish is a Catholic. She says she won't sleep with anyone before marriage. She says she likes me very much, but she means to go to her marriage bed a virgin. Can you believe that?'

'Yes, I believe it. Why not? D'you think every woman in the world has got to fall flat on her back just because you look her way?'

'You didn't,' Atherton pointed out in an effort to change the subject.

'You never made a play for me. Not a serious one. Not,' she added sternly, 'that it would have made any difference if you had. I'd never go out with someone in the Department, and I'm surprised that you do. I've never understood why you've made such a dead set at Polly.'

'I like her,' he said.

'Can't you like her without trying to get her into bed? Why do you have to knock off every woman you meet?'

He shrugged. 'It's a challenge. One must do something.'

'That's a disgusting thing to say!'

'Oh, come on, Norma – the women I chase are just as eager for it as I am.'

'So where's the challenge?' Norma countered with spirit. Atherton looked down at his hands, thoughtfully rubbing the back of one with the forefinger of the other. 'You don't really mean any of that cobblers, anyway,' she said, looking at his bent head. 'You're quite a nice bloke really. I don't know why you pretend to be a bastard. It doesn't suit you.'

'Ah well, when the woman you love loves someone else, what can you do?' he said lightly. She regarded him thoughtfully, a doubt forming in her mind and a question on her lips. He looked up. 'Won't you chuck your Tony and give me a chance, lovely Norma?' he pleaded winsomely, laying a hand on her thigh.

'Oh, bugger off,' she said explosively, leaping out from under his touch. She went back to her own desk to the accompaniment of his laughter, but as she reapplied herself to her work, she wondered all the same.

Slider arrived to find his office furniture under sheets and two men in Matisse-dotted overalls up ladders.

'It's the painters, Guv,' McLaren told him helpfully as he

was passing. He held a polystyrene cup in one hand and a greasy paper bag in the other.

'Thank you,' said Slider. 'I was wondering. And what's that?'

'Just a hot sausage roll,' McLaren said defensively, edging the bag back out of his line of vision.

'You know Mr Barrington has forbidden eating in the CID room,' Slider said sternly.

'That's all right, Guv. I hadn't forgotten. I'm going to eat it in the lav.'

He was sidling off, when Slider remembered. 'By the way, what happened about Mrs Stevens? Was she able to add anything more?'

McLaren's face fell. 'She wouldn't ID the man she saw from Slaughter's photo. In fact, she still insists he had a camel coat and fair hair – she says she saw it glitter in the lamplight. I suggested maybe it was a bald head shining, but she says she knows the difference between a glitter and a shine. She won't be budged on it. But the good news is I've got her to agree it was Wednesday morning, not Thursday—'

'Got her to agree? So she'll change her mind back again just as easily?'

'No, sir,' he said in wounded tones. 'I didn't push her. She remembers that when she went to make herself a cup of tea straight afterwards she was nearly out of milk. She gets three pints a week, delivered on Monday, Wednesday and Friday. So it couldn't have been Thursday, or she'd've had half a bottle left.'

'That's the good news, is it?'

'There's more. She thinks he *was* carrying something, a bag of some sort, but she's not sure what.'

'Thinks he was. Not sure. And he had fair hair. And a camel coat.' Slider sighed. 'Whoever he was, he wasn't Slaughter.'

'No, but it's a start though, isn't it Guv? I mean, we've got something to follow up now.'

'Absolutely. Well, go follow it. And – McLaren?'

'Yes, Guv?'

'For God's sake do your top button up. And get rid of that bag before somebody sees it.'

'Okay,' McLaren said easily, and legged it down the corridor. Slider turned back to contemplate his office, and found Atherton approaching from the other direction.

'We've checked on the key, and it is there, as Slaughter said,' he greeted his superior. Pausing he looked in through the door. 'Oh, I see the painters have arrived.'

'Is that what it is?' Slider said gratefully. 'Oi – you up the ladder!'

The painter turned at the waist. 'What's up, mate?'

'How long are you going to be?'

'Couple of hours or so. Be done by lunchtime,' the man said cheerily.

'Wonderful! And what am I supposed to do until then?' Slider asked rhetorically.

'How should I bloody know?' the man up the ladder said agreeably, and turned back to his work.

'No need to get emulsional about it,' Atherton said. He eyed his boss with sympathy. 'Looks like a clear signal from on high to get out on the street, doesn't it, Guv?'

'On high? From God, you mean?'

'One step down. Titian here is acting on Mr Barrington's orders, after all. Which reminds me of the limerick:

> *While Titian was mixing rose madder,*
> *His model reclined on a ladder.*
> *Her position, to Titian,*
> *Suggested coition,*
> *So he nipped up the ladder, and had 'er.'*

136

Slider grinned unwillingly. 'Are you trying to tell me something?'

Atherton opened his eyes wide. 'Me, sir? No, sir. But you can't work in your office, now can you?'

Slider grunted. 'There is one urgent interview I need to do, which would be better done in person than on the telephone.'

'Well, then.'

'Can I rely on your discretion?'

'It's the better part of my valour,' he assured him gravely.

Joanna answered the door warm, sleepy and in her dressing-gown. In less than a minute she was wide awake and Slider was in her dressing-gown.

'What is all this?' she queried indistinctly, running a hand up and down the front of his trousers.

'Don't you really know?' he asked in amazement through a mouthful of her neck. 'You must let me show you.'

'Oh I must,' she agreed. They sidled like dressed crabs down the passage to her bedroom, where her rumpled bed was still warm. Without breaking step they undressed him and clambered into the nest.

'Umm!' Joanna said some minutes later. 'I should go away more often.'

'Wrong,' Slider said, pulling her head close and burying his face in her hair. 'You smell like a hill.'

'A what?'

'Bracken and warm earth.'

'Gee, thanks!'

'That's the best sort of hill. I'm very partial to them. I like to lie on my back in the bracken and stare at the sky.'

'How poetic,' she said. She pressed her nose into the underside of his chin, all she could reasonably reach in that position.

'Whereas you smell like the most expensive sort of coloured pencils. I won some as a school prize, once, in my junior school. Lakeland, they were called. Six beautiful coloured pencils in a tin box.' She kissed him. 'I loved those pencils.'

He kissed her back. 'I loved my hill, too.'

'How's the case going?'

'As smoothly as a pig on stilts.'

'That well? I thought you'd got your man, my dear mountie.'

'Oh, we've got him, but it's hard work putting together the sort of evidence we're going to need. We can't find anyone who saw him at the scene of the crime, and that makes me nervous. All we've got is a woman who thinks she saw a red or blue or brown car parked in front of the shop, and another woman who saw a man coming out of the alley at the back of the shop who couldn't possibly be the suspect, but who might be almost anyone else in the known universe.'

'So do you think you've maybe got the wrong man?' she asked sympathetically.

'I don't know. By his own admission, no one else could have done it. Yet he still says he didn't do it. I just don't know.'

'I see.' She ran her hands up and down his back. 'So what are you doing here, Inspector? Shouldn't you have your ear to the grindstone and your nose to the wheel? What would your new boss say if he saw what you were doing?'

'He's having my office painted at the moment, so I can't use it.'

'What, now? In the middle of an investigation?'

'To be fair, he may have looked at the duty roster and seen that I'm on lates today.'

'Ah, I wondered how you could spare the time. I should have known you'd never play hookey just to see me.'

138

'There's a distinct note of regret in your voice as you say that,' he said sternly.

'All the same, painting your office at a time like this——!'

'Yes. He has a firm grasp of the trivial. Whereas I——' He felt new stirrings, to his own faint amazement. 'I have a firm grasp of you.'

'So you do. I don't know how you keep it up,' she said with admiration.

'Polyfilla,' he said.

A further pleasant interlude later, he sat up and sighed. 'I hate to eat and run, but I had better get back.'

'Was that all you came for?' she asked sternly, shoving a hand through her rumpled hair. She looked like a bronze chrysanthemum in a high wind.

'Well, no, not entirely. There was something I had to tell you. I'm afraid there's a bit of a problem with the concert.'

'Don't tell me,' she sighed. 'You're going to have to work.'

He told her, and watched with a sinking feeling as the expression drained out of her face.

'No,' she said at last.

'No what?' he asked nervously.

'I won't have it. You're not coming to *my* concert with your wife. It isn't fair.'

He could hardly blame her, and she had always been patient and understanding before, but he wished she had not chosen this moment to become immovable.

'Tell her,' she said. 'Just tell her.'

'I can't. Not now. Not over this. She's so excited and pleased about it. I can't take that away from her. I can't let her down.'

She turned on him angrily. 'You don't seem to mind letting me down!'

'I do, of course I do,' he said helplessly, uncomforted by

139

the knowledge that thousands of men must have trodden this path before him. 'But you know about her and she doesn't know about you, so—'

'Do you think I don't know that?'

'Do you think I want to hurt you?' he countered.

'I don't know,' she said stonily. 'I don't know what you want any more.'

She got up and pulled on her dressing-gown, turning her back on him. He groped around in the muddy pool for words. All he found was grit.

'I want what you want. But you've got to let me do it my own way.' She didn't answer. 'You wouldn't want me if I didn't care about Irene, would you?' She shrugged unhelpfully. 'I will sort things out, I promise you. As soon as I can.'

'You've said that before.'

'I mean it. I was all prepared to talk to her last night, but she jumped in first with this stuff about the concert, and I just couldn't be so cruel as to spoil it for her. If you'd seen her face, all lit up with excitement – oh Jo, we'll have the rest of our lives together! Don't begrudge her this one poor little thing.'

'It's all so pathetic and futile,' she muttered angrily.

'To us, not to her.'

She turned. 'All right,' she said. 'You're so good at seeing both sides of every question, so here's the compromise – and it's my only offer, so you'd better not try and haggle.'

'Compromise?' he said, hoping to God the relief didn't show in his voice.

'You can tell her you've got to work, and that you'll come later if you can. And then you can sit backstage with me. I'm not in the concerto, so we'll be together then, and in the interval. And she'll have her concert. You said she said she'd sooner go without you than not at all.'

'You mean I don't appear at all? What about the reception afterwards?'

'We'll both miss it. We'll go for a drink instead.' She watched his struggling face. 'Take it or leave it. It's my best offer.'

'I'll take it,' he sighed; and tried to comfort himself with the thought that Irene's pleasure in the evening didn't really depend on him. Maybe he could persuade her to get the Crippses to invite someone else for her escort. 'I hate this situation,' he said at last.

'It's your situation,' Joanna said, for once unmoved by his plight.

There was a large envelope for him at the desk when he got back to the station.

'University College Hospital.' O'Flaherty handed it over, looking at the return address. 'I hope you haven't been having secret tests, darlin'?'

Slider grinned. 'No panic. It's just the Tooth Fairy's report.'

'Who's that, Ben Whittaker?'

'Yes. Do you know him?'

'Me? I'm a poor ignorant lad from the land of the bogs and the Little People. How would I know a man with letters after his name? I've just heard of him, that's all.'

'He's a nice bloke. I saw a lot of him at the time of the Spanish Club fire, when we had thirty-seven barbecued bodies to identify. At the end of each day we used to go and get pissed together in a little pub in Foley Street, just to take our minds off.'

'In dem sort a circumstances men become friends,' Fergus said gravely. 'Like Nutty and me in the trenches. When you go t'roo hell together, it forges a bond.'

'In your case the bond must have been a forged one. You were never in the trenches.'

141

O'Flaherty looked dignified. 'All right, we went t'roo Police College at Hendon together.'

'That's close enough.'

Slider headed instinctively for his office, but swerved away as the smell of paint met him half way up the corridor and went to the CID room instead to peruse the report. Ten minutes later he was telephoning Cameron.

'The fish bar corpse, Freddie—?'

'Yes, old boy? It's fresh in my mind.'

'If nowhere else. I've had the orthodontal report. Have you ever heard of mongoloid pits?'

'Ancient Siberian funerary rites? Mass graves in Tibet?'

'No, seriously.'

'Seriously? Of course I have. They're grooves you get on the back of the incisors of people of Asian origin. Are you telling me our corpse had 'em?'

'According to Whittaker.'

'He should know. Well well! That's an interesting thing.'

'But Freddie, wouldn't you have noticed if the corpse was Asian?'

'Oh, certainly. But you see, these mongoloid pits are a genetic thing – passed down in the blood. You wouldn't have to be a full-blooded Tibetan to have 'em – only that you'd have to have some oriental blood in you somewhere. And I suppose our victim could have had a dash – no reason why not. Slight build, sallow skin, scanty body hair. We haven't got the face, eyes or hair, which might have told us a bit more. The eyes particularly.'

'He doesn't look particularly Chinese from his photograph,' Slider said.

'He doesn't have to. He only had to have some Asian forebears somewhere in his history, and there's nothing impossible about that as far as my findings are concerned – if that's what you wanted to know. Did Whittaker say anything else?'

'The teeth were in excellent condition, only three fillings, no crowns or prostheses. He agrees with you about the victim's age. He says there were traces of blood in the capillaries, which is usually a sign of violent death. Oh, and he says that he doesn't think the fillings were done in this country.'

'Doesn't he? Why, are they made of some exotic alloy?'

'No, he says the amalgam they use is the same in all affluent countries these days. It's more the method of filling – a matter of style. He thinks they were done in Japan or Hong Kong, most probably Hong Kong.'

'It's wonderful the advances they're making in the forensic branches these days,' Freddie said admiringly. 'Now all you've got to do is find the dentist.'

'Well, we know from Leman's passport that he visited Hong Kong several times. He must have had his dental work done while he was there.'

'Sensible man,' Freddie said. 'I was in Hong Kong once – had a suit made. Quickest work you ever saw. If the dentists there are anything like the tailors, they probably do fillings while you wait.'

In accordance with his agreement with Joanna, Slider telephoned Irene during the afternoon to tell her that there were new developments and that he was afraid he wouldn't be able to get to the concert on time.

'I don't want to spoil your evening. Why don't you see if Marilyn can get someone else to go with you?'

'No, no, she doesn't want anyone else, and nor do I. Don't worry, Bill, we all knew this might happen.'

He didn't want her to be reasonable and sympathetic. It made him feel a rat. 'I'm sorry—' he began, but she jumped in.

'Your job has to come first. Really, don't worry about it. Just come when you can. Look, I'll get Marilyn to leave your ticket at the box-office, and you can come later, whenever you finally get finished.'

'I won't be in dinner jacket.'

'It doesn't matter. I'm sure lots of people won't be. Your work suit's all right. But do come, Bill, even if you only get there for the second half, or for the reception afterwards. Promise you will come.'

'If at all possible,' he said unwillingly. 'If I'm finished in time.' And she seemed to be satisfied with that.

So here he was, much later, sitting in the dimly-lit artists' bar backstage at the Festival Hall, fulfilling his promise to Irene only in that he was in the building – giving her no pleasure by it. He was denied the pleasure of watching Joanna play, wearing her best long black and looking so grave and important and talented up on the platform (he had learned by now not to call it the stage) and exercising her inexplicable, dazzling skills. He was even denied the pleasure the music might have given him, since although it was relayed into the artists' bar, it was always turned down very low so as not to disturb the musicians' conversations or poker games.

And he doubted whether he was going to give Joanna any pleasure by his presence either. When the overture was finished and the musicians not needed in the concerto came offstage, she appeared and joined him on the banquette in his dim corner, accepted the drink he had got in for her, and sipped it in silence. For once in their lives they had nothing to say to each other.

In the end he told her about the day's developments.

'So what will you do now? Circulate the dental description to all the dentists in Hong Kong?' Joanna asked.

'Not immediately. It would be rather slow and expensive, and it may not be necessary. I'm going to wait until we get the result of the genetic fingerprinting from the handkerchief. If that gives us a positive match, we won't need the teeth.'

'But on the face of it, the tooth business sounds like more evidence of identification,' Joanna said. 'Teeth cannot lie. And there can't be all that many people who go regularly to Hong Kong.'

'It would be a long coincidence,' he agreed. 'Unfortunately, Suzanne Edrich wasn't able to help us one way or the other. She doesn't know anything about Leman's background or family, and he never said anything to her about having Asian forebears.'

'You still don't know who his next of kin is?'

'We're circulating his description and photograph, but no one's come forward to claim him yet. But he was obviously a secretive man. He didn't mean anyone to pin him down.'

'That's men all over. They're afraid of being tied down.'

She said it flippantly, but Slider glanced at her partly averted profile and sighed, going to the root of it. 'I'm sorry. This isn't my idea of a good night out either.'

She turned to look at him, and seemed in long debate with herself as to whether to pursue the subject. In the end she said, 'This can't go on, Bill. It's ridiculous and undignified and hurtful. No one benefits.'

'I know,' he said. 'I know it's not fair on you. And I will sort things out—'

'You keep saying that,' she said quietly. 'Why is it so hard?'

'Should it be easy to hurt people?'

'You hurt me. Why not Irene?'

Now she had got him into the position of justifying something he didn't want to justify, arguing a case that was impossible to argue. 'I don't want to hurt anyone,' he said

145

helplessly. 'And it isn't just Irene. You don't know what it's like to have children—'

'No. How can I?' she said, staring into her empty glass.

'I'm sorry. That wasn't fair.'

'None of it's fair. Life isn't fair.' She took a resolute breath. 'I want to marry you, Bill. If that isn't what you want, then say so, and let's stop making ourselves and everybody else unhappy.'

'It is what I want.'

'Then—' She shrugged and let it hang.

'I'll speak to her tomorrow,' he said firmly.

'Why not tonight?' she asked suspiciously.

'No, it's better in daylight. Nothing is ever really resolved by emotional conversations late at night.'

'Well, as long as—' She broke off as a thunder of feet heralded a posse of musicians skidding into the room and throwing themselves at the bar. Joanna half rose in instinctive reaction. 'That's the first half over,' she said. 'I'd better get in the queue if you want another drink.'

'I'll do it,' Slider said, standing up. 'Same again for you?'

By the time he reached the end of the queue it had already reached the door. The first comers were plainly getting in huge rounds for all their friends: it was going to be a long wait. Slider leaned against the wall, looking across the room at the woman he loved, the only woman he had ever loved. *You hurt me. Why not Irene? He* had not tried to explain it to her because he doubted if he could make it sound sensible, but the reason he always protected Irene rather than her was not only because of the status quo, but because he didn't really, most of the time, see Joanna as separate from him. And just as he had been taught as a child to offer the chocolate cake to the guest and take the plain bun himself, so he would always feel driven to give Irene more consideration because she was the outsider, and take the gristly bit for the himself-and-joanna entity.

It was only at moments like this, when he deliberately detached himself to look, that he saw Joanna as a discrete entity, capable of suffering in ways quite different from his own. And it—

'Bill, you made it after all! I'm so glad!'

His heart contracted so violently with fright that it actually hurt him. His head whipped round, painfully wrenching a vertebra in his neck, and he found himself staring at Marilyn Cripps, standing inches away from him, very much *en fête* in grey tulle and sequins and with what looked horribly like real diamonds round her neck and at her ears. Behind her the dark-jowled David Cripps in a dinner suit looked like a Mafia boss gone soft; and beside him Irene was wearing her one long dress and an ecstatic smile. She had too much blue eyeshadow on, and more on the left eyelid than the right, and he ached to whip her away behind a screen and wipe it off before anyone noticed. He didn't want her shown up in front of the she-Cripps, whose maquillage might have been painted on by Michelangelo on a particularly good day.

'Darling,' Irene said, oblivious to her lopsidedness, 'have you only just got here?'

'Good thought to meet us backstage! Did you pick up your ticket, old man?' David Cripps asked. 'We left it downstairs but they said they'd be closing quite soon. Doesn't matter if you didn't,' he went on, taking Slider's stunned silence for a negative. 'They never check the tickets going back in for the second half anyway.'

Slider's tongue seemed to have turned to sand and trickled down into the bottom of his neck. He couldn't get so much as a croak out.

'Well, I think we'd all like a drink, wouldn't we?' Cripps went on, craning his neck to assess the length of the bar

147

queue; but at that moment the leader of the orchestra, Warren Stacker, came up to them with an official smile stitched to his lips and his arms out in a gathering-up gesture.

'Ladies, gentlemen, I'm afraid you must have taken a wrong turning,' he said with a sort of PR cheeriness barely masking exasperation, like the doorman at the Ritz turning away a party of German students in shorts and backpacks. 'The Corporate Sponsor's Bar is at the other end of the corridor. Let me show you. This bar is for the artists only.'

'Is that right? I'm a new boy, I'm afraid. Haven't done this before,' David Cripps said heartily. 'Have we made a *faux pas?* Mustn't disturb the geniuses at rest, must we, ha ha!'

They were being shuffled inexorably away, through the gathering press of musicians trying to get in, by Stacker's outstretched, sheepdog arms. Slider, who had not made a single voluntary sound or movement since the first Cripps hail, flung a desperate glance back towards Joanna as his feet, in the interests of remaining directly under his body which was being shoved along willy-nilly, scuffed forwards. He could just see her through a gap in the crowd, a single glimpse of her white, set face above the black evening dress telling him that she had seen it all, before he was shoved out of the bar and into the corridor.

Cripps was still burbling merrily about being in the wrong place and ha-haing and rubbing his hands.

'Not at all, not at all,' Stacker said pleasantly. 'A lot of people make the same mistake. It is confusing backstage. We really ought to put larger signs up. This way – straight ahead.' He met Slider's eye curiously. Of course he knew all about Slider and Joanna, and was having no trouble in putting two and two together; especially as Irene, as soon as space allowed, slipped her hand through Slider's arm and beamed at him with an unmistakably proprietorial smile.

148

'You were waiting in the wrong place, darling,' she said.

'Yes,' Slider agreed desperately. And it ought to have been his safeguard, he thought. If the others had gone to the Sponsor's Bar as they should have, this wouldn't have happened. He bet, savagely, that it was the she-Cripps who had brought them all blundering into the wrong place and ruined everything. Of all the futile, stupid, rotten luck! What an awful bloody farce! And what would Joanna be thinking now?

10

A Wish Devoutly to be Consummated

The rest of the concert passed in a uncomprehending blur. He heard nothing of the music, only stared until his eyes watered at the small black and white blob that was Joanna on the platform, willing her to hear his thoughts. Afterwards there was no escape. Irene took his arm again, and the Crippses led the way with confident step to one of the hospitality rooms where a bar was laid on and uniformed staff handed round trays of cocktail snippets to the assembled corporate, and frequently corpulent, guests.

Here Cripps was in his element. He plunged into business talk with his colleagues while Marilyn graciously presented Irene to the colleagues' wives and Slider tagged along like a subnormal child, always two exchanges behind the conversation. The agony was soon to be intensified, as a door at the rear of the room opened and members of the orchestra began to drift in. Slider knew how much they hated being dragooned into these sponsors' receptions, and when he saw Joanna amongst them, he knew it meant trouble.

She didn't look at him, heading like her colleagues first for the bar, and then allowing herself to be fastened on by one of the organisers. As the crowds thickened and the noise level rose, he lost sight of her. Marilyn Cripps was introducing him to people now, evidently having decided his profession and rank could be turned into a social asset after all. Warren Stacker drifted by and was seized and lionised – 'We're in the right place now, aren't we, ha ha!' – but he was too experienced at the game to be held against his will. With another curious glance at Slider, he scraped them off onto the principal clarinet and escaped. Two minutes later the principal clarinet attempted to emulate his leader's example and unloaded them rather more clumsily onto Joanna.

'And do you play the clarinet as well?' Marilyn asked loudly and clearly, as though she thought Joanna might be deaf or foreign.

'No,' Joanna answered. Her voice sounded tiny next to Marilyn's, as though she were a Lilliputian talking to Gulliver's wife. 'I play the violin.'

'Oh, my husband once had to investigate a case about a violinist,' Irene burst in, placing her hand once more with proprietorial pride on Slider's arm. 'He's a detective inspector in the CID.'

Joanna's eyes shifted for the first time to Slider. Her face was as expressionless as a chair. 'Really? That must be an interesting job.'

Slider felt as though he were sitting by an open fire in a castle – one side of him burning hot, the other side icy.

'The poor girl was murdered, the violinist, I mean,' Irene burbled on. 'Perhaps you remember the case? It was a couple of years ago now, but it was in the papers at the time.'

The agony of having Joanna look at him as if she didn't know him was ousted abruptly from Slider's mind by the more urgent pain of trying to remember whether Irene was likely to have heard Joanna's name in connection with the case. As the dead violinist's best friend, she might possibly have been mentioned at some point. Joanna must be in an even worse fix, not knowing what Irene might or might not know about the murder of Anne-Marie Austen. At the moment she was looking politely blank, but at any moment someone was going to remember that it was this very orchestra which had been at the heart of the case.

'Actually,' Irene said, turning back to Slider, 'I think this was the orchestra she played for, wasn't it, darling?'

Slider opened his mouth without the slightest knowledge of what he would hear himself say, but Marilyn Cripps, redeeming herself for ever in Slider's books, interrupted.

'I don't think we want to discuss such a morbid subject, do we?' She didn't care for conversations she hadn't initiated. Tell me, isn't the orchestra going abroad soon, on a tour? It must be so nice for you to be able to travel all over the world.'

'Excuse me,' Slider muttered desperately to Irene. 'Must find a loo.' It was all he could think of to get away. He just couldn't stand here between Irene and Joanna like this. It was giving him vertigo.

He didn't find a loo. He didn't look for one. He just stood outside in the empty corridor and held his head in his hands and tried to think what to do, and while he was standing there he saw Joanna come out of a door further down and walk away towards the stairs. She had her fiddle case in her hand and her coat over her arm: leaving, then. He went after her at a half run, and caught her just on the other side of the swing doors.

'Joanna!'

She turned, backing a step at the same time as though to stop him touching her. The gesture was not lost on him.

'Where are you going?' he said, the first thing that came into his head.

'I'm going home,' she said, as if it were none of his business. Her face was like wax.

'Jo, I'm sorry,' he said. 'There wasn't anything I could do. You saw what happened.'

She looked at him searchingly for a moment as though she were going to speak, and then turned away again in silence.

He caught her arm. 'Aren't you going to say anything?'

She sighed, and detached her arm, and then said patiently, as though explaining something to an unpromising child, 'If you really believe there wasn't anything you could do, then there's nothing to say.'

'But – what do you want me to do?' he asked in frustration.

'Whatever you were going to do.'

'What do you mean?' She was actually walking away and plainly didn't mean to answer him. He went after her and caught her again. 'What do you *mean*?'

'I'm tired,' she said. 'I'm going home.'

There seemed hope for him in the words, he didn't know why. 'I'll phone you tomorrow,' he said, releasing her arm. She started forward again like a wind-up toy.

'No, don't,' she said.

'Don't what?'

'Don't phone me,' she said. 'I don't want you to phone me.'

And then she was gone.

He went slowly back to the reception. Nothing had changed, no one but Irene had even noticed his departure.

'Did you find it?' she whispered as he rejoined her.

'What?'

She was too polite to mention water closets in public,

153

even in a whisper. 'Are you all right?' she asked in a different voice.

'Yes. I suppose so. Why?'

'You look funny.'

'I'm tired, that's all.'

'Have you got your car here?' she asked.

The question put him on his guard. Was it a trap? How did the car fit in with his cover story? 'Yes,' he said after only a moment's hesitation. 'Why?'

She squeezed his arm and smiled at him in a way that in any other woman he would have thought was meant to be seductive.

'If you've got your car, we don't need to wait for Marilyn and David. We can go home when we like.'

'I thought there was supposed to be a meal afterwards, a restaurant or something?'

'We don't have to go to that. There are other people going now, they won't miss us. I can tell Marilyn you're tired, and we can go straight home.'

She *was* being seductive. Slider shuddered, and she squeezed him again in response. 'As soon as I can catch her attention,' she murmured encouragingly, 'I'll make our excuses.'

Atherton lounged against the window, beyond which the day was white and blank, sunless and windless, neither hot nor cold, as though all weather had been cancelled out of respect for some national catastrophe. Slider felt that ozony sensation of internal hollowness which comes in the aftermath of a great shock, the sense that various functioning bits were missing and that his head had somehow come adrift from his body. He also felt slightly sick, but that might have been because of the residual smell of paint.

At the end of the recital, Atherton made a soundless whistle.

'Christ, what a mess,' he said. His face was screwed up with sympathy. 'I just don't know what to say.'

Slider hadn't even told him the last and maybe worst bit, about making love to Irene last night. Or having sex, whatever was the proper name for what he had done. When it came to it, he hadn't known how to reject her advances, so unexpectedly confident were they, and his body had let him down by apparently not being able to discriminate between the proper object of desire and the lawful.

It was the first time he had done it with Irene since he met Joanna, and he felt terrible afterwards for a whole range of reasons, not least among them that Irene had been glowingly happy this morning: it was many years since the kitchen had been so smiled in before eleven a.m. And he had no idea whether she was still taking the Pill. He rather doubted it, given that they had not done it for so long, but she hadn't suggested any precautions on his part, even supposing he could have obliged if she had. Supposing she fell pregnant? Now there was a man-sized worry to get his teeth into!

Even to Atherton, the closest thing he had to a friend, he couldn't tell that bit.

'I rang her as soon as I got out of the house this morning,' he said instead, 'but she wouldn't talk to me.'

'What, did she slam the phone down?'

'She said she was sorry but it was all over between us, and that she didn't want to see me again. She said if I couldn't see how farcical the situation had become she was sorry for me.'

'Ouch!' said Atherton, wincing.

'I tried to argue, but she said she didn't want to talk to me any more, and put the phone down. When I rang again a bit later her machine was on. I think she must have gone to work by now.'

155

'It sounds bad. What are you going to do?'

'I don't know. I've never been in a situation like this before. Do you think she means it?'

Atherton looked at him, and shook his head. 'How can I know that?'

'You've known so many more women than I have,' Slider said desperately. He'd take any reassurance just at the moment; any rag that would stop the bleeding. 'What should I do? How can I explain to her?'

Atherton thought. 'It's hard to be persuasive on the telephone. You could write her a note, perhaps. Send it with some flowers.'

'Flowers?' Slider frowned. 'That's a bit naff, isn't it?'

'Women are naff,' Atherton said. 'When it comes to their emotions, they're like children – they have no taste.' Slider looked disbelieving, and Atherton shrugged. 'Well, you asked me. I speak as I find, as the man with the geiger-counter on the beach said.'

'Should I go round there, perhaps?' Slider mused. 'Is that what she'd expect? Or does she really want me to stay away?'

Atherton came to his feet. 'Don't you think it would be an idea to sort things out with Irene first?'

Slider looked startled. 'What – before I know how things stand with Joanna?'

'If you really mean to leave home and move in with her—'

'But then supposing I did that and Joanna didn't want me?'

Atherton did not reply, only shrugged again – a gesture which said a great many things Slider didn't want to hear.

'I'll ring again this afternoon,' he said at last. 'And if I don't get her, I'll try going round there this evening.'

It was a long time to wait to hear his fate. 'What you need now,' Atherton said, kindly, on his way out, 'is something to occupy your mind.'

* * *

156

It came soon enough, in a telephone call from Tufty.

'Bill!' he boomed. 'I've got the report on the material from that handkerchief you sent in! The genetic lab boys really pulled their fingers out on this one. It was semen, as I think you know. Unfortunately—'

'Oh no. Don't say it!'

'I'm afraid the sample wasn't terribly good,' Tufty bellowed sadly, 'but they managed to get a partial profile. The thing is, it doesn't match up with the victim.'

'You mean they couldn't get a good enough match to swear to identity?'

'No, no, quite the reverse! Well, to be fair, almost the reverse. What they've got is nothing like the profile of the chip shop body. The sample wasn't good enough for them to be able to swear an identity *with* anybody, but they can tell you quite categorically that the material in the handkerchief didn't come from the victim.'

'Damn! Slider said in frustration. 'What was Leman doing with a handkerchief full of someone else's semen in his bed?'

'I hate to think,' Tufty shouted cheerfully. 'Never been that way inclined myself.'

'And I thought all our troubles would be over when we got that result,' Slider said. 'Oh well, back to the drawing board, I suppose.'

Every clue seemed to run away into the sand. Now it was going to have to be the dental report, and a long wait while it circulated the thousands of dentists in Hong Kong; and he was so disillusioned by now, he wasn't even sure that would produce a result. The presence in Leman's flat of another man did add weight to the theory that he was bisexual, but it introduced an unwelcome extra element of doubt: an unknown lover who might have had cause for jealousy, reason to commit murder. The defence – if this colander of a case ever came to court – were going to love that.

He took out a copy of Slaughter's statement and read it again, though he knew it almost by heart now, hoping it might yield some new idea to him. But there was so little material there. Slaughter had a simple story, and weak though it was, he stuck to it manfully. Leman had come to the shop, suggested going for a drink with him, went home with him. They danced and flirted. They quarrelled. They made it up. He walked Leman to his car, walked around the streets for a while and then went home. He had never seen Leman outside of the shop before. He did not kill him. He had no idea how the body came to be in the black sacks. No one else had access to the shop.

As a defence, it had the strength of lunacy. As for the case against Slaughter, he had motive, means, opportunity, and no alibi, and he himself swore no one else could have done it. All Slider didn't have was a confession, or any solid proof. It was all theory – and there was so much he didn't know about the victim, too. Peter Leman had been up to something, that was for sure – probably smuggling, and even more probably drug-smuggling. Of course, that didn't make any difference now he was dead, but Slider wished he knew all the same. Not knowing maddened him.

He was still staring at the wall deep in thought when the phone rang again.

'Mr Slider?' It was Suzanne Edrich, in a state of considerable excitement. 'Mr Slider, I've just had a phone call from Peter!'

'Peter?'

'My Peter! Peter Leman! He isn't dead after all!' She made a sound between a laugh and a sob. 'Isn't it wonderful? I can't believe I really thought it was him who was murdered!

158

I should have known he was still alive. I'm sure I did really, deep down. Oh, I'm so happy!'

Her voice clotted and she sobbed again into the receiver.

'Where are you?' Slider asked.

'I'm at work,' she managed to say through the strange noises she was making into the receiver. 'He phoned me here. He wouldn't ring me at home, because of my parents.'

'Do you know where he is?'

'He wouldn't say. It has to be a secret, he says. Oh, but he's alive, that's all that matters!'

Not by a long chalk, Slider corrected inwardly. 'All right, Miss Edrich, I'm going to come and see you right away. Stay where you are, don't talk to anyone else, and if Peter rings you again, try to find out where he is, or get his number – or failing that, try to keep him talking until I come. Do you understand?'

'Yes,' she said, and added some more incoherent phrases of joy before ringing off. Slider slammed the phone down and was on his feet yelling for Atherton before it had stopped jangling. In the best detective stories, he remembered saying to Tufty, the suspect is never the suspect and the corpse is never the corpse. The thing was coming to pieces in his hands. If Peter Leman was alive, what price their case now?

Suzanne Edrich had let go and had a jolly good cry, and had enjoyed it so much that she threatened at any moment to spill over again. Slider had to question her very carefully to keep her juices confined, or they'd have got nothing out of her but salt water.

'Are you sure it was him? Are you absolutely positive?'

'Yes, of course. I couldn't possibly mistake his voice. It was Peter all right,' she said radiantly. 'He said "Hullo, Suze," – he always calls me Suze. And I said, "Oh God, Peter, I thought you were dead!" But I feel now that I didn't, not really, not deep down,' she said gravely. She was working up for a full-blown attack of mysticism, Slider could see. Her previous affection for Peter Leman had been given a tremendous boost by her brief and dramatic experience of widowhood, and now he was back from the dead he had been promoted to the One Great Love of her Life.

'Was he surprised when you told him that you thought he was dead?'

'Well, he must have been, mustn't he? I told him all about it, anyway – about the body and that fish-shop man and your questions and everything.'

'What did he say about himself? Did he tell you where he's been?'

'No, he only said that he was in hiding—'

'In hiding?' Slider said explosively. This was beginning to sound like a practical joke.

She looked a little surprised. 'Yes. He's hiding up. He says he's doing a job for someone, and he has to keep out of the way for a while, and no one must know where he is. But he said he had to call me because he didn't want me to be worried,' she said radiantly. 'He really does care for me, you see.'

'What sort of job is he doing? Do you mean something criminal?'

'Of course not! Peter wouldn't do anything like that,' she said indignantly.

'What else would necessitate his hiding up?' Atherton interrupted in an appeal to logic.

'Well, I don't know!' she said rather crossly. 'I told you, he said it was secret. It wouldn't be secret if he could tell me, would it? And he said no one must know I'm his girlfriend either. But I thought I'd better tell *you* he wasn't dead so that

160

you could call off your enquiries – only you must promise not to tell anyone else.'

'Who are we not to tell? Who is he afraid of?'

'He didn't say. I keep telling you, he said it has to be a secret. But he promised to tell me everything when it's all over.'

Slider and Atherton exchanged glances. This was straight out of the pages of a 1930s romance, and not a very well-written one at that.

'Miss Edrich, just think about it logically. He must be involved with some sort of criminal activity. There isn't anything else that would have to be kept secret, now is there?'

'What about military secrets? Or the Secret Service? Or industrial secrets, for that matter?' she said indignantly. 'I think you're horrible to jump to the conclusion that Peter's a criminal – but I suppose that's the way your minds work, if you're policemen,' she added with some contempt. 'I wish I'd never told you, now. I thought you'd be pleased.'

'Oh, we are, of course we are,' Atherton said hastily. 'It's wonderful, too, that he thought of phoning you first of all. He must really love you.'

She purred under the flattery like a tea-kettle. Slider could only watch in admiration. 'Well, I think he does.'

'And if he's going to be in hiding for some time, he won't be able to bear not to speak to you again, will he? I mean, how else will he be able to cope with being apart from you?'

'Well, he did say he might call again,' she admitted modestly.

'And when he does, you know it's terribly important that we should have a chance to speak to him. We don't want to make any trouble for him, but there are one or two things we desperately need to know.'

She looked doubtful. 'Well, I don't know. I could ask him, but I don't know if he'll agree. I wouldn't want to put him in danger.'

'That's the whole point,' Atherton said. 'He is in danger, and he needs our protection. But we can't protect him if we don't know where he is.'

'Yes, that's true,' she said. A few minutes more of Atherton's play-acting, and she was agreeing to any kind of telephone link they liked. It was a masterly performance.

'Now all we've got to do is to convince Barrington the expense is necessary,' Slider said as they drove back to the station.

'How much of that load of cobblers do you believe?' Atherton asked.

'I don't know,' Slider said gloomily. 'She's so convinced she's in a Humphrey Bogart movie, there's no relying on anything she says.'

'Except that Leman's alive.'

'Yes. That bit would have to be true.'

'Slaughter always said he didn't kill Leman.'

'Yes. No wonder he stuck to his guns over that – he could tell the truth with perfect conviction. But then who did he kill? The corpse must be someone.'

'Maybe he was a Chinaman after all? We know the victim had Asian blood. We just don't know how much.'

'But Leman's got to be involved in it somehow. We've got to get hold of him.' Slider sighed. 'I don't know what we're going to do about Slaughter. We'll have to drop the charge against him. The question is, do we make other charges in their place? We're still left with the fact that the murder was done in the chip shop and that no one but Slaughter had a key.'

'Murder of a person unknown,' Atherton said. 'I'm glad I'm a lowly sergeant. I wouldn't like to have to make difficult decisions all day long.'

* * *

162

'Let him go,' said Barrington decisively. 'If the victim isn't Leman, we've got nothing on him.'

'Except physical evidence at the shop, sir,' Slider said. 'No sign of forcible entry. No one else's fingerprints.'

'All the same, until we know who the victim is, we can't connect him with Slaughter. And if we let him go, my guess is he'll do something really silly and give himself away.'

'Yes, sir.'

Barrington raised feral eyes to Slider's face. 'I'm very, very unhappy about this, Slider. You've wasted precious time following a false trail. Now we've got it all to do again. So get your finger out! I want no mistakes this time. I want to know who the victim is, and what Leman's got to do with it. If he's not the victim, maybe he's the murderer. He could be in it with Slaughter, had you thought of that? Maybe Slaughter lent him the key, and now he's shielding him. But first you've got to find him! Find Leman!'

Slider outlined his plans for putting a relay into Suzanne's phone so that her calls could be monitored. Then as soon as Leman calls, we can put a trace on it.'

'All right,' Barrington said. 'I'll authorise it. And put somebody on to watch his flat. He might come back there.'

Slaughter took hold of the seat of the chair on which he was sitting with both hands, as if he thought they were going to pick him up bodily there and then and throw him out into the street. 'I don't want to go,' he said. 'I want to stay here.'

'We're releasing you, Ronnie,' Atherton said patiently. 'Don't you understand? We're dropping the charges against you. You're a free man.'

Slaughter looked from Atherton to Nicholls with the eyes of a cornered rat. 'Free?' he said blankly.

'That's right. You're free to go. You can go home.'

'No!' he said determinedly. 'I'm not going.'

'You can't stay here, laddie,' Nicholls said kindly. 'We need your room.'

Opposition seemed to make Slaughter determined. 'I won't go,' he said. 'You've – you've made a mistake. I did kill him. All right? I killed Peter Leman. That's what you've been wanting me to say, isn't it? I hit him on the head like you said, and then I chopped him up and put him in the sack. I did it! I killed him!'

Atherton exchanged a glance with Nicholls, and said gently, 'It wasn't Peter Leman, Ronnie. The body in the sacks. It wasn't him. Peter Leman's alive.'

'Peter? He's—' Slaughter's eyes filled with tears. 'Peter's not dead?'

'Not even a little bit. He's alive and kicking. That's why we're letting you go.'

'Peter's alive,' Slaughter said dazedly. 'Peter.'

'That's right,' Nicholls said breezily. 'So up you get, laddie, and let's have you out of there. It's warm and sunny outside. We'll give you a nice ride home in a car, eh? It's a shame to walk on such a lovely day.'

Slaughter's expression hardened, and he gripped his seat more tightly. 'No, I'm not going. I did it. I killed the other bloke.'

'What other bloke?' Atherton asked with diminishing patience.

'The dead bloke. The one in the sacks. I killed him.'

'All right – who is he, then?'

'I don't know,' Slaughter muttered.

'You don't know. So how can you say you killed him if you don't even know who he is?' Atherton said kindly. 'Come on, now Ronnie, let's have you out of there.'

He grew hysterical. 'I killed him, I tell you! I did it! Gimme a statement, I'll sign it! Anything you like, only don't make me go out there again!' And he burst into noisy tears.

It was some time before they got him quietened down again, mopped him up, and detached him from his seat. Nicholls talked to him kindly, and at last he seemed resigned, and was even vaguely comforted by the prospect of a car ride right to his own front door.

'What will I do now?' he asked quietly as he shuffled docilely towards the back yard where the cars were parked, accompanied by Atherton to see him off the premises and the PC who had been detailed to drive him home. 'Will I go back to the shop?'

'Not for the moment. You can't open the shop yet, I'm afraid. Not until we're sure we've got all the information we need out of it.'

'Like, clues, you mean?'

'Yes, that's right.'

'So I just stay at home, right? And, like, wait?'

'Yes, I should do that,' Atherton said. He had been threatened by released arrestees before now, but never asked for advice. 'We'll let you know when you can open the shop again.'

Slaughter shook his head. 'No, Mr Cate will do that,' he said. 'Mr Cate will decide. He'll tell me what to do. I'll just go home and wait, then.'

11

Breakfast and Villainies

What with one thing and another, it was late before Slider
got home, his mind aching with the events of the day, and
raw with the fresh sting of his last, unhappy interview with
Joanna. When she had opened the door to him, he had thought
that she would refuse to talk. But after looking at him for a
long moment, she sighed and said, 'All right, come in. I
suppose it all has to be said once.'

He followed her in, and she led him into the sitting-room,
where they had eaten and drunk and made love and talked
so many times, done everything except as now to have a
formal conversation, sitting too far apart to touch each other.
He felt at a disadvantage like that. His mind, in any case,
was still partly occupied by the case, and a large part of the
rest of it was simply consumed with longing to take hold of
her and sink his face into her neck. To sit here unlicensed
to touch her, and have her look at him with that unsmiling,
frozen face, made him want to throw back his head and howl
like a dog.

'Jo, why?' he said at last. 'Nothing's changed.'

'Yes, it has,' she said.

'Not for me.' She seemed unwilling – or perhaps unable – to amplify. 'What, then?' he urged at last.

'I hadn't seen *her* before. She wasn't real.'

'She was just as real to me. I love you, I want to live with you. That hasn't changed. I'm ready to do it. Don't stop now, just when everything's on the brink of being all right.'

She looked at him clearly. 'Not tonight, now – it's too late. Not tomorrow – you'll be working late. Not at the weekend – the children will be around.'

His own words delivered back to him were like smacks in the face.

'Don't,' he said. 'That's not fair.'

'I'm not being unkind. I just want you to see it as it is, the truth. I know you weren't just making excuses. If you had been, everything would be quite different.'

'They weren't excuses, they were reasons.'

'I *know*,' she said quickly. 'That's the point. And the reason you haven't been able to do it all this time is that you know it's wrong. You made promises, you took on responsibilities, and you can't just shrug them off. And I,' she finished sadly, 'should never have asked you to.'

'I have a responsibility to you, too,' he pointed out.

She shook her head. 'Not the same. Not really.'

'It's real to me.'

'Well,' she said. She began to speak, changed her mind, lifted her hands from her lap and tucked them under her arms, a defensive gesture, hugging to comfort herself. 'Yes, I suppose that's why it has to be me who decides. And I've decided I can't ask you to do something that's so hard for you, something that you believe is wrong.'

'You're not asking me. I am capable of making my own decisions about my own life.'

'You decided last night.'

'I didn't. I couldn't help that.'

She sighed. 'If it's that hard for you to do, maybe you shouldn't do it. If you could have come to me gladly – but not like this. Not—' She seemed to search for words, and then said again flatly, 'Not like this.'

He could not move her. In the end she asked him to go, and seeing what it cost her to ask, he got up obediently. But at the door he found himself overwhelmed with disbelief. This couldn't be all. He turned again and said, 'You'll change your mind.' Half statement, half question. Half plea.

'No.' She met his eyes, and almost managed to smile. 'But thank you for not suggesting that we just go on as we are. That takes real greatness. You are a great man, Bill.'

He felt as though he had a tennis ball stuck in his throat. 'I love you,' he managed to say despite it.

'I love you, too,' she said. She stepped back, like someone who had just cast off a boat, and he thought it was so that he should not try to kiss her. There was nothing to do but go. 'Good luck,' she said when he was half way down the path. He would have liked to say something but the tennis ball prevented, so he lifted his hand in a futile sort of gesture and concentrated on not stumbling or walking into the gate-post in the fog which enveloped him.

By the time he got home, everyone was in bed, and he thanked God for the small mercy, because he didn't think he could bear to speak to anyone. He couldn't go to bed – he'd never sleep. Besides, he didn't want to get in beside Irene. He didn't want to sleep beside her ever again. He couldn't think why it hadn't bothered him before. He would move into the spare bedroom, sleep alone from now on. Why hadn't he done it before? It would be a modicum, the smallest modicum possible, of honesty. Irene wouldn't mind. Barring the aberration last night (was it really only last night?) his company in bed had meant nothing to her for years, and she often complained that he woke her up with his comings and goings and late phone calls. He would use work as the excuse, so as to save her face – and for the children's sake.

He should have moved into the spare room long ago. For tonight, the sofa would do. He wasn't going to start morrissing about with sheets now. The sofa – or couch, as Irene called it, as though it were some exotic divan upon which an odalisque might quite easily be found reclining – and the whisky bottle. If ever a man needed a small glass of Lethe, it was him, and now. God, what a life! The case going to pieces all around him, Barrington telling him off like an inky schoolboy, and Joanna – no, he'd better not think about Joanna or he'd start weeping, and he had the perilous feeling that if he started he'd never stop.

The case, think about the case. Leman must be the clue, the link. The more he thought about it, the more it seemed that there was some sort of conspiracy going on, and that Slaughter was being used. The innocent, or perhaps only partly innocent, catspaw. The alternative was that Slaughter had gone to the shop after leaving Leman and had met the victim there – by chance or be pre-arrangement – and had murdered him for his own reasons, and that Leman's presence earlier in the evening in question was pure coincidence.

Well, the essence of a coincidence was that it was coincidental, and therefore theory number two was just as likely as theory number one. But it was in any policeman's nature to be suspicious of coincidences, and if Slaughter had committed the murder, why did he say he didn't know who the victim was when he was so gaily confessing to anything and everything?

Why had Leman taken the chip-shop job when he plainly

169

had plenty of money from other directions? Why had he not told the Abbotts that he was minding the Acton flat for a friend? Why had he taken on the pub job so suddenly? Why had he left it early to go to the chip shop? All those things could have been deliberate ploys to make it look as though he was missing, to support the illusion that Ronnie had murdered him – and if that were the case, Leman must know something about the real victim, the real murder. That was theory number one.

Well, from the procedural point of view it didn't really matter. They still had to find Leman, whether to prove he was involved or he wasn't.

And they still had to identify the victim, damn it! Perhaps he was Chinese. There was the Hung Fat Restaurant almost next door. Of course everyone there had been questioned as a matter of routine, and had said they knew nothing, but it was always hard to get trustworthy statements out of people who didn't speak English, or pretended not to. They would all have to be interviewed again.

Hadn't there been another mention of Chinese men somewhere in the case? It escaped him for the moment, but the motif had come up before somewhere—

He was flung out of his train of thought by the telephone bell. He leapt across the room to grab it before it woke Irene. It was Paxman, who was station sergeant on night duty.

'A call this late must be an emergency,' Slider said. 'What's up, Arthur?'

'That joker you released this afternoon?' Paxman said.

'Slaughter?'

'That's right. Just had a call from his place of abode. Looks as though the silly bugger's topped himself.'

'God, that was quick work,' Slider heard himself say.

'Found in his room with his throat cut,' Paxman amplified.

'Who's on night duty in the Department? Mackay, isn't it?'

'Yes, he's gone, and the area car. And Atherton's on his way.'

'Right, thanks. I'm leaving now,' Slider said.

'Why these silly buggers can't wait until daylight I don't know,' Paxman said genially.

'If they waited until daylight they probably wouldn't do it,' Slider pointed out. He put the phone down and went out into the hall to pick up his car keys.

'Bill?' Irene was half way down the stairs, still tying the belt of her dressing-gown. Her sleep-ruffled hair made her look softer and younger than her daytime sleekness.

'I've got to go out again. Emergency call,' he said.

'Bill, I need to talk to you,' she said, still coming down.

He felt a strange mixture of irritation and panic – a cross between wanting to snap, 'Not now, woman!' and put his arms up in front of his face in the form of a cross.

'It'll have to wait,' he managed to say with an approximation of normality. 'We've got another corpse on our hands, I'm afraid. I don't know what time I'll be back. You know how it is.' And he grabbed his keys and legged it like one John Smith. Even as he backed the car out into the road, he could see Irene standing at the door watching him go, softly implacable as Nemesis. She would be there when he got back. That was marriage for you.

The house was lit up as though for a party, the front door open, cars drawn up outside, pretty flashing blue lights . . . there ought to have been a small bunch of balloons tied to the railings, Slider thought as he spotted Atherton's immaculate four-year-old Sierra double-parked by it. On the bathroom landing a strange man was being voluble and indignant to Mackay, and at the next landing Mandy was in her nextdoor neighbour's room, seated on the bed between WPC Coffey and a cross-looking dark girl in a negligee, weeping violently.

Slider toiled on up, and found Atherton on the upper floor with the local doctor who had been called in to pronounce life extinct. Not that there was any doubt about it. Slaughter was lying in a huddle in the far corner of his room under the wash-basin with his throat cut from ear to ear. There was blood in the basin, smears of it down the outside of the white porcelain, and pools of it on the floor. Lying in the basin was a large, sharp, black-handled kitchen knife, plentifully bloodied. Slaughter himself was in pyjamas, black nylon with a pattern of small, random red and white squares. His feet were bare. Slider looked at them, and then away again. There was something so pathetic, so horribly, vulnerably human about feet – knobbled and calloused and marked by a lifetime of unsung service.

Dr Wasim was departing. 'I've taken the temperature. Life extinct about an hour and a half, I should say. Immediate cause of death suffocation from the severed windpipe. No other exterior signs of violence.' He gave a small, taut smile. 'I'll leave the rest for Dr Cameron. Would you like me to look at that unfortunate young woman downstairs before I go?'

While Atherton saw him off, Slider picked his way delicately over to the body. The story was written there, easy to read. He had stood over the sink to cut his throat, presumably out of consideration for others, hoping not to make a mess. Having made the cut, he had dropped the knife and collapsed, smearing the outside of the basin with his bloody hands, and sunk to the floor.

'It was Mandy who found him,' Atherton explained, coming back. 'She was downstairs in her room – immediately underneath, if you remember – entertaining a gentleman friend. As soon as he left she went over to the sink to make herself a cup of coffee, and a drop of blood fell on her. She looked up and saw it dripping through the ceiling. You see how it is, Guv—'

He saw how it was. Below the sink the floor was covered with a square of lino. Through this the various water and waste pipes were let through holes, and through holes cut in the floorboards below.

'The cold water pipe goes straight through into Mandy's room. She said she can see the light through it when her room's dark and the light's on up here. So the blood—'

The blood, finding its own level, had trickled down and through the corresponding hole in Mandy's ceiling – just two significant drops before it thickened too much to drip.

'Who's the bloke downstairs? Is that her customer?'

'No, he'd already gone. That's the man who was in with the other girl, Maureen. They rushed out when Mandy started screaming to see what the hullabaloo was about. He's most indignant now because he feels he was being public spirited in staying with the girls until the police arrived, and now we're demanding his name and address, which he isn't keen to give.'

'What about the knife?'

'It's fairly old and used, and there are two others matching but in different sizes in the cutlery drawer.'

Slider grunted, bending over the body and carefully lifting the head. The cut ran from high up under the left ear to the base of the right side of the neck – the typical direction of a right-handed suicide – and had severed all the great vessels in one clean sweep – not typical of the average suicide. Slaughter's eyes were open, and had the grey and clouded look of a stale fish on a slab. Slider laid him down gently and stood back, looking around.

'It's not usual for a slitter to make it first go,' Atherton remarked. 'And that is a very deep and clean cut. No haggling.'

No haggling. Like the dismembered corpse where it all began. 'Yes; but he was used to handling knives,' Slider said. 'And there's no sign of disturbance or struggle.' The room was as monastically neat as before, except that the bedclothes were thrown back, and there was a dent in the middle of the pillow. 'He was in bed,' Slider said aloud, his eyes moving from bed to sink and back.

'Yes. Doesn't that seem odd to you? I mean, to get undressed and go to bed, and then get up to commit suicide?'

Slider shook his head. 'Not impossible. Got undressed and went to bed as a matter of routine, then lay there unable to sleep, thinking, going over and over things in his mind until it just got too much for him. Flung the bedclothes back and got up—'

'Scribbled a suicide note,' Atherton put in, gesturing towards the mantelpiece.

Yes, there it was, propped up beside the photograph of Mum. It was a smudgy fly-leaflet advertising a local disco – LADIES! YOU MAY ENTER 'FREE' AFTER NINE O'CLOCK ON FRIDAY'S AND SATURDAY'S – and the note was written on its unprinted back.

I got mad and killed him it said in pencil, the clumsy, cramped handwriting of the unaccustomed. *I can't stand it any more. God forgive me.*

Slider looked round again, more carefully. Ah, there was the pencil on the floor, just under the table, as if it had rolled off the mantelpiece and fallen. It was one of those tiny, thin jobs with the plastic stud on top, that lives down the spine of a diary. The size of the lead corresponded with the thickness of the writing. That was all right.

'Have to test that for fingerprints, and the note. And the knife, of course,' Slider said. But there was something odd about it. He couldn't put his finger on it, but something . . .

174

'They're on their way,' Atherton said. 'Photography, finger-prints, forensic, the whole circus. But it looks all right on the surface of it.'

'Yes,' said Slider.

Atherton looked at him more closely. 'Are you all right, Guv?'

Slider pulled himself up. 'Just tired,' he said. 'I thought I wouldn't sleep so I had a large glass of whisky before I got the call.'

'I wish I'd thought of that,' Atherton said.

'We'd better go down and have a word with Mandy and – what's the other one's name again?'

'Maureen O'Rourke. Not from Oiled Oiland, though – she's got a Shepherd's Bush twang you could cut with a knife.'

Slider glanced again at the pyjama'd huddle under the sink, the straggling back hair and the mute, reproachful feet, gnarled and discoloured like old potatoes.

'I wish you hadn't used those particular words,' he said.

It was morning when they finally emerged from the station, gritty-eyed and weary. The streets were full of people on their way to work and delivery vans double parked in front of shops just to annoy. Slider felt hollow of frame and stuffed of head, but he had gone through tiredness and out the other side. He knew from experience that he could go on like this now all day if he had to. It was the thought of going back to Ruislip that daunted him, and reminded him, with a sinking sensation, of the present state of play in his personal life.

Atherton, close by him, read his expression and the faltering step, and said, 'How about coming back to my place for breakfast? I don't know about you, but I could do with a really good meal. Scrambled eggs and bacon – you like the way I scramble eggs. And I've got some really good sausages from that shop on the corner of Smithfield Market, what's it called—?'

'*Simply Sausages,*' Slider heard himself say from about a hundred yards away.

'That's right. I got a whole lot last time I was at the Old Bailey. There's a pork and apple job so delicious it would make a strong man weep. How about it? A real gutbuster?' He saw that Slider was still hesitating, and added cunningly, 'I'll cook while you make the coffee. You make better coffee than me.'

Transparent device, Slider thought with an inward smile. His voice seemed to be half way to Brighton by now.

'Yes, all right. Thanks.'

Atherton made the coffee first, and Slider sat on the high stool in the tiny kitchen with Oedipus kneading his lap and purring like a hypocrite, and sipped while Atherton assembled the ingredients for breakfast. Slider usually drank tea, since he could never care for instant coffee and the other sort was not available at home or in the canteen, so Atherton's brew revived him like intravenous Benzedrine.

They talked about the night's events.

'Well, now we've got no victim and no suspect.' Atherton said, breaking eggs into a bowl. 'It takes all the running you can do in this case to stay in the same place.'

'Barrington wasn't pleased,' Slider said. 'But after all, it was what he wanted – to let Slaughter go and see if he incriminated himself.'

'Instead of which he exsanguinated himself.'

'Did he?'

'Well, didn't he?' Atherton said. 'After all, he'd every reason to kill himself.'

'You've changed sides,' Slider observed.

'You argued away all my objections. Besides, neither Mandy nor Maureen heard anything, and I can't believe if Ronnie was dragged out of bed and slaughtered that he wouldn't have yelled or struggled.'

'He might have been too frightened. Or he might have known the murderer and trusted him. Suppose he'd got up and gone to the sink to fill the kettle or something, to make a cup of coffee for his guest, perhaps, and the murderer just came quietly up behind him and cut his throat before he knew what was happening?'

'He would have had to do it from behind to make it look like a suicide cut,' Atherton acknowledged. 'But even so, surely Mandy must have heard something? She said she could hear Slaughter moving about and thumping on the floor the night he had Leman back there.'

'Yes, but by her own account she didn't even hear the body hit the floor, and it must have done that whether it was suicide or murder. When you consider what she and Maureen were up to—'

'Yes,' Atherton frowned. He pulled out the grill pan and turned the sausages with a fork. The smell wafted out and Oedipus dug his nails into Slider's knee in sensuous reaction. 'And Mandy had the radio going, too, didn't she? But look – if it was murder, the murderer must have gone down the stairs to get out. Someone must have heard him.'

'Perhaps someone did. But hearing and registering aren't the same thing, and in that house men are creeping in and out all the time. He only had to wait his moment for the coast to be clear—'

'Could he have got out before Mandy came running upstairs?'

'Why not?' Slider shrugged. 'The blood would take a little while to trickle through, and Mandy must have stood staring at it and the ceiling and making exclamations before she actually sprang into action.'

Atherton pondered. 'How would the murderer get in? You can't slip those electronic latches with a credit card.'

'Either by ringing Slaughter's bell, if he was known to him, or by waiting for someone going in or out and slipping in with them – though I don't suppose he'd want to risk being recognised.'

'But Mandy didn't hear his bell, and she did when we rang it that day.'

'But that day she was waiting for a customer. Last night she had one already in there, grunting in her ear and pounding the bedsprings. I don't suppose she'd have noticed anything much less than a good-sized articulated lorry bursting in through her walls.'

'Hmm.' Atherton beat the eggs with black pepper and a fine, free, practised movement of the wrist. Slider watched admiringly, completely relaxed now. He had handed over responsibility to his sergeant for the time being. His mind coasted, viewing everything with the clear detachment of sleeplessness.

Atherton added a little grated nutmeg, and tipped the beaten eggs into the pan. 'If it was murder, the murderer must have had blood at least on his hand and wrist, even doing it from behind. Someone will have seen him in the street.'

'Large gauntlets,' Slider said. 'Motorcycle gauntlets, that's what I'd use. The sort with the big cuffs that come half way up your forearm.'

'Wouldn't he have been a bit conspicuous, wearing those?'

'Not if he had a motorcycle. Or he could have carried them in a bag of some sort, put them on for the murder and taken them off again.'

'You've got an answer for everything,' Atherton smiled

unwillingly. 'All the same, Mr Barrington's quite happy for it to have been suicide—'

'Well he would, wouldn't he?'

'—and there's no real reason why it shouldn't have been.'

'Except the note,' Slider said. 'There's something about that note that bothers me. Where did he get the leaflet, for instance?'

'He picked it up in the hall when he came in. Those kind of things are put through every letterbox in the land every day of the week.'

'The disco ones are more usually stuck under people's windscreen wipers.'

'Maybe. Maybe not.'

'And the pencil – where did he get that? He didn't have a diary.'

'He could have picked it up anywhere,' Atherton said reasonably. 'Someone dropped it on the street, in a bus, in his shop – on the stairs.'

'Yes,' said Slider, dissatisfied. 'He could have.'

Atherton looked at him askance. 'But you don't think so?'

'I don't know why, but it bothers me. The letter, and the fact that he was so scared of being released. I think this was what he was frightened of.'

'Well, if it was murder, who, and why?'

'Leman, perhaps. Whatever this "job" is that he's in hiding for must have involved Dave's Fish Bar. Perhaps killing Slaughter is part of it.'

'But then he must be doing it *for* someone,' Atherton said, dissatisfied. 'And that would mean we're nowhere near a solution.'

'Or perhaps it was a revenge killing for whoever it was that Slaughter killed at the chip shop – the whole thing a tangle of homosexual jealousy. We've got to find some of his previous pick-ups, find out who he knew, and if any of them are missing.'

'What a lovely job! Tracing nameless contacts through the gay bars of London could take the rest of our lives,' Atherton said. Slider didn't reply. Atherton looked at him for a moment, and then shrugged. 'Breakfast is ready. Do you want some more coffee?'

The delicious food revived him, set his mind running at normal speed again, and woke from its numbness the pain of the Joanna-situation.

Lingering over his last piece of toast and marmalade, Atherton asked delicately, 'Do you think she means it?'

'Oh, she means it all right. She wouldn't say things like that for effect.'

'No, I don't think she would,' Atherton said slowly. 'But what are you going to do, then?'

'What can I do? Just – go on, I suppose.' He played with his knife, swinging it round on his plate like the secondhand of a clock. 'I don't think I've really taken it in, yet. I can't believe I'll never see her again.'

'Nor do I,' Atherton said briskly. 'There's got to be a way to sort it out.'

'It would be wrong. She's right about that. But on the other hand—' He paused, frowning in thought. 'Five years ago I wouldn't even have thought of it. The children were younger – Irene hardly ever went out – they all depended on me so much more. But now Irene has her own friends and her own interests, and the children – well, you know what kids are like these days.'

Atherton didn't and said so.

'They're all the time doing things – friends' parties, clubs, school visits, I don't know what else. They practically need

180

social secretaries. If ever the phone rings these days you can bet it's for one of them. And when they are at home, they don't want to talk to you or be with you. They shut themselves up in their rooms, demanding their privacy – you have to knock before entering these days. They're like hotel guests, really. I can't believe they'd care one way or the other if I went.'

Atherton looked at him steadily. There was nothing for him to say in this argument. In the Central Criminal Court, it was Slider vs. Slider.

'But is that really true? Or am I just rationalising what I want to believe? And in any case, does the fact that they don't care about me – if it is a fact – justify me in abandoning my responsibilities?'

'She was right about one thing – it is much too hard for you,' Atherton said.

'You mean, I shouldn't leave them?'

Atherton slid away from the role being thrust upon him. 'I can't advise you. It's not my place.'

'But you have an opinion?'

'Not even that. Only a philosophy of life.'

'Well?' Slider demanded.

Atherton shook his head. 'It wouldn't help you.'

'Tell me anyway.'

'All right. It's this; "Live each day as though it were your last. One day you're bound to be right."'

Slider stared a moment's incomprehension, and then an unwilling smile tugged at his lips. 'You're a fat lot of help!'

'I did warn you,' Atherton grinned.

They were suddenly both embarrassed by the feeling of warmth between them.

'Thanks for letting me maunder on,' Slider said gruffly.

'Any time,' Atherton replied lightly. 'I think I offer a very reasonable maundry service.'

They both got up, and began to clear the plates. Oedipus, on his chair between them, teetered this way and that, trying to see where the bacon rinds were going.

'And now I suppose it's back to the real world,' Atherton said. 'There's a thousand interviews waiting for us out there, and a whole new lot of house-to-house enquiries.'

'Is that what you call the real world? It doesn't look very believable from where I'm standing.'

'I daresay you haven't had much practice,' Atherton said kindly. 'Why sometimes I've believed as many as six impossible things before breakfast.'

12

And Flights of Bagels

'The Chinese connection,' Slider said as they headed back to the station.

'The Tooth Fairy didn't say Chinese specifically, only Asian,' Atherton pointed out.

'But then there's the fact that the eyes were missing, and the scalp. Why that, if the idea was only to prevent identification? Couldn't it have been because the eyes and hair would give away the fact that the victim was Chinese, or part Chinese?'

Atherton grunted, concentrating on the gleaming, elderly Vauxhall Cresta in front. The driver was wearing a hat – always a danger signal in Atherton's book – and had his left indicator flashing while hand-signalling right. 'It's a long shot,' he said. The Cresta turned left, and Atherton shot past with a blast on his horn.

'But then there's the Chinese Restaurant practically next door – and so many chip shops these days are run by Chinese. I can't help wondering, you see, what the chip shop had to do with it.'

'Your conspiracy theory?' Atherton said.

183

'There's still the fact that Leman took the part-time job for no obvious reason.'

'Maybe it was just for pleasure. Some people like chip shops. If only we could speak to the bastard we might find out.'

'We'll get him when he phones Suzanne again. With that new equipment it only takes thirty seconds to trace back a call.'

'If he phones again. But I must say the alternative theory sounds much more attractive – and I'd be willing to bet Mr Barrington will prefer it. If Leman really was bisexual—'

'We don't know that he was. There's only his night with Slaughter to go by, and that may have been a set-up.'

'What about the handkerchief in the bed?'

'But that might have been Leman's semen. We only know that it wasn't the victim's.'

'Oh yes, I'd forgotten.'

'Besides, I've remembered now where I heard the Chinese mentioned before: it was Mandy. Do you remember, she said that the room next to Slaughter's was empty, but that—'

'That there was a Chinese man staying there, yes,' Atherton said.

'And that they had a lot of them – presumably one after the other. It might all be a coincidence, but since we're starting again from scratch, I don't want to miss out anything.'

'Fair enough, Guv. D'you want me to go back and talk to Mandy again?'

'No, I'll do that. I want you to go to the Hung Fat and try to get something out of them. I know it's hard work, but—'

'Actually,' Atherton said thoughtfully, 'I think I know a way to go about it.'

After redisposing his troops for the new fray, and before departing for Holland Park, Slider telephoned Irene.

'It was an all-nighter. Our prime suspect and sole witness has been offed, and the case is wide open again. I'm sorry, but I don't know when I'm likely to be back.'

'It's all right, I understand,' she said kindly.

Who was this mild-mannered woman? Slider wondered internally. Did she wear a blue body-suit and red wellies under her neat floral dresses? Where was the Irene 'Slugger' Slider of yesteryear, veteran of a thousand light-heavy marital bouts – he light, she heavy?

'There is just one thing,' she said, almost diffidently.

'Yes?' Slider said cautiously, feeling his jaw.

'Did you remember that we were supposed to be taking the children to Box Hill today?'

'Oh, Lord, I'd forgotten!'

'For a picnic.'

'I'm sorry—'

'No, no, it's all right. I was just wondering if you'd mind if Ernie Newman took us instead.'

'Instead?'

'Instead of you. You see, I don't really want to risk going a long distance in my car – you know that trouble I've had with it overheating – and when I talked to Ernie he said he'd love to take us.'

'When did you discuss it with him? I've only just told you I won't be home,' Slider said, perplexed.

'Oh, he phoned up this morning and I happened to mention that you'd been called out and I doubted whether you'd be back in time, and he said he hadn't been to Box Hill for years and he loved picnics and, well, I think he finds weekends a bit lonely since Nora died.'

Lame dogs, now, was it? 'Of course I don't mind. You fix it up just how you like.'

'All right. Thanks.'

It sounded less than rapturous. 'I'm sorry I can't take you,' he said 'You'll tell the kids I'm sorry, won't you?'

'Oh, they know what your job's like,' she said.

He thought she was a little subdued and remembered her appearance on the stairs this morning. 'What was it you wanted to talk to me about? You said this morning—'

'Oh! That. Yes. No, it doesn't matter. Another time will do. I'll expect you when I see you, then, shall I?' And she said goodbye and rang off rather abruptly.

Mandy was swollen-eyed, voluble with a mixture of shock and indignation. Slider found her migrated to the larger bedsit of the midnight-haired Maureen: the two of them were sitting on the bed drinking endless cups of instant coffee and emitting Silk Cut smoke in a blue pall like the twin exhausts of an elderly Jaguar.

'I just can't stay in that room,' Mandy explained with a violent shudder. 'I keep thinking about it, seeing that blood dripping down from the ceiling, God it was awful! And then when I went upstairs, and poor Ronnie was just lying there, just—'

'Don't think about it, Mand,' Maureen said warmly, patting her hand.

'I can't help it! I just keep thinking about the poor sod, all alone up there, bleeding to death, and we never knew anything about it.'

'He would have died very quickly,' Slider said.

'That's what I said,' Maureen said triumphantly. 'I said he wouldn't have had time to feel nothing, not with his throat cut right through like that – oh, sorry Mand! Well, but when I think of him being murdered up there, and the murderer creeping past our door and we never knew nothing about it, it gives me the willies. I mean, I don't know as I want to stay here much longer, what about you, Mand?'

'It won't be the same,' Mandy mourned. 'And this was such a nice house.'

'What makes you think it was murder?' Slider asked, intrigued.

'Well—' The question seemed to puzzle Mandy. 'I just thought it was. When I see him lying there covered in blood—'

'I mean,' Maureen took over the explanation for her, 'old Ronnie wouldn't do a thing like that. I mean, he wouldn't have had the balls for one thing. He was a real softy. Remember that fuss he made when he had a splinter, Mand—?'

'Yeah, and I had to take it out for him. You'd think it was major surgery.'

'And anyway, what would he do it for? He'd have to have a reason. I mean—'

'He was all right,' Mandy added. 'He liked his job and everything. He wasn't an unhappy person, was he, Maur?'

'No, that's what I'm saying! I mean, he used to chat to us and everything. If he'd been feeling really rotten, he'd have come and told us, wouldn't he?'

Slider didn't feel tempted to go into that, or into what Atherton called the conspiracy theory. Instead he offered the easier explanation.

'He left a note,' he said.

'A note?' Maureen said.

'A suicide note,' Slider elaborated. ' "I can't stand it any more" – that sort of thing.'

'What, Ronnie did?' Maureen said blankly.

'So it seems,' Slider said patiently.

'Ronnie left a suicide note?' Mandy came in now like the chorus in Gilbert and Sullivan. Yes he did, he did, he did it, yes he did. Did he do it? Yes, he did it, yes he did!

'We found it on the mantelpiece.'

'But – but who wrote it for him, then?' Mandy asked in an utterly foxed voice.

187

'What do you mean, who wrote it for him?' Slider asked, giving in to the general trend towards gormless incomprehension.

'Well, Ronnie couldn't write,' Mandy said.

'I mean, he couldn't read or write,' Maureen amplified earnestly. 'He was, like, illegible.'

'That's right,' Mandy confirmed with a nod.

Slider looked from one to the other. 'Are you sure?'

'Course!' said Mandy. 'He was really sensitive about it—'

'Ashamed.'

'He didn't like anyone to know. But he used to come to me sometimes to ask me to read things to him – like when he got an official letter or anything. Me or Maureen—'

'We was the only ones what knew. I had to read his poll tax thing for him once, didn't I, Mand? He couldn't read anything, and he couldn't write except just to write his own name, like, that was all.'

Mandy said. 'The poor bloke really hated it, being, you know, whatsitsname. So he never let on to anyone, only me. And Maureen, because she was in the room once when he come down to ask me something. But we promised never to tell anyone.'

Slider was silent, piecing things together. That was why the note had made him uneasy. It had chafed against his previous perception that there was no reading matter in the room, not a book or newspaper or letter. A man who couldn't read or write naturally would not accumulate paperwork, and would be the last person in the world to pick up a handbill about a disco, or a dropped pencil. He had not written that note – which meant that it was a forgery, left there to suggest suicide by someone who didn't know Ronnie's secret. Someone who had murdered him by cutting his throat from ear to ear.

188

Unless Mandy and Maureen were lying – but they seemed completely in earnest. He remembered belatedly the original purpose of his visit, and asked them about the Chinese man upstairs. They were willing enough to talk, but could not tell him anything useful. There had been three who had taken that room. The first had been there for ages – that was before Maureen came – but Mandy had never got friendly with him. He would nod if they passed on the stairs but she didn't recollect ever speaking to him, except to say hello.

The others had only stayed a short time, the last one just six weeks. He had left, ooh, when was it, Maur? It was the Monday, wasn't it? The Monday before all this had started with Ronnie and the police and everything. Yes, that's right, Monday last week. No, they had never spoken to him. He came and went at different times, and kept himself to himself. They did not know his name or where he went to.

Did he ever get letters, phone calls?

Not that they remembered, no.

What about visitors? Did they ever see him with anyone?

No, no they didn't think so. Wait a minute though, Maur, what about that time they'd been coming back from the Seven Eleven one afternoon and they saw him getting out of a car on the corner of Notting Hill Gate? Oh yes, and it was a foreign car, wasn't it? With a funny number plate.

What did they mean, funny?

Oh, with funny letters and numbers. And red, it was printed in red.

Had they seen who was driving it?

No – no, not really. It was too far away. The Chinese bloke had just got out and walked off down Pembridge Road, and the car drove off. It was a man driving, though, wannit Mand? Yes, a man. In an overcoat.

Slider pondered this unhelpful, intriguing news. The only

189

connection he could make in his mind was with the man in a camel coat who had been seen coming out of the alley.

'What colour overcoat was it?' he asked.

They looked at each other. 'Black?' Maureen said.

'No, it was blue,' Mandy said firmly after a moment. 'Dark blue. Not navy, though – a bit lighter than that.'

Slider contemplated this new information without enthusiasm. He began to feel that he was going to be on this case until retirement.

Atherton dialled the number of the Blue Moon Chinese Restaurant and Take Away and after a long wait was answered by a breathless male voice.

'Harrow? Broo Moo Lestoh Ta' Awa', We crosed ri' now.'

'All right, Kim, you can cut the Nanki Poo crap. I'm not a tourist,' Atherton chuckled.

The voice became expansive and cockney. 'Is that you, Jim? How's it going, mate?' Kim Lim – known as Slim Kim – was an old and useful contact of Atherton's from his Bow Street days, when he had chopsticked his way in nightly excursions from one end of Soho to the other. 'Long time no see!'

'You don't need to talk pidgen to me. How's the noodle business?'

'Not what it used to be, but then what is? Rent going up like a rocket, hardly a tourist in sight. Who'd be in catering?'

'Don't give me that shinola. I know the restaurant's only a front for your opium den. You and your dad are the two richest men west of Regent Street.'

'Believe that'n you'll believe anything,' Kim said cheerfully. 'By the time we've paid protection to the Tongs and the Bill, there's hardly enough rice left in the bowl to feed a Peking Duck. What can I do for you, anyway?'

'I want to bum a favour off you. I've got to interview a

Chinese family – restaurant proprietors – who don't speak English, or pretend not to—'

'Same thing.'

'Exactly. So I wondered if you would come and translate for me. You're the perfect man for the job. You understand how to conduct an interview and you know how to speak to them – they being your own people.'

'How many times have I got to tell you, I'm not Chinese, I'm Malayan.'

'But you speak the lingo.'

'Now who's talking pidgen. What dialect?'

'Cantonese, I think.'

'There's Cantonese and Cantonese. Still, I can only give it a try.'

'Thanks, Kim. You're a prince! Can you come now?'

'Yeah, all right. Shall I come to the station?'

'Please. I'll stand you lunch afterwards.'

'All right. No cheap Chinese crap, though. Somewhere nice.'

'What about the kosher place on the corner of Goldhawk Road?'

'Ace! I'm really into all that! They do this pickled fish thing—'

'I know. They pull out all the stops, and one of them is the Lox Angelicus. "And suddenly there were with the bagels a multitude of the heavenly host."'

'What? You're raving.'

'Skip it. Goodbye, sweet prince.'

'See you soon. God bress!'

Atherton knew a Stonewall when he saw one, even if it was speaking in hieroglyphics. Slim Kim Lim and his pal Jim accepted the offer of tea, and sat at one side of a table in the dimly lit restaurant while Mr Hung Fat and the eldest Master Hung Fat sat at the other side being inscrutable. Mrs Hung Fat and a Miss Hung Fat stood behind them in distaff silence and watched the conversation go back and forth like spectators on Centre Court.

Kim spoke a great deal, Master Hung Fat very little, and Big Daddy hardly at all. Atherton hardly needed telling that they were repeating all their former advices – that they saw, heard and knew nothing. There was only one little moment of excitement, when the lady of the house suddenly leaned towards her husband and broke into a patter of anxious talk, with little fluttering hand movements. It lasted until he turned and silenced her with a few stern words, and dismissed her to the kitchen, whence she departed with her daughter hanging sympathetically on her arm.

Kim extricated them shortly afterwards. Outside in the street Atherton addressed him urgently out of the corner of his mouth as they walked away, aware that they were probably being watched from behind bamboo curtains.

'What was Momma Fat going on about? Poppa shut her up pretty quickly, didn't he?'

'Yes, she broke ranks there for a minute,' Kim said dubiously. 'Trouble is, she dropped into a different dialect, and I couldn't latch onto it.'

'You probably weren't meant to.'

'I think she wanted to tell us something, and he was telling her to keep her mouth shut. One bit of what she said sounded like someone's name.'

'So there is something to know,' Atherton said, gratified. 'How can we get it out of her?'

'Is there a back way into the restaurant? A kitchen entrance?'

'Yes, there's an alley. You go round this corner—'

'I don't think she'd be too surprised if we turned up at the back door,' Kim said wisely. They turned the corner and slipped into the alley like a couple of burglars. It was a narrow, dank and malodorous passage, serving all the shops except Dave's, which had its back access from the other end. They had only crept half way down it when a slight figure emerged from the back door of the Hung Fat, looked both ways, and came hurrying towards them.

It was the daughter. She laid a hand on Kim's arm and spoke in a rapid and urgent undertone in Chinese. He replied briefly, and then turned to Atherton.

'It's the goods, Jim. Her mother's sent her to—'

'I tell him,' the girl interrupted quickly. She spoke English with hardly an accent, and only a trifling difficulty with l's and r's. 'My mother wanted my father to tell you, but he said no, it was a family matter, and we do not talk about family to outsiders. But my mother is worried, and she thinks you may be able to help. It is my brother-in-law, you see – my elder sister's husband. Well, he is half English anyway, so my father does not like him. He did not want her to marry him, but there were reasons—' She paused and shrugged, to show there were family matters even she would not discuss.

'What's his name, your brother-in-law?' Atherton asked quickly.

'Lam. Michael Lam. My sister married him two years ago and they have a little boy, and now she is pregnant again, but he has disappeared.'

'Disappeared?'

'Yes. He went away on Tuesday night, to go to Hong Kong on business for my father. He said he would telephone from his hotel on Thursday and he would be back on Saturday. But he did not come back, and when my brother telephoned the hotel they said he had not been there, and the man he was supposed to meet on my father's business says he did not come. So now my father thinks Michael has run away because he is a worthless person, and he never wishes to hear his name spoken again. But my mother is afraid something has happened to him, and she wants you to help to find him because my sister cries all the time and her baby will be born without a father.'

She looked nervously behind her, and Atherton saw that he must order his questions quickly.

'You say he left to go to Hong Kong – did he actually get on the plane?'

'I don't know. He left here alone in his car to drive to the airport, and that was the last time we saw him.'

'Heathrow?'

'Yes.'

With rapid questions he elicited the details of the flight time and number, the number and description of the car, and a description of Lam, scribbling frantically against time.

'And where did he—'

Behind them, the mother looked out from the kitchen door and called something soft and frantic.

'Oh, quickly!' the girl said, making little pushing movements with her hands. 'You must go! Don't let my father see you!'

'One last thing,' Atherton said desperately as Kim pulled him away. 'Where did Michael have his dental work done?'

'For Christ's sake,' Kim muttered.

'It's important,' Atherton hissed.

The girl was backing away, looking frightened. 'I don't know. I will try to find out.'

'Tell anyone at the police station. My name's Atherton.'

She nodded and was gone, and they hurried away. Atherton half expected a well-thrown kitchen knife between the shoulder blades, and when they got out into the street, he found his hands were sweating.

'What was all that about his dental work?' Kim asked indignantly as they headed for Atherton's car. 'You don't want to know about his tailor as well, by any chance? Or where he went to school.'

Atherton shook his head. 'We've got a corpse,' he said tersely. 'Unidentifiable, except that we know from the teeth it's probably Eurasian.'

'Local?'

'It was found in the back yard of the fish bar,' Atherton said with a jerk of the thumb in the direction of Dave's. 'On Wednesday morning.'

Kim whistled softly. 'What a bummer,' he said.

Slider found Kathleen Sullivan in the basement, where she had a flat, a laundry room and a supply room. She was ironing, a fag clamped in the corner of her mouth and her eyes screwed up to avoid the rising smoke. Every now and then a little ash would tumble onto the ironing-board. Sometimes she noticed and brushed it away, and sometimes she ironed it firmly into the blouse of the moment.

'The Chinese boy? Oh, he was very nice, very respectable. Lee Chang, his name was. He was only here a short while though. Yes, he left last Monday.'

'Suddenly?'

'Oh no. He gave a fortnight's notice. There was nothing funny about it. Packed his stuff Monday afternoon and off he went about six o'clock.'

'And before that?'

'I can't remember his name, the one before. Had a lot of x's in it. Of course, they change the spelling these days, don't they? I remember the days when Peking was Peking. I never got to know him, really − kept himself to himself. A bit unfriendly − but perfectly respectable. And then we had one a couple of years ago – Peter Ling. He was here a long time. I got very fond of him. He used to say I was like a mother to him. Gave me a box of chocs when he left – Black Magic. Not that I like them,' she confided, flinging the green blouse over a chair back and hoiking a red one out of the basket. 'Too many hard centres. Dairy Box, now, that's the chocs I like – but how was he to know? It's the thought that counts, that's what I say.'

'That room up there – next to Ronnie's – you seem to keep it specially for the Chinese, don't you?' Slider said conversationally.

She was unconcerned by the question, speaking in jerks as she thumped the iron up the blouse's armpits. 'Just the three. Coincidence, probably. Or maybe they pass the word around, I don't know. I'd sooner have *them* than a lot of others I can think of,' she added emphatically. 'They don't make trouble, and they leave the place clean.'

'So they just turned up, looking for a room?' She grunted through the cigarette, which might have meant assent or merely indifference. 'How did they know it was vacant? Was it advertised?'

'*I* don't know,' she said robustly. 'Not my business.'

'Well, whose business is it?' No answer. 'Who sends along the new tenants when a room becomes vacant?'

'I look after the house, clean it, change the sheets. I'm paid to mind my own business. I've been here ten years – d'you think I want to be thrown out on the street?' she said angrily, smacking the iron down onto the red blouse's death throes.

He decided to try a little pressure. 'Mrs Sullivan, you've got at least three girls in this house who are operating as prostitutes. Mandy says it was you who interviewed her when she came for the room, and that you knew what her trade was.'

She put down the iron and actually removed the cigarette

from her mouth to face him and say, 'Look, mister, this is a clean house and no trouble. What the girls get up to is their business. If they want to sleep with a different man every night, it's not against the law.'

'Prostitution isn't illegal,' Slider agreed, 'but running a brothel is, and so is living off immoral earnings.'

'Now you listen to me! I've never taken a penny from any of those girls, and nor would I! I'm a good Catholic, and I wouldn't dirty me hands with the wages of sin. You want to mind what you're saying to a decent woman.'

She seemed genuinely outraged, but Slider thought he detected a shadow of fear behind it. He pressed his advantage home. 'I believe you, Kathleen, but the magistrates may not, especially as you've got one or two little things on your record already.' This was a shot in the dark, but it seemed to be on target. She was silent, looking at the ironing-board in a troubled way.

'I've no wish to make trouble for you. All I want is a bit of help. You answer my questions honestly, and you've nothing to worry about. Don't forget I'm investigating a very serious crime. You don't want to get mixed up in that, do you?'

'What do you want to know?' she asked in a subdued voice.

'About the Chinese boys,' he began.

'If it's Lee Chang you're wondering about,' she said quickly, looking up, 'you're barking up the wrong tree. He was as respectable as they come – American, he was. He worked up at the NATO base.'

'At Northwood?' Slider said, and she nodded; but even as he said it, other things were beginning to click into place. Northwood was practically next door to Chorleywood. And someone had mentioned Chorleywood before, in this very house. 'Tell me about the rooms – what happens when they become vacant?'

'The first and second floor rooms I deal with,' she said with obvious reluctance. 'I advertise them, or sometimes I know someone who's wanting a room. It's down to me who I take in.'

'But not the top floor rooms. Ronnie's room and the one the Chinese boy had.' She shook her head. 'What happens about those?'

'People are sent.'

'Who sends them?'

'The owner.'

'And who is that?'

She opened her mouth and shut it again. She seemed to want to tell him, but not to be able to get it out past some powerful taboo.

'I'll help you out, shall I?' Slider said kindly. 'Mandy said you told her the owner was very rich, and had a big house in Chorleywood. A big, Hollywood-style house with a swimming pool, is it?'

She found her voice. 'I've never been there.'

'No, you wouldn't have, would you? No wonder Ronnie was so reliable and grateful – he owed him everything, didn't he – his job and his home? Poor Ronnie. He must have felt really bad about letting him down. So bad, he preferred to kill himself.'

'That's right,' she said.

'Funny thing, though,' Slider said conversationally, 'that this great man wants the fact that he owns this house kept secret. You'd think with all the good he does – providing clean accommodation at a reasonable rent – that he wouldn't be so coy about it. You'd think he wouldn't mind people knowing.'

'You won't tell him I told you?' she said anxiously.

'You haven't told me anything,' Slider pointed out. 'Not even his name.'

That's right, I haven't,' she realised with relief.

'And what's more, I'm not going to ask you,' he said. 'Aren't I a nice copper? And in return, you aren't going to tell him I was asking, are you?'

'I know when to keep me mouth shut,' she said tersely.

'Yes, you do, don't you?' said Slider.

13

A Fistful of Dolours

The turning off the main road dropped steeply through a wood for a couple of hundred yards, between high banks overhung with trees so that it was like driving in a green tunnel. Then suddenly the horizon opened out to a view over the Chess Valley, the road did a right-angled bend, and there was the entrance to Colin Cate's house, set back a little off the road – a pair of massive, wrought-iron, electronically operated gates, backed with heavy duty wire mesh to prevent an anorexic burglar slipping between the bars. Beyond the gates the drive curved between high banks of rhododendrons. You couldn't see the house.

Slider pulled up on the gravel in front of the gate, and saw the security camera mounted on the top of the gatepost swing round to goggle at him. He climbed out of the car and breathed in the sweet country air of May, heard a wood pigeon burbling in a tree close by, blackbirds, sparrows and chaffinches making a pleasant background noise further off, and somewhere out of sight within the grounds several dogs barking excitedly.

He walked up to the gates. They surprised him a little, for despite what Barrington and Fergus had said, he had not quite grasped how rich and powerful a man he was dealing with. Ordinary mortals, even pleasantly well-off mortals, did not protect their property to this extent. The gates were impregnable to anything much less than an APC with a determined driver, and there was an enamel plate screwed on high up showing a silhouette of a Dobermann Pinscher and the words DANGER! GROUNDS PROTECTED BY LOOSE DOGS. The idea of loose dogs made him wrinkle his nose: he made a mental note to watch where he was stepping.

The camera was still poking its long nose at him, and he saw set into the gatepost an intercom grille and buzzer. He pressed the button, and after a moment the grille hissed and spat and said, 'Yes? What do you want?'

'I'd like to see Colin Cate, please,' Slider said, feeling, as he always did when speaking to a wall, faintly hilarious. 'My name is Slider – Detective Inspector Slider. It's about—'

'Yes, all right,' the grill squawked. 'Drive in.'

Slider got back in the car and started the engine as the gate began slowly to open. He drove through, and saw in his rear-view that it began to close immediately behind him. He followed the drive past the rhododendron walls and it led round the curve to the car park, a flat, tarmac platform set into the hillside, which surrounded it on two sides and was terraced with low walls and shrubs and a zigzag of steps leading up. He noted that there were a bright red BMW and a maroon Ford Sierra already parked there, side by side and nose to the wall. With a vague instinct of self preservation he swung round and parked with his tail to the terrace wall and his nose facing outwards for a quick getaway.

He got out. Facing him was the open side of the platform, a view past the trees over the valley into the blue distance. It was quiet, and the sun was straight and hot, making him think of high Alpine meadows. Turning, he looked up at the terraced hillside and saw, some fifty feet further up, just a glimpse of the house, a red roof and a glint of windows amongst the greenery. Should he go up? He thought of the loose dogs and hesitated, and then saw that someone had appeared at the top of the steps and was coming down to meet him. It was Colin Cate, dressed in slacks and a dark blue open-necked shirt. Wound round his hand he had the lead-chain of a very fit-looking, larger-than-average Dobermann.

Slider stood still until Cate arrived in front of him. Cate's eyes were screwed up against the sun, but he was smiling a pleasant if slightly quizzical smile. The dog leaned against its collar and panted, its frilled pink tongue dripping between the white, white teeth, its yellow cat's eyes gleaming as it strained to reach him. It was smiling, too, an unpleasant if slightly anticipatory smile.

'Hullo! Bill, isn't it? What brings you here?' Cate said. 'New developments?'

'I'd just like a few words, if that's all right,' Slider said neutrally.

'Must be important to bring you out here on a Sunday.'

'Oh, I don't live very far away,' Slider said. 'I hope I'm not disturbing your family lunch?'

'As a matter of fact, I'm on my own.' He turned towards the steps, inviting Slider to follow. 'Come and have a drink by the pool. I was doing some paperwork. The wife's gone to visit her mother for a week or so.' They climbed. 'Are you married?'

'Yes.'

'Kids?'

'Two. A boy and a girl.'

'Just right. I've got too bloody many. Two boys by my first wife – live with their mother – and three by my present encumbrance. Two boys and a girl. Away at school – cost me a fortune. Makes you wonder sometimes why you do it, doesn't it?'

It was all as genial and pleasant and open as could be. Slider followed him up the steps, trying not to let the tension of his mind seep into his body, mindful of how sensitive guard dogs are. The house, when they came in sight of it, was modern, perhaps ten or fifteen years old, low and sprawling, set on several levels to take advantage of the hillside, and with huge windows to take advantage of the view. At the front corner of it was a curious structure like a square tower, and through its large windows Slider could see a man sitting and staring out at them.

'You said you were on your own, sir?' Slider said cautiously. Cate looked to see what he was looking at, and smiled.

'Except for the security guard. Someone has to watch all those damned cameras and answer the door bell.'

Cate did not take him into the house, but down a path to the side, through a shrubbery. The sound of barking came nearer, and the shrubbery broke to reveal a large, wire-mesh compound in which half a dozen Dobermanns were running back and forth in a bored way. They broke into a fusillade of barks at the sight of the men, and one or two put their great paws up against the mesh to give them the full benefit of their physique.

'Lovely animals, aren't they?' Cate said. 'I breed 'em – hobby of mine. Do you like dogs?'

'Yes,' Slider said. 'If they're well-trained, working dogs. I don't like yappers or lap-dogs.'

203

'A dog is only as good as the man who trains him,' Cate said.

'I suppose you could say the same of men,' Slider offered.

At the back of the compound was a long, low shed, presumably the kennels, and a separate small building, brick-built, with a chimney from which smoke was rising. As they passed down-wind of it, a fearful smell met them which had Slider and the Dobermann sniffing, though probably for different reasons.

Cate looked at Slider sidelong with an amused smile. 'Whiffs a bit, doesn't it? It's the dog's grub – a mixture of meat, offal and cereal. We boil it up ourselves in a huge copper. It's called pudding.'

'Oh yes,' Slider said. 'Like with foxhounds.'

'That's right. Do you hunt?'

'No,' said Slider. I will make you hunters of men, he thought. 'But I was brought up on a farm. We used to send our dead cattle to the local hunt kennels.'

'Well, it's nice to know you can go on being useful even after you're dead, isn't it?'

They left the smells and the dogs behind, turned another corner, and came out by a large, kidney-shaped, sapphire blue swimming pool, sparkling in the sun, and equipped with diving board, changing-rooms, sun-loungers, and wrought-iron tables and chairs.

'Take a pew,' Cate said, waving towards a table. Slider sat, and Cate led the dog to the other chair, made it sit, and then dropped the lead. 'Stay,' he said. The dog looked at him, and then turned its head to fix Slider with an unwavering stare. 'What do you want to drink? Fancy a Pimms? I've got a jug all ready made up.'

'Yes, thank you, that'll be fine,' Slider said. He'd never seen the point of Pimms, but he'd take whatever was quickest.

He didn't really want this interview to be drawn out longer than necessary.

One of the changing-rooms must have been a bar, for Cate emerged from it in short order with a jug, two glasses and an ice-bucket on a tray. 'You don't want all that fruit business, I hope?' he said cheerfully. He put down the tray and poured out two glasses, added ice, and handed one to Slider. 'That's just nonsense to keep the women quiet. Now when I mix a Pimms, it's a man's drink. Cheers!'

'Cheers,' said Slider, and drank. The Pimms turned out to be fire-water, and bit him on its way down. 'Very nice,' he said.

'Like it?' Cate sat opposite him. 'The secret is equal parts of Pimms and gin, and a splash of bitters before you add the lemonade. And not too bloody much lemonade, either.' He drank, put down his glass, and said, 'Right, now what did you want to see me about?'

'The house that Ronnie Slaughter lived in – I understand it belongs to you,' Slider said, not making it a question.

'Who told you that?' Cate asked pleasantly.

'Ronnie did,' said Slider, putting the blame where it could do no harm.

'Did he? Did he?' Cate sat thoughtfully. 'Yes, poor Ronnie!'

'It wasn't meant to be a secret, was it?'

'Of course not. How could it be?' Cate said. He sipped his drink and put it down again, resting his hand beside it. Slider glanced at the skull ring and away again. 'I own quite a lot of property one way and another. My father said to me when I was a boy, Colin, he said, if you ever get money, buy property. You can't go wrong with it.' He smiled with pleasant self-mockery. 'I never forget I wasn't born with a silver spoon in my mouth, you see. And on the whole, my father was right. On the whole.'

'It must have been useful to be able to offer Slaughter a room as well as a job,' Slider said.

'What do you mean by that?'

'Well, it can be hard to find somewhere to live in London. Firms often lose promising employees because they can't find a flat they can afford.'

Cate looked him over carefully. 'If you've got something to ask me, Inspector, ask it. I don't like innuendo.'

'I wasn't implying anything, sir,' Slider said. 'You must be sorry to have lost Ronnie. You said yourself he was a good manager.'

'He was,' Cate said shortly. 'But I don't think you came here to talk about Ronnie's accommodation problems. What is it you want to know?'

'About the Chinese men who stayed in the room next to Ronnie's.'

'What about them?'

'It just seems an odd coincidence that there should have been three of them, one after the other, and odd coincidences start me wondering. You'll understand that, having been a copper yourself. I suppose it's curiosity that makes us take up the job in the first place, isn't it?'

Cate nodded, which might or might not have been acknowledgement of the point. 'It's not as great a coincidence as it seems, I'm afraid. There was Peter Ling, who worked in one of my computer shops – he was Chinese to look at, but he came from North Kensington actually. The second man, Chou Xiang Xu, was attached to the Science and Technology section of the Chinese Embassy, over here looking into new computer developments. A business colleague of mine at IBM asked me to put him up. And the third one, Lee Chang, in fact was American, attached to the NATO base at Northwood, and a friend of mine put him on to me because he knew I sometimes had rooms to let. He was only there for a few weeks. Now is there anything sinister in that?'

'Nothing at all. I didn't think there would be,' Slider said with perfect truth. 'I was just puzzled by the coincidence, that's all.'

'*Apparent* coincidence,' Cate corrected.

Slider sipped his drink. 'It's a lovely place you've got here,' he said.

'Yes,' Cate assented. 'I'm always surprised it can be so rural so near to London.'

'My wife would love us to move out to Chorleywood,' Slider said. 'Ruislip is getting a bit rough these days. Have you had much trouble with break-ins here? I was very impressed with your security arrangements.'

'If an ex-copper can't keep himself safe, who can?' Cate said amiably. 'I've worked hard for what's mine, and I mean to keep it. My dad had one fish and chip shop, that was all, in Westbourne Park Road. We lived above the shop, Mum, Dad and four of us kids, and everything smelled of frying fat. We used to fry in dripping in those days, of course, and you could never get the smell out of your hair. I went to the local council school, and the other kids used to make fun of me – called me the Greasy Pole. I was skinny in those days – well, there wasn't much to eat except left-over fish and chips, and I couldn't stomach 'em, after smelling 'em all day. I swore to myself one day I'd be rich, and never have to eat fried fish again.'

Scarlett O'Hara again, Slider thought. As God is my witness, I'll never be hungry again.

Cate drained his glass and fixed Slider with the look of one who has reached the point of his whole narrative. 'I started off as a potato boy – just like poor old Ronnie Slaughter. I left school when I was fifteen to work in my Dad's shop. Now I own eight of 'em – besides the other bits and pieces. I've never looked back. I felt sorry for Ronnie, and I tried to do him a favour, but I suppose I should have left him to struggle on his own. You can't help people, they have to help themselves. He let me down.'

'Let you down?'

'He killed that boy, Leman, didn't he?' Cate said. 'Well, at least he's paid for it. Better than wasting the taxpayer's money bringing the case to court. I'd have thought Barrington would have closed it by now.'

'Yes sir,' Slider said. 'There is just one thing I wanted to ask you. You told me that Ronnie Slaughter wrote to you in reply to your advertisement for the job of manager of Dave's Fish Bar?'

'Yes. What about it?'

'I wondered if by any chance you still had that letter? It would round things off nicely if we could match his handwriting against the suicide note, just to be absolutely sure. All we have is his signature on a statement, and you know yourself, sir, that that isn't enough to go by.'

Cate looked thoughtful. 'No, I'm afraid I wouldn't still have it.'

'I was afraid of that,' Slider said.

'However,' Cate went on, 'I think I do have a note from Ronnie upstairs in my office somewhere. I remember seeing it the other day when I was looking for something. It's only short, but it may be enough. I'll go and get it, if you'd like to have a look at it.'

'Yes, thank you, if you don't mind,' said Slider. Cate got up and went into the house, leaving Slider and the dog facing each other. The animal's unwinking stare took the edge off the excitement he would otherwise have been feeling. Was he

208

about to get his break-through after all? He almost smiled in anticipation, and the dog shuffled its bottom an inch nearer. Its muzzle was now only three inches from Slider's left knee, and the drippings from its tongue were wetting the toecap of his shoe.

At last Cate came out, carrying a piece of paper.

'Sorry to have been so long,' he said. 'I couldn't put my hand to it at first. Here you are. Not very exciting reading.'

Slider took it and put it down on the table in front of him. It was a page which had been torn out of a small, ruled pocket note-book, written in pencil in what appeared to be the same clumsy script as the suicide note.

Mr Cate, we need 90 skinless cod, 25 kilos mozza meal, and 25 kilos rice cone for the special order. Also 100 steak pies. Thanks. Ronnie.

'It was some stuff he wanted me to order for a big party because it was too short notice for the usual supplier,' Cate explained.

'I see,' Slider said. 'But can we be sure it was him that wrote it, though? It might have been one of his assistants writing to his dictation.'

Cate smiled expansively. 'Ah, well as it happens, you're in luck there. I remember that on that particular day I was going to call in at the shop on my way past in the afternoon, during the closed period, and I asked him to leave me a note of what he needed. But I arrived earlier than I expected, and he was still there, writing the note.'

'You actually saw him writing it?'

'Yes, as I came in,' said Cate.

Slider smiled. 'Thank you,' he said. 'That's very useful.' He stood up to take his leave. 'I'll take this with me, if I may. Put it to the handwriting expert, see if it's the same as the suicide note. But I'm sure I'll find that it is.'

Cate took up the dog's lead again, and as Slider met his eyes there was something quizzical in them. He wondered if he had overplayed his hand. But all Cate said was, 'I'll see you out.'

'Thank you, sir. I'm sorry to have disturbed you.'

'Oh, you haven't disturbed me,' Cate said pleasantly.

As Slider came in from the yard he bumped into O'Flaherty on his way back from the front shop.

'Barrington's after you – bing-bonging the place down. There's a bounty in gold offered for the first man t' sight you.' He grinned. 'How about dat? Moby Dick spotted by a Dopey Mick.'

Slider made a disgusted face. 'What's he doing in, anyway?'

'It's his little way, so I'm told, when there's overtime bein' clocked up. He's been in this hour, doin' his Demon King impersonation, poppin' up here and poppin' up there. You never know where he'll be next.'

'Oh well, I suppose I'd better go and see what he wants.'

'Put newspaper down your trousers,' Fergus advised his retreating back.

Barrington's room smelled of sulphur, and flickers of lightning were playing round his brow when Slider presented himself.

'What the devil are you playing at?' he demanded angrily, without preamble. 'Sir?'

'I've just had a telephone call from Colin Cate, saying you've been round there bothering him with inane questions. And after I specifically warned you that we had to tread carefully with him! We've already let ourselves down with him once, and you have to go plunging in, spoiling his weekend, annoying him, and making a complete fool of yourself, *and* me, *and* the Department! Now he thinks we're a bunch of clodhopping bozos. What the hell did you go barging in there for? Why didn't you clear it with me first?'

Slider was surprised. 'I didn't think I needed permission to follow up a line of enquiry, sir. We've always—'

'I don't care how you've done things in the past!' Barrington said, his eyes as yellow and baleful as the Dobermann's. 'My predecessor may have run this place like a boarding house, but that's not my way. I'm in charge of this investigation, and you do not go annoying respectable members of the public without checking with me first.'

'Sir,' Slider said woodenly. It was proving an invaluable monosyllable in his relationship with Mad Ivan.

Barrington stood up and went to look out of his window, a movement of restlessness by a man of action unwillingly confined. Probably at that moment he would have liked to have thumped somebody. 'And what was this "line of enquiry" anyway, which was so important and urgent?' he asked, his back intimidatingly to Slider.

Slider told him. Half way through Barrington turned back to look at him with wild incredulity.

'Are you seriously telling me that you went badgering Colin Cate – *the* Colin Cate – for that? Are you trying to tell me that you think – I just don't believe this!' he interrupted himself with a hand gesture and a short pacing walk one way and then the other – 'You think that *he* murdered Slaughter and faked the suicide note?'

'He said he actually saw Slaughter write that note, sir. He must have been lying, and why would he do that if not—'

'You take the word of a slut of a call-girl rather than him? A half-witted tom tells you that Slaughter was illiterate, and that's enough to make you believe Colin Cate is a murderer?' Barrington shook his asteroid head again in disbelief. 'I really think you must be sick in the head, Slider. Perhaps you need a holiday. Perhaps I ought to take you off this case – it seems to be getting too much for you.'

Slider kept his hands down at his sides, and his eyes on his shoes.

'Did Mr Cate say anything more about the note, sir?'

'There wasn't anything *to* say. I didn't know any more than he did what you wanted it for. He was very polite about the whole thing, in fact – he just said he couldn't understand why such routine enquiries were being carried out at overtime rates. Reminded me that we are accountable to the taxpayer. But I could tell he was angry, and with good cause – oh, and yes, it seems you didn't tell him that we've discovered Peter Leman is alive after all.'

Slider was startled. 'No, sir.'

'No, sir? What does that mean? You don't think he has the right to know that an employee of his we thought had been murdered was alive and well? He was pretty annoyed about that, too. He said he couldn't understand why you didn't tell him, unless you suspected him of something, and that if you suspected him, he wished you'd have said so openly. He could have told you then that he didn't leave the house at all on the night Slaughter died, or on the night of the chip-shop murder, and that he could show his security guard's records to prove it if you were really worried.'

'Did Mr Cate volunteer that, sir?' Slider asked, intrigued.

Barrington glowered. 'Yes, and I'm ashamed that an officer under my command should have made him think it was necessary. He couldn't be more willing to help in any way he can with this investigation, but you go and set his back up, behaving like an amateur gumshoe in a second-rate movie!'

Try as he might, Slider couldn't bring himself to slip a 'sorry, sir' into the space Barrington left for it. He stood silent and thoughtful, and after a moment, Barrington went on.

'Let me make this clear, Slider: I don't expect you to bother him again on any pretext. If anything comes up that he ought to know about, or if there's anything you need to ask him, you come to me. Do you understand?'

'Yes, sir.'

'Very well. And for Christ's sake get on and find out who the victim was, so that we can close this case. If we can't cover ourselves with glory we can at least try to be cost-effective. There is such a thing as budget, you know.'

'Yes, sir.'

'I'm not pleased with the way you're handling this case, I don't mind telling you. I shall have to consider whether or not to replace you. So bear in mind that you're on probation now. Don't screw up again.'

Slider was sitting at his desk when his phone rang, and simultaneously Atherton burst in, with Mackay close behind him.

'It's Leman, Guv,' Atherton said urgently, gesturing towards the telephone. 'Rang up asking for you.'

'Get a trace on it,' Slider said, reaching out his hand to the instrument.

'We're doing that.'

'Good. Keep quiet, then. I'll put it on Talk.'

He picked up the receiver and pressed the button at the same time. 'Detective Inspector Slider,' he said.

Leman's voice emerged small but clear from the loudspeaker. 'Is that Mr Slider? It's Peter Leman here. Suzanne's boyfriend. You know, Suzanne Edrich.'

'Yes, I know who you are. I'm glad you've called me. We've got a lot to talk about. Do you want to give me your number in case we get cut off?'

'I'm not that daft,' he said. 'I told Suzanne – and I suppose she told you – that I'm in hiding.'

'Yes, so she said.'

'Well I'm not about to tell you my number then, am I? Talk sense.'

'So why did you call me?'

'I saw it in the newspaper this morning that Ronnie had topped himself. Is that true?'

'It's true that he's dead,' Slider said.

'What, you mean it wasn't suicide?' Leman's comprehension was suspiciously quick. Slider didn't immediately answer him, and the voice rose in manifest fear. 'For Chrissake tell me! Was he murdered?'

'It's possible,' Slider said. 'His throat was cut. We don't know if it was suicide or murder.'

'Oh, Christ,' Leman muttered. 'Oh, Jesus. Listen, I've got to tell you – I suppose you think I did it, but I didn't. I've been here all the time, ever since Wednesday—'

'Where's here?'

'Don't make me laugh. Listen! I didn't kill Ronnie. My orders were to pick him up at the chip shop, take him for a drink and go home with him, that's all.'

'Why did you have to do that?'

'The bloke I work for doesn't give you reasons, and you don't ask. You just do what you're told.'

Sounds like Barrington, Slider thought wryly. 'And who is he?'

'I'm not telling you his name. D'you think I'm daft? I shouldn't even be phoning you, but I had to find out about Ronnie. I didn't kill him, you know. I quite liked him in a way, old Ronnie, even if he was thick. He was all right. I never knew they were going to top him, poor old bastard. If I had—'

'You wouldn't have had anything to do with it?' Slider hazarded.

Leman muttered something profane. 'My boss – I've worked for him for a long time. There's never been anything like this before.'

'The night you went for a drink with Ronnie, there was a murder committed at the chip shop. What was your connection with that?'

'Look, I didn't phone you to answer your questions. I just did what I was told.'

'But you knew about it, didn't you? Why were you told to go into hiding?'

'*I* don't know! I never knew there were going to be bodies everywhere. That's not my scene.'

'So tell me who you were working for.'

'I can't. It's not safe. I shouldn't even be talking to you, only Suzanne told you about me, silly bitch. I told her not to tell anyone, but she had to go and open her big mouth.'

'You can't trust women,' Slider said sympathetically.

'You're dead right. I wish I'd never – the thing is, you've got to keep away from Suzanne. My boss – he doesn't know I've got a girlfriend. If he knew – well, he wouldn't be too pleased. I wasn't supposed to get mixed up with anyone while this was going on. So just keep away from her, all right?'

'Do you think she's in danger?' Leman didn't answer. 'If you think she's in danger you must tell us. We can protect her.' There was an unidentifiable sound at the other end, and then the dialling tone.'

'He's rung off,' Mackay said.

Atherton looked at Slider. 'What was that last thing – that noise?'

Slider met his eyes. 'I don't know.'

'It was a sort of glugging noise,' Atherton said. 'Like someone gargling.'

They waited. A minute later Beevers appeared waving a

piece of paper like a short, hairy Anthony Eden. 'Got it, Guv!' he said in triumphant tones. 'It's an address in Hanwell.'

'Let's go!' snapped Slider, jumping to his feet, snatching the paper from Beevers and thrusting it at Atherton. To Beevers, 'You and Mackay, organise some uniform backup, fast as you can. Then get to Suzanne Edrich and stay with her.'

14

Morning Brings Fresh Counsel, as They Say at the Old Bailey

It was a narrow, dirty, crowded road of Victorian terraced cottages, built before the motor-car was invented, choked with parked cars. The house itself was shabby and neglected, with filthy lace curtains at the windows, paint peeling off the door, rotting window frames, rubbish sacks propped against the mangy remains of a privet hedge. It was two storeys high, but built to such a small budget that the upstairs windows were almost within reach. In such houses Victorian working men had raised families of thirteen, and thought themselves blessed.

The front door was pushed to, but not latched. Atherton prodded it open cautiously with the end of a pencil, and they went in to an uncarpeted hall with the staircase straight ahead; cheap patterned wallpaper and brown paint. The two downstairs rooms were empty and unfurnished, but in the scullery at the back was a stained porcelain sink, encrusted gas stove, and a small table bearing dirty crockery and the evidence of take-away meals. It smelled of damp and old fried food.

'Upstairs,' said Slider. Upstairs was a bathroom, cleaner than the rest and smelling of soap, the bath still dropleted from recent use, a damp towel hanging up and a frill of dried lather on the bar of pink Camay. The front bedroom was empty. The back bedroom contained a single bed, a cheap wardrobe, a small chest of drawers, an armchair, a stack of paperback books, a telephone, and Peter Leman. He was lying across the bed, his legs dangling over the far side, his hands flung back, his throat cut from ear to ear. Like Anne Boleyn, he had only had a little neck, and it had been cut right through to the bone. His eyes stared at the ceiling, wide and brown, dully shining like those of a stuffed deer in a country house trophy room.

'Too late,' said Slider expressionlessly.

In the small, stuffy room the halitus of fresh blood was sickening. It had soaked Leman's white shirt and the bedclothes he lay on. There were even splashes on the wall where the last pumpings of his heart had flung it from the severed arteries. His flung-back left hand was minus all four fingers, which seemed to have been removed at the knuckle with a very sharp knife. In the centre of the palm of his right hand was a round, red mark like a small bruise.

On the floor beside the bed was a plastic mac, also bloody, and a pair of rubber gloves. The missing fingers they found just under the bed, where they had rolled, or been flung.

'He had his back to the door. He was sitting looking out at the garden while he telephoned,' said Atherton after a moment. 'What a mug. And chummy crept in from behind, well protected against the splashing—' Slider heard his dry throat click as he swallowed. 'But why cut off the fingers? Unless he tried to grab the knife as it came round in front of him?'

The noise they had heard over the telephone, Slider thought,

218

was the gurgle of Leman having his throat cut. If only he had telephoned sooner. Well, they could take the bug off Suzanne's telephone now. That would ease the budget and please Mr Barrington. Except that they got further from a solution every day – further into the soup.

'And then there were three,' he said aloud. 'You'd better go down and radio in from the car.'

Later, very late, in a dim corner of the moodily lit Anglabangla Indian Restaurant – which had lately tried to shove its image upmarket by adding karahi to the menu and landed its less sophisticated customers in the burns unit of Charing Cross hospital – Slider ordered Chicken Bhuna and Atherton the suspiciously-named Meat Vindaloo. They were both so hungry by then that they were quite likely to eat it when it came.

'There's something going on,' Slider said, turning his lager glass round and round on the spot.

Atherton ate another papadum, much as a starving horse eats its bedding. 'That much is obvious. But what?'

'Everything seems to operate in a vacuum. Nothing leads to anything else – and yet it must all be connected, or why has any of it happened?'

'Cheryl Makepeace found a finger in her chips. Ronnie Slaughter called us in. We found the rest of the body,' Atherton mused. 'Was he carried along by inevitability, or was he so thick he thought he could get away with it? Or was he, conversely, completely innocent?'

'Or only comparatively completely innocent,' Slider added. 'He accepted the suggestion that the body was Peter Leman without too much strain on the credulity.'

'Even while protesting that he didn't kill him. Yes. And he was certainly with Leman that night. In this whole messy case, that's the one thing we know for certain. But why?'

'You heard Leman say he was told to make friends with Slaughter that night and go home with him. And he said he'd been in hiding ever since. I think we were meant to think that Slaughter had killed Leman. I think Slaughter was set up to take the fall.'

'Someone would have been taking a lot of chances,' Atherton said doubtfully.

'Why? It convinced us, after all. It was only Suzanne blowing the gaff that spoiled it. And there again, it can't be coincidence that someone has shut both of their mouths – Slaughter's and Leman's. Someone has something serious to hide.'

Atherton looked restless. 'Ronnie could still have committed suicide, you know. Out of remorse or fear over the original murder – we don't know he didn't commit that. Or simply because everything was getting on top of him. He wasn't the brightest person in the world, but he was sensitive. Maybe he really couldn't take any more. Maybe the suicide note was quite genuine.'

'But then how do you explain the second note?' Slider frowned. 'The one Cate gave me, which looks like the same handwriting as the suicide note, subject to confirmation from the experts. Cate said he *saw* Ronnie write it, which is impossible.'

Atherton shrugged. 'Reluctant though I am to credit anyone above the rank of inspector with any sense, Mr Barrington could be right about that. We've only got Mandy's word that Ronnie was illiterate, and she could be lying, or mistaken. Or Ronnie could have lied to her, just pretended to be illiterate, for some reason—'

'What reason?' Slider said incredulously.

'Cry for attention, maybe. An excuse to go to her room and sit with her, thigh to thigh, heads bent together over the same piece of paper. A poor, lonely guy – an ugly poor lonely

220

guy – who has no friends and can't afford a tart and simply wants a little human warmth and sympathy. So he pretends he can't fill in his Community Charge form and takes it to the tarts to do for him.'

'Except that they seemed quite willing to talk to him without excuses,' Slider said. 'And there was the fact that we found no reading or writing materials in his room at all. And do you really think that Ronnie was bright enough to act a part like that?'

'He was acting a part all his life, wasn't he, pretending not to be a ginger.' Atherton dipped a fragment of papadum into the raita. 'And look at the alternative. Did Colin Cate – an ex-copper, rich, smart, influential, sitter on committees and adviser to Parliamentary review bodies – did this man really troll up to Ronnie's bedsit, slaughter him with his own hands, and fake that suicide note? And then when you came asking for a corroborative piece of handwriting, pop upstairs and write you another? Honestly, Bill, it just doesn't seem likely to me. A man like that, assuming he wanted a bit of dirty biz done – and I don't rule out the possibility of almost any human bean being crooked, with the exception of you and me – but a man like that would surely have paid someone else to do it.'

'Maybe,' Slider said. He took a draught of lager. 'Maybe,' he added, more doubtfully. 'But the more partners you have in crime the more likely you are to be caught. The safest way is to do it yourself – as any copper or ex-copper knows.'

'Well, then,' Atherton added relentlessly, 'there's the fact that the first time you met Cate, he said that Ronnie had written to him to apply for the job. Why would he lie about that, at that point?'

'He could have been telling the truth then and lying later. Someone might have written that application for Ronnie.'

'Besides, he's got an alibi for the night in question.'

'Only a guilty man needs an alibi.'

Atherton grinned. 'You have got it bad.'

'All right, what's your theory?' Slider asked, nettled.

'You told me never to theorise ahead of my data,' Atherton said piously.

'No I didn't, that was Sherlock Holmes. Just give me an explanation to keep me out of Colney Hatch for a few more hours, will you.'

'I think I'll wait until we find out more about Michael Lam. He's my favourite for the dismembered corpse stakes.'

'Talking of dismembered corpse steaks,' Slider said, as the waiter came just at that moment with their food, and plonked it down in front of them on two plates. No poncing about with heating apparatus at the Anglabangla. Atherton inserted a fork into his brown mess and discovered that Meat was really the only description for it. However, when he looked closely at it nothing looked back, and he reasoned that the heat of the vindaloo sauce would kill whatever it was, if it wasn't already dead.

He had his own vision of the kitchens of the Anglabangla: six large buckets keeping warm, three of amorphous lumps labelled Chicken, Meat and Prawn, and three of curry sauce, labelled Hot, Medium and Mild. Whatever you ordered required only two swift movements of the ladle onto the plate. The rest of the twenty minutes between ordering and being served was sheer artistic embellishment on the part of the staff.

Slider transferred a forkful of medium hot lumps from his plate to his mouth and swallowed absently.

'Well, I don't care who the corpse is,' he said finally. 'I think Ronnie was murdered, and the three deaths are connected. And I think Cate has got to be in it somewhere.'

222

'The King of the Chip Shops. You see him as a sort of Eminence Grease, do you?'

'I don't know if someone's pulling his strings, or if he's the puppetmaster. I'd be sorry to think an ex-copper could be involved in anything as stupid as multiple murder, but I do think Ronnie was illiterate, and Cate lied about it to make us believe in the suicide. And Leman was killed because he was in a position to finger somebody. But who, and what the hell it's all about, I can't imagine. It must be something big to be worth all those bodies.'

They ate in silence for a while. Then Slider sighed.

'There's so much to be done – and Barrington's not going to like it. Cate's last Chinese tenant, Lee Chang, worked at the NATO base. I suppose that accounts for the foreign car Mandy saw giving him a lift home.'

'The dark blue overcoat could be an airman's greatcoat,' Atherton offered helpfully. 'And American cars have number-plates printed in red.'

'But what's the connection?' Slider worried.

'Just what Cate said, maybe,' Atherton shrugged. 'Didn't you tell me that he holds an advisory brief on security for the base?'

'He liaises between the military and the local police security teams, as I understand it. One of his many consultative positions. He's on every committee known to man.'

'There you are, then. Why shouldn't he know someone at the base who asks him to find a chap somewhere to stay?'

'Oh, I know,' Slider said. 'I know it holds together. But I just have the feeling that it shouldn't have to.'

'I know what it is,' Atherton said wisely, soaking his rice into the brown and steamy. 'You don't like Cate because Mr Barrington is so hot for him. And you don't like Barrington because he didn't like Dickson.'

'Yes, and there's another thing – why is Barrington so against our late lamented boss?'

'Because Barrington is ex-army parade bull and Dickson was an egg-on-the-tie man, and the one sort never understands the other.'

Slider was silent, unaccepting. Atherton sighed inwardly and let it be. They ate. When the waiter came with more lager which they hadn't ordered, Atherton said, 'And there's the other thing, of course.'

Slider came back from a long way away. 'What thing?'

'The other reason you feel low. Joanna.'

'Oh.'

'Have you spoken to her again?'

Shake of the head. 'It wouldn't be fair. It would make it harder for her.'

'It might make it easier for you.'

'I can't take advantage like that.' He put his fork down wearily. 'I worry about her, though. At least I have my work to occupy me.'

'She has hers,' Atherton pointed out.

'It isn't the same. It doesn't use up the same bit of her brain.'

'She'll survive,' Atherton said.

'I know.'

'And so will you.'

'I know.'

'Doesn't help, does it?' Atherton said sympathetically. He eyed Slider through the artful catering gloom. 'You look worn out. Why don't you go home and snatch a few hours' sleep?'

'I think I will,' Slider said. 'As long as whoever they are can hold off from killing anyone else for a few hours.' He looked at Atherton tentatively. He would not normally have

224

tried to talk about Atherton's private life with him, but men who have been through a meal at the Anglabangla together feel a kind of brotherhood. 'How are things with you and Jablowski?'

'Oh, there's nothing doing there,' Atherton said lightly. 'She told me yesterday she's met someone else. Bloke called Resnik, from the Holloway CID.'

'Yes, I know him,' Slider said. 'Midlander. Big, gloomy man with bushy hair.'

'If you say so. I've never met him. He's a DI, apparently – step up for her from me. She met him at the Polish Club, and he's a Catholic, so they speak each other's language.'

'You're upset about it,' Slider perceived.

'Hurt pride, that's all,' Atherton said. 'I'm a shallow, superficial kind of bloke, not the sort to have really important feelings.'

Irene was surprised, seemed almost fluttered, to see him.

'I didn't think you'd be back. After Sergeant O'Flaherty phoned about the second murder, I thought it would be another all-nighter.'

'The troops are doing the routine work,' he said dully. 'I need to think things out a bit.'

'Yes, of course,' she said.

'Kids in bed?'

'Yes.' She hesitated. 'Do you want something to eat?'

'No, thanks. I had a curry with Atherton.'

'I thought I could smell it on you,' she said, not unkindly. 'Why don't you have a bath? It might relax you. You look done in.'

'I think I will,' he said. A wave of sadness passed through his intestines like wind at the thought that he would never share a bath with Joanna again. Never sit with her while she bathed, mixing black velvet and feeding her cheese and onion crisps. He felt lonely and defeated. For the first time he doubted his ability to solve a case which seemed so complicated and contradictory; and worse, he wondered if there were any point in it. Tomorrow there would be another, and he would still be without Joanna. Was there any point in anything at all? Perhaps he could run away, drop out?

But Irene and the children would still have been let down, and Joanna would still be shut off from him, and the likes of Peter Leman would still be sprawled across their own beds stinking of butchery, with parts of their bodies exposed to view which God had never meant to be seen. There was no escape. You just had to get on with things. Ain't nothin' but weery loads, honey.

He realised that Irene was still watching him, as if she expected him to say something else. Oh, God forbid, was it time for one of her searching conversations about the State of their Marriage? He didn't think he could bear that now. He had braced himself to go through with it, but he didn't want to have to talk about it as well.

He looked at her cautiously; sidelong, but more closely. She looked different: less varnished-sleek; pinker, almost fluffy. What had she been up to? Oh yes, he remembered, today had been the day of the picnic on Box Hill. Could it be that she had enjoyed something that did not involve shopping? He made himself enquire after it.

'Did you have a nice time today, by the way?'

'Oh, yes,' she said eagerly, and then the eagerness seemed to run out. 'Yes, very nice,' she repeated woodenly.

'I'm sorry I couldn't come with you,' he said, in case it was that.

'It's all right. Ernie was wonderful. He thought up all sorts of games – the children loved it.' Why did she sound as if that didn't please her? 'He brought food, too. I told him he didn't need to, that I'd do it all. But he brought things from that kosher deli in Northwood – you know the one. Smoked salmon and cream cheese bagels, and some savoury dumpling things, and some special sort of cake.'

'That was nice of him,' Slider said.

'Yes,' she said. No smile with it. She looked more as if he had offered her mortal hurt. 'Matthew really liked it – better than my dull sandwiches. Ernie's car is much more roomy than mine anyway,' she added, as though that were an explanation.

'Yes, well it would be,' Slider said. He wanted to get away now, afraid of what other comparisons might be coming up. Ernie doesn't have to work ridiculous hours, Ernie earns twice as much as you, Ernie knows all the high-ups and belongs to two golf clubs and three bridge circles. Piss on you, Ernie, he thought defiantly, you couldn't tell Perpendicular from Decorated without a guide book, so there. To get away he yawned hugely and falsely, and half way through it turned into a real yawn, tangled up his reflexes and nearly choked him.

Irene took the hint. 'Go and have your bath. Put some Radox in it.'

'I will,' Slider said. 'Are you going to bed now?'

'Yes.'

'Good. Don't stay awake for me.' He hadn't yet broached the subject of the spare bedroom. He might have to fall asleep on the sofa again. 'I have a lot of thinking to do. I might be some time.'

She nodded and went away upstairs without a word. Slider didn't know where the new Irene had come from, but she was certainly much easier to live with than the old one.

★ ★ ★

227

Dickson's house was a perfectly ordinary 1930s North Harrow semi in a perfectly ordinary tree-lined suburban road. The only difference was that it had not been visibly altered or modernised. It had its original 'sunburst' front gate and its original door and windows, and the same little tarpaper-roofed, wooden-doored garage with which the original developers had sought to outdo their rivals in enticing people to move out to Metroland.

Dolly Dickson was at work in the front garden when Slider arrived. She straightened up at the click of the gate-latch. She was wearing a smock and a shapeless skirt, a battered straw hat and gardening gloves. She looked as timeless as the house.

'Begonias,' she said. 'They were Bob's passion, but I've never liked them. Fleshy, unnatural-looking things. I try to keep them up for his sake, but they seem to be dying.' She smiled deprecatingly. 'I wonder if I'm subconsciously doing the wrong things so as to kill them? I do hope not.'

He had forgotten her voice, soft, pleasantly modulated; posh accent. He remembered absorbing somewhere – he didn't remember where – that she had come from a large, impoverished but definitely 'county' family. For a copper, Dickson had married well above him.

'I don't know about begonias,' he said. 'I don't much like them either.'

'I found myself stroking one the other day and talking to it. Bob was so attached to them. Time for coffee, I think,' Mrs Dickson said, stripping off her gardening gloves. Her hands were brown and freckled like her face, but the skin of them was loose where the skin on her face was tight and shiny. She looked as though she were wearing a second pair of gloves under the first. Slider wondered if she had lost a lot of weight recently.

She caught him looking, and distracted his attention.

228

'What's in that intriguing box you're holding?' she asked with a nod in its direction.

'A cake,' Slider said. The shop girl had tied it with that thin raffia ribbon and made a loop for his finger, and he held it rather shamefacedly, like a ten-pints-a-night man caught wearing an apron. 'I didn't know what else to bring you,' he apologised.

'It's very acceptable,' Dolly said, with the effortless graciousness of the lifelong committee woman. 'Coffee is so dull without something to eat. Let's go in.'

They went in through the front door. The house seemed empty and silent, smelling of lavender wax and carpets, with a suggestion of sunlight in some other room, and a ticking clock somewhere not quite heard. It reminded him of the few occasions when he had come home from school early: a house entered at an unaccustomed time gave him that feeling of strangeness, as if he had interrupted it on the verge of some unimagined metamorphosis.

Inside the house was as *virgo intacta* as outside – no knock-throughs, extensions, removed fireplaces, replacement doors. It was expensively furnished, but with the taste of twenty-five years ago. Everything was of good quality, designed to last, and gave the impression that it had been bought after solemn consideration, placed just so, and never moved again. Not for Dolly Dickson the frenzied bouts of furniture moving and the restless urges for new wallpaper or structural alterations which consumed Irene. Hers was a spirit at peace with its Cintique.

She led him through into the kitchen, which was full of sunshine. Everything was spotless and neat as if it had just that day been installed, though the original range, now unused, still stood in the original fireplace, and the cream and green wall tiles were of a sort not made since the war. The back door was open, and beyond it the garden was so orderly it looked like a painted cyclorama. Slider gazed at the neat lawn and crowded flower beds so as not to have to look at the single mug and plate on the wooden drying rack by the sink, which he supposed represented Dolly's solitary breakfast. Loneliness was such a huge thing, and lurked in such tiny symbols, it made him feel dizzy.

'The garden looks wonderful,' he said.

'I'm trying to keep it that way.' She put her gloves down and took the kettle to the tap. 'Of course it was Bob's passion – he spent every minute of his spare time out there.' She smiled out at it, as though it might smile back. 'For myself, I'd have liked something a bit less formal, more flowing. But it was always his garden rather than mine.'

'It looks like a lot of work,' Slider said.

'It is. I'm probably only experiencing the tip of the iceberg as yet. But I feel I ought to keep it the way he liked it.' She brought the kettle back and plugged it in. 'I suppose I might have to get someone in to do the lawns and hedges. But for the moment it's good for me to have something to do, to keep my mind off things.'

'We all miss him,' Slider said.

She looked at him consideringly for a moment. 'Yes, I believe you do. Bob was always very fond of you, you know. I wish we had had the chance to get to know each other more, but the Job doesn't seem to be like that. So few occasions to mix socially. And Bob was such a shy man. He found human contact such a struggle, poor lamb!' She arranged jug, filter and cups, and spooned coffee from a Lyons tin into the filter. 'It's the way he was brought up, of course. When I was a girl at home, there were people in and out all the time, tennis parties, weekend guests. But I had three elder sisters and two brothers.' She looked at him. 'Were you an only child?'

'Yes.'

'So was Bob. I sometimes think perhaps only lonely people become policemen. What do you think?'

It was obviously a question not meant to be answered, so he didn't. The kettle boiled and she made the coffee. 'Now what about this splendid cake of yours?' she said. 'Should we put it on a plate, do you think?'

Slider allowed himself to be domesticated, waiting until they were sitting at the kitchen table with cups and plates and pastry forks and napkins disposed about them before he approached his question. Even then, it was she who primed him.

There was something in particular you wanted to ask me,' she said, cutting the cake.

'Yes, there was, if it doesn't upset you too much to talk about it.'

'If it's about Bob, I shall talk about it gladly. I seize any excuse to mention his name. People don't like to, you know, when you've been bereaved. Almost as if it's bad luck.' She placed a slice of cake on Slider's plate and eyed it critically. 'Is it from the Polish bakery by the station?'

'Yes,' Slider said. He thought of Jablowski taking up with DI Resnik; and then of Ernie Newman plying his children with kosher delicacies and Polish cheesecake. Free-association, sign that his mind was tired. Practically free fall.

'I thought it looked nice. Shop cake is so often disappointing, isn't it? So what is your question?'

'I ought to mention first that it isn't an official enquiry,' Slider said. 'In fact, I've been forbidden to follow up on this.'

'I understand,' Dolly said, with an amused look. 'Being forbidden always set up Bob's back, too.'

'I want to know all I can find out about a man called Colin Cate.'

'Ah,' said Dolly. Her eyes grew grave.

'Especially about the incident in 1982 when two DCs were shot.'

'Field and Wilson,' she said. 'That was a dreadful business. I don't think Bob ever got over what happened to those two boys.'

'But there was no question of blame, was there? It wasn't his fault?'

'Some people thought it was. And I dare say he blamed himself.' She looked across at him. 'You would, wouldn't you? Even if there was nothing you could have done to prevent it.'

'Yes, I suppose so. Can you tell me exactly what happened? Did Bob talk to you about it?'

'Oh, yes. Not all in one go, but in dribs and drabs over the years. I suppose you know it was a stake-out of a pub where they believed drug dealing was going on?'

'The Carlisle, yes.'

'Colin Cate was in charge of the operation. Do you know him, by the way?'

'I've met him briefly. Twice.'

'He and Bob never saw eye to eye. It's only fair to tell you that from the beginning, because naturally I will be prejudiced against him. Anyone Bob didn't like, I didn't like.'

'Do you know why he didn't like him?'

'Bob hated the idea that it's not what you know, it's who you know. Cate relied heavily on contacts – in both directions. He was a very successful policeman, because he knew a great many criminals – had a whole network of informers, if legend is to be believed. And he went very quickly up the ladder because he knew all the important people above him. He was a great socialiser, which of course Bob wasn't. Dinner-dances and that sort of thing bored him stiff, but you would always see Colin Cate in the centre of a lively group, keeping his seniors amused. I felt awfully sorry for his wife,' she added

232

thoughtfully, stirring her coffee. 'His first wife, I mean. He married her when he was very young, and then found he'd outgrown her, that she wasn't important enough or glamorous enough to be the wife of a rising star. So he divorced her and married a wealthy young woman who could wear clothes.'

'What was he like to work with?'

'Full of energy, no detail too small, that sort of thing. And a great disciplinarian. Unquestioning obedience to orders. Bob thought Cate didn't leave enough room for individual responsibility and initiative, and of course he was always one to act on instinct – Bob was, I mean – which was anathema to Colin Cate. *He* liked to have every tiny detail under his own thumb.'

'So what happened at the stake-out?'

'It's only hearsay, remember,' she said acutely. 'I only know what Bob told me, and after all these years I may remember wrongly. And it concerns your DS, Ian Barrington.'

'I understand all those things. But I need to know. Please – your version.'

'Very well. The plan was quietly to draw a loose net round the pub, and then tighten it quickly, going in by all the doors at once. Everyone had their orders. Bob's were to stay out in the road as a backup, and to catch anyone who managed to slip the net. He didn't like it, I can tell you. He wanted to be part of the action, and he believed that Colin Cate had put him in the back row as a punishment. So he was restless, you see, and looking around for some way to be more involved.'

'I understand.'

'Now the pub is on a corner plot on a fork of the road, as you know. It had doors to the street on three sides, and the fourth side had a little yard with gates and outbuildings, and there were fire doors leading into it from the back of the pub. Ian Barrington was to cover the yard, and as far as

Bob understood, his orders were to stay outside in the yard and just catch anyone who came out. They didn't expect any of the customers to come out that way because it led to the staff quarters and kitchens and storerooms. There was a door through from the bar, but it was in the corridor beyond the lavatories and it was in a dark corner and marked private.'

'Fair enough. One or two might make it that far, but not a crowd.'

'Quite so. But now, you see, Barrington said afterwards that Colin Cate had changed his orders just before it all began, told him that he was to wait thirty seconds after the raid started and then go in through the fire doors and go straight through to the bar, to make sure no customers did, in fact, get out that way. But no one told Bob that. He saw the main force go in through the street doors, and while he was pacing restlessly up and down hoping for something to happen, he looked into the yard and saw that Barrington and his men were nowhere to be seen, and that the fire doors were apparently unguarded. So he did what any man would do – any man with initiative—'

'He took two of his men and went to investigate.'

'Field and Wilson,' Dolly said. 'Jack Field was mad about motorbikes, poor boy. His one ambition in life was to buy a Harley Davidson and take it to Germany where there was no speed limit and see how fast it would go on the autobahn. And Alan Wilson – he was shot in the stomach. A dreadful place to be wounded. He lingered in hospital for months, and he was never the same afterwards. He had to leave the police force. I don't know what became of him.'

'But the raid,' Slider prompted her gently. 'What happened?'

'It all happened so quickly. Bob led them in. There was a passage, quite dark, no lights on. He could hear the noise of

234

the raid from up ahead of him. There was no one in the passage, but there were doors to either side, and a staircase a bit further along, leading up to the staff bedrooms. Bob headed for that, leaving the boys to check what was behind the doors. He'd just started up the staircase when the two men came bursting out from one of the doors – between him and his boys. Bob shouted something, and the two men looked round – startled, I suppose. Then Bob's foot slipped.' She sighed, her fingers tightening unconsciously on the cup handle. 'He was turning, you see, and the stairs were uncarpeted. His foot went out from under him and he fell forwards – up the stairs, if you understand me—'

'Yes,' said Slider.

'And at the same moment he heard the shots. One of the men shouted 'Let's get out of here,' or something like that, and Bob scrambled up to see Field and Wilson on the ground, and the two men running out of the door. He went to his boys, of course. Some people suggested afterwards that he should have gone after the two felons, but he knew they were armed, and his own men were hurt.'

'Quite right. Getting himself killed wouldn't have helped.'

'And besides, he'd recognised them when they looked round at him.'

'Jimmy Cole and Derek Blackburn.'

'That's right.'

'But you said it was dark in the passage?'

'It was light enough for that. There were street lamps outside and the doors were open.' She looked distressed. 'Of course the defence counsel at the trial made all they could of the darkness, but he was only ten feet from them. Besides, they never denied they were there, only that they had fired the shots.'

'Bob didn't see which of them fired them?'

'No. The staircase was enclosed, you see. And he'd fallen forwards, face down. He only heard the shots.'

'He didn't actually see the gun?'

'No. But there was never any doubt about it. The gun was found in Blackburn's bedroom the next day. Colin Cate himself took a team to search the house, and the gun was there under some clothes in his wardrobe.'

'There was no doubt it was the right gun?'

'None. The ballistic evidence was quite clear. Even the defence didn't challenge it. It had been wiped clean of fingerprints, but it had been recently fired, and the bullets they recovered matched it.'

'And what happened afterwards? There must have been an internal investigation into the shooting of the two DCs.'

'Yes, there was. Well, no blame was officially attached to anyone. But afterwards Barrington said that it was all Bob's fault for not following his orders. If he'd stayed out in the road, Field and Wilson wouldn't have been shot. He and Bob had a dreadful argument about it, and Barrington gave him to understand that such was also Cate's unofficial view. So there was no possibility of their ever being able to work together again. Bob put in for a transfer, and that was that. But I understand that Colin Cate left the force soon afterwards, and did rather well for himself in business.'

So that *was* why Barrington hated Dickson, Slider thought; and, in particular, hated his indiscipline and laxity. Unquestioning obedience to orders, that was the way to salvation.

'But if Cole and Blackburn said they didn't fire the shots, who did they claim had done so?' he asked after a moment.

'They didn't offer any explanation,' Dolly said. 'Have another slice of cake. It's very nice, isn't it? No, they couldn't suggest who might have shot the two DCs if they didn't. They

236

never even tried to claim that they were elsewhere. They said they'd been having a quiet drink when the raid started and they simply tried to run for it. It was such a thin story the defence counsel didn't put them in the box, and the jury had no doubts about their guilt. They were only out for two hours.'

Slider was silent, running the new ideas through his mind. There didn't seem to be any great mystery about it, except perhaps as to why Cate had changed Barrington's orders at the last minute. But on the face of it the change was for a good reason. And it was perhaps slightly odd that Cole and Blackburn had offered no better defence – but then, since they were caught bang to rights, what defence could they offer?

'I haven't helped you much, have I?' Dolly asked, breaking into his reverie.

'Yes – yes a great deal,' Slider said. 'But there is just one thing more. I understand why Bob didn't like Cate, but was he generally liked, by the other people who worked for him?'

'You didn't like Colin Cate,' she said decisively. 'He preferred to be obeyed and reverenced. *Oderint dum metuant,* you know.'

'Sorry?'

'Caesar Tiberius. Let them hate me as long as they fear me.'

'Ah! And was he reverenced?'

'Oh yes, I think so. He was a very effective officer, Bob always said, and that's what counts, isn't it? I think Ian Barrington modelled himself on him, but then poor Ian had scars that went very deep, and Cate was a very handsome man. Charming, too, when he wanted to be.'

'Did he charm you?'

'No. But then he didn't try. I was just a lowly inspector's wife – he had nothing to gain from me. And he never had

237

any time for women anyway. He was a man's man, and his charm was a man's charm. Maybe that's why Bob didn't care for him,' she added as though she had just thought of it. 'There was a lot of woman in Bob, in the best possible way. There is in you, too. Do you like him?'

'No,' Slider said, a little embarrassed at the turn of conversation.

'There you are, then,' Dolly said with a satisfied nod.

15

Some Day My Prints Will Come

'All right,' Slider said, 'Let's have a look at what we know. Atherton, tell us about Lam.'

'Michael Lam set off from the Hung Fat restaurant in his car at about eight o'clock on Wednesday evening for Heathrow. He checked in for his flight, which was to leave at eleven-thirty, and the ground stewardess concerned says that to judge by the seat allocation he must have checked in amongst the first, when the check-in opened at eight-thirty. He subsequently caught the flight, but the business colleague who was waiting to meet him in Hong Kong says he didn't arrive. He says he saw every person who came through from that flight, and Lam wasn't among them.'

'He missed him,' Mackay shrugged. 'It happens all the time.'

'It's possible of course. But Lam didn't arrive at his hotel, or contact the man at any point as he was supposed to, he didn't catch his booked flight home, and he hasn't been in contact with his family since.'

'So he disappeared during the flight, is that what you're saying?' Norma enquired sweetly.

'I'm just establishing what we know. I haven't got round to theorising yet,' Atherton said loftily. 'Point number two – Lam's car has been discovered in the short-term car park at Terminal Three. If his original intention was to go to Hong Kong on Tuesday evening, returning Saturday, why not the long-term car park? Three to four days in the short-term costs a fortune. Indeed, why take the car at all? The Tube would have been more sensible. He didn't have much luggage, only a small shoulder-bag.'

'But we do know he caught the flight,' Jablowski said.

'We know *somebody* caught the flight,' Atherton corrected.

'I thought you weren't going to theorise,' she complained. 'You've got him down for the corpse, haven't you?'

'We tried the cabin crew with a photograph of Lam, and they don't think he was amongst the passengers, though they can't be absolutely sure.'

'I should think not, indeed,' Norma said, amused. 'They were on their way to Hong Kong, remember.'

'Why do you think he was the victim, then?' Mackay said, still catching up.

'He was Eurasian, and he fits the description of the victim as far as height, build and age go. And he is missing.'

'That's what we said about Leman, and look where that got us,' said Norma.

'He could be anywhere,' Jablowski said. 'He might just have done a bunk when he got to Hong Kong.'

'I would, if old Hung Fat was my father-in-law,' Norma agreed.

'Of course he could,' Atherton agreed. 'That's why we've still got to get an ID. We've got the name of his dentist from his sister-in-law, and we've sent off the dental profile. His dental work was done in Hong Kong, but it was two years ago, and businesses tend to act like mushrooms over there – up one day and gone the next. Still, we shall see. And if

240

there's no joy, we could try taking a blood sample from his baby, if the mother will allow, and do a genetic fingerprinting. That ought to give us a fix.'

'Assuming for the moment and for the sake of argument,' Slider said, 'that Lam is the victim, why did he come back to the shop, why was he killed, and who went to Hong Kong in his place?'

'It's probably a nice, simple family matter,' Beevers said. 'You know what these people are like about family. How about someone was banging Lam's old lady, Leman maybe, and he met him at the fish bar to have it out with him, and lost the fight?'

Hoots greeted his theory.

'Except there wasn't a fight!'

'Why would an adulterer go to a midnight meeting with the bloke whose wife he was jumping – unless he was suicidal?

'And who took the Hong Kong flight in your theory?' Norma asked derisively.

'His murderer, of course,' Beevers said, unmoved. 'To get away from the scene of the crime.'

'You just said it was Leman, you twonk!'

'Maybe he came back. They do, don't they? Revisiting the scene of the crime.'

'Honestly, Alec,' Norma said, quite kindly, 'I've worn dresses that were more intelligent than you.'

'Well, I've known villains do that,' McLaren supported his sex through a raspberry Rowntree's Fruit Gum. 'When I was at Lambeth we had this bloke—'

Slider stepped in. 'We need to know a lot more before we can start this kind of theorising. Atherton, I want you to get hold of Mrs Lam, find out everything you can about her husband, who he knew, where he went, what he did. This business of his in Hong Kong, for instance—'

'That was legit,' Atherton said. 'He was meeting this colleague of the old man's to discuss the supply of dried and tinned ingredients for the restaurant. He'd done a couple of trips like that.'

'Hmm. But there must have been a reason the old man didn't approve of him. Maybe he was up to something else on his own account. Let's find out.'

'Okay, boss. What about the Leman murder?'

'Mr Barrington's handed that over to the local lads, with Mr Carver liaising. So far they've discovered that a man was seen coming out of the house at about the right time for the murder—'

General exclamations and wolf whistles.

'—but he was wearing a motorbike helmet with a dark visor, so he can't be identified. He was carrying a leather bag – presumably containing the knife and protective clothing – but unfortunately nobody noticed the number or make of the motorcycle.'

Sympathetic groans.

'And Freddie Cameron has done the post, and he suggests that the mark on Leman's palm may have been where he was holding some small, round, hard object at the moment he was killed, and clenched his hand tightly enough to bruise it. In that case, presumably the murderer opened his hand and retrieved it, whatever it was, which leaves Mr Carver's people with the problem of discovering what it was and why it was so important.'

'We wish them joy of it, don't we, girls and boys?' Atherton said brightly.

'Meanwhile, we've still got Slaughter to follow up. He can't have lived his entire life in a vacuum. Someone else on Planet Earth must have known him, so let's see if his history yields any information. Beevers, Mackay, McLaren and Anderson

– I want two teams trawling the most likely gay bars and clubs. Take mugshots with you of everyone in the case and follow up any lead however trivial. Jablowski, I want you to find out who owns the Acton Lane house and the Hanwell house. Contact the Community Charge office – I don't want the owner or owners alerted. Norma, I want you to go and talk to Suzanne Edrich. She must know something more useful than Leman's inside leg measurement. Ask her especially about that last trip to San Francisco in April.'

'Yes, Guv.'

'And when you get back, you can help Jablowski go back over all the door-to-door reports again – that goes for all of you. Every spare minute. If there's anyone we missed because they were out or away or unhelpful, go get 'em. And I want everyone whose windows overlook that alley visited again. Someone must have seen something.'

Unenthusiastic chorus of assents.

'It's going to be one of those cases,' Slider said. 'The essence of police work: step by step, sheer slog. No flashes of genius or strokes of luck are going to get any change out of this situation. Let's get to it.'

'And where will you be doing your slogging?' Atherton asked as they began to disperse.

'I'm going to start from the other end,' Slider said.

Slider's vigil in a small and obviously unused office was finally broken by the entry of an endlessly tall, bony young man in the uniform of the US Air Force who introduced himself in an accessible sort of way as Captain Phil Bannister and how-can-I-help-you?

Too tall for a pilot, Slider thought. Must be bright in some department to have got promoted so young. He only looked about twenty-two, but that might have been the ears. Or the ears might have been the clinically short haircut. He had the appearance, which Slider had noticed before in young officers in the American forces, of being somehow extra clean over and above perfectly spotless. He made Slider feel like Columbo.

'I'm Detective Inspector Slider of the Shepherd's Bush CID,' Slider said, showing his brief. Bannister took it and inspected it gravely, and handed it back with a touch of uncertainty. Slider didn't blame him. He didn't find them very convincing either. Technology was having a hard time catching up with the life of an ID card in a hip pocket. Why did so many policemen have big bottoms? It was one of Life's insoluble little mysteries.

'Okay,' said Bannister, as though prepared to overlook its shortcomings, 'what can I tell you?'

'I'm interested in a man called Lee Chang, who I believe worked here until quite recently.'

'Yeah, they said you were asking about Lee, but they didn't say why. Is he in trouble?'

'I hope not. What I'm hoping to do is to eliminate him from an enquiry. You worked with him, did you?'

'He was in my section, which I guess you'd loosely call operational computers, but as a civilian he wasn't directly under my command. But, yes, I guess you could say I worked with him. He seemed a nice guy. What did you want to know?'

'Could we start with when he came here, and where he came from?'

'That's easy. He was here for six weeks from April seven through May eighteen. He was loaned out to us by his company, Megatrends Warmerica Inc – have you heard of them?'

'I'm afraid not.'

'Oh, big, big software house in Santa Clara. But *megabig* in the products development field! Lee's been with 'em for a

244

couple of years now, very highly rated by his people, so I understand. Real whizz kid. He started off as an electronics engineer, went into the micro side – used to work for Intel at one time – and then went over to software, so he knew the business from an all-round angle. That's why they sent him to us. He was here to install a new strategic planning program for us and get it running, sort out any glitches and so on. Well, he did his job and he went, and that's all. I'm kinda sorry to lose him. He was a great guy – full of laughs.'

'When exactly did he leave?'

'Like I said, May eighteen – that was the Monday. He finished up around three-thirty and we all said goodbye and – away he went!' He flattened his right hand and made it take off into the big blue yonder.

'Do you know where he was going when he left here?'

'I guess he went home,' Bannister said, puzzled.

'Home to the States? That very day?'

'Oh, I get you! Well, as far as I recall, he said he was gonna take a couple of days out shopping in London, and then head back to San Francisco on Wednesday or Thursday.'

'And then he would report back to his company, I suppose?'

'I guess so. No, wait, I remember now he said he had some leave coming that he was gonna take right after he got back. I don't know if he'd have to let them know how the job here went off first, but after that he was heading off on vacation.'

'You suggested he was a very friendly man. Did he have any particular friends? Anyone he spent time with outside working hours?'

'I don't know about that,' Bannister said, shaking his head. 'He was friendly in and around the base, but I don't know if he met anyone outside. I could ask around for you.'

'Please, if you wouldn't mind. And also if anyone has a photograph of him.'

'Oh, I can give you a photograph. He had to have one taken for his security card.'

'You run a security check on everyone who works here, I imagine?'

'Certainly. But the people at Mega would have checked him out before they sent him anyway. They wouldn't have put him on a new product installation like this if there was anything funny about him.'

'I understand.'

'Has he done something wrong?' Bannister asked with a concerned frown. 'He didn't have access here to any sensitive material, of course, but if there is any question of a security problem we ought to know about it.'

'It isn't anything like that,' Slider said with a reassuring smile. 'A man in the same house where Chang was staying committed suicide in rather peculiar circumstances, and I'm obliged to check on everyone who may have come into contact with him. It's purely a domestic police matter, you see.'

'I see. Okay. Well, if anything develops that we ought to know about—'

'Of course. I'll make sure you're informed at once.'

'Meanwhile I'll get you that photograph – do you want to wait for it?'

'Yes, please. If it's no trouble.'

'Not at all. And I'll ask around the guys if anyone saw anything of him out of hours.'

'Thank you. Oh, there is one other thing.' Bannister paused and looked enquiring. 'Chang was staying in a bedsitter in Notting Hill Gate—'

Bannister beamed. 'Yeah, I gave him a lift home once on my way to Grosvenor Square. Quite a way to travel every day!'

So that was the man in the dark blue overcoat, Slider thought with minor relief. One less thing to check up on.

'The room he rented belonged to a man called Colin Cate, who you may have heard of?'

'Oh, yeah, everyone here knows him. Well, he kinda liaises on security, so he gets round all the departments one way and another.'

'I see. I just wondered how Chang got to know him. Did someone here suggest to Chang that he contact Mr Cate for accommodation?'

'I'd have to ask around about that, too.'

'I suppose he must have been staying in a hotel to begin with?'

'That would be on his personal record. Do you want me to look it up for you?'

'If you would I'd be grateful. Also his home address in America, and his next-of-kin.'

'Sure. I can let you have those. I didn't know Colin let out rooms,' he added with a puzzled smile. 'He seems to be into all kinds of things, doesn't he?'

'He's an all-round businessman,' Slider said warmly, and Bannister relaxed.

'Yeah. I wouldn't trust a man who didn't respect money, myself – would you? But I didn't get the impression that Lee and Colin were particularly friendly. I mean, I've been there when Colin's come into the department, and there was no kind of—' he hesitated, not quite knowing how to phrase it.

'Special relationship?' Slider offered.

'Right! I mean, you'd expect him to say, "Hi, Lee, how's the room? Comfortable? Anything you need?" Something like that. But I never heard him say anything to Lee at all. Or the other way around.'

'Well, maybe Cate didn't like people to know he let out rooms. May have thought it sounded a bit downbeat for such a successful man.'

'Maybe so. Yeah, that would explain it all right,' Bannister said, comforted. 'Okay, well I'll go get that photograph for you.'

While he was gone, Slider sat very still, his eyes fixed on the skirting board, his mind working furiously. Computers again. Cate had a chain of outlets called Compucate. And there had been one other mention somewhere of computers, but he couldn't bring it to mind. Some other connection . . . No, it was no good. It would come to him if he left it alone. The Chinese connection and the computer connection. He must find out whether Chang had reported back to his company, or indeed anywhere.

What was it all about? He was willing to bet Cate was in it right up to his eyeballs, though, whatever it was. If only he could investigate Cate properly, instead of pussyfooting around the periphery. But he'd get there, he'd get there. A man who didn't like Bob Dickson couldn't be all good.

Bannister came back at last with a neat manilla folder – military efficiency allied with personal cleanliness. 'Everything you want's in here – photo, addresses and all.'

'Thank you,' said Slider. 'I'm very grateful.'

'Also I've asked in the department whether anyone saw anything of Lee outside the base, but they all say no. He used to head right off home when he finished his shift. Jimmy Demarco says he invited Lee to Sunday lunch once at his place – thought the guy must be lonely all on his own – but he wouldn't come. Just said he had things to do. That seems to be how it was.'

'I see.'

'As to your other question, about how he knew to ask Colin Cate about accommodation, I can't give an answer. No one in the department knows. But it does seem that he went straight to the bedsit, not to an hotel first. Is it important to know? Would you like me to ask around the other departments?'

'No, no, please don't bother. It doesn't matter at all,' Slider said hastily. General enquiries about Colin Cate would almost certainly go straight back to Colin Cate, and Slider would find himself swiftly promoted to Permanent Latrine Orderly.

'Okay. You're the boss. Anything else you want any time, just let me know.'

'You've been most helpful. I really am grateful.'

'You're welcome.' Bannister beamed. 'I'll see you off the base. I hope you find out that there's nothing wrong with Lee, though,' he added, ushering Slider out into the corridor. 'He really seemed like a nice guy.'

He didn't say the same about Colin Cate, Slider thought, as he got into his car.

His enquiries of the Chinese Embassy were less fruitful. Any questions about personnel would have to be put through the correct diplomatic channels. But he only wanted to know whether a certain person had actually been officially in England at a certain time. No information whatever could be given about employees past or present. Very sorry. The Great Stonewall of China in full working order again.

He decided to go back to Mrs Sullivan and put a little pressure on her. He wished he could confront Cate and threaten him with living off immoral earnings or running a disorderly house or something if he didn't answer a few questions, but he didn't think Barrington would be too frightfully keen on that idea. All he got out of Kathleen Sullivan, however, was that Lee Chang had come to the house straight from the airport, and that she had been told the day before by 'the owner' – whom she still coyly refused to name – to expect him, and how long he would be staying. That did not, however,

249

necessarily give the lie to Cate's own account, for the 'friend at the base' could have asked him about accommodation before Chang arrived. But then the friend would have had to know Chang, and know that he would want accommodation. And, as Bannister had said, it was a long way to travel each day. Surely Harrow or even Watford would have provided better, cheaper, more convenient rooms than that top-floor bedsit in Notting Hill?

As to Peter Ling, she remembered that he had left the house about two years ago because he was leaving Compucate to open a shop of his own in the same line of business. She didn't know where the shop was, except that she thought it was somewhere in Fulham, or what had become of him. Why did he have to leave the house? Because the accommodation was dependent on the job. Had Ling been resentful about that? Well, towards the end he and his boss hadn't seen eye to eye about things, so he'd pretty well had to go anyway, new business or no new business. What things were those? Mrs Sullivan couldn't say.

Wouldn't say, more likely, Slider thought. He also doubted that if it ever came to a court of law he could bring her to swear to anything very much. She seemed to be a very loyal employee. She also had a healthy fear of Cate's disapproval, which said a lot both for her common sense and for Slider's case.

He went back to his car, and after a moment's thought, drove round to the offices of the *Hammersmith Gazette*. He looked up his little friend in the photographic department, and she obligingly looked up Cate in the morgue and found a good deal on him, including a decent *Gazette* photograph of him arriving at the Town Hall for the Mayor's New Year Ball. While she was making him a couple of prints of it, he went across the road to a telephone box and rang the factory.

250

He got Jablowski. 'I want you to do something for me.'

'Yes, Guv?'

'Ring Pauline Smithers at Fulham Road nick – she's the DCI – and ask her, as a favour to me, to find out about a Peter Ling who opened a computer supply shop somewhere in Fulham about two years ago. I need to get in touch with him. And ask her not to tell anyone I've been asking. Tell her I'll ring her later and see if she's got anything.'

'Righto. Anything else?'

'Did you find out who owns those two flats?'

'It's a property company called Shax—'

'Shacks? Hovels would be more appropriate.'

She spelt it. 'Address in Northfields. Do you want it?'

'Yes, please.' He wrote it down. 'Any more news?'

'Norma's drawn a blank with Suzanne Edrich. Leman didn't tell her anything about his trip, wouldn't even let her see him off. The only interesting thing she said was that when Leman phoned her from hiding, he said that when the job he was involved in was over, he'd be so rich he'd never have to work again.'

'That big, eh? Anything else happened?'

'Only that you've been asked for – but I take it I don't know where you are?'

'You don't. I haven't told you.'

'Oh – no more you have.'

'I haven't rung you, either,' he warned.

'Are you kidding? I value my skin.'

'Good girl. I'll be in later.'

He collected his prints and, on the principle of clear as you go, headed down King Street, Chiswick High Road, along the A4 and up South Ealing Road. He missed Lawrence Road the first time because it was so narrow and almost entirely obscured with motorcycles which had spilled over from the display window of the dealership on the corner. He went round the block and found that there was nowhere to park in Lawrence Road, went round again, left the wheels on Junction Road and walked down, and discovered that the registered office of Shax appeared to be the upstairs portion of a Victorian two-pony stable across a yard from the motor-cycle shop, the lower half of which was dragging out a dishonourable existence as a shelter for bits of rusty bike nobody wanted any more. Whoever had named the company Shax had a sense of humour.

To Slider's entire and unconcealed surprise, he found the office open, and manned. It contained a battered but once handsome desk supporting a white sea of paper which he guessed, like a glacier, probably only moved at the rate of an inch a year; a green filing cabinet with a telephone on top of it; a rickety enamel-topped table containing tea-making equipment and two chipped mugs liberally smeared with heavy-duty oil. It also contained a tall, well-built young man in spectacularly dirty overalls. His hands were black to the wrist, his face smudged and smeared with grease, his hair long, straight, blond, and tied in a pony-tail at the back, and his left ear pierced and dangling a cute single earring in the shape of a skull.

He was holding in his hands an oily cylindrical piece of metal of unimaginable but evidently motor-mechanical purpose, and he turned when Slider entered and fixed him with a pair of china-blue eyes.

'Help you?' he said shortly.

'This is the office of Shax Limited, isn't it?' Slider asked with his most boyish smile.

The young man didn't answer, but as if the question had necessitated the action he turned away and rummaged in the overflowing waste-paper basket, pulled out a sheet of crumpled paper, spread it over one part of the lava flow on the desk, and placed the cylindrical object tenderly on top of it.

'What do you want?' he asked without noticeable friendliness.

'You own two properties I'm interested in.' He gave the Acton Lane and Hanwell addresses.

'They're not for thale,' the young man said. A spot of pink appeared over each cheekbone, which was really not unbecoming.

'But you do own them?' The man didn't answer. Slider thought he probably didn't much like saying the word yes. It must be a hard cross to bear in the land of the bikers, to have both a lisp and heavenly blue eyes. 'I wasn't thinking of buying them, anyway,' he went on. 'What I'm really interested in is who lets them out.'

'What do you want to know for?' the man asked after a short internal struggle.

Slider got out his ID card, and the young man, after a glance at it, raised his eyes apprehensively to Slider's. 'What's your name, son?' Slider asked gently.

'Peter,' he said. Then, 'Peter Davey.' He seemed frozen with apprehension, and in spite of his size made Slider feel quite fatherly towards him.

'All right, Peter. I'm not here to make any trouble for you, I just want you to answer a few questions.'

'I don't have to. I haven't done anything,' he said defensively.

'I know you haven't. Just tell me who lets out those two houses I'm interested in. Who has the say-so on who goes into them?'

'I do. It'th my job. They're my houtheth. Thith ith my company.'

'Come on, now. I know that isn't true. I know that you

253

are working for someone, and that he wants you to keep his name secret. He's told you never to tell anyone about him, hasn't he?'

'I don't know what you're talking about,' Davey said, turning his head away like a naughty child. Slider noticed that his right ear looked very sore, with a ragged tear right down the lobe which, from the surrounding swelling, must have been done within the last couple of days.

'The thing is, Peter,' Slider said comfortably, 'that this man is in big trouble, and the time has come when you have got to stop protecting him. Because believe me, he won't protect you when we come to take him away. He'll drop you in it good and hard, so unless you help me now, you'll go down with him.'

The pink had spread all over the cheeks now. Davey's lips were set in a hard line, and he stared resolutely at the wall.

'You don't want to go to prison, do you?' Slider said softly. 'It isn't very nice in prison for people like you.'

He turned his head now, his eyes flashing. 'What do you mean by that?'

'Good-looking young men, particularly blue-eyed good-looking young men, have a rotten time in prison. They get waylaid in the showers by gangs of the meaty boys, and—'

'You bugger off!' he shouted suddenly and surprisingly. 'I don't know what you're talking about. You can't threaten me! I haven't done anything, and I'm not telling you anything, and you can't make me!'

Slider, marvelling at what a long sentence could be constructed impromptu entirely without the letter s, sighed inwardly and tried again.

'Look, son, I'm trying to help you, that's all. Just tell me who the real owner is, and I'll go away. All right? And I won't tell him you said anything, I promise.'

'I haven't thaid anything!' Davey snapped.

Slider drew forth one of the prints. Pray tell me, sweet prince, if this print's of your prince. 'Is this the man?' he asked. He held it out towards Davey, who had turned his face away again and was staring in front of him. Slider could see his chest rise and fall with his rapid breaths, and a sort of anger stirred in him against whoever was using him. This boy was like a frightened rabbit. He thought of the slight Leman, another Peter, head dangling like something in the butcher's shop and his brown hare's eyes glassy with untimely death.

'Just look at it, Peter,' he said kindly. 'There's no harm in just looking, is there?'

He held the print out steadily, and after a long moment the pale blue eyes swivelled irresistibly, and then the head followed a half turn.

'I've never theen him before in my life,' Davey said, turning his face away again.

But it was too late. He had looked, and a look told everything. Slider put the picture away and quietly took his leave.

16

Busy with the Fizzy

Mrs Lam turned out to speak English, once she was away from the restaurant. Atherton was lucky, and managed to waylay her as she wheeled her baby out from the alley in a very smart new pram. She was nervous and reluctant to talk to him, but her anxiety for her husband was now great enough to make her risk it. She told him she was taking the baby for an airing in Wormholt Park, and consented to his accompanying her. So it was there, on a bench with the pram before them, looking like a very mismatched married couple, that they conducted their interview.

She had first met Michael through some relatives of her father's who ran a fish and chip shop. Atherton had already learnt from the late lamented Ronnie Slaughter that fish and chip shops, like pre-Norman England, suffered invaders in waves: first the Italians, then the Greeks, and lately the Chinese had all taken the national dish to their bosoms and made a go of the business. Micky had been employed by the relatives concerned to help in the shop, and had been brought along by them to a large family party. There Mrs Lam – her name was An-mei, which she had already Anglicised effortlessly to Amy – met him and fell in love.

He was a lively young man with a great gift of the gab. Reading between the lines Atherton saw him as one of those slick, showy creatures, given to gold jewellery and unsubtle chat-up lines; but to Amy, strictly brought up by a tyrannical father, he seemed like a breath of fresh air. Her father must have seen some potential use in him, for he allowed the marriage, but Amy's vision of freedom dislimned on the day of her betrothal when it was announced by the patriarah that she and Michael would live with the family and work in the restaurant.

It had been all right at first. Micky played up to his father-in-law, worked hard and minded his tongue. It did not last, though, for Micky was not used to hierarchical living, and spoke his mind too freely, getting into arguments with the old man. He wanted too much time off, as well, for himself and for Amy; and when Amy showed herself incapable of defying her father, Micky had taken the time off himself and left her to endure the storms alone.

'But he was doing it for me, you understand,' she explained anxiously to Atherton. 'I did not realise at first, and was not kind to him, but he told me that he was doing jobs for another man and putting the money aside for me and the baby, so that we could leave my father's house and set up in business of our own. But my father discover this, and he was very angry. He took away the money Micky had made, and make him work very hard. So after that Micky was more careful, and pretended to do everything my father wanted. But still he worked for this other man, and he put the money where he said my father could never find it.'

'Who was the other man, do you know?'

'Micky never told me his name. He said he was a very

257

important man with many businesses, and that he would be a good friend to us and make us rich.'

'What sort of jobs was your husband doing for him?'

'I don't know. Micky didn't tell me and I would not ask. It meant being away, sometimes just one night, sometimes two or three, and Micky had to be very clever to get my father to agree. Usually he made some business for my father at the same time so that he would not suspect – buying things for the restaurant and so on.'

'How often was Micky away, then?'

'It was not very often. Only twice last year, but the man paid him very well. Micky put the money into a savings account and hid the book in a very safe place where my father would never find it.' She glanced shyly at Atherton and smiled. 'You will not tell? It is inside the baby's nappy. No man would ever look in such a place. That is why Micky thought of it. He is very clever. We have twenty thousand pounds saved now. Soon it will be enough for us to leave my father's house completely.'

'The trip your husband was making to Hong Kong last week for your father – was that to be combined with a job for this other man?'

Her cheeks went pink. 'He told me not to speak of it.'

'I understand. But now that Micky is missing, you must tell me everything, or I cannot help you. You want to find out what has happened to him, don't you?'

'Yes, of course. But—'

'I won't let your father know anything about it, if it can be helped,' Atherton assured her. 'Please, tell me all you know.'

She nodded gravely, and was quiet a moment, assembling her thoughts, or perhaps debating with herself over what was the right thing to do. Then she said, 'Micky was very excited about the trip. He said that it would be the last he did for this man, because it was so important and would pay him so much money that he would never have to work again. He said that he and I and the baby would be able to go away on our own and be rich and happy far from my father.'

'Did he say what the job was?'

'No.'

'But it was to be done in Hong Kong?'

'Yes. I think so. It was Micky who suggested the trip to my father, not the other way around, so I think it must have been on this other man's business that he was going.'

Atherton thought a moment. It was frustrating to know so much and so little. He wasn't even sure, though he had an idea, where his guv'nor's suspicions were leading. 'Are you sure he didn't tell you the name of this other man?'

'Quite sure,' Mrs Lam said. 'He was an English man, that's all I know. When he spoke about him to me, Micky used to call him something in Chinese which means White Tiger – I suppose because he was a powerful man. I think he didn't want me to know the real name, so that I would not be able to betray him by accident.'

'Very wise,' Atherton said. Then, 'Do you know how much Micky was to be paid for this last job?'

Her cheeks grew pink again. 'He said two million dollars,' she said with quiet pride. 'American dollars, not Hong Kong.' Atherton whistled softly, and she looked gratified. 'He would be an important man with so much money. My father would have to listen to him then.' She stood up. 'Now I have to go. They will be waiting for me, and I must not make my father angry.'

'I'll walk back with you,' Atherton said, rising also.

'Please not. It will be better if I go alone. You will find Micky for me, won't you?'

'Yes,' Atherton said, a little absently, his mind revolving the sum of money. Was it genuine? Was it a lie? And if so, by whom to whom? 'Anything else you can remember, anything at all, please let me know. Particularly if you remember any names your husband might have mentioned.'

'I will try,' she said sadly, 'but I am sure he did not.'

Pauline Smithers had known Slider since his first posting, was five years his senior, and had been one rank above him for the whole of their acquaintance; and that she was only a DCI proved how slow promotion had been for both of them. She had always had a soft spot for Slider, a fact he had known without knowing what to make of it. His own diffidence had led him to be careful of being too friendly with her, and it had been left to her to make all the running. Their present easy terms were a monument to both her perseverance and her tact. Whenever their paths had crossed, they had gone for a drink or a meal together. She had never met Irene, though she knew more about her than Slider would have realised he had told; Slider had no idea even whether Pauline was married or not.

She received his telephone call with cheerful caution. 'Hullo, Bill! So what's all this cloak-and-dagger stuff? Are you moon-lighting or something? Some old pal looking for a divorce?'

'Nothing like that. It's just a line I'm following up, but there's someone who doesn't see eye-to-eye with me about it.'

'In other words, you've fallen foul of Mad Ivan,' she said wryly.

'I don't know what you're talking about.'

'Oh come on, Bill, this is me! It's all right, no one's listening. Actually, as soon as I heard he'd gone to your nick in Dickson's place I thought there'd be trouble. He's not your kind of guy.'

'There isn't any trouble,' Slider said doggedly, and then, with a sigh, 'Does everyone in the Met know about this bloke except me?'

'Probably,' she said cheerfully. 'You've always had your nose to the grindstone. Makes it difficult to keep your eyes on the horizon at the same time. But Bill, really, are you all right?'

'Yes, really,' he said. The concern in her voice was both flattering and alarming. He didn't want himself seen as a case for pity. He didn't want other people discussing his problems, real or imagined. 'All I wanted was a bit of information without letting the world know about it. It's no big deal.'

'Ah, yes, the information,' she said lightly, going along with him. 'I just love the way you threw that one at me. Ask old Pauline to find a man in Fulham who opened a shop two years ago. Don't give her anything else to go on. No sense in making it too easy.'

'You found him,' Slider said, smiling. 'I can tell by your voice. I knew you wouldn't let me down.'

'It was only your dumb luck,' she said, and he could hear that she was smiling too. 'There are two or three lads in our Department who are computer crazy, and when I threw the name at them casually, they threw it right back with an address and telephone number. Seems your Peter Ling has a weakness for coppers – gives us very generous discounts. It's well known round our shop that if you want anything in the computer line you go to Ling's. He's apparently very knowledgeable and has all the contacts. Can get you anything you want practically at cost.'

'So it won't have roused any suspicions, your asking?'

'Not at all. It'll just give me a reputation for liking to play with PCs.'

'I always knew that about you anyway. Give me the address, will you?' He wrote it down. 'Thanks, Pauline. You're a prince.'

'Dumb luck, as I said.'

'Well, thanks, anyway. We must get together one of these days – I owe you a drink at least.'

'Any time. Just give me a ring.' A faint pause. 'Bill, is everything all right? I mean, with you generally? You can tell Aunty Pauline, you know.'

A pause of his own. 'I wish I could. Maybe I will one day. When I've got this case out of the way. I could do with a friendly ear and a bit of female advice.'

'Ah, I thought there was something! Well, the ear's here and switched on, whenever you want it.'

'I'll give you a ring,' he promised.

'Bye then,' she said, reserving belief. 'And Bill – be careful.'

It was too late for Ling's shop now – he wouldn't get there before it shut. That would have to wait until tomorrow. The American end, though – given the time difference, it would be a suitable moment to make some telephone calls. What he needed was a phone in a quiet place where he could not be disturbed. He thought automatically, and then wistfully, of Joanna. In a brief spasm of self-indulgent imagination he saw himself knocking at her door, being taken in, furnished with a drink, a sofa and the telephone, and afterwards offered supper and the luxury of Joanna to discuss it all with. He thought so much better when he thought aloud to her.

But her door was closed, and that was that. He turned his mind away from her as one determinedly pulling the tip of his tongue away from a mouth ulcer. The pain of thinking about her was more pleasant than not thinking about her, but every touch delayed healing. He didn't want to go home. He was getting almost superstitious about going home. In his own office he would be bound to be disturbed. That left Atherton.

He drove back to the station, parked down Stanlake Road,

and went in cautiously through the yard. Atherton's car was still there. He paused at the charge room door and saw Fergus perched on the edge of the desk eating a bacon sandwich and reading the *Standard*. He looked up as Slider appeared, and his face creased itself with concern.

'Where in th'hell have you been, Billy me darlin'? Haven't they been draggin' the lakes and rivers of Shepherd's Bush for you all day?'

'Oh, I've been busy,' Slider said vaguely. 'Fergus, can you get Atherton on the phone for me? I don't want to go up there in case somebody sees me.'

Fergus sighed gustily. 'You're cookin' trouble for yourself. Yerman Barrington's been havin' a conniption – wants to wind his case up and can't lay his hands on half his team.'

'He wasn't meant to. I need a couple more days. I'm getting somewhere at last.'

'Maybe you'd be better off not gettin' there,' Fergus warned. 'As the Chinese philosopher says, it is better to travel hopefully than to book yourself into the Deep Shit Hilton for a mid-week mini-break.' But he balanced the remaining half of his sandwich delicately on top of his tea-mug and reached for his telephone all the same. 'I'll give Boy Blue a bell for you, if that's what you want.'

'Mmm,' said Slider, deep in thought. He had to come back from some distance a moment later to register that Atherton was being pressed to his ear by O'Flaherty's meaty paw.

'Is something going on, Guv? Aren't you going to make an appearance?'

'I've still got some lines to follow up. What's been happening your end?'

Atherton told him about Amy Lam's story. 'It accords with what Leman said to Suzanne about being involved in a really big job, and being rich enough never to work again. I think you're right and it must all be connected after all, though for the life of me I can't see how.'

'Nor can I, yet, but now we see the direction we've got to keep going.'

'Yes,' Atherton said. 'More so than ever now. We've had a response from Hong Kong.'

'The dental profile?'

'Yes. The chip-shop corpse was definitely Michael Lam.'

'Ah!' said Slider.

Atherton was puzzled at the response. 'Is that what you expected?'

'I don't know. No, on the whole I think I thought that Lam really had gone to Hong Kong. I don't understand it yet – but I will. It's coming slowly.'

'What do you want us to do, then, Guv?'

'Do?'

'Mr Barrington's been in and out all day,' Atherton said delicately.

'Just – just don't say I've been in touch. I need a bit more time.'

'What about the Lam identification? Mr Barrington wants us to find a connection between him and Slaughter, so we can write it off as Slaughter murdering Lam and then committing suicide.'

'It's all right. Go along with it for now. I'm nearly there, I tell you. I'll sort it out with Barrington tomorrow.'

'But—'

'I need to make some phone calls. Can I use your house?'

'Yes, I suppose so. Yes, of course. You've got your key with you?'

'Yes, I have. Thanks. I'll see you later.' Slider put the phone down, and turned to face O'Flaherty's Atlantic-wind-roughened facade. 'You haven't seen me,' he said.

'I know there's no point in tellin' you,' Fergus said, 'but mountin' a crusade in his memory never did any dead man a tither o' good.'

Slider didn't even hear him. 'Didn't you say Seedy Barry ran a garden centre in Brunei Road?'

'That's right.'

'Do you know where he lives?'

'Right next door. One o' them converted council houses. You can't miss it – all over trellises and climbin' plants.'

'Thanks,' said Slider.

O'Flaherty watched him go thoughtfully, and then reached for his telephone.

There was nothing overtly seedy about Barry, and Slider concluded that his nickname referred to his present calling rather than any physical shortcomings. In fact he was really rather dapper, and apart from a few missing teeth he did have quite a strong resemblance to Leslie 'Oh Ashley' Howard in his heyday.

When Slider arrived at the much becreepered house, he found Seedy was expecting him.

'Come in, sir,' he said, holding the door wide. 'Mr O'Flaherty said you was coming, and I was to tell you what you want to know. Mr O'Flaherty's done me and mine a lot of favours over the years, and what he says goes with me.'

He closed the door and led Slider through into the lounge – a bright and cheerful room with a cherry-red carpet, wallpaper patterned with large orange circles, an imitation red-brick fireplace housing the electric fire, and the largest collection of brass ornaments and horse-brasses Slider had ever seen. There was a magnificent new three-piece suite in emerald green cut moquette, and in pride of place on the wall behind the sofa was a framed reproduction of the Chinese lady with the green face.

'Sit down, then, sir,' Seedy said kindly, gesturing towards

265

the sofa. Slider sat obediently, facing the brasses. There was a hatch in the wall to his right, and through it he glimpsed a fluorescent-lit kitchen and a woman tracking in and out of sight. There was an agreeable smell of boiling potatoes. 'My wife,' Seedy said, seeing the direction of his glance. 'We have our tea early, I'm afraid.'

'I won't keep you very long. I don't want to disturb your meal.'

'That's all right, sir. Stay and eat with us. There's plenty.

'Oh no, really, thanks—'

'It's no trouble.' Seedy cocked a knowing eye at him. 'Mr O'Flaherty said I was to look after you. Said you probably hadn't eaten all day. P'raps you'd like to join us.' Without waiting for Slider to answer, he stood up and moved towards the hatch. 'Nice bit of boiled bacon, pease pudding and potatoes, how about it?'

'No, thank you. Really. I've still got a lot to get through tonight. Thanks all the same.'

'Up to you,' Seedy said, gently closed the sliding door of the hatch and returned to sit in the chair diagonally opposite Slider, and said, 'All right then, what did you want to know? Tea'll be ten minutes, more or less.'

Slider nodded. 'It's about Jimmy Cole. I understand you know him?'

'Knew him before and after. Knew him when he was a kid, and I was sorry to see him get himself into trouble. He was a nice enough boy, but impressionable. Well, he paid dear for it, and I hope he's going to go straight from now on. I've told him I'll help him get a job. I've got plenty of contacts in the nursery business, and there's nothing better than an outdoor life when you've just spent ten years inside.'

'Ten years isn't much for killing a policeman,' Slider said neutrally.

266

Seedy eyed him sharply. 'It wouldn't be. And I've no time for that sort of thing, I'll tell you straight. I've done me crime and I've done me time but I never held with violence, and if I thought Jimmy had anything to do with shooting those two coppers, I wouldn't give him the time of day now. But the fact is everyone knows Jimmy never went near a gun in his life, never mind pull the trigger. It was that scumbag Blackburn done the job. Jimmy never even knew he had the shooter on him, I'd bet my life on that.'

'What do you know about that business?' Slider asked. 'There was something funny going on, wasn't there? I mean, what were Cole and Blackburn doing there anyway? I don't believe they were just having a drink.'

'Well, sir, from what I heard there were two jobs going on in the Carlisle that night. There was the regular drugs dealing, which the Bill were onto; and there was something else going down which nobody knew about except Jimmy and Derek Blackburn. But something went wrong, and instead of being out and away before the Bill turned up, Jimmy and Blackburn got caught up in the raid, and that's how come the shots got fired. Blackburn afterwards always swore he'd been fitted up, though, and he went on yelling double-cross until someone closed his mouth for him, permanent.'

'I thought he died in a brawl inside?' Slider said.

'That's the way it was,' Seedy said enigmatically. 'He'd only served three months. He was never a popular man – a foul mouthed, violent bastard if ever there was one. Well, three inches through the liver was enough to cure him of that. And there was more than one person interested in shutting him up. Word was someone was paid to do it, but no one ever owned up.'

The hatch was pulled back. 'On the table!' a woman's voice called from within the kitchen.

'Sure you won't stay?' Seedy asked, standing up. 'There's plenty.'

'No, thanks. I want to go and see Jimmy Cole now.'

'As you please. You'll want his address.' He walked out into the tiny hall and bent over the telephone table to write on the message pad, 'Tell him I say he's to tell you what you want to know. And tell him I'll be in touch with him in a day or two about that job. It's time he got himself something to do. Satan finds, as they say.'

'Thanks. I'll tell him.'

'I'll see you out,' said Seedy, a statement of undoubted fact since the hall was only two-foot-six wide and five foot long. Slider squeezed past him to the door, and Seedy added, 'He's gone back to live with his mum since he came out. No need to worry her with all this. Best take him down the pub if you want to ask him questions.'

Jimmy Cole's mum lived in Shirland Road, which was less than a mile from Atherton's house. Slider decided to go there first and put his American enquiries in hand, seeing he didn't know how long the next interview would take him. He had had a spare key to Atherton's house for two years now, and regarded it – rightly – as a very great gesture of affection and trust on Atherton's part. He wished he could have reciprocated, but Atherton had never been popular with Irene; and besides, he could think of no possible reason why Atherton would ever have wanted to go out to Ruislip, which agreeable suburb probably ranked in Atherton's estimation with the ditch he wouldn't be found dead in.

Slider let himself in, returned Oedipus's greeting, and fell in with his loud insistence that they retire together to the kitchen. Oedipus trotted ahead of him, tail straight up like a lightning rod, led him to the fridge, and then sat down and stared hard and meaningfully at its closed door. And they say cats don't communicate, Slider thought. He opened the fridge and found an opened tin of catfood, removed the front end of Oedipus from the lower shelf where it was investigating a hunk of pate wrapped in clingfilm, closed the fridge door, found a fork in the cutlery drawer and transferred the Kit-e-Kat to Oedipus's bowl. Oedipus sniffed it, gave him a hurt look, and then settled down resignedly to eat.

In Atherton's neat, elegant drawing-room, which smelled faintly of pot-pourri and rather more definitely of damp, Slider sat on the sofa, drew the telephone towards him across the coffee table, and laid his notebook beside it. He opened it at the page where he had copied in the names and numbers of Lee Chang's employer, landlord, and next-of-kin (a sister in Washington – both parents were apparently dead, and he had not married). He checked the time again by his watch, and began dialling.

Jimmy Cole's local pub turned out to be another Watney's house, and Slider sighed as he stood at the bar and watched two pints of the fizzy being drawn. Why didn't his investigations ever take him where they sold Charles Wells or Shepherd Neame?

Cole sat in a corner seat, smoking phlegmatically. He was an undersized creature with a bad complexion, thin, greasy hair, and a vacant look, and Slider had struggled to see in him the nice enough lad that Seedy Barry had mourned. But he had accepted Slider's arrival on his doorstep with docility, and when Slider brought the pints back and settled down to question him, he answered willingly. Slider got the impression he was glad of the attention. Jimmy Cole's one claim to fame was that he had once been on trial for murder, even if in the end he had gone down for nothing more than aiding and abetting.

Derek Blackburn, Slider gathered, was Cole's hero. They had lived in the same street, gone to the same school – though Cole was younger by four years – and Blackburn had gone out with Cole's older sister Pamela, on an on-off basis, for several years.

Blackburn had begun his life of crime virtually as soon as he could walk by stealing sweets from the corner shop. By the age of nine he had graduated to stealing car stereos, and thence to housebreaking where people were obliging enough to leave a window open. He specialised in old people's flats and bungalows, and was not averse to a bit of violence, as long as his victim was unlikely to fight back.

Amongst his peers he gained a reputation for violent temper, and for being quick to take offence and start a fight. He also slapped girls around – 'took no nonsense from them' was the way he put it himself – an attitude which was admired by his acolytes but not much emulated, since the girls in their group tended to slap right back. Pamela Cole broke finally with Blackburn after he blacked her eye outside a pub, but they remained on civil terms, and Blackburn continued to visit the Cole house as Jimmy's friend.

In April 1982 Blackburn came to call, took Jimmy up to his bedroom, and asked if he would be interested in working with him. He had a job on, he said, working for someone he called the Big Man, and he needed a driver. Blackburn, oddly enough, had never learned to drive, not even unofficially. There was something wrong with his coordination, and TDA remained the one common crime it was impossible for him to commit.

Jimmy, on the other hand, though he could barely read and write, had been able to drive anything of which he could reach the pedals for as long as he remembered. Blackburn would pay Jimmy out of what he made. He had already done

one job for the Big Man, and he paid really well. Jimmy wouldn't regret it. Slider gathered that Jimmy would have worked for nothing, just for the glory of being Derek's partner.

'And what was the job?' Slider asked.

'We had to collect some stuff from this pub and like drive it to this other place right out in the country. Easy job, Derek said – walk in, walk out.'

'What stuff was it?'

'I dunno. Derek never said. Just a box of stuff.'

'What size box?'

'I dunno. The way it turned out, I never saw it.'

'All right, tell me what happened.'

'Well, we like nicked this car and left it round the corner. Then we went in the pub and this bloke was s'posed to like give us the stuff but he never shows. Well, we been waiting hours, and Derek's getting antsy. Then the phone goes and—'

'You mean the pay phone on the wall by the bar?'

'Yeah. Well, the barman goes and answers it and he goes to Derek, "It's for you." He was like pissed off about it, the barman, 'cause he don't reckon people getting calls, 'cause he don't like having to answer it. But like Derek takes the call, and then he comes back and says we gotter go.'

'Who was the call from?'

'He never said. Anyway we goes out, like, as if we was going to the bogs, but there's another door there marked private, what goes out into the back way.'

'Yes, I know.'

'Well, Derek, he says the Bill's all round the place and there's gonner be a raid any minute, only he's had the tip-off, right? And there's this storeroom just inside the back door, and we've got to get in there, and when we hear the raid starting, we wait exactly one minute and then make a run for it, and there won't be no one covering the back door. Then we gotter climb over the garridge roof and down the wall the other side and we're clear.'

Slider was silent, deep in thought. Cate had changed Barrington's orders at the last minute, told him to wait thirty seconds then go in at the back door and straight to the bar, which would have left the back door unguarded. What was going on here? How could that have been coincidence? Who knew about the change of orders in time to tip off Derek Blackburn?

'Go on.'

'Well, we goes into the storeroom, and we hadn't hardly shut the door when the noise starts out the front, like in the pub, shouting and breaking glass and all stuff like that. So Derek starts counting—'

'Counting?'

'Well, it's dark in there, he can't see his watch. So he goes I'll count up to sixty, and that'll be like a minute. Well, he ain't finished when we hear the back door bust open, and all these people go running past. Then it goes quiet and he finishes counting and he reckons they've gone, so he says come on, and we gets out.'

He paused, not from any narrative genius but because he was not used to talking so much and his mouth had become dry. He took a swig of his beer and lit another cigarette from the butt of the last one.

'Go on. What happened?' Slider prompted when he had finished this ritual.

'I ferget where I was,' Jimmy confessed.

'You and Derek came out of the storeroom into the corridor.'

'Oh, yeah. Well, it was quiet out there, and we thought there was no one around. But when we come out we see these two coppers standing in the passage by the door.'

'Were they in uniform?'

272

'No, ornry close. But we knew they was coppers. Anyway someone shouts out behind us, and we looks round and there's another of 'em just up the stairs. I was so scared I just stood there, but Derek grabs me arm and shouts come on, and then there was this bang and flash and the coppers in front of us fall down.'

'Just a minute – how many bangs?'

'I dunno. Two or three. It all happened so fast. I was that bloody scared I nearly shat meself. I never had nothing to do with no shooters before. So when them coppers go down me and Derek runs for it, out the back door, and over the garridge roof like we was told. Then we gets back to the car and I drives back to Derek's.'

'All right, let's just go back to the gunshots for a moment,' Slider said. 'When you and Derek came out of the storeroom, it was dark in the passage, wasn't it?'

'Yeah. Not pitch black, like, but dark.'

'And you were looking at the two detectives anyway, so you didn't see Derek put his hand in his pocket and bring out the gun.' Cole stared uncomprehendingly. Slider went on, 'He grabbed your arm and shouted "Let's get out of here", and the shots were fired and the two detectives fell to the ground. Derek fired the shots so that you could escape.'

'Derek never had no gun,' Cole said.

'The gun was found in his room the next day.'

'It was the cops put that there when they come to search,' Derek said. He said he never had no gun. He was fitted up.'

'Well, he would say that, wouldn't he?'

Jimmy Cole stared in silence, his face working painfully as he struggled with the unaccustomed effort of thought. 'Yeah,' he said suddenly, the blockage clearing with a rush. 'But I know he never fired them shots. I know because they come from behind me.'

'What?'

'Yeah,' he said with growing confidence, "cause I felt one come past me, like, right past me ear. It kind of buzzed like a fly or sunnink right past me ear.'

'Came past you? Are you sure?'

'Yeah, course I'm sure.'

'What did Derek say about it?'

'He never said nothing about it.'

'You didn't discuss the shooting with him? Even though you saw two policemen gunned down?'

'I was like upset, and Derek, he was white as a sheet. But he never said nothing, not while I was driving him home.'

'What happened when you got back to his house? Did you go in?'

'No. He got out, and he said to me to go home, and he said to me, he said not to worry, everything would be all right. He said nobody had nothing on us, and if anyone was to ask, we'd gone to the Carlisle for a drink, and then run out the back when the Bill bust in, and that's all.'

That, Slider thought, was the oddest thing of all. If Blackburn had shot two policemen, he ought to have been working out some kind of story with Cole, or else to have been planning to make a run for it. On the other hand, if Blackburn hadn't fired the shots, it was surely beyond belief that he would not discuss it with Cole. Above all, when they were arrested, why did neither of them mention this strange story?

'You didn't say anything about this to the police,' Slider said at last. 'About the shots being fired from behind you.' Cole shook his head. 'Why was that? You were arrested for shooting the two policemen—'

'I told you,' Cole interrupted, 'Derek says to me to say nothing. See, after I went home, like, that night, Derek phones me up and he says it's all taken care of. We got to say we was having a quiet drink, and we don't know nothing about no shooting, and he says no matter what they ask you, you just keep saying that, and it'll all be taken care of.'

'Taken care of by whom?'

Cole shrugged. 'Derek says everything'll be all right as long as we don't say nothing.'

And what Derek said was plainly law. 'But it wasn't all right, was it? You did ten years. And Derek got life.'

Cole struggled with the logic, but it was beyond him. 'I never had nothing to do with no shooting. I just said what Derek said to say. And he said we'd be took care of all right as long as we kept our mouths shut.'

'But Derek didn't keep his mouth shut, did he?' Slider asked. 'When he was in the Scrubs, he started to complain that he'd been fitted up.'

'Yeah,' said Cole.

'And now he's dead.'

'Yeah.' The thought seemed to depress him. 'Maybe that's why—'

'Yes?' Slider encouraged.

Cole struggled again, mouth open. 'Maybe with him complaining and that, maybe they reckoned we hadn't, like, done what we was supposed to. Maybe that's why I done ten years.'

'You think that if he'd kept his mouth shut, you'd have got out sooner?'

'Well, he said we'd be took care of,' Cole said simply. 'Maybe like Derek messed it up for me. I never thought of that before.'

You were taken care of, Slider thought, you and Blackburn both. Blackburn was dead. Cole, who knew too little to be a danger to anyone, who was too stupid to be believed whatever he said, was tucked away for ten years.

'Have you got any idea who it was that Derek was working for? Who tipped him off about the raid? Who told him he'd be all right if he kept his mouth shut?' Cole had been shaking his head all through this, and Slider pressed on, 'Are you sure he never let a name drop, or a hint? You needn't be afraid to tell me now, you know. You must have some idea who it was?'

'No, I don't know who it was,' Cole said, and then, meeting Slider's eyes, 'I'd tell you if I did. Barry says I've to tell you everything.'

'Did you ever hear a hint while you were in prison, from another prisoner, for instance? A suspicion about who was behind it?'

Cole shook his head again. 'I dunno if Barry might know,' he added. 'He knows everyone. He might've heard.'

Barry was obviously slated to take Blackburn's place as Jimmy Cole's instructor, boss, and hero. Well, he must be better for him than Blackburn.

17

What Cate Did

Having enjoined Cole to absolute silence on the subject, and
advised him to see Seedy about a job, Slider saw him home
and then went back to his car. The beer had blown him out,
and acting on his empty stomach and his tension it was giving
him heartburn. There was a tight knot of pain under his ribs
which was probably wind but felt like an impending heart
attack. He was aching with tiredness, and thought longingly
of Joanna. Would she be home, awake, thinking of him? He
wanted her so badly he was hallucinating the smell of her
skin. He wanted to bury himself in her up to the eyebrows
and never come out again.

He had been driving without direction, but now he saw a
telephone box up ahead beside the road. He stopped alongside
it, put on the handbrake, reached for the ignition. In his mind
he had run on ahead, gone into the box, shoved in the money,
dialled, heard her answer. But there he stopped. What could
he say to her? Take me back, and I promise I'll leave Irene?
But he couldn't leave Irene. That was what it had all been
about, wasn't it? Joanna had known it before him. He couldn't

do it. It was wrong, that was all, and there was enough wrong in the world without him adding to it.

He put the car back in gear, took off the handbrake, drove on. Irene had done nothing to deserve to be hurt. She had always been a good and faithful wife, and if he didn't love her, that was his fault, not hers. And the children – all the experts said they preferred having their own two parents, however ill-matched, to a break-up. All right, so he knew what he had to do. He had to go home, and try to be a good husband and father in the time that was left.

But not yet. The prospect filled him with such a sense of emptiness that he could not face it. Besides, he rationalised instantly, he had to discuss the case with somebody – not with somebody, with Atherton. He had to keep him up to date on developments. And he had to check Atherton's answering-machine for replies from America. He would ring home from there, and explain that he would be working all night again.

'So you think the Big Man, whoever he was,' said Atherton, 'was reassured by Cole's complete stupidity, and didn't feel anything needed to be done about him, one way or the other?'

'It's a fact that he hasn't been able to do any harm,' Slider said. He was sitting in the big armchair with one of Atherton's magnificent club sandwiches on a plate on his lap, and a glass of whisky on one broad arm of the chair. On the other arm Oedipus was sitting. He had his eyes tightly shut as though to avoid temptation, but his diesel-engine purr gave him away.

Slider was aware of a sense of comfort – of having been comforted, perhaps. Atherton had taken him in, had agreed that he should stay the night, had fed and watered him. And when he had phoned Irene, she had been understanding. She didn't mind at all, she said – and by the way, did he think he'd be home tomorrow evening? Probably not; why? Oh, it was just an invitation to supper with Marilyn and David and Ernie Newman. It was a last-minute invitation, but Bernice was free to babysit. David and Marilyn's photos from their holiday in Turkey had come back and they were going to show them. Why didn't she go anyway, without him? Well, she'd quite like to, if he really didn't mind. And Slider had said, with perfect truth, that he didn't, and that he was glad she wouldn't be left alone at home for yet another evening.

So with Irene at least partly off his conscience, he was able to enjoy Atherton's hospitality, and unburden his mind of one part of the problem.

'Anyway, would you put Cole in the box with any confidence?' he continued.

'The CPS certainly wouldn't,' Atherton said, 'which is more to the point. But if Cole was telling the truth about the shots, it means that there was someone else in the passage. Unless you're suggesting that it was Dickson fired the shots? No, cancel that,' he added hastily as Slider looked up. 'Of course it wasn't him.' He took a bite of his own sandwich, and Oedipus's eyes opened a yellow crack to watch for falling prawns. 'But then, who?'

'The way I see it,' Slider said slowly, 'is that, assuming for the moment that Cole is telling the truth, Blackburn must have known who fired those shots. Either he saw the man and recognised him when he looked round, or he had a telephone call later that night about it. My feeling is that it was both. If he didn't know who had fired the shots, I can't believe he wouldn't have said something to Cole on the drive home. But he simply told him to keep his mouth shut. Later that night he telephoned and confirmed the instructions. He was completely confident that it would be all right, and went on being confident until he found himself banged up in gaol and no appeal in the offing. Then he started to complain loudly and vociferously.'

'And got knifed.'

'Very professionally. All right, then who did he see in the passage? It must surely either have been the Big Man, whoever he was, or someone who worked for him, otherwise why the confidence?'

Slider put down his sandwich and looked steadily, if a little reluctantly, at his friend.

'I think it was Cate. Look,' he ticked off on his fingers, 'he discovers Blackburn's still inside the pub when the raid is about to start, because the man with the goods hasn't turned up. So he tips Blackburn off, gives him alternative instructions, which involve escaping from the back door. Barrington's orders about covering the back door were changed just before the raid started. Dickson messed it up by not following his orders to the letter. Cate afterwards blamed Dickson for Field's death, saying he should have obeyed his orders and stayed outside.'

Atherton shook his head unhappily. 'Go on. If it was Cate, why do you think he shot the two detectives?'

'We know he went in at the front when the raid started. He probably met Barrington coming through from the back, and went out there just to check that his two pals were safely off the premises. He'd have to order a thorough search at some point, or it would look odd. Maybe he meant to see them getting away over the roofs and give the alarm when it was just too late. I don't know about that. But when he came through into the end of the passage what he saw was disaster – the two DCs between his men and the door. I think he fired off a couple of rounds in sheer desperation, probably meaning to scare Field and Wilson so that Blackburn and Cole could run past them, but he hit them instead. In the event, that did just as well, because once he'd planted the gun in Blackburn's wardrobe – and remember, he went in person to do the search – he could be sure Blackburn would go down and be put away where he could do no harm. And afterwards, when Blackburn started complaining – it's easy enough for someone with criminal connections to get a man inside done away with, especially if he's a foul-mouthed, unpleasant sort of a bastard.'

There was a silence when he stopped speaking, except for the ticking of the clock and the purring of the cat. Then Atherton said, 'It's the whole cloth, Guv. I can't see anyone believing it. I don't really believe it myself. You've no proof that Cate ever did anything dishonest in his life, much less was involved with criminal activities. He's a respected businessman now – all right, I know you don't have much of an opinion of businessmen, but he's well-respected in police and government circles too. The only suspicious circumstance is the change to Barrington's orders, which coincided with Blackburn's instructions for getting out. But someone could have overheard Cate telling Barrington, and dashed off to phone.'

'Only another policeman. No one else could have got near enough to hear. And how could he have got away from everyone to use the phone?'

'How could Cate?'

'He was the guv'nor. He could walk away from any group, and they'd think he was going to another. He only had to nip round a dark corner. He had a mobile phone when I saw him in the golf club. He could have had one that night.'

Atherton tried again. 'But surely if what you believe is true someone must have suspected something – Barrington, at least. Or Dickson.'

'I think they did, I think Barrington suspected very badly, and that's why he's so protective of Cate now, and admires him so much. The more he admires him, the more he can

281

put those suspicions away in a box he never opens. Cate is the untouchable to him. And I think Dickson also suspected, maybe suspected before that day that Cate's many connections with the underworld were more than just for information-gathering. Possibly he voiced some tentative doubts to Barrington – which is why Barrington hated him so much. And perhaps why Dickson distrusted the top brass. And perhaps—' He stopped.

'Perhaps why top brass was always so down on Dickson?' Atherton guessed shrewdly. 'Come on, Bill, that's going too far. If you're beginning to suspect grand conspiracy—'

'Not grand conspiracy. Just a huddling together in the face of a cold wind.' He stared at his hand, rubbing it thoughtfully. 'You can have doubts about someone almost without knowing it, and then feel guilty because you've doubted him. And Cate was very charming and popular, which Dickson never was. Given a choice of who to support—'

Atherton finished his sandwich without tasting it, stood up, reached for Slider's glass. 'Refill?' He crossed to the table, poured more whisky for both, and returned to his seat. 'Well, what are you going to do with this?' he asked at last.

'Nothing,' Slider said. 'I've thought and thought, but I can't see that there's anything to be done. The only remaining witness is Cole, and he doesn't know much, and would never be believed anyway. And as you say, I've no proof of anything, and if I can't convince you that my suspicions are reasonable, I'll never convince anyone else.'

'Then – all this was for nothing?'

'I had to do it,' Slider said. 'Once I'd started wondering—'

'Yes, I see that.'

'And injustice to Dickson.'

Atherton did not concur with that. Dead was dead. Nothing could improve Dickson's lie now.

282

'But it's important anyway,' Slider went on, 'as part of the whole picture about Cate. I think he was a dodgy number when he was in the Job, and when he left it, I think he went on being dodgy. And I think he's up to something very big at the moment which we happen to have stumbled across the corner of. It wouldn't surprise me if he hadn't set the whole thing up on Dickson's ground for the very reason that Dickson would be the last person to accuse him of anything publicly – or the second-last, I should say. Because when Dickson died – well, Barrington's appointment was very quick, wasn't it? Suppose somebody had put in a word for him – someone with the ear of the Commissioner, and with both reputation and influence in elevated circles? What do you think?'

Atherton sighed. 'Honestly?'

'Honestly.'

'I think you're mad. No, I think you're tired. I think you ought to down that scotch and go to bed. You can have my bed, if you like, and I'll sleep on the sofa. You need a good night's sleep more than I do. And tomorrow—'

'Tomorrow I may get some answers from America,' Slider said. 'And I've got one more person to see – someone who may have quite a lot to tell me about Mr Cate. But there are some things I'd like you to do for me.'

'You're incorrigible,' Atherton said. 'All right. What?'

'Ask your friend Kim if there's any way he can get information out of the Chinese Embassy without going through the Foreign Office. I want to know whether Chou Xiang Xu was here officially or unofficially and why, what his position was, and where he is now if possible.'

'All right. What else?'

'Try Mrs Stevens with a picture of Cate. It occurs to me that she might have mistaken silver hair for blond, given those yellow street lamps.'

For the first time Atherton looked shaken. 'Yes,' he said thoughtfully. 'And if anyone would be likely to have a camel coat, it would be Cate, judging by what you've told me about his taste.'

'That's what I thought,' said Slider.

He was sitting outside the shop in his car at half-past eight when Peter Ling arrived. Ling had the key in the lock when Slider got out of the car, and he looked round and a fleeting expression of fear crossed his face which made Slider stop dead a few feet off and reach for his card.

'Peter Ling? I'm Detective Inspector Slider of Shepherd's Bush CID.'

Ling smiled a little, but his eyes did not relax. 'I was afraid you'd come to rob me,' he said.

'Sorry if I startled you,' Slider said.

'You read things all the time,' Ling said. 'I suppose you're after a discount?'

'No, nothing like that. I'd just like to ask you a few questions.'

'Oh,' he said uncertainly. Then, 'You'd better come in.'

There was nothing particularly Asian about his looks, except for his very thick, very black hair, which he wore blow-waved elegantly upwards at the sides, and his dark eyes which, though they showed no epicanthic fold, seemed somehow to lack eyelids. He locked the door of the shop behind them, and said, 'You'd better come through to the back. If anyone sees me through the window they'll want the shop opened.' He led the way through, and glanced back to say, 'You'd be surprised how many policemen I get in here. You all seem to be computer-mad these days.'

'I understand from the lads at Fulham that you give them extra discount?'

284

'Self defence,' he said with another tight smile. 'If they're in my shop all the time, I'm less likely to be robbed.'

In the back office Ling gave Slider a chair and took another for himself. 'Well, what can I do for you?' he asked.

'I want to know everything you can tell me about Colin Cate.'

An extraordinary expression came over Ling's face, of fear, suspicion – distaste? Slider wondered what his first words would be: a denial, or perhaps just the inevitable, 'Why do you want to know?' But in fact Ling said nothing, and after a pause, Slider realised he didn't intend to say anything, and that they would sit here in silence until the world turned to coal unless Slider did the next bit of talking. Most people can't bear a silence, and feel obliged to put something into it – a fact of human nature of the greatest possible benefit to policemen. Ling's was self-control on a grand scale – or was it perhaps caution?

Slider put his hands on his knees and his cards on the table. 'I'd better tell you straight away that this is not an official enquiry. No one knows I'm here, and I don't want anyone to know. Anything you tell me is in confidence. But I have a strong suspicion that Colin Cate is mixed up in something illegal, and I want to get to the bottom of it. I also think he did the dirty on an old friend of mine, and I'd like to get to the bottom of that, too. You see I'm not hiding anything from you. I've put you in a position do me a lot of harm if you're a friend of his—'

'No,' Ling said harshly. Slider paused. No, what? In the end, since Ling seemed deep in internal debate, he had to ask it aloud.

'No, I'm not a friend of his,' Ling answered with some vehemence.

'But you were once, weren't you?'

'I don't think so,' Ling said. 'An employee, certainly. A dependant, perhaps. In his debt. In his power – but a friend? Colin didn't have friends.' He looked at Slider for a long moment, as if to gauge his calibre, and then he said in a manner so without overtones it was almost demure, 'We were lovers.'

Even after Shax, it was a surprise to hear it confirmed. Oddly, the first thing that crossed Slider's mind was to wonder if Tufty knew, and what the golf club would think. And then he wondered briefly and blindingly about Barrington, and quickly shoved the thought as far away to the back of his mind as he could manage without a broom-handle.

'I see,' he said neutrally.

'Do you?' Ling countered. Slider wondered if this was going to be one of those tedious emotional conversations where every fill-in word was analysed and flung back challengingly.

'I hope to. Why don't you tell me everything, from the beginning? Start with how you first met.'

'He bought the computer shop I was working in. The bloke who started it – Dave – was computer nuts, but he had no business sense, so he got into trouble. Colin came along looking for something to put his money into, bought Dave out, made me manager, and set Dave up as manager in a new shop. That's how the chain was born,' he added with what might have been irony. 'Compucate's – the last word in computer know-how.'

'It sounds entirely laudable,' Slider said. 'Wealth creation. Job creation.'

'That's right. He was a man of the eighties.' Ling looked down at his hands. 'I wasn't ungrateful. And of course he liked people to be grateful.'

'Was that why—?'

'No,' Ling said quickly, looking up. 'Do I look like that sort of person?'

Slider shook his head, at a loss. 'How did it happen, then?'

'He used to come in the shop just about closing time to ask how things were going. It was his baby, that first shop, but he was more interested in it as a business – it could have been selling knitting wool for all he cared. Although he always liked gadgets. He liked machines.' He paused and looked enquiringly as Slider stirred.

'It's all right, I've just thought of something.' He had just remembered the other computer reference he hadn't been able to pin down: Leman's publican boss saying that Leman knew his way round a circuit board all right. 'It's nothing important. Please go on.'

'Well, one day he asked me why I was so fascinated by computers, and I told him they are the greatest power of all. The man who controls the computer controls the world, I said. He seemed very struck by that and asked me if I could teach him. So I did. He was really keen,' Ling added with a small, reminiscent smile. 'And quick, too. He never had to ask anything twice. He had a wonderful brain. Well, I suppose he still has. I don't know why I'm talking as if he was dead.'

'Because he's dead to you, perhaps?'

Ling looked struck with this piece of psychobabble. 'Yes. You really do understand, don't you?'

'You see and hear a lot in this job,' Slider said gravely. 'So it was while you were teaching him about computers—?'

'He'd come through to the back of the shop after I locked up, and we'd sit down in front of the screen together.' One day our hands met accidentally on the keyboard and something electric passed between us, Slider thought. 'We'd go for a drink afterwards. Then one day it was a meal. Afterwards he took me to this house he owned, that was let out as bedsits. There was an empty room – I was still living at home, you see. And after that he said why didn't I move into the room so that we could see each other whenever we wanted.' He shrugged. 'So I did.'

'Did he charge you rent?'

The question seemed to offend Ling. 'It was for his convenience as much as mine. Once the shop started doing well and I was on profit-sharing I could have afforded to rent a place myself, but I preferred to save the money towards buying somewhere later on. The financial question never came into it. We loved each other, you see.' The animation left his face. 'He really did love me. I don't suppose you'll believe that, but—'

'Of course I do,' Slider said, obedient to the cue.

'I was his first,' Ling said dreamily. 'He'd never even thought about it before – it came as a complete surprise to him. He was married and everything. He had a struggle to overcome his prejudices. But when he did, it was wonderful. And we were faithful to each other. That's why it lasted. It's the ones who aren't exclusive who get into trouble.'

'Did you give him a ring?' Slider said on impulse.

Ling looked suspicious. 'Why do you ask that?'

'I noticed he was wearing a ring in the shape of a skull. I thought it was an odd thing for a man like him to wear.'

'He thought it was cute, or funny, or something. He saw it on a stall in Portobello Road one day. We were just mooching about looking for bargains. Anyway, he bought this ring and had two copies made in gold, and gave one to me. He always wore his, and I wore mine till we broke up, and then I gave it back to him. I wasn't sorry about *that*, at least – I always thought it was ugly. Not me at all.'

'So why did you break up?'

'He changed. I don't know why, but he got harder. He started dabbling in things I didn't like. And he started going with other people. I wasn't going to stand that. What did he think I was? He told me to put up and shut up, but I wasn't having it, even if he did employ me. Then he asked me to do something dishonest, and that was the end of that. We had a blazing row, and he sacked me, and told me to get out of the house as well. So I was glad I'd saved up the money after all. I put it into this business, and went back to living with my mum and dad. They'd moved down here by then, to Fulham.'

'Did they know about your relationship with Cate?'

'Dad didn't. Mum sort of guessed, but she'd never say anything. She's quick on the uptake, Mum is. It was her that showed me the bit in the newspaper about Ronnie Slaughter topping himself. 'You got out just in time," she said. "He'd have driven you to it in the end."'

'You knew Ronnie, of course?'

'He lived next door to me in the same house,' Ling said with a shrug. 'But he was very shy. He hardly ever spoke to me. And I think he might have been a bit jealous of Colin visiting me there. He worshipped Colin, you see.'

'How do you mean, worshipped?'

'What d'you think? Poor old Ronnie got the fuzzy end of the lolly all his life. It's no fun being gay when you look like him. Then Colin picked him up out of the gutter, gave him a good job and a nice place to live, treated him like a human being. Ronnie would have died for him. Or killed. He'd have burned down Buckingham Palace if Colin asked him to.'

Slider nodded thoughtfully. Killed for him, or died for him? Or perhaps even both. 'How did he meet Ronnie in the first place?'

'Hanging around the Crooked Billet. Ronnie was, I mean. Colin used to go there a lot. I suppose he still does,' he added bitterly. 'He must make his pick-ups somewhere. Though I suppose he's still got his regulars tucked away in bedsitters.

Caged rabbits – visit them at his own convenience on his own premises, the way he used to visit me.'

'Have you ever heard of a man called Peter Leman?' Slider asked on impulse.

Ling nodded, biting his lip. 'He's one of them. He worked at one of the shops for a while, till Colin picked him up. He was the first Colin was unfaithful with. I like to think he chose him because he looked a little bit like me.' His eyes slid sideways. 'Of course his name isn't really Peter Leman. Colin made a new identity for him, called him Peter after me, and Leman – that's an Old English word for sweetheart, did you know that? He called him that because he knew I'd find out. He just wanted to hurt me.'

'Do you know what his real name is?'

'No. He was one of Colin's waifs and strays. He set him up and just made a puppet of him, gave him everything. That's how he does it – makes them dependants. He likes them grateful, you see.'

'Why?'

'So that they're his willing slaves. Nice to have someone to get their hands dirty on your behalf, don't you think? And he can play them off one against the other, too – do as I say or I'll chuck you and go to X instead. And of course he likes to be sure they keep their mouths shut.'

'About what?'

Raised eyebrows. 'You don't think he wants people to know he's gay, do you? That would put the lid on all his committees and clubs, wouldn't it? The highly respected pillar of the community. The golf club would probably ask him to resign.'

'Oh, surely that sort of thing is quite acceptable nowadays?'

'Much you know,' Ling said shortly, and relapsed into a brooding silence.

'What was the dishonest thing he wanted you to do that caused the final break-up?' Slider asked after a moment.

Ling came back slowly. 'Oh – he wanted me to put something through the books to clear it. He said it was just a technicality, to speed up the export licence, but when I started asking questions, he clammed up and told me to mind my own business. I told him it was my business, and that I wasn't going to put my name to something I didn't know all about, and he said all I needed to know was that he was boss, and I should do what I was told. So then I knew it was something dodgy, and I refused point blank, and that was that'

'What was it he wanted put through the books?' Slider asked.

'A consignment of hardware for the Iraqi government. That was before the invasion of Kuwait, of course.'

'What sort of hardware?'

'Oh, just ordinary office computers. There was nothing against selling to Iraq as long as it wasn't military equipment. That's why I reckoned there must have been more to it than met the eye.'

'You think the computers might have had a military application?'

'Why not? Everything depends on computers nowadays. Like I said, the man who controls them controls the world. There's nothing you can't do if you've got the right gear.'

'So I suppose if you got hold of the right gear, you could get a high price for it?'

'Sky's the limit.' Ling grew animated. 'Listen, those new fighter planes can launch a missile and put it through one window of an office block a hundred miles away. You don't know it's coming. You don't even know the plane's there. You never see it. It never sees you. Just suddenly, out of the blue – voomp!' He made a mushroom cloud with his hands.

'Pin-point accuracy. All done by on-board computers. And what controls those computers? A microchip. A little bit of silicone not much bigger than my thumbnail.'

Slider was silent, things falling into place in his mind. He formulated his next question slowly, carefully. 'If you were to hear that Colin Cate was involved in some kind of illegal deal, something to do with computers, something that was worth so much money that it was planned months ahead – something so important it was worth killing three people to protect—'

Ling's lips grew pale. 'I don't want to know about it,' he said quickly. 'Don't tell me anything. I don't want to know.'

'Could a microchip be worth that?' Slider said, leaning forward. 'A stolen microchip?'

Ling's eyes were distant, viewing a desolate landscape. 'Say someone developed a new chip – something to do with weapons systems – or with an anti-missile defence system – a completely new capability – that's happening all the time. And say someone else managed to steal that chip before it could be put into production—'

'A prototype?'

'Yes, if you like. If someone stole that prototype and could get it to someone else who wanted to produce it—'

'Who? Who would want to do that?'

He shrugged. 'It would have to be a government, because of the funds and facilities involved – an individual or a company just wouldn't be that powerful. But it would have to be a country outside of the cosy UN circle, with a government able to put the thing to work in secret and make sure people kept their mouths shut about what they'd got and where it came from.'

'A country like Iraq?'

'Iraq couldn't do it. Not now.'

'What about China?'

'Yes. They've got the facilities and the money, and they want the capabilities. China would buy.'

'And how much would they be prepared to pay?'

He shrugged again. 'Write down a number,' he said elliptically.

'Millions?'

'Billions,' said Ling.

18

Lam to the Slaughter

When Joanna opened the door, she had a numb and congested look to her face as though she had been asleep, and she stared at Atherton with a just-woken sort of blankness.

'I thought I'd come and see if you're all right,' he said.

'Oh. Yes. Well, that's nice of you. Come in,' she added with belated hospitality. She led him into the living-room. There was music scattered about on the floor, and her fiddle was propped upright in the corner of an armchair with the bow laid across the chair arms. 'I was just marking in some bowings,' she said, scuffing the sheets together with a bare foot. She stopped in the middle of it and looked up at him. 'Would you like a drink, or is it too early? Silly question. What would you like?'

'Have you got a beer, by any chance?'

'I think there's a lager. Will that do?'

'Yes. Fine.'

'All right. Make yourself comfortable. I'll just . . .' she said vaguely. She scuffed the sheets further out of the way, and then went out towards the kitchen. Wandered, was perhaps the right word.

Left alone, Atherton stooped first and gathered up the music and put it in a pile in the armchair with the fiddle, then looked around the room for information. She had never been houseproud, but there was an air of neglect about the room. The dust was thicker than usual on the surfaces; there were dead flowers in a vase on the bookcase; opened and unopened mail littered the telephone table; an empty mug stood on the mantelpiece; and a record lay dumb on the turntable of the record-player, its empty cover forlornly on the floor. He walked over to look at it. Elgar's second symphony, a reissue of the famous Barbirolli-LPO recording. Strong stuff, he thought. Good for weeping to if you felt that way inclined.

She came back in with a glass of lager in one hand and a whisky in the other. She had obviously taken the opportunity to splash water over her face, for it looked a little less puffy, though shinier, and the edges of her hair were damp.

'Here we are. It's only Sainsbury's. I hope you can drink that,' she said with a fair approximation of cheerfulness.

'Thanks,' he said. 'Cheers.'

'Cheers.' She sat in the corner of the Chesterfield with one foot tucked under her, and he sat correspondingly at the other end so that he could face her. 'Well.'

'Well,' he said. 'How are you?'

'Did Bill send you to find out?'

'He doesn't know I'm here. I came because I wanted to know.'

'I'm coping.'

'Really?'

'Just about. Fortunately I've got quite a lot, on at the moment, including this beastly school concert.' She gestured towards the music. 'There's about eight of us do it. We go into schools that have school orchestras and we sit in and lead the sections. We rehearse in the morning then give a concert to the rest of the school in the afternoon. We do about three a year and it's horribly hard work and we don't get paid, but it's supposed to encourage the young entry. Though why in God's name we want to encourage more of the little beasts to become musicians when there isn't enough work for us all as it is, is beyond me. Still, it seems to be the thing to do. The worst part about it is having to stay to school dinner with them. I still have psychological scars from eating school dinners. Do you remember spam fritters, or are you too young? I can never quite work out how old you are.' She took a breath and looked at him. 'I can hear myself talking. Will you for God's sake say something and stop me.'

'I don't know what to say. I didn't think you'd take it this hard.'

'Oh, you thought I was just a careless little homebreaker did you? Desperate for a man, and any man would do?' Before he could answer she waved a hand back and forth in the air, rubbing out the words. 'No, cancel that. I can't think of any reason in the world why I should be rude to you.'

'Because I came here asking for it. I've given you my opinion unasked before now. I was always willing to interfere.'

'You were against us in the beginning,' she said. 'You wanted me to leave him alone. I'm not sure now you weren't right.'

'He really loves you.'

'I know. But it doesn't seem to be enough, does it?'

Atherton stirred restively. 'Oh, come on, you must have known it would be hard for someone like him to break away.'

'Yes, of course I did. But not this hard. I thought by now he would have argued the whole thing out with himself and come to his decision, but it never seems to get any better.'

'And now you don't want him any more.'

'Of course I want him. But he's got to want me – so much,'

296

she anticipated his protest, 'that the price seems worth paying. I just don't think he thinks it is.'

Atherton shook his head, not in negation but to indicate it was all beyond him.

'How is he? How's he taking it?' she asked after a moment.

'Well, he's keeping busy, like you. But I don't know whether he's coping. I was against it at the start,' he said, meeting her eyes, 'but now I wonder whether you really can break it off. I don't know whether he can manage without you.'

'He did before we met.'

'You don't miss what you've never had. It's different now. He's got used to sharing everything with you.' He sighed, not wanting to say the sort of things he was saying. 'This job – it takes a lot out of you. We each have to find a way to cope.'

'And what's yours?'

'Sometimes I get so sick of it,' he said reluctantly. 'The squalor and the stupidity and the waste. People think it's a glamorous job, but it's not. A lot of it's boring and a lot of it's just plain nasty. And most of the villains are so utterly stupid and gormless—'

She nodded encouragingly.

'Often I wonder why I'm doing it – when it seems more nasty than usual. But then I think, someone's got to.' He half smiled. 'And then when I'm being less self-deceptively noble, I think, what else could I do? Once you're in it's hard to get out. It's your family, you see. More than that, it's your – your justification. When you're a copper, you're larger than yourself because you're part of the whole. Out there, on the outside, you'd just be you, all on your own, very small and alone. So you stay in.'

'Yes,' she said. 'I do see that.'

'I bear it better than Bill because I'm detached,' he said, and hearing that that didn't quite explain it, he raised his

297

hands before him like a man demonstrating the size of a fish, trying to take a grip on what he meant. 'You see, to us there are two sorts of people – those who commit crimes, and those who don't – and the difference is absolute, it's fundamental. To me, I'm different from a criminal in such a fundamental way that I don't take any colour from them. But Bill doesn't really see himself as separate from the misery he works in. To be truthful, he doesn't see himself at all. The ability to stand back from your own personality and view it as if it were a third party is not a universal gift.'

'No,' she agreed. 'Not universal and not a gift.'

'I don't know about that,' he said, waving away what he thought was an irrelevant aside. 'But he hasn't got it. And what it means is that he needs you far more than you will ever need him.'

'Don't be so sure about my needs.'

'I know that you can watch yourself suffering and rationalise it. I don't think Bill can do that. And that makes it harder.'

'It's in his own hands,' she said helplessly. 'It always was.' Atherton said nothing. 'You're worried about him. What's he done?'

Atherton sat forward, clasping his hands between his knees. 'He was always an independent sort of worker. But our new boss likes everything done by the book. Now Bill's gone off trying to hunt down a man our boss thinks is the bee's knees. I think he's going to get himself into trouble.'

'What do you want me to do about it?'

'He's been in trouble before, of course, but I'm not sure this time if he'll be able to cope. I'm not sure, now, if he'll even want to.'

'What do you want me to do about it?'

'Nothing. I don't know. It's not for me to say—'

'You think I ought to take him back, tell him that he doesn't

298

have to leave home, that I'll just be his mistress – is that it?' He didn't answer, looking at the carpet angrily. 'But that wouldn't work either. That wouldn't make him happy.'

'At least you'd be giving him the choice,' he flashed. 'What choice does he have this way? You're blackmailing him!'

He stood up and walked over to the fireplace, and kicked the bottom of the surround, though he managed to pull his kick at the last moment and damaged neither his toecap nor the wood.

'There's no right answer,' she said.

'I know,' he muttered, his back turned to her. 'That's what makes me angry – not being able to do anything about any of it.' She didn't say anything. 'Well, I suppose I'd better get back,' he said. 'I just slipped out for a moment, just to see how you were.'

'Thanks,' she said. Her voice sounded so peculiar that he turned to look at her at the same moment as she stood up, and seeing her expression he moved towards her and took her in his arms. She held on to him tightly. A woman he'd never seen before had once held onto him like that, when he had broken the news to her that her husband had been killed in a car accident. There was no sex in it, or even affection. He might have been anyone.

'I suppose we'll just have to wait and see how it comes out,' he said kindly. She wasn't crying, just holding on to him, her arms round his waist, her face pressed against his chest. He held her quietly, and after a while bent and laid his lips against the top of her head.

The Crown and Sceptre, Melina Road, was a Fuller's pub, thank heaven. Atherton was already there when Slider arrived, seated at a corner table facing the door, with two pints in front of him.

'Thanks,' Slider said.

'For the pint or my presence?' Atherton asked tautly.

'Both,' Slider said, taking the top two inches down.

'I'm putting my neck on the block for you,' Atherton grumbled. 'I hope you're at least going to tell me what it's all about.'

'I am now. I'm sorry for the way it's happened, but I don't see what else I could have done.'

'I can give you a list, if you've got an hour or two to spare.'

'Sorry,' Slider said again. 'First tell me what's been happening back at the shop.'

'We've broken the news to the Hung Fat crew that Michael Lam is dead. That went down extremely well. One of the sons asked on behalf of the father who the murderer was, and Mr Barrington authorised us to say that it was Ronnie Slaughter, who has since removed himself from the stage.'

'Barrington's still going down that road, is he?'

'It's a pleasant lane through a smiling and sunlit countryside,' Atherton said. 'I don't think old Hung Fat was a hundred percent convinced, though. He said a large number of things in Chinese to his son, of which his son only translated about a quarter.'

'Talking of translating—'

'Yes, I spoke to Slim Kim. He's pretty sure he can find out about Chou Xiang Xu. He's got a friend in the business whose daughter Sun-Hi works at the embassy, and if this bloke came over officially it can't be top secret or anything. He spoke to Sun-Hi this morning and she agreed to make enquiries.'

'Right. What about Mrs Stevens?'

'She gave it six on a scale of ten. Too far away to be sure, but it could be. And she took to the silver hair idea without too much trouble.'

'Suggestible, isn't she.'

'She was never going to be a star witness,' Atherton concurred.

'Any news from America?'

'The woman you spoke to at Chang's firm called this morning just after you'd left. I don't know how you sweet-talked her into it, but she managed to get hold of the concierge at his apartment, who confirmed that Chang said he was going straight off on vacation after his trip to England, and that he hadn't come back in between. She sounded worried, and asked if she ought to tell anyone, like the police or her boss. I said she shouldn't, but whether that will stick or not I don't know. If it doesn't—' He let the inference hang. Oh, and one little nugget you'll particularly enjoy – we've tracked down the car Mrs Acropolis saw parked by the alley, and it was nothing to do with our case.'

'How lovely!'

'As you say. It was a dark red Capri belonging to the mate of a man called Leroy Parkes who lives in the flat below hers. The mate had called on him on his way home from a party, and Parkes didn't want to say anything because his mate hasn't got insurance or tax. Mackay got it out of him, and it all checks out And that,' Atherton said, putting down his glass and looking seriously at Slider, 'leaves you, my dear old guv'nor, and the question of your future career, if any, in the Metropolitan Police Force. There are those in high places who wonder not a little what you've been doing for the past two days.'

'I've got a problem,' Slider said.

'Tell me about it!'

'No, seriously. I think I know what happened now. What I don't know is whether Barrington is involved. If he is, I can't go to him with what I know.'

'Well, I see that,' Atherton allowed doubtfully.

301

'And if he isn't involved, he's going to tell me I haven't got any evidence – which I haven't, not good enough for the CPS. And there's information I need that I can't get without his help.' He brooded a moment.

'Two brains are better than one,' Atherton suggested.

So Slider recounted the interview with Peter Ling.

'A microchip?' Atherton said. 'It's possible.'

'It's more than possible,' Slider said. 'Look – Cate has a string of computer shops. He has government and quasi-government contacts. He has the run of the NATO base. He must have known how important and valuable a prototype microchip could be.'

'You think he stole one?'

'I think Lee Chang stole one. He had the knowledge and the contacts; he'd worked in microelectronics, and he was based in Silicon Valley where all the big firms are. How he and Cate got to know each other I don't know, but Ling said Cate went every year to the Computech Convention in California, which is an enormous trade and science fair—'

'Yes, I know.'

'You've heard of it?'

'Not everyone is computer ignorant, you know,' Atherton smiled.

'Oh. Well, I imagine Chang met Cate there – perhaps on several occasions.'

'Maybe it was a holiday romance,' Atherton said. 'He seems to have liked small, slim orientals.'

'Perhaps. Anyway, one day Chang told him about this chip and how valuable it would be if it fell into the wrong hands, and Cate then offered to do all the planning and disposing if Chang would do the initial stealing.'

'Yes, but—'

'Let me go on. Cate knew from having been a copper how

302

a plan can fall through because of one little thing going wrong. So his idea was to have double and triple lines of defence. To begin with, the chip couldn't be smuggled out of the States by Chang, who had to be squeaky clean to get in and out of the NATO base. I think that's why Peter Leman went to San Francisco. He had no connection with anyone, and no one was watching him or checking up on him. A microchip's a pretty small thing and easily hidden if no one's looking for it.'

'So why did Chang need to come to England at all? And in any case, how could he possibly arrange his attachment to the NATO base just for his own convenience?' Atherton got his question in at last.

'Oh, he didn't, of course. I think it was the fact that he was coming to England that made the whole plan possible. As to why he was needed – someone who understood the thing had to do the sales talk. No one's going to fork out billions of dollars without a bit of convincing that the goods are worth it. I think Chang was probably thrown in for the price, to set the thing up for the purchasers – and as a kind of hostage.'

'You think he went to China?'

'He had to disappear very thoroughly. Sooner or later he would be connected with the missing chip, and then the whole of the western world wouldn't be big enough to hide him in. Inside communist China he could make a new life for himself, safe from Uncle Sam's revenge.'

'So what had Michael Lam got to do with it? What was all that malarky in the chip shop?'

'Michael Lam was Chang's passport out of Britain. Cate recruited Lam and got him to do some little carrying jobs for him to get him acclimatised and test his trustworthiness. It was Lam who set up the trip to Hong Kong on his father-in-law's behalf, remember. On the night itself, his instructions were to set off for the airport and check in early, and then come back to meet Cate at the fish bar to collect a little package to be taken to Hong Kong on Cate's behalf.'

'Why couldn't he have the goods in advance? Why did he have to come back?'

'You mean what reason was he given? Probably that the goods wouldn't be available until later. Cate couldn't bring them to the airport – they mustn't be seen in public together. The chip shop was a nice private place to meet, where Cate would have a perfect right to be if spotted. And anyone who might recognise Lam wouldn't think anything of seeing him hanging around that alley, even at night.'

'All right,' Atherton said. 'Then what?'

'Lam has to get back to Heathrow to catch his plane, so the meeting at the chip shop can't be too late. But the shop is open until eleven – although Cate knows Ronnie has shut up early on occasion. So Peter Leman is sent along to lure the poor dope out for a drink, making sure he gets out before half past ten, and that they're seen together in some public place – of which more later. As Ronnie and Leman go out of the front door, Cate and Chang come in at the back—'

'How?'

'Cate has a key to the back door. And Leman unbolts it while Ronnie's attention is elsewhere.'

'But Ronnie swore it was bolted when he came in the next day,' Atherton objected.

'Yes, I know, and that bothered me for a time. But you see I couldn't think why Cate would make such a point of not having a front door key, except to prove he couldn't have got in, and only Ronnie could have done the murder. If you remember Ronnie's reactions to the mention of Cate's name – I think Cate must have warned him on several occasions of

304

the dire consequences if he ever left the back door unbolted. Ronnie, according to Peter Ling, adored Cate, and would do anything rather than let him down. He was also afraid of him. Now I think when we asked him if the door was bolted, he was too scared to say no, in case it got back to Mr Cate that he'd been and gone and forgotten. And I think Cate was banking on that.'

'He may simply not have remembered whether it was or not, and assumed it was. He wasn't very bright,' Atherton said. 'But look, if he had remembered and/or sworn that it was unbolted, where was Cate then?'

'Cate had an alibi – his security guard is ready to swear he didn't go out that night. And the lock on the back door is only a Yale – it could be slipped by anyone. Why should anyone think Cate was involved at all?'

'Hmm. All right, go on.'

'Where was I? Oh yes, Cate and Chang wait in the chip shop until Lam arrives back from the airport. They let him in, and kill him. Chang takes Lam's identity, passport and the microchip, and heads off for the airport in Lam's car to catch Lam's flight. Of course at the other end the genuine contact waiting for Lam doesn't see him, because he isn't there. Lam disappears, and so does Chang. Two for the price of one.'

'Meanwhile,' Atherton said, 'you're telling me that Cate did the cutting up?'

'Who better? He knew the place and the apparatus, and he'd spent his formative years cutting up fish in his father's shop. If Slaughter could do it, so could Cate. Then he concealed the body in the rubbish sacks, all except the bits which might give a hint to the corpse's identity. He washed everything down, and wiped the knives clean, and left everything as Slaughter would expect to find it. The plan, I think,' Slider added slowly, 'was for the body not to be discovered at all, and there was a good chance of it. The dustmen would have thrown those sacks into their truck without examining them, and they would be offloaded onto a corporation dump, where they're moved around by mechanical grab. No one is very interested in getting into close quarters with the stuff. And there are all sorts of scavenging animals that live at the dump – gulls, rats, crows, probably even foxes—'

'I get the picture,' Atherton interrupted hastily.

'If any part of the body was discovered at the dump, it would be hell's own job to discover where it had come from. But there was a second line of defence: if it was discovered before it left the chip shop premises, we, the investigators, would pretty soon discover that it could only have been Ronnie who committed the crime.'

'In which assumption Ronnie unwittingly helped us by pretending the place was his,' Atherton said. 'He wasn't very bright, was he, our Ronnie?'

'Just bright enough for us to suppose he might think of wiping his prints off the knives and then put fresh ones on in the morning,' Slider said ruefully. 'I knew there was something wrong about the fingerprint situation, but I couldn't—'

'Put your finger on it? But talking of fingers, what about the one in the chips? Sheer bad luck, do you think?'

'A bit of that, and a bit of serves-'im-right. I think Cate put the hand through the chip-cutter out of a nasty little-boy's desire to see what would happen. Maybe he'd been fascinated by the thought all his childhood, and now was his chance to find out. But one finger went astray. Whether he didn't notice, or whether he noticed and searched but had to leave before he could find it I don't know. I suspect the latter. He wouldn't have been too worried. If it did turn up, the second line of defence came on line. It was supposed to be Slaughter who did it, and as soon as we started investigating Slaughter, we'd find out about Leman.'

'Yes, Leman of the two addresses,' Atherton mused. 'He courted Slaughter, went out with him, went home with him, and quarrelled with him. Perfect motive for a murder.'

'He looked just enough superficially like Lam for the pathologist to accept the identification. He had no background, so no one would miss him and ask awkward questions. But on the other hand, he had gone out of his way to establish his disappearance, should anyone come asking. I think Leman was supposed to lie low until Cate saw which way our investigation went. Then, if he wasn't needed for the role of corpse, he could have resumed his identity.'

'And if he was to be the corpse, he'd have had to disappear permanently.'

'Yes. Well, everything seemed to be going quite well for the conspirators, until all of a sudden we released Slaughter. If we had doubts about him, they had to be resolved. So Slaughter committed suicide, leaving that very poignant note, and the case was nicely wound up. All Barrington had to do was to sign on the dotted line and accept the bouquet. Unfortunately for Cate, Leman wouldn't stay dead. He wasn't quite as faithful and dependent as Cate had imagined: he had an unlicensed girlfriend, of whom he was rather too fond, and an irrepressible desire to talk.'

'So Leman had to be rubbed out, before he could do more damage?'

'Yes,' said Slider. 'And if you look at the timing, it happened immediately after Barrington insisted on telling Cate that Leman wasn't dead after all.'

'Ah,' said Atherton. 'That's why you wonder whether Barrington's involved or not?'

'Not only that. He's been telling me to keep off Cate's back right from the beginning – ending up with forbidding me to investigate the man at all. Look at it from Cate's point of view – it would be extremely useful to have a Barrington on your team. Or perhaps in your power.'

Atherton shook his head. 'I don't know. As much dangerous as useful, I'd have thought.'

'You think so? But if I had been prevented from asking questions about Cate, we'd have had nothing to go on at all.'

'Except his slip about Ronnie's literacy,' said Atherton.

'Yes. Ronnie concealed that well from his hero.'

'And you really think Cate popped into the house and wrote another note, just to convince you the first one was genuine?'

'No, I'm sure he didn't. Barrington might have recognised his writing, even if he disguised it.'

'Then—?'

'I think the security guard wrote both of them. I think it was the security guard who killed Slaughter – Cate was rather too well known in that house to slip in and out without the chance of someone recognising him. And he and Cate are each other's alibis, if such things could be supposed to be needed.'

'Yes,' said Atherton. 'I see. And I suppose the security guard killed Leman, too.'

Slider thought of the other Peter, blond, smouldering, devoted, jealous. He thought of the round, red bruise in Leman's palm and the torn and swollen lobe of Davey's right ear. He thought of the skull earring in Davey's left ear, and Leman's missing fingers – easier to chop them all off in one swift movement to retrieve the ring, than mess around taking just the one. And none of it, none of it would matter if they could not get the evidence against Cate. It was no use knowing things in your gut – you had to prove them.

And what did he have to go on? Cate had lied about how

he first met Slaughter, lied about the note. There was his probable connection with Shax – would Peter Davey crack if leaned upon? Maybe – maybe not, if he had killed Leman. The ring and the earring. The connection with Lee Chang and with Chou Xiang Xu were both normally accountable, if a little coincidental. The most he had to accuse Cate of was being gay, which wasn't a crime, and of owning a house in which three girls had sex for money – and it would be impossible even to prove he knew about that unless Kathleen Sullivan spoke up.

And yet if he did nothing, and he was right – which he knew he was – and it all came out? Or if there were more deaths? Suppose Cate got nervous and started eliminating everyone who knew anything about him?

'What do I do?' he asked aloud. 'There are all sorts of reasons why Barrington might be protecting Cate. They might have been lovers once. They might be brother masons, or belong to some other even tighter organisation. He might have been implicated with Cate in whatever happened at the Carlisle. He surely must at the very least have wondered about that, but he never seems to have asked any awkward questions.'

Atherton was looking grave. 'You have to take all this to him – what you've told me, everything. It's the proper procedure. And he's asking where the hell you are anyway. You can't never go in to work again.'

'No,' Slider agreed dully.

'If he isn't protecting Cate, he must at least follow up some of the questions. And if he is—'

'Yes?'

Atherton bit his lip. 'I'll be standing there with you. If it looks iffy, we'll take it higher up. As high as we have to.' Slider only looked at him. 'It's the only way,' he insisted. You have to do what's right, Bill. To do anything else would make nonsense of your life. The only reason we're coppers is that we're different from *them.*'

'Is it? I don't know,' Slider said. 'I don't think I know any more why I do it. It's my job, that's all. It's just a job.'

Atherton was silent, watching him steadily, aware of many of the conflicts seething in that slightly bowed head. The bowed head concealed from him Slider's other line of thought, which was that, even leaving aside the question of DC Field, Cate had proved himself ready to kill a man in the course of his master plan, and just as ready to kill two more to protect its outcome. And if Barrington, either innocently or with malice aforethought, told Cate that Slider was asking questions about him, what price Slider's continued presence on this fretful globe?

'You're right, of course,' he said. 'There's nothing else to be done.' He raised his head with an unconscious sigh. 'We'd better have something to eat first. Don't want to face Mad Ivan on an empty stomach.'

Atherton seemed relieved at this return to normality. 'D'you want to eat here? There's just time before the kitchen closes. I'll go and get a menu.'

'Oh, don't bother. Just order me anything – whatever you're having. As long as it's not fish and chips.'

'If this case has taught me one thing, it's that chips are bad for your health,' Atherton said, standing up.

19

Guess Who's Coming to Pinner?

As Slider turned the corner of Old Bailey and Ludgate Hill he saw Joanna coming towards him from the direction of St Paul's. She spotted him at exactly the same moment and stopped dead, and reading in that no rejection he walked on up to her. The last week of June had turned cold, perhaps in compensation for the extra-benign May, and a gritty wind swirled round their ankles while a dark grey sky threatened them overhead.

'What are you doing here?' he asked.

She gestured vaguely behind her. 'Concert at the cathedral. We've just broken for lunch. What about you?'

'Lunchtime too. There's a case on in number five court that I was involved in,' he said, gesturing towards the Central Criminal Court building. 'I was supposed to be called this morning, but they're making a pig's ear of it. I suppose they'll get round to me sooner or later.'

They were silent, staring at each other. 'You've lost a lot of weight,' Joanna said. His dark blue suit, which he always wore in court, was hanging noticeably loosely on him.

'Yes,' he said. He reached up and touched his head. 'I've got a lot more grey hairs too.'

'I can't tell in this wind,' she said. 'It's been pretty tough for you, I imagine. I've read one or two little bits in the papers.'

'They haven't let much of it get out,' he said, 'but all hell has been let loose. I've been up to my neck for the last month. Coming here's been rather restful, really.'

She nodded. 'Jim told me a bit about it. He's been to see me once or twice.'

'Jim? Atherton?'

'Of course Atherton.' She smiled at his absurdity. 'How many Jims do we know?'

'You've been seeing Atherton?'

'Oi,' she said, protesting at his choice of words. 'He comes to see me now and then.'

'Why?'

'Because he likes me and I like him. And because he's the only person in the world I can talk about you to.'

'Oh.' The last words seemed to him faintly comforting. She put a hand up to field her hair out of her eyes. It was longer – she evidently hadn't had it cut for a while. He said, 'Look, shall we get out of this wind? Could you – do you fancy a spot of lunch? There's a pub just along here—'

He expected her to refuse, but after a moment she nodded. 'I'll have to keep an eye on the time, though.'

'Yes, me too,' he said defensively. She turned and they walked back up the hill together, awkwardly, far apart in case they might brush accidentally. It was a horrible pub he never went in – modern, built for tourist through-put, full of young people from the offices, loud music, keg beer, overpriced plastic sandwiches. On the other hand, no one he knew would come in here, and he had walked up this way in the first place to get away from them.

He bought drinks and sandwiches, and then they shoved their way through to a corner and managed to get the reversion to a couple of warm, just-vacated seats at a table awash with spilt beer and piled with dirty plates. It seemed, somehow, right that they should meet at last in such unpropitious surroundings. Surely the gods' envy would be appeased and they would look away for a few moments?

'It's a horrible pub,' Joanna said, as if she had read his thoughts. 'No one would ever think of looking for us here.'

'It's good to feel safe. Everyone at the court is trying to winkle information out of me,' he said.

'Does that mean you aren't going to tell me?'

'Oh no, you're different. If you really want to know—?'

'Of course I do!' A young couple came to play the fruit machine which was right next to them, so she shifted her chair closer to his and leaned towards him. The piped music and the electronic warbling of the machine would have foiled any listening device known to man, let alone human ears. 'You know I won't tell. So tell.'

He told.

Barrington got up abruptly from his desk, and walked back and forth across the room in front of his window. It made him hard to see, big and black against the bright May sunshine, stroboscopic as he cut in and out of the shadow of the glazing bars. Finally he turned and dropped his fists threateningly on the desk top. 'You've no evidence for any of this. No evidence at all.'

'No, sir,' Slider said.

'It's all suggestion. Innuendo.'

'Yes, sir.'

'Don't agree with me, damn you!' Barrington bellowed. Slider could see he was worried. The granite face revealed nothing, but the eyes were thoughtful. There must have been occasions – *must* have been – when he had asked himself questions. But perhaps not these questions.

'All I ask, sir, is that some enquiries be made. Some we can carry out, but others – concerning a possible missing microchip, for instance – will have to go through other channels.'

'You don't want much, do you?' Barrington enquired fiercely.

Atherton put in his word. 'Sir, if Chang is innocent, and he's really gone on holiday, it ought to be easy enough for the FBI to find him. But if he is missing—'

'When I want your input, I'll ask for it,' Barrington snapped. But now Atherton could see he was shaken, and that shook Atherton.

'At the very least, there are some things that need explaining,' Slider said gently. 'Mr Cate lied about how he met Ronnie Slaughter. He lied about that note he said Ronnie had written in his presence. And his ownership of the properties involved in the case is at the least an odd coincidence—'

'Alleged ownership,' Barrington interrupted. 'You have no evidence that he has anything to do with Shax.'

'I think Peter Davey would tell the truth if he was leaned on,' Slider said. 'The mark on Leman's palm could be matched to his earring. And there's the question of the ring. Why would Leman's fingers have been cut off if not to retrieve—'

Barrington straightened up abruptly, and a look of great bitterness crossed his face. 'You just couldn't do as you were told, could you? You had to disobey orders. Indiscipline is at the bottom of every evil in society today.'

'Sir,' Atherton protested, unable to help himself.

Barrington spared him only a glance. His attention was all

on Slider. 'It will be out of our hands,' he said. 'Once you start asking questions of US military intelligence—'

If there is such a thing, Atherton added silently to himself. In the face of deep peril, it is the custom of Englishmen to make jokes.

Barrington released Slider from the burning glance, and turned his cratered face away towards the window. Was it imagination, or did his silhouette already look diminished? 'Go away and write me a full report. Have it on my desk by the end of the afternoon. I'll read it and think about it. That's all I can promise.'

'What about Mr Cate, sir?' Slider asked, with the air of a man reluctant to kick another when he's down, but forced by circumstance at least to prod him with a toecap.

Barrington did not look round. His eyes were fixed on the shining spaces of the Uxbridge Road beyond his clean windows. 'He's not going anywhere,' he said shortly. 'Even if he wanted to, he couldn't get far. He's too well known.' They waited for more, but all he said was, 'Just get out, will you?'

It was while they were still writing that the call came through for Atherton from Slim Kim, and he took it in Slider's room, where they were working one on either side of his desk. The smell of paint was almost gone now, but Slider still found the pale blue of the walls unnerving. It made him feel as though he was in the non-critical ward of a mental hospital, and he felt enough like that in any case not to want any help from his decor.

'Interesting,' Atherton said when he put the phone down. Officially Chou was attached to the Science and Technology branch at Maida Vale, which is what Cate said. He was over here to buy computers and software for his department. But Sun-Hi, Kim's little friend, says that he was only recently transferred there from the Ministry of Defence. He was with them for a long time. He speaks very good American, and he did a summer course in Political Economy at UCLA last year.'

'Very interesting,' Slider said.

'It still doesn't prove anything,' Atherton pointed out.

'No. It's all just suggestion. But how much do you have to suggest before it becomes suspicious?'

'Depends, I suppose, on who you're suggesting about.'

'Yes, I know,' said Slider. 'But three people are dead—'

'Only one of them known to be connected with Cate,' Atherton said. 'I don't think we're going to bring this one home. I don't even think Barrington is going to take it up.'

'He knows Cate is guilty. You can see it in his face.'

'Knowing isn't proving.' He chewed the end of his pen. 'Do you think they *were* – you know?'

Slider shook his head. 'Not my business.'

Atherton tried to be cheerful. 'Never mind, if we don't get him, someone else will, sooner or later. You said Tufty warned you about him. And he wasn't exactly a careful conspirator. He'll trip himself up one day. In the meantime, there are other villains. And once this report is in, the rest of the day's our own.'

'I'd better report to Barrington straight away about Chou,' Slider said, getting up. 'I don't want to annoy him any more at this stage.'

But he found Barrington had gone out not long after he and Atherton had left him, saying he'd be back later. And by the time Barrington did return, the first reports had already come in about a fatal shooting at Chorleywood.

'Apparently,' Slider said to Joanna, 'Mrs Cate arrived back home from holiday to find she couldn't get in. The security gates were double locked and she couldn't raise anyone inside.

She had to go to the local cop shop to get them to override the circuit, and when they managed to get in they found Cate lying dead beside his car and the security guard ditto at the top of the steps. Each had been killed by a single shot from a long-range rifle. It looked as if the guard must have seen Cate fall, and locked the system from the control box before running out to see what was happening. Then of course they shot him as soon as he was in clear view.'

'Unsporting,' Joanna said expressionlessly.

'Ungentlemanly. Well, they found my name in the guard's occurrence book as the last outside visitor, and then the local DCS remembered that Cate and Barrington were chums and members of the same golf club, so he telephoned through to us to let him know. Of course when Barrington finally got back and heard the news the Shah finally bit the spam. There was no hope for him after that of keeping the whole thing quiet, even if he had wanted to.'

'So who killed Cate?' Joanna asked.

'We don't know. He and his security man were both shot with the same XL-type long-range rifle. It's a type that's commonly used and freely available. Criminals have them. Our own SAS and Anti-Terrorist Squad both use them at times. The IRA have stolen plenty of them. And for the same reasons foreign intelligence services like them – even the CIA on occasion, when they don't want to leave their calling-card. So it could really have been anyone. It could have been a business associate or an enraged lover, or for all I know Mrs Cate might have found out about his proclivities and hired a hit-man.'

'Did they break in, or what?'

'They didn't need to. The range of the rifle is such that they could have done it from the road if they could have got a clear sight. But it looks as though the shots were fired from

317

the top of a tree on the next property, which was easily accessible. Cate's neighbours didn't go in for the same degree of security.'

'And who do you think it was?'

He glanced automatically around before answering. 'My own personal preference was the Chinese government. They had the most to lose, and if I were them I'd have wanted to get rid of a conspirator as unsafe as him. He was leaking all over the place, and the questions were being asked too close to home. Our enquiries in Hong Kong and at the embassy must have made them nervous.'

'You were right about it all, weren't you?' she said, almost anxiously, as though it mattered that he should have been.

'Yes, I was right,' he said, and sighed unconsciously. 'It hasn't made me flavour of the month. Some little questions I'd been asking in the States about the missing Lee Chang met up with some great big questions they were already asking about a missing microchip, and there was an almighty explosion. The Home Office and the Ministry of Defence were both involved – they were badly embarrassed because they'd put so much trust in him – and Special Branch, M13, C13 – you name it! Then we had the Americans accusing the Chinese and the Chinese being righteously offended, and the Foreign Office in the middle trying to keep everything quiet – there was almost a diplomatic incident. It was absolute hell. The reverberations are still going on – fortunately at a level well above my head.'

'Oh, Bill! No wonder you look so worn.'

'In a way, though, that wasn't as bad as the storms closer to home.'

'Barrington?' He nodded. 'Was he involved?'

'It seems not. But I still have my doubts about him. He must at some point have at least suspected that Cate wasn't completely straight. I think what upset him most, though, was what was revealed about Cate's personal life – his little love-nests, where he kept his lads. Caged rabbits, Peter Ling called them. They were very much of a type – young men alone in the world, strays who'd cut themselves off from their families, or didn't have any to begin with. He picked them up, gave them a home and a job and a complete new identity, even a new name sometimes. He recreated them. That way he had complete power over them.'

'He must have been mad,' Joanna said dispassionately.

'Yes, probably,' Slider said absently. 'Three of them were called Peter, that was the odd thing. He wondered whether Cate had really named them all after Peter Ling, or whether there had been another Peter before him, a more fundamental Peter – in childhood perhaps – who was at the bottom of all his strangeness. Well, they'd never know now. Cate had died and taken his mystery with him.

'You don't think that he and Barrington—?' Joanna asked, breaking into his musings.

'No, I don't think so. Though I wonder whether Barrington didn't have suppressed feelings about him.'

'If he did, and realised it, that might account for why he took it all so badly.'

'Perhaps,' Slider said. He had wondered that too. He had also wondered whether perhaps it had been Barrington who had fired those two long-range shots – Barrington who was a fellow member of the Shooting Club, had been a noted marksman in his army days. He had worshipped Cate and been let down by him. Had he wondered all those years whether it was just coincidence that Cate ordered him to leave his post at the Carlisle at the very moment the two villains were making their escape? Had Slider's new questions and revelations made him think again, brought him to a conclusion? No one had ever asked where Barrington had gone that afternoon and early evening. Perhaps no one but Slider had wondered.

'So I gather from Jim they're not exactly throwing bouquets your way?' Joanna was saying. 'It does seem unfair, when you've solved the case – three murders.'

'That's the way it goes. The whole thing had to be hushed up. Officially Slaughter murdered Lam and then committed suicide out of remorse. And Peter Leman's murder was a completely unconnected incident.'

'Peter Davey really did do that, didn't he?'

Slider grimaced. 'You and Atherton have been having some talks. Yes, he did. It was on Cate's orders, but he was jealous enough to have wanted to do it anyway, especially when he was told to retrieve the ring, which of course was a match to the one Cate wore. The trouble's going to be making up a court case without bringing all this other stuff into it. There's plenty of evidence against Davey, but juries always want a motive, and once Cate is mentioned as the lover of both, it's bound to start other questions being asked. He was such a pillar of society.'

'And the very first murder – Michael Lam – that was Cate?'

'I think he struck the blow. He was tall and powerful, while Chang was small and slight. Probably Chang distracted the victim's attention while Cate came up behind him.'

'And then he cut him up.' She made a face. 'He must really have been mad.'

'Once the body's dead, it's no different really from cutting up any carcase, like a butcher.'

'You don't believe that,' she said.

'How did you guess?'

'So what did he do with the bits that were missing – the hands and hair and whatever?' she asked.

'Cate bred Dobermanns for a hobby,' Slider said, looking into the amber depths of his beer. 'He had a copper in a little hut where he cooked the dogs' pudding – that's a mixture of meat and meal. He even had a machine for grinding up bones for bonemeal.'

Joanna made a sound which might have been acknowledgement.

'The copper was heated from below by a small furnace, of course. He burned the clothes in there. Forensic cleaned the whole thing out and examined everything minutely, and they found some buttons which we reckoned were from Lam's clothing. They didn't find any human remains at all, though. Well, there'd been a lot of pudding cooked since then.'

'Oh, Bill,' she said. 'Thank God somebody shot him.'

'I'm not allowed to agree. But it was a tidy solution. Even if we'd investigated him thoroughly, we might not have been able to assemble a good enough case against him. And if we had got him sent down, he'd probably only have done ten or twelve years. Still,' he added thoughtfully, 'I'd have liked the opportunity to question him. There are things we still don't know, and I like to know everything.'

There was a silence, at the end of which he looked up at her, and found her looking at him with an intense and searching look.

'Oh, Jo,' he said helplessly, 'I do miss you so much.'

'Me too.'

'I mean, I miss just being with you and talking to you. It's so – everything's so uncomfortable without you.'

'I know.'

'Couldn't we just – I mean, it doesn't have to be—'

'Don't say it,' she pleaded.

But he had to. 'Couldn't we just meet sometimes as friends? Do we have to cut ourselves off from each other so completely?'

'We aren't just friends. We never have been. That's the whole point.'

'But it seems so stupid that I can't even talk to you.'

'Would that satisfy you? Just to be able to talk to me?'

He read the warning in her unsmiling expression. 'No, not satisfy, of course not. But it would be better than nothing, wouldn't it?'

'Do you really feel that?' she asked, looking at him as though she didn't know him. 'How can you feel that?'

He dropped his hands on his knees, defeated. 'I don't know. I don't know what to think or what to do any more. It's like being lost in Hampton Court maze, and the man on the ladder's gone home to tea.'

She almost smiled. 'Oh, Bill!'

He looked at her. 'You don't know it all yet.'

'Well, tell me then. What else don't I know?'

'Yesterday, I had an interview with Barrington. At his request. About the Cate business.'

Barrington had not seemed at ease. He didn't quite fidget, but he gave the impression of wanting to.

'You did a lot of work on this case,' he said at last. It didn't sound like the beginning of a commendation, nor was it. 'I have the feeling that you went into it for the wrong reasons. You wanted to prove something. Your loyalty to your old boss – well, we don't need to go into that. Loyalty is a virtue, but misplaced loyalty is a weakness.'

He seemed to see belatedly where this last track would lead him, and stopped. Slider wondered whether he had been hauled over coals, and how many and how hot. When a big man goes overboard, the splash swamps a lot of smaller fry. It was important to be far enough away from the point of entry – or small enough to bob on the surface until the waves die down.

'It seems to me, Slider, that we have a problem,' he said, and he smiled. It was an uncomfortable smile to be on either side of. Slider would sooner have had a door between himself and it. 'I'm staying on here,' Barrington went on – a revelation, though perhaps he didn't mean it to be, that there had been some doubt on the subject. 'I like the view from my window. I like the view from my desk. I don't want it spoiled by having to look at your face every day.'

'Sir?' Slider said rigidly, a man gratuitously insulted. He wasn't going to make it easy for him.

'I don't think we can work together, not after all this. I think you might say we have a personality clash. You're not my kind of copper, Slider, I have to tell you that. And seeing you every day might remind me of the ways in which you have disappointed me since I started here.'

Slider said nothing. He had the absurd head's-study desire to laugh again. Is it going to be whops, sir? Or do I get off with lines this time? It was a purely hysterical reaction, he knew. He might be looking the end of his career in the face at this moment. It was not a laughing matter. But crikey, he wished he'd thought to put an exercise book down his shorts before he came in here.

Barrington, getting no reaction from his victim, looked down at the folder on his desk before him, and he turned a page or two in a nervous way. Slider deliberately didn't look at it. He concentrated on the portrait of the Queen. One couldn't laugh at the Queen, now could one?

'It's on your record that you turned down promotion to DCI once before, giving as a reason that you preferred to stay in a less administrative rank. Well, I'm happy to tell you that you are going to be given a chance to reconsider that decision.'

'Sir?' All desire to laugh at an end. This was serious. This was real life intruding.

'There is a vacancy at Pinner. You can be transferred there by the end of the month. It's quite nice and handy for your home, isn't it? That is right, you live in Ruislip?'

'Yes, sir.'

'Just down the road, you see. Won't that be nice?' Slider said nothing. 'I can't force you to accept it,' Barrington went on, 'but I am very strongly recommending that you do. I don't think you'd enjoy life here with me very much. I am a very resentful sort of person. I harbour grudges.'

'Sir.'

'You'll find the extra money very useful, too, I'm sure.'

'Yes, sir.'

'Retirement looms closer every day for all of us.'

'Yes sir.'

'So you'll think about it?'

'Yes sir.'

'Don't take too long about it,' Barrington said, and then, apparently irritated by Slider's lack of reaction, dismissed him curtly. 'That's all.'

Slider left, *risus intactus*. A hollow victory.

Joanna didn't react to the story either. She sat looking at him with thoughtful, troubled eyes. She thinks I'm going to use it to blackmail her, Slider thought with a flash of insight. He wanted to cry out in protest at the very thought. He wanted to scoop her up in front of his saddle and gallop off with her very fast and very far.

'I don't know what to do,' he said, when it was clear that she wouldn't speak.

'I can't advise you,' she said.

'No,' he said. 'I didn't mean to ask you to.'

'It's a promotion,' she said, with an air of being scrupulously fair about it.

324

'Yes. And the extra money is always useful. But the days can be so long at those outer stations. I like to be busy. I like it at Shepherd's Bush.'

She looked down and then up again. 'Irene would like having you closer to home, I expect.'

Desperation broke through. 'Oh, Jo, is there no hope for us?'

That roused her. 'It's your decision! It always was! Don't ask me those questions and look at me with those sad-dog eyes!' She made a getting-up movement. 'I've got to get back. I mustn't be late.'

'Wait, please; just a minute more.' She subsided. He reached across the space between them and took her hand, and she let him, though suspiciously. 'I love you so much. Please tell me – do you still want me?'

'Of course I do, you stupid sod,' she said desperately. 'But only if I have all of you. I'm not going to share, not any more.'

He shook that away. 'No, I know. I didn't mean that. But if I do – if I did sort things out with Irene – would you take me back?'

'Yes. But you've got to do it first.'

'I know. I know. I wouldn't try to cheat you. You don't think that, do you?'

'I really have got to go,' she said, standing up. He stood up too – perforce, since he had hold of her hand. She looked at him painfully. 'I love you,' she said. 'I miss you. All those things. Don't think it's easy for me, being away from you. I only get through it at all by boring the pants off Jim, bless him, talking about you. But I won't share you. Don't get my hopes up if you don't think you can do it.'

'I don't think I can not do it,' he said. 'Life is too short.'

She looked at him intently a moment more, and then pulled her hand away. 'Thanks for lunch,' she said, and left him, pushing her way through the throng in a manner that left him in no doubt he wasn't meant to follow her.

He drove home feeling hopeful, feeling hopeless. The thing to do, he thought, was to stop treating Irene like a passive object in his life and talk to her, really talk to her about the whole thing. She had accepted his move into the spare room with surprising docility – had heard his rehearsed speech about pressure of work and late nights and disturbing her without a murmur. Perhaps he would find, if he talked to her, that she wouldn't really mind it as much as he had supposed she would.

And the children – well, researchers always found the answers they wanted. He was absent so much; and when he was at home they stayed in their own rooms or went out to friends' houses. They never wanted to talk to him or play with him or anything. It surely couldn't make much difference to them if he moved out? It wasn't as if it was an unusual thing any more. Lots of their schoolfriends must have parents who had divorced.

Divorced. It was a cold and knobbly word, uncomfortable whichever way you grasped it. And after all, once he had broached the subject he couldn't take it back, unsay it if it turned out that Irene couldn't bear the idea.

But it made no sense to go on as they were, the three of them. And for no particular reason he could fathom he suddenly thought about Atherton. He hadn't told Slider that he had been visiting Joanna. These little missions of mercy – how many of them had there been? Was he so very fond of her, then? More than fond? Oh, don't be silly. They had never been attracted to each other that way. They just shared the same kind of sense of humour and had read the same books, that's all.

It started to rain again, cold, steady rain out of a sky as grey and blank as a tarpaulin. Miserable June weather. The wipers smeared the dirty spray-water back and forth, obscuring and then revealing the view, like a mind changing itself monotonously between two possible courses of action. Thank God he was nearly home.

He turned into his road, and there was the familiar, loathed, ranch-style executive chicken-coop he lived in, wedged in between all the other coops just like it. There was a strange car on the hardstanding in front of the garage, which irritated Slider twofold, firstly because he had to park out in the road, which made it a longer, wetter dash to the front door, and secondly because he didn't like coming home and finding visitors there. He liked to know about visitors in advance so he could prepare his mind for them.

Then as he got out of the car into the rain he realised that it was bloody Ernie's car, and that was close to being the last straw. Ernie was a pompous bore, and he'd never understood what Irene saw in him. She actually seemed to like his company. He ran across the grass to the front door and let himself in, shaking himself like a dog on the front doormat. He heard Irene call from the sitting-room.

'Bill? Is that you?'

'Yes,' he called back. Silly question. Who else would it be? Still, he was in the business now of placating Irene. He smoothed his damp hair down and went to the sitting-room door prepared to be polite if it killed him. Ernie was sitting bland and complacent in the armchair opposite the door like a semi-animated pudding. Irene was standing in the middle of the room looking irresolute and flustered – probably thought he was going to be rude to Ernie. Well, he'd show her. 'Hullo,' Slider said to her equably. And then, 'Hullo, Ernie. How nice to see you.'

327

Ernie gave a sort of equivocal smirk, but Irene, for some reason, looked upset at his words.

'I'm glad you're back early,' she said, not looking it a bit. 'I've got something I want to talk to you about. Well, we have, really.'

'We?' Slider asked, puzzled.

'Ernie and me,' she said.

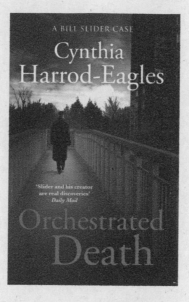

A BILL SLIDER CASE

Cynthia
Harrod-Eagles

'Slider and his creator
are real discoveries'
Daily Mail

Orchestrated
Death

Detective Inspector Bill Slider – middle-class, middle-aged, and middle-of-the-road – is never going to make it to Scotland Yard. He's spent most of his working life at Shepherd's Bush nick, and stopped minding long ago about being passed over for promotion.

But then the unidentifiable body of a woman turns up on his patch, and suddenly Slider and his partner Atherton have a chance to prove themselves.

As they wrestle with an investigation, in which the only clues are a priceless Stradivarius and a giant tin of olive oil, everyone – most of all Slider himself – is wondering whether this latest crisis will make or break the steely-eyed detective.

*

'Slider and his creator are real discoveries'
Daily Mail

A BILL SLIDER CASE

Cynthia
Harrod-Eagles

Death
Watch

The lot of the working copper is getting harder: new
regulations, regular rousting by the top brass, a budget
tighter than a Victoria corset and a DC who thinks he's in
a John Le Carré novel makes it a trying time for
Detective Inspector Bill Slider.

Then when a noted womaniser dies in mysterious fire in a
sleazy motel and the whole of his murky past comes to light,
Slider begins to question whether this was suicide . . .
or murder.

And that's not the only thing Slider is questioning. As soon
as he's solved the motel mystery, Bill is going to have to put
his own house in order . . .

*

'Sharp, witty and well-plotted'
Times

There's a changing of the guard at Shepherd's Bush
police station. But unfortunately for Bill Slider, incoming Detective
Superintendent Barrington has something to prove and no desire to
make friends with his subordinates.

Luckily – or rather, unluckily – Slider has work to be getting
on with, and soon the discovery of a dismembered corpse plunges
him into west London's seedy underworld.

But something's not sitting right. Why did Barrington have
an axe to grind with the old Detective Superintendent? The more
Slider learns, the less he likes it, and the less he can believe
solving the case will win him friends in high places . . .

'An outstanding series' *New York Times*

'Sharp, witty and well-plotted' *The Times*

'A class act. The style is fast, funny and furious –
the plotting crisply devious'
Irish Times

CAN
$15.9

A BILL SLIDER CASE
Cynthia
Harrod-Eagles
Death
Watch

A BILL SLIDER CASE
Cynthia
Harrod-Eagles
Orchestrated
Death

FSC
The Mark of
Responsible
Forestry

visit littlebrown.co.uk

ISBN 978-0-7515-7535-4
UK £8.99

9 780751 575354 >
CRIME FICTION

THE
CRIME
VAULT
.COM

Cover photography: Figurestock & Shutterstock Cover design: Nick Castle